# ABSOLUTE ANGER

Brian T. Seifrit

Author web-site: www.booksbybriant.ca
Contact Email: briantseifrit@gmail.com

Absolute Anger

Published by

ISBN: 978-1-7773169-4-5 Paperback
ISBN: 978-1-990215-15-5 Hardcover
ISBN: 978-1-7773169-5-2 eBook

This book is dedicated to the memory of Arthur John Seifrit and Arthur Henry Taras, both of whom are now stars in the sky. May your spirits continue to soar in the great unknown and may peace be with you as you go. God Bless…

'Let go and let God.' Anonymous.

Special acknowledgements go to my children, Dayton, Desarae, Christopher, and Garett, to my adorable wife and to all my siblings, to my belated mother Jane Seifrit and my mother-in-law Clara Reid.

# One

Henderson left O'Brien his usual call sign: a little sticky note attached to his coffee mug, inviting him to his office as soon as he arrived on shift. Pouring his first coffee of the day, O'Brien tossed the stupid little note into the wastebasket. He wondered what Henderson wanted this time. He had a full roster already with crappy assignments and could only guess what Henderson was expecting of him now. He slowly approached Henderson's office and before he could even knock, Henderson was waving him in.

"O'Brien," Henderson started as O'Brien sat down, "do you want a real assignment for a change? I have a pretty good one for you if you're interested?"

"Oh, what's that?"

He knew exactly what Henderson was doing. Chances were the so-called assignment was one of the many that no one else wanted.

"Remember those murders that took place out near Hudu Park? Well, some new evidence has come in and I think you are just the guy to go over it. What do you say?" Henderson asked with hope.

"New evidence? Exactly what kind of new evidence?"

Henderson tossed a brown envelope onto his lap. It held some pictures of the crime scene. In the right bottom corner of one was a big black circle.

"Is this the evidence you're talking about?"

He looked more closely at the photo he held in his hand. "Sure is."

"What is it supposed to be? I can't seem to make it out."

"Look closely, O'Brien. It's a dental plate. Can you believe that? This is just the break we've been looking for."

O'Brien looked again. Sure enough, it was a dental plate. The only thing was it hadn't been found yet. Someone had just recently spotted it in the picture and brought it to Henderson's attention. This, of course, meant a three-hour drive back to the crime scene. O'Brien contemplated for a few minutes.

"I'll take it," he said with conviction. "You're right that this is the break we've needed. If I can find that plate, maybe we'll be able to get a lead on the killer."

"The only downside is that the case is three weeks old. Who knows what's tramped all over the crime scene by now," retorted Henderson.

Deep down O'Brien knew he was right. The good thing was that with the photo he had a general idea of the location of the plate by the circle on the picture.

"I'll find it. If not, we can have this picture magnified and possibly get an ID on the dentistry."

"I suppose," Henderson nodded as O'Brien exited his office. "Make sure," he yelled as O'Brien made his way back to his own desk, "that you report to me directly if you find anything."

"I know the procedure," O'Brien muttered as he sat down at his desk.

Gathering up the reports on the murder, he checked them over and then headed out of the dank building. The sun sucked the moisture from his skin like a ravished puppy suckling. The hot dry air made his eyes burn, leaving him with the impression that they were melting. *Ah, it was great to be home,* O'Brien thought. He hadn't lived there for almost twenty years. He had operated a small PI agency back east for the past five years, but got sick of the everyday rat race of the city. Finally, he had decided to move his family back home to the beautiful mountain air of the Kootenays.

He had been working for Henderson & Co. PI Agency ever since. The pay wasn't bad, but he wasn't in the business for the money. The true payoff for him had always been when he had solved a case. This one, though, he knew was going to be different.

The drive out to Hudu Park that day was a pleasant one. He made himself believe that he was going there on different business. The killings of the two girls had really hit home for him. With kids of his own, he couldn't fathom the pain and heartbreak, the girls' parents had suffered and were still going through.

The murders took place south of the Hudu Park sawmill amongst the old lumber piles in the mill's stockyard. A twelve-foot chain link fence had been constructed to keep people out. Somehow, the two young girls had managed to get in. *Were they locked in,* he wondered. The old paddle-lock and chain that kept the gate closed appeared as though it had not been opened in months when the investigation was first started. Something was being missed, and O'Brien was determined to find out what it was.

He pulled into the Hudu Park general store around 1:00 in the afternoon. The heat was extreme. He was glad that, at least, a mild breeze was beginning to blow mussing his shoulder-length dark-blonde hair. The air was scented with the fragrance of freshly cut grass and wood. In the distance he could hear the sawmill buzzing and he wondered how the workers were coping with the heat. When he entered the little store, old man Curtis met him.

"Hey O'Brien, what brings you out this way?" he asked.

"Business, Ted, business," O'Brien replied.

He had known Ted Curtis since he was a kid back in the early 70's. O'Brien had grown up in Hudu Park. Even after all the O'Brien children moved on with their lives, his parents continued to reside there for another twelve years. Things were different then.

"Business?" Ted asked with curiosity. "Still working the Fogerty case, eh? That was a bloody tragedy," Ted added as he looked to the ground and shook his head.

"It sure was."

O'Brien moved over to the pop machine and grabbed a coke.

"By the way, Ted, do you recall anything unusual that day?"

"Not particularly on the day the bodies were found. I told one of Henderson's guys that prior to that day… I can't rightly remember if it was Wednesday or Thursday, however, just before I closed on whatever day it was, a guy came in. Never bought a thing, though; only used our restroom," Ted responded as he stroked his chin.

"Is there anything else you can tell me about this guy, colour of his hair, eyes, that sort of thing, or even what he was driving?" O'Brien questioned as he took a long sip from the ice-cold coke he held in his hand.

"Heck, O'Brien. I can't remember what I ate for breakfast yesterday let alone try to remember what happened last week."

O'Brien chuckled at old Ted's response.

"It's been three weeks, Ted. It didn't happen last week if that's what you're speculating."

"It's been three weeks!" Ted exclaimed. "Well then, that proves it; I'm losing my mind."

O'Brien reached into his pocket to get some change to pay for the now-empty pop, but Ted raised his hands.

"This one is on the house, O'Brien. It's going to get a lot hotter by day's end. You'll be back for another. Maybe by then I can come up with some answers to those questions. I know this much for sure: I remember he said he was from up north, said he was going to get on at the mill. He also drove a pumpkin-orange Dodge half-ton. Does that help you a little?"

"It could. I'll have to check a few things out. You said orange Dodge half-ton, right?"

"That's right. Pumpkin-orange, if I can reiterate."

"Thanks Ted."

O'Brien nodded as they walked to the door and exited into the afternoon rays. Ted stopped short of O'Brien's car, bringing his hand up to his chin once again, as though he were in deep contemplation.

"You know," he began, as O'Brien walked to the driver's side of his car, "come to think of it, I do recall something else that struck me as odd. In the back of his pickup, he had a length of chain link."

"Chain link?" O'Brien asked with interest.

"Yeah, you know, for fencing?" Ted responded with sincerity.

"I know what it is, Ted. Thanks very much."

O'Brien quickly opened the car door and retrieved his notebook. He wrote down the few pieces of information that Ted had shared and then tossed the notebook back onto the seat. He waved to Ted and told him he'd be back later.

Driving the short distance to the stockyard, he had one thing on his mind; he would walk the entire perimeter of the two-acre yard paying close attention to the chain link fence. He had a theory; although it sounded corny, he knew it was a possibility. Someone could have cut the fence and fixed it again if they had the tools and the material. First, he had a dental plate to find.

Parking the car a short distance from the gate, he could see the police tape fluttering in the wind. He was relieved to see that it remained intact. The gate was locked with a police lock and he reached into his pocket for the key. After unlocking the gate, he entered the ghostly yard. The grass had grown another few inches since he had last been there and it was now up to his knees. *Great, this is going to be a real treat,* O'Brien thought.

Coursing his way towards the police tape, he walked around the old remnants of lumber piles and dilapidated outbuildings. In the north outermost corner there were poplar trees growing madly. The grass on the other side was almost as tall as the fence itself. *That would be a good place to cut through, commit the crime and slip back out,* he thought as he looked on. *No one would even notice the repairs.* He stopped for a minute as he averted his smoky-blue eyes and contemplated. Finally, walking the distance to the crime scene, he put on a pair of latex gloves. With picture in hand, he tried to guess where the dental plate might be found. The depth of the grass didn't help much, but he continued with the search. He knew it was going to take a miracle to find the piece, and there he was without a metal detector.

The picture wasn't that useful either. He worked the scene for over an hour with nothing to show for it except a bad case of sunburn, dry mouth, and sore fingers. The entire crime scene may have been only 10 feet by 10 feet; he looked at the picture again and did some calculations. The girls' feet were pointing in the direction he was standing. The plate, according to the picture, was a short distance from her left foot. O'Brien knelt down again, to where he guessed it might be. He searched carefully, but once again found nothing. It wasn't until just before the sun was going down that he caught the shiny glimmer. Reaching over, he picked it up between his fingers. There was the evidence that would point to the murderer. Putting it into an evidence bag, he tucked it into his shirt pocket. Looking to the north corner of the large fenced yard where the poplars were overgrown, he ruminated. If the killer or killers had carried out what he thought they might have, the north corner would have been the likeliest spot for access because of its obscurity.

Approaching the north end, he could hear Beaver Creek as it churned by. It brought back memories of his childhood. He tried to smile, but because of the circumstances why he was there, no smile crossed his face. Looking over the fence, he walked east, south and west. However, found nothing that would indicate that a piece had been replaced or altered. It was a dead end. Somewhat discouraged, he walked back to his car. It was almost 6:00 p.m. according to his Timex. Deciding that he better get a move on if he wanted to talk to Ted again before heading out, he looked one last time at the crime scene and walked away.

Ted invited him to dinner, and if he liked he could spend the night. O'Brien wasn't one to turn down a good meal, but to spend the night was out of the question. He had a lot of work back at the office. Henderson would want him there first thing in the morning. Ted was a little disappointed that he couldn't stay and he hummed and hawed for a while until his wife told him to shut up.

"Let the boy be, Ted, he's got work to do."

"O'Brien, she said, "you don't pay any attention to Ted. You know how he gets?"

O'Brien smiled and nodded.

"Yes, I do."

After dinner, coffee, and pie, he thanked the Curtis' for their hospitality, gave Madge a kiss, and told her how much he loved her blueberry pie. He promised that once he finished up with the case he would pop out again with his wife and kids. He was a bit disappointed that Ted really didn't have anything else that he could remember about the night of the murders. The orange Dodge half-ton that he mentioned would have to be looked into. It reminded O'Brien of a highway department vehicle. That would explain the chain link in the back of the pickup. Ted's memory was certainly not, what it used to be.

After driving for almost two hours, O'Brien passed a pumpkin-orange half-ton going in the direction of Hudu Park. It was definitely not a highway department vehicle. Slowing down, he turned on to the shoulder, signalled, and turned out again into the direction the truck was travelling. The orange truck turned left at Champion Lakes Provincial Park and headed towards the camping grounds. Following the vehicle, he phoned ahead to the office. He had one of the guys check out the license plate number. They came back telling him that it was registered to a Norm Bradley who was wanted for felony assault. There was a Canada-wide warrant for his arrest. O'Brien let the guys know that he was following the said felon and that they had turned up onto Champion Lake road. He requested them to send backup.

Town was about an hour and a half away. He knew it would take at least two hours for someone to come. Pulling in opposite the camping ground, O'Brien walked over to the picnic area. Because of the time of day, he knew they would be doing a night arrest and those always bothered him.

He noticed a park Ranger walking around so he introduced himself and inquired about the Dodge half-ton. The Ranger told him that the owner had been camping at site nineteen for almost a month. He said there were no complaints about him from other campers. The guy had paid in advance and was rather pleasant.

O'Brien informed the Ranger that a warrant had been issued for the man and that for safety reasons he shouldn't allow anyone else in the park, except his backup. The Ranger agreed and went as far as to detour traffic three miles down near the bottom of the main highway.

O'Brien grew impatient after the first hour of waiting and decided to walk the distance to the campground. Casually walking past site nineteen, he noticed that the orange truck wasn't there. He asked the people camping in the adjoining site if they had seen the occupant of campsite nineteen.

They answered that they had and that he and his girlfriend were over at the boat launch. They pointed him in that direction.

The campground was overgrown with cedar and pine. The boat launch, too, was covered in a canopy of large evergreens. O'Brien walked over to it looking for the truck and driver to no avail. On a hunch, he hiked up a recently-driven dirt road, staying hidden amongst the shadows. At the half-mile mark, he faintly heard a muffled cry.

Standing motionless, he listened. He paid close attention to the cries he heard and realized that they were cries for help. Drawing his gun, O'Brien began to run; he couldn't wait for backup now. He had to do something and he had to do it fast. As O'Brien came around the bend with his pistol ready, the headlights from a vehicle blinded him. Jumping out of the vehicle's path, he rolled to the ground pistol in hand. The truck stopped. A gun fired in his direction and O'Brien fired back as the truck again sped off.

In a clump of trees, he could see the silhouette of a woman sitting on the ground, her head tucked into her knees. Approaching the victim, he realised she was a young girl of about fourteen. Her clothing was torn and she looked beaten up. Helping the young lady up, he assured her that she would be okay as he dialled 911.

Crying, the young lady told him how she met her assailant on the beach earlier that day. They had smoked a couple of joints and he had left, promising her that he would return later and they could scoot off and smoke a couple more. She said that she had trusted him.

O'Brien had no words for her and simply shook his head. After walking the young lady back to her parents' campsite, he explained what had taken place and that an ambulance would be by shortly to take her to the local hospital. Her parents were horror-stricken. She owned a few good cuts and bruises, but luckily, she hadn't been raped.

Making his way back to his car, he called his backup. So far, the truck had not been seen.

*"Where could it have gone?"* he questioned himself in a low whisper as he did a quick drive through of the campground, but found nothing. Finally, his cell phone rang and the voice of Hal Beady was on the other end.

"O'Brien, the suspect spotted us. He is high-tailing it back your way."

"Thanks, Hal. I'm on my way."

Hurtling his car into over-drive, he quickly headed in the direction of the main highway. Spotting the truck speeding in his direction, he skidded to a halt and exited the car. Pulling out his gun, he was quick to realise that he hadn't reloaded it. With only four shots left, he knew he needed to make every one count. When the headlights beamed on him, the driver sped up cutting across the highway heading directly toward him. Hal's car was approaching fast, but he was still too far away to do any good. O'Brien braced himself for what he knew was going to happen next.

As the truck came within range, O'Brien had no choice and fired all four shots into the front window on the driver side. Still the truck bore down on him. Within only a few yards of where he stood, it finally darted out of control and veered over an embankment with a loud crash. Dust and smoke billowed in the air as screeching tires and smashing metal echoed. Hal pulled up behind it and skidded to a halt. Jumping out of his own car with his pistol drawn, he cautiously approached and checked on the driver.

"O'Brien," he hollered, "nice shooting! He's dead."

Dental records and DNA tests proved that Norm Bradley, wanted for felony assault, was also the Fogerty girls' killer. Case closed.

# Two

It was 4:00 a.m. when the phone rang. It was Henderson.

"O'Brien?" he asked.

"Yeah, it's me," O'Brien said reluctantly as he tried to wipe away the cobwebs.

"Listen. Some guy claims he has found a body that appears to have been mutilated."

"Mutilated, what do you mean mutilated?" O'Brien questioned as he sat up in bed.

"Just like I said, mutilated," retorted Henderson.

"By what? Man or beast?"

"Why do you think I'm calling you, O'Brien? Now get out of bed and down to the north side train yard. That's where the body is and that's where you're going."

Henderson always got that way when he couldn't answer a question. O'Brien silently chuckled to himself knowing he had chafed Henderson a tad.

"I'm on my way," he replied as he hung up the phone and slowly rose.

After dressing, he kissed his wife goodbye, checked on the kids and walked out into the cool morning. The moon shone in the early dawn like a dim light bulb and the air was pleasantly scented.

When he arrived at the train yard, he was greeted by the local police.

"What have you got, Ray?" he questioned the constable as he put on his gloves.

"Looks like some guy either jumped or was thrown from a train."

Lifting the white blanket that covered the body, O'Brien peered at it. It did look as though it had been torn up by something. There were a few dogs that ran around that area of town. The wounds he was looking at though didn't look like marks from a dog. O'Brien covered the corpse again and looked at Ray.

"I hate Mondays," he commented as he rose.

Ray smiled.

"You're going to hate them even more. A dispatch just came through. This mess is going be left to you guys."
"It figures," O'Brien responded as he scribbled something in his notepad.

The coroner arrived at 5:30 a.m. and trucked off the body. O'Brien stuck around the crime scene looking for further evidence. He talked with all the train engineers that had been on duty the night before. No one had seen or heard a thing. The guy who had found the body and called it in couldn't be found. Henderson's office did manage to trace the call. It was from a pay phone. They dusted it for prints but nothing showed up. It was going to be one helluva week.

Returning to the office around 10:00 a.m., he was surprised to see that Henderson was still there. Henderson had already pulled a nightshift and everybody who knew him knew that if he didn't get his sleep he was easily perturbed. O'Brien hadn't even made it to his desk before Henderson was calling out to him.

"O'Brien. Where have you been? Get in here." Henderson yelled, as he waved O'Brien into his office.

O'Brien closed the door behind him as he entered and walked over to Henderson's desk.

"Shouldn't you be home getting some sleep?"

Henderson glared at him with his nostrils flared. O'Brien could hardly contain his smile. He was probably the only one in the agency who got away with jibing old Henderson.

"Never mind that right now, O'Brien. What do you got for me on the corpse that was found?"

"Nothing other than I think it's more than a murder. I think somebody tortured the victim."

He could tell Henderson was about to blow a fuse.

"What are you trying to tell me, O'Brien?" he clamoured.

"Whoever called it in was certainly right. It looks like something or somebody has mutilated the victim," O'Brien replied as he slumped into a chair.

"Are you trying to tell me that we could be dealing with a possible lunatic? Give me a break, O'Brien," Henderson retorted as the blood vessels in his neck protruded.

That happened every time Henderson got mad.

"I'll tell you this much," O'Brien began with conviction, "the marks on that body aren't from an animal."

That much he knew for sure whether Henderson believed him.

Henderson took a deep breath and was about to say something when his phone rang. It was the coroner. He had determined the cause of death to be loss of blood. The corpse was four days old. There were six unidentified tears throughout the body. The coroner couldn't rule out that they were man-made. Henderson hung up the phone, a look of concern on his face.

"O'Brien, we got ourselves a maniac running around. You were right."

"I figured as much," O'Brien sighed and began to stand.

"All right then. I want you to put out a memo to all the police agencies. This madman may have struck elsewhere. Any information we can get on other homicides such as this will be of assistance. I'll contact upper law enforcement agencies myself and see if they have any files that might help."

"Will do," O'Brien said as he exited Henderson's office and walked over to his desk.

He turned on his computer, typed a short memo, and sent it to all the agencies in his address book. Within the hour, he received two replies. In a city north of Fruitmont called Grandbluff, ten years prior there was a case that was similar. Some guy had called the police and reported finding a body that appeared to have been mutilated. When the police arrived, they too found a body but not the caller. They had also traced the call to a nearby pay phone where no prints had been found. The case had been put on the shelf because of lack of evidence and any witnesses. The body had been designated as a transient and the man had been buried as a John Doe.

O'Brien reported the Grandbluff incident to Henderson who immediately made arrangements and dispatched O'Brien. His flight would be leaving for Grandbluff at 3:00 p.m. allowing him three hours to retrieve some clothes from home and to let his wife and kids know that he had been called away.

O'Brien patted his kids on the head and kissed his wife goodbye as he stood in the doorway getting ready to leave. He was just stepping out when the phone rang. It was Henderson. He couldn't believe it. Henderson had already put in a double shift and now it was going on eighteen hours.

The phone call was to inform him that Henderson had received a memo from the FBI. Another body had been discovered in a train yard in Copeland, USA. It, too, had been mutilated.

Both Henderson, and O'Brien, were becoming increasingly convinced that, they were dealing with a serial killer or a cult of some kind. O'Brien's flight plans had been changed, and now he was expected to catch the 4:20 p.m. flight to Copeland, USA. Henderson dispatched Hal and Rory to Grandbluff. When O'Brien landed in Copeland, he was supposed to meet up with an FBI agent named Riley who would take him to the second scene, a simple enough task.

Tracy and the kids drove him to the Airport and watched as he boarded flight 215 to Copeland. He was fortunate enough to get a window seat and looking out the little window; he waved and blew a kiss to his wife and kids.

The big jet engine rumbled to a start and within minutes, they were airborne. O'Brien watched as Fruitmont disappeared from view. Turning his attention to the case at hand, he opened the file and briefly went over it. He concluded that all he really had was the cause of death and a corpse with no name, a missing murder weapon, and unidentified marks on a body dead four days. He looked over the folder again. *I've got nothing,* he thought. That's exactly what he had, nothing, a big fat zero. He could only hope that the crime scene in Copeland would produce some evidence.

The flight took three hours and in that time, O'Brien went over everything not once or twice but easily a half a dozen times. The only thing that kept popping up was the timeframe. It was obvious that the victim was not from the area of Fruitmont, otherwise he would have been discovered sooner. The only feasible thing was that the victim had been murdered elsewhere and transported. O'Brien tried to come up with some answers, but there weren't any, not yet at least, not for this case.

The plane landed in Copeland at 7:15 and as he made his way through to the checkout, he kept his eyes peeled for someone named Riley. He hated it when Henderson set him up like that. O'Brien didn't have a clue on who Riley was or even what he looked like. Finally, he spotted a guy standing near the exit of the airport dressed in a suit. His instincts told him that the guy standing at the exit was the guy he was supposed to meet. He walked over to him and asked if his name was Riley.

"Yes, it is," he replied, "and you must be O'Brien?"

"That's right."

O'Brien showed Riley his credentials.

"Nice to meet you, O'Brien. Your boss speaks quite highly of you. I hope you're as good as he claims you are."

"What did Henderson say to you? He hasn't said a decent word about me to anyone," O'Brien commented as he put his ID back.

"Let's just say he thinks you are the one that can solve this crime. The FBI doesn't want to get involved, not yet anyway. We have more pressing cases."

O'Brien knew exactly what Riley meant. The FBI was going to wait for the little guy to do all the leg-work. Then, as always, they would pull rank and take over the investigation. It nauseated him the way the FBI operated. It was probably for that reason that he had always hated working with them.

"It's getting late. We better get a move on," O'Brien responded with dislike.

"Follow me," Riley said as he exited the double glass doors. Riley drove the five miles to where the corpse had been found. Rarely did the two speak to one another. The crime scene was much like the one in Fruitmont, except that the body had already been removed and was on ice at the Copeland morgue.

Investigating the scene, O'Brien began to devise a scenario in his head as he slipped on his latex gloves. Obviously, the killer or killers were travelling by train and obviously, the killer or killers had a greater motive than just to kill. O'Brien looked over the scene a few more times without Riley's help. Riley had decided to sit in the car, and drink coffee, yakking on his cell phone. Satisfied that there was nothing more he could do in the dark, O'Brien walked back to the car.

"Come up with anything?" Riley asked as O'Brien opened the passenger side door and sat down.

"Both scenes, I'd say, are related. Whoever is doing this is certainly sick," O'Brien responded.

"I know. Wait until you see the corpse."

Riley turned the key in the ignition and fired up the car.

"Lead the way."

O'Brien slipped on his seatbelt. Riley nodded and off to the Copeland city morgue they went. It was on the outskirts of Copeland and was surrounded with a wrought iron fence and gate. Riley buzzed the bell and identified himself. The gate swung open and they drove the short distance to the big, grey building.

At the building's front door, they were met by the coroner, a tall, lanky man in his sixties with a limp.

"Come in, come in; how are you this hour, Agent Riley?" the old man asked.

"Not bad," replied Riley. "This is O'Brien, a Private Investigator from Canada. His detective agency up there in the great white north is investigating a similar crime to the one committed here in Copeland."

"Nice to meet you, detective."

"Nice to meet you too, sir."

O'Brien shook the old man's hand.

"I guess you would like to see the body now?" questioned the old coroner.

"Yes I would, thank you," responded O'Brien.

"It's in terrible shape. I hope you have a strong stomach."

"I do."

"This way then, O'Brien."

He led O'Brien down a flight of stairs and through a darkened corridor. The stench of embalming fluid at times was overpowering and it left a bad taste in O'Brien's mouth. The coroner opened a big metal door which led into a holding room. He walked over to one of the gurneys and undid a rubber body bag. As soon as the zipper opened, the smell of decayed and rotting flesh was prominent. O'Brien did everything to prevent himself from puking.

"How long has this man been dead?" he asked with great disgust.

"I suppose a little over a week."

"What have you determined to be the cause of death?"

"He bled to death. He probably died within a couple of minutes."

"What do you think the purpose of that would be?"

"Well a dead body won't bleed," replied the coroner as though it were a simple riddle. With that said O'Brien stepped back and bumped one of the empty gurneys. He hadn't thought about that! If he was hearing the coroner correctly, someone or something was killing people for their blood. *Jesus Christ,* O'Brien thought aloud.

"Pardon?" asked the coroner.

"Oh, nothing…sorry. I was just thinking. Can I use your phone? I have to call the coroner in Fruitmont to make sure he does all the right tests on victim one."

"No need. Womarz and I have already spoken. That victim too was still alive and suffered a great deal before finally dying."

"Does the FBI know about this?"

"Not to my knowledge. I haven't mentioned it."

"Please don't."

"I won't, O'Brien. I, too, have a dislike for the FBI and their antics. I have helped them in many cases and more times than not they have tried to discredit me. I have practised medicine longer than most of them have been in the Bureau, yet, on occasion, they still rile me."

"I hear you, Doc; I hear you."

O'Brien looked up at the clock on the wall and saw it was closely approaching 10:00 p.m. He realised that he had been awake for over seventeen hours.

"Listen, I have to get to a hotel. Can you suggest one?"

"Sure can. You might want to stay at the Cobbler Hotel. It's not far from here. It also has all the amenities and serves a great breakfast."

"Thanks."

O'Brien turned and left the cold, dead room. He met Riley upstairs and had Riley drive him to the Cobbler.

"Are you sure you don't want to stay at the Hilton?" Riley asked almost arrogantly.

"The Cobbler will do."

"Suit yourself."

Once at the Hotel, Riley bade O'Brien good luck and said he would be leaving in the morning. O'Brien nodded and thanked him. They shook hands and Riley sped off.

The Cobbler was no gem, but the price was right. The clerk handed O'Brien the key to room # 29 upstairs. It was a double room with all the modern amenities of home. It was exceptionally clean and lightly scented with pine. O'Brien immediately called home to let his wife know that he was alive and well. They talked for a few short minutes and he told her that he would probably be home by mid-week. He gave her the name of the hotel where he was staying and said that he'd try to phone Tuesday night before the kids were in bed.

"You always say that, O'Brien," Tracy responded. O'Brien could almost see her eyes rolling back in her head as she said that.

"I will this time, I promise," he chuckled.

"You better," she said.

He could tell by her tone that she was smiling. It brought a smile to his face as well.

"I love you."

"I love you back," she replied.

They said their goodnights shortly thereafter.

By midnight, O'Brien was completely exhausted, not only from lack of sleep, but also because of the lack of food. Tracy had always tucked away food items in his briefcase so he retrieved them. Sure enough, tucked inside were two packages of instant coffee, some jerky, and a bag of unshelled peanuts. *Leave it to the wife.* Nibbling on some of the finger food, he made a cup of coffee with hot tap water. He hadn't noticed the electric percolator until he had downed the first cup. It was sitting on the TV stand along with coffee and condiments.

"Oh well," he muttered as he shrugged.
Retrieving his overnight bag, he slipped into his jogging pants. Tossing his clothes onto the bed, he stretched out beside them.

The alarm on his watch went off without a hitch at 7:30 a.m. By 8:15 a.m., he was down at the cafe eating eggs and pancakes and slurping coffee. He thumbed through the Copeland yellow pages looking for a reputable car rental place. The only one listed was Copeland Car & Truck Rentals. Their ad stated they would deliver within thirty minutes, 'If the rental fees were put on a credit card'. O'Brien fished in his pocket for a quarter to make the call. Some snooty old lady answered.

"Copeland car and truck rentals; please hold."

*Terrific,* O'Brien thought. He sat on the phone waiting for almost ten minutes before the old lady came back on.

"Copeland car and truck," she repeated.

"Yeah, hello. I'd like a rental car for a couple of days."

"How long exactly, sir, will you need the rental for?"

"I don't know exactly how long I'll need it for."

"Sorry, sir. I need to know exactly how many days you will need it."

Not even when he explained to her that he was a detective from up in Canada and that he was down in Copeland on a criminal investigation, did she lighten-up.

"You may very well be the King of England, sir. Without the exact number of days or hours that you will be in need of the vehicle, I cannot rent it to you."

"Look lady," O'Brien said with conviction while trying to keep his cool, "I would like to rent a car."

"I realise that, sir, but..." O'Brien cut her off at that point and finally told her that he would need it for two days.

"Very well, sir. What card are you using today, Visa or MasterCard?"

"I'd like to put it on my Visa, please."

"What is the card's number and expiry date?"

O'Brien read off the numbers and the expiry date.

"Thank you, sir," she replied, "We will send one over directly."

O'Brien looked at his watch; the time read 9:00 a.m. If Copeland Car and Truck Rentals were true to their word, a car would be delivered to him in thirty minutes. O'Brien waited. Sitting back down at the little table where he had eaten his breakfast, he ordered another coffee. As he downed the last swallow, one of the waitresses came over to him.

"Detective O'Brien?" she asked.

"Yes."

"There is a phone call for you from Copeland Car and Truck Rental."

"Thanks."

O'Brien stood, pushed his chair in, and went over to the phone.

"Hello."

"Yes. Mr. O'Brien, I'm afraid the only car we have available is a truck."

"That will do," O'Brien replied.

Whether it was a car or a truck didn't matter; he needed wheels.

"I'm sure it will; however, it costs an extra fifteen dollars a day."

"That figures. Send it over anyway."

"Very well, I'll send it over as soon as it comes in."

"What do you mean when it comes in?"

"It's not due back until 11:00."

"And you have nothing else?"

"No, sir, we don't."

"Fine."

"Thank you for your patronage, detective."

O'Brien hung up the phone and paid his breakfast bill at the counter. He walked up to his room and jotted down a few notes. Turning on the idiot box to catch the morning news, a chill ran up his spine when the newscast stated that a body in the Hinton, Alberta area had been found near a railway track. It had been grossly mutilated. Picking up the phone, he immediately called Henderson.

"Have you heard the news?" he asked when Henderson finally picked up.

"Sure have, O'Brien. Sounds like we have an epidemic on our hands."

"Yeah, south of the border and right on through to Alberta. It's almost as if there is more than one killer and each killer is going in the opposite direction of the other riding the rails."

"That's a probability and we better start moving on it fast. I'm going to send one of the others to Hinton today. You do what you can down there in Copeland. If you come up with anything new be sure to ring me. I'll either be here or at home," replied Henderson.

"Right," O'Brien said as he hung up the phone.

At 11:30 a.m., there was a knock on his door. It was Copeland rentals.

"Detective O'Brien?"

"That's right."

"Hi, I'm from Copeland rentals. I brought you your rental. It's the black Dodge. The tank is full, but you'll have to keep an eye on the oil. It burns it up quite quickly."

"What kind of operation are you running?" O'Brien asked with a smile. "First I'm told that you have no cars left. Then you bring me a truck at fifteen extra dollars a day that burns oil."

"I'm sorry, sir. I only work there."

"Yeah, yeah. I've heard that one before."

The kid handed O'Brien the keys, smiled, and left. O'Brien looked out his window to the truck. To his surprise, it was a nice looking four-wheel drive truck. *Well, that won't be so bad,* he thought. The first order of business, he decided, would be to return to the crime scene and do a more thorough search, then get back over to the morgue and speak with the coroner again. Forced to stop off at a nearby gas station, he purchased four quarts of oil. The truck certainly did burn it quickly.

An hour later, he was at the crime scene. Slipping on a pair of gloves, he paid close attention to the surrounding area. The body had been found some three or four yards away from the tracks or in his terms, 9 to 12 feet away. The train through Copeland travelled in only one direction, west. The impact spot where the body first landed was east of where the body was found. This proved to O'Brien that the victim was only a corpse when it was hurled from the locomotive.

The problem was that if the victim had been dead for over a week, as the coroner suggested, why was there no tissue, hair, or minute blood samples found at the point of impact? Surely, a body that had been festering for even only a couple of days would rip open and spew pieces of flesh. So far, that was not the case. A question burned inside him and one he had yet to answer.

Kneeling down again near the point of impact, he looked at it closely. The way it appeared made him think of another possible scenario. Perhaps the killers created the crime scenes making it look as though the victims had been thrown from a train. O'Brien wondered if that was feasible. The more he thought about it the more it began to make sense.

The 'who' and 'why' questions remained. Retrieving his 35mm camera from the truck, he began snapping pictures of the impact point. His hope was that after the pictures were developed he would see something in them that he wasn't seeing now. Next stop would be the morgue.

# Three

It was getting on to 3:00 p.m. when O'Brien finally found his way back to the morgue. He stopped off at the front gate and pressed the buzzer.

"Who is it?" a voice answered.

"It's Detective O'Brien."

The gate unlocked and swung open. As he began driving the distance to the building, the truck suddenly became overheated and all the idiot lights came on. He managed to drive it up to the front doors cursing the entire way. The truck made a screeching sound, stalled, and sent up clouds of black smoke. O'Brien popped open the hood and then stepped out. The coroner was standing beside him with a smile on his face.

"Looks like you need a tow?" he stated sarcastically. "You rented this from Copeland rentals, didn't you?"

"As a matter of fact I did; why?"

"I can't believe they're still renting it."

"What do you mean by that?"

"This old truck blows more engines than a whore blows Johns," the coroner replied with a raspy snicker.

"How do they get away with that?" O'Brien was curious.

"They keep repairing the motor so it will run for a while. It gets inspected then they put it back on their lot and rent it to guys like you."

"Guys like me," O'Brien retorted as though he had been insulted.

"Yeah, you know, people from out of town," the coroner responded. "It's nothing against you, O'Brien. It's just the way they do business."

"Is that right? Good. They can pay for the tow themselves."

O'Brien slammed the hood shut.

The coroner looked at him and smiled.

"Come on in, O'Brien," he said, "we'll deal with that problem later."

He led O'Brien into the parlour and offered him one coffee, then another. By the time the pot was finished O'Brien had gained new insight on the case. The coroner described a good scenario. He believed that the perpetrators were selling blood to donor clinics. There was a big market for plasma because of all the shortages and problems the Red Cross was having with their blood supply.

O'Brien hadn't even thought of that. The coroner back in Fruitmont, Womarz, said that the marks were unidentifiable. O'Brien wondered if maybe the marks were from a medical instrument. If that were the case, Womarz should have been able to identify such an instrument. After all, he was a medical examiner.

There was a lot O'Brien needed to figure out. He thanked the coroner for his time and said that if any more questions arise he would see him again before he left Copeland. The coroner called a tow truck for him and he met it outside. The driver looked at him and with a grin from ear to ear.

"You're from out of town, aren't you?"

"Yes I am and yes I rented this from Copeland rentals and yes I know this truck blows more engines than a whore blows Johns," O'Brien replied smugly.

The driver looked at him and chuckled.

"You know," he began, "if all my tows had the same sense of humour as you, my job would be a lot easier and pleasant. Every time I've picked this old boy up, I've been sworn at, threatened, and even blamed."

"Why is that?" O'Brien asked to make conversation.

"I've been contracted out by Copeland Rentals to do all their towing. I guess people associate me with them. Nevertheless, I'm not in any business relationship with them other than, of course, the towing. If this were my truck, it would be in a junkyard. This year alone I've towed it over a half dozen times."

There was a short pause as the driver hit a lever and the truck creaked as the tow bar tightened up.

"By the way," he said reaching out his hand, "I'm Chuck."

"Hi Chuck, my name is O'Brien. I'm a private investigator from up in Fruitmont."

"Fruitmont? What brings you to Copeland?"

"I'm not at liberty to say."

"You're here because of that body they found, aren't you?"

"Like I said, Chuck, I'm not at liberty to say."

"No matter," he said. "Do you need a lift?"

"Yeah, please to the Cobbler Hotel."

"Sure thing; hop in."

Back at his room, O'Brien phoned Copeland Rentals and complained about the piece of work that they rented him. He asked if he would be getting a refund.

"Sorry, sir, we have a 'no refund' policy. It's stated in the contract you received."

"What contract?" O'Brien asked.

"The contract you picked up at our office, sir."

"Listen, lady. I paid for that rental with my Visa. The vehicle was dropped off at my hotel. I don't have a clue where your office is."

"The delivery driver must have dropped off the contract with you then, sir."

"Look."

O'Brien was a little hot under the collar.

"I received no contract nor was I informed of your 'no refund' policy which I think is a total crock."

"I'm sorry to hear that, sir. We've been in business for over thirty years and our policies have rarely changed. The only way you would be entitled to a refund is if the problem you have with the rental was our doing."

"What do you mean if it was *your* doing? Whose doing do you think it was? Mine?"

"Very well, sir. Can you tell me what the problem was then?"

"I can. It is simple. The engine blew."

"And why did the engine blow, sir?"

"Because, the piece of crap, burns more oil than Chong smokes joints."

There was a short pause on the other end.

"I'm pulling up your information now, sir. You rented truck number six, a black Dodge 4x4, correct?"

"I don't know what number it was, but yeah, it was a black 4x4?"

"That's right, sir. And the delivery driver did mention to you to keep an eye on the oil levels, didn't he?" the lady questioned.

O'Brien felt like telling a line of bunk, but the kid who delivered it did tell him to keep an eye on the oil.

"All right, lady, you win. The kid did tell me to keep an eye on the oil level," O'Brien responded as he changed the tone of his voice to a more passive one.

"So then do you still feel you are entitled to a refund, Mr. O'Brien?"

"No, but how about another vehicle?" O'Brien asked apologetically. There was a brief pause on the other end.

"Mr. O'Brien, we do have a 1987 Toyota Camry coming in later this evening. Would that suffice?"

"Yes, Ma'am, that will do," O'Brien replied respectfully.

"We'll deliver it to you in the morning then. Now how long will you need it for?"

*Not this again,* O'Brien thought, but he knew the procedure.

"I'll need it for one, no make that two days."

"So, you'll have it back to us by Thursday at 5:00 p.m.?" came her reply.

"That's correct. What happens if I turn it in on Wednesday?" O'Brien questioned.

"You'll still have to pay for the extra day."

"I see. Yeah, send it over in the morning. Can you tell me what time I should expect it?"

"We open at ten a.m., so between ten and eleven I would guess."

"All right. Thanks, then."

O'Brien hung up the phone. Looking at his watch, he realised it was going on 7:00 p.m. He still had time to take a quick shower before phoning home and being able to talk to his kids. Picking up his overnight bag, he headed into the bathroom. Looking in the mirror, he noticed how desperately he needed a shave; his five o'clock shadow was looking more like a four-day beard. Turning the shower on, he stepped in. The water felt good and he could taste the salt from his skin as it trickled into his mouth. Gurgling with water a couple of times, he reached for his toothbrush and brushed his teeth.

The shampoo he had brought with him, he noticed, somehow had popped its lid. The contents were now spewed out inside the plastic bag. *Thank God, it didn't spill all over my clothes,* thought O'Brien. Adding a small amount of water to the bag, he poured it over his head. The bottle was probably only a quarter full when he'd packed it. The little amount that spilled by now had turned into a dry, pasty crust inside the bag. By adding water to the bag, he was at least able to lather up his hair. *What a day...* he thought as he scrubbed. After showering and having a shave, he called home. The phone rang once, then twice, and finally Tracy answered.

"Hello, sweetheart," O'Brien said in his best Bogart voice.

"Hey, Bogey; how goes the battle?"

"Could be better if you were here beside me," replied O'Brien. "So, are the kids still awake?"

"Probably, but they're not here."

"What?"

"They're at Grandma's. Your nieces are down. Mom figured it to be a good time to take the boys."

"Oh really," O'Brien said with disappointment.

"Yeah, isn't it great?"

"I suppose. So, do you want to go out dancing then?" O'Brien joked.

"Are you in town?"

"Sorry, sweetie. I'm still in Copeland."

"Awe you buggar. Why did you ask if I wanted to go dancing then? I guess I should've known. When was the last time you danced, anyway?" Tracy asked.

"I'm dancing right now," O'Brien snickered.

"Yeah, as if. You don't know how."

He could tell by her tone that she had her pouting face on. They talked for about an hour and he thanked her for putting the finger food in his briefcase. He told her that he was planning on catching either the late flight home on Wednesday, or the early flight on Thursday. He told her about the incident with the rental truck, and how he had tried to get a refund, but with no success.

Tracy laughed.

"You're just too honest, O'Brien."

"I know, but that's why you love me, isn't it?"

"That's part of the reason."

"Oh. What's the other reason?"

"If you don't know, I guess you'll have to wait until you get home to find out the other reason."

O'Brien smiled. He knew exactly what the other reason was. Finally, they said goodnight. He had one more call to make and that was to Henderson. He called the office on the chance that Henderson was still there and, lo and behold, he was.

"Pulling another eighteen-hour shift?"

"Not by choice," Henderson answered. "These idiots can't run this place without me, especially when you're not around."

"Are you giving me a compliment?"

"Never mind compliment, it's the truth. How is it going down there?"

"Not bad. I have few more possible scenarios for you."

"Please no, O'Brien. No more of your gruesome ideas. The cult theory isn't good enough for you anymore?"

"It's still a possibility, but it's not the only one I'm thinking of now."

"All right then; give it to me."

"Before I do that, how did Hal and Rory make out in Grandbluff? Did they come up with anything that I should be informed of?"

"Those two guys couldn't solve a crime if it bit them in the ass, excuse the pun."

"Come on, Henderson, you know that ain't true. Hal is one of the best detectives you've got. He's been in this business for a long time. Rory is also good at what he does. You know well enough that both those guys live and breathe their work."

"I suppose you're right, but do you know what those guys are trying to tell me now?"

"What's that?"

"They seem to think that someone is running around killing people and selling their blood on the black market."

"Well then, I guess you don't need to hear my theory."

"No, O'Brien, not you too?"

"Put it this way, Henderson. That's not such a bad theory. There currently is a Canada-wide blood shortage. With all the problems, the Red Cross is having with their blood supply. That's not to mention that it's a quick way to make a few bucks."

The long pause at Henderson's end told O'Brien that he was probably shaking his head.

"Good God, I need a holiday."

"That probably wouldn't hurt. When was the last time you had one?"

"Never mind that. I can't believe that you also think someone is running around with a thirst to sell blood."

"It's not my only theory. It's just the theory I have today."

"Keep it up, O'Brien; keep it up. Keep pushing my buttons," Henderson retorted.

O'Brien knew then that he had pissed Henderson off and he couldn't help but smile. Henderson always hated it when O'Brien taunted him.

"Listen, I'm only funning with you."

"I know that, but you're still a jackass."

"Yeah, but I'm not always a jackass. You, on the other hand, will always be fat."

O'Brien could tell by the way that Henderson was breathing that he was likely snickering on the other end.

"O'Brien, when you finally make your way back here I'm going to give you the worst possible case I can come up with... because you're an ass."

"That's all right. I'm used to getting all the crappy cases anyway," commented O'Brien.

With that, Henderson chuckled. O'Brien told him what his flight plans were and that he'd be back at the office Thursday or Friday at the latest. Then they said goodbye.

O'Brien hung up the phone and switched on the TV. The news headlines were plastered with news about a possible serial killer or cult that was running around killing people to make a few bucks with their blood. It was a circus. O'Brien shut the thing off. He knew the newscasts weren't going to help much. He decided to walk down to the café to have a late snack. He was craving a big T-bone, but he knew that the kitchen was probably closed. A piece of pie and coffee would have to do.

Sitting down at the same table he had used that morning, the waitress came over and took his order. He ordered two pieces of blueberry pie a glass of milk and coffee. A short while later the waitress returned.

"Here is your order, detective," the waitress said as she set the pie down.

"Thanks."

"No problem. Is there anything else I can get for you?"

"Nah, that's fine, thanks."

O'Brien averted his eyes to the piece of luscious blueberry pie.

"Just holler if you want anything else."

"I will."

O'Brien savoured every piece as he slowly finished. The coffee and milk topped it all off. Sitting for a few minutes, he let the evening snack digest. Then he stood and walked over to the cashier to pay his bill. Thanking the waitress again for her service he tipped her. The short jaunt back to his room that night felt good as he walked up the stairs.

The cool evening air was tainted with the smell of diesel exhaust as a big rig passed by, breaking the stillness of the night. Looking at the time, he was surprised that it was going on to eleven bells. Inhaling deeply, he stepped inside his room. Slipping his shoes off, he walked over to the desk, pulled out the chair, and sat putting his feet up. As he leaned back in the chair, to his surprise, it broke. Falling over backwards, he landed on the floor jarring his back. He lay there for a few minutes grimacing in pain until finding enough pain tolerance to stand.

Slowly he waddled over to the bed and slumped into it. He knew that in the morning he was going to pay, for that blunder, not to mention the twenty-dollar chair. He had been shot in the back in his younger days when he was still a rookie. The bullet made dust out of one of his thoracic vertebra. At that time, the doctors all figured he was going to die or, if not, they assumed he would be in a wheelchair for the rest of his life. Somehow, he was lucky and the doctors were able to reconstruct. Even though it had happened fifteen years ago, sometimes it still caused him a great deal of pain, especially when he fell out of chairs. Not that he made it a habit or anything. It's just that this wasn't the first time he had fallen on his back.

As he lay in bed, he slowly began moving his back muscles hoping they weren't going to seize. That would be the last thing he would need. *Hasn't my day been lousy enough?* O'Brien wondered. Then he heard Tracy's voice talking in his head.

"It's your own fault O'Brien. How many times do I have to tell you not to lean back in chairs? Think about what you're teaching the boys."

It brought a smile to O'Brien's face because that's exactly what she would have said. Heck, she had probably said that to him a million times. Closing his eyes, he began to think about how much Tracy meant to him. She always backed him as he pursued his career. When he was running his own agency, she was the brain that kept the clients coming back. God, he was lucky to have a woman like her at his side.

His mother had always said to him, "You know how lucky you are Tyler to have a woman like her, someone who puts up with all your crazy antics and sense of humour and still stands by your side?"

"I know," he would always reply.

O'Brien smiled as he reminisced. Tracy and he had been married for almost fourteen years and she certainly had put up with a lot. O'Brien knew that back then as he did today. The two of them had met in a bar when he was a rookie, about eight months after he'd been shot. A month later, they were married. It wasn't a big wedding. They invited some friends to be witnesses and they were married by a Justice of the Peace. It cost about five hundred dollars out of pocket expenses. It was the most meaningful five hundred dollars O'Brien had ever spent. If he could change anything in his life, that wouldn't be it.

As he lay there on the bed, memories of his father fluttered his mind. He'd slipped into God's hands in '98 at the age of sixty-seven due to heart failure. While he was growing up, O'Brien's dad was probably the biggest influence in his life, although the two rarely saw eye to eye until O'Brien was in his twenties. He bred into O'Brien what was right and what was wrong. It was because of his dad's influence that O'Brien wasn't able to tell that lady at the Copeland Car & Truck rental a line of hooey.

"Honesty is the best policy in all that you will do, son," his dad always said or "Get back on that horse and ride." What his dad meant by that was no matter how hard life gets, if you fall, get back up again. These words had helped O'Brien recover after being shot. Although his old man wasn't fond of O'Brien's career choice, he never batted an eye. *I miss him,* O'Brien thought as he smiled.

Around 1:00 a.m., he was finally able sleep. His back didn't seem to be bothering him as much as he expected it to and sleep found him quickly. He was awakened the next morning by the sound of someone knocking on the door.

"Who is it?" O'Brien responded as he covered his head with the pillow.

"Copeland Car and Truck."

"What time is it?" O'Brien asked.

He had left his watch on the desk the night before and it was out of his reach as he lay there in bed.

"11:00 a.m." came the reply.

O'Brien sighed and sat up, then walked over to the door and opened it.

"Here are your keys," the kid said as he handed them to him.

Rubbing his eyes, O'Brien asked which car it was. The kid pointed to a purple jalopy.

"You got to be kidding?"

"No sir, that's the one. A 1987 Toyota Camry just came in last night."

"All right then, thanks," O'Brien said as he began to turn and close the door.

"Oh yeah, I'm supposed to tell you that the contract is in the glove box."

"Sure thing."

O'Brien closed the door. He walked into the bathroom and brushed his teeth. He couldn't believe what time it was. *Boy, did I sleep well,* he thought to himself.

He didn't bother with breakfast that day. Instead, he headed to the car and fired it up. First order of business today would be finding a Blood Donor Clinic. He needed to know if such clinics made it a practice to buy blood from private vendors. If they did, then maybe as the coroner implied, someone was killing people for blood. It was a long shot; still, it was a shot.

It didn't take him long to find the Red Cross building. After getting a parking spot near the front doors, he entered the clinic.

He introduced himself and asked if he could speak to someone in charge.

"Is there something I can help you with?"

"Maybe. Does the Red Cross buy blood from private vendors?"

O'Brien knew it was a shot in the dark, but he had to ask.

"On occasion we have, but not recently."

"Really. When you have bought from a vendor who usually supplies you?"

"It's hard to say. Pat usually picked it up. It's not something we get in the mail, you know?"

"I'm aware of that," O'Brien replied. "When Pat picks up the plasma on those occasions, where does he or she get it?"

"Pat is a she. I'd have to look it up. It's been so long."

"That's all right. By the way, what's your name?"

"It's Pete, Pete Tennison."

"Thanks a bunch for your help, Pete. You may have shed some light on a bit of a dilemma I was having."

"Glad I could be of help."

O'Brien thanked him again, then turned and walked outside. His gut instincts told him that he was barking up the wrong tree. Still, he was compelled to scribble the information he had obtained from Pete into his notebook. Starting up the car, he drove into a nearby McDonalds and ordered some lunch. He decided to catch the early flight home the next day. He had all the information he could obtain from Copeland; there was no need to stick around. Finishing his burger and fries, he headed back to the Cobbler. He phoned the airport and made a reservation to catch the 10:00 a.m. flight back to Fruitmont on Thursday.

Then he phoned Copeland Car & Truck Rental and asked if they could pick the car up at the hotel and drive him to the airport in the morning. They informed him that wouldn't be a problem, but he would still have to pay for the full day on Thursday. O'Brien teasingly told the lady that if the driver got him to the airport on time, he'd even throw in a tip. He went through his notebook for the rest of the day scribbling out theories here and there. By 9:00 p.m., he was ready to crash.

True to their word, Copeland Car & Truck Rental picked him up in time to make his flight. As he exited the car, the driver made it a point to remind him that he had promised to throw in a tip. O'Brien looked the driver in the eye.

"I did say that, didn't I?"

"Yes you did, sir," the kid replied.

"My tip then is this: don't believe everything you hear."

The kid looked at him in disappointment and somewhat hurt.

"I'm just kidding," O'Brien chuckled as he reached into his pocket and pulled out a red back. "Here's fifty bucks. Don't spend it all in one spot."

The fifty was more than a day's rental on the car, but O'Brien figured the kid deserved it.

The kid's eyes grew as big as saucers and he smiled.

"Thanks, man."

O'Brien nodded and entered the airport terminal. His flight took off on time and by 3:00 p.m.; he was on his way home from the airport in Fruitmont.

# Four

The drive from the airport seemed to take forever with red lights, green lights, and all that stop and go jive. It didn't matter though. O'Brien was just glad to be back in Fruitmont. Before heading home, he went to the office to punch a few things into his computer. Tracy, he knew, would be expecting him by now because he hadn't arrived on Wednesday. She knew, also, that when he returned from afar he always stopped off at the office first. It was always his policy to take care of business. That way he could leave his work at the office and not take it home with him. It was something he did by choice.

O'Brien was surprised to see that Henderson's car wasn't in the parking lot. He pulled into his usual spot and exited the car. Entering the glass doors to Henderson & Co. PI Agency, he was pummelled by an array of questions from the crew working that night.

"Hey O'Brien, what did you come up with in Copeland?" asked Hal.

"O'Brien, do you really think there is a bunch of lunatics running around offing transients to make a couple of bucks by selling their blood?" another asked.

"Who do you think would do such a thing?" asked Rory.

By the time O'Brien finally made it to his desk, he had answered probably fifteen questions all with the same answer.

"I'm working on it."

O'Brien got Hal and Rory to come over to his desk. He let them know in more certain terms what he had found out. He asked whom Henderson sent to Hinton and when they were expected back. O'Brien was pleased to hear that Henderson had sent Thom Beard. Bluebeard they all called him, not because he wore a beard, but because the name suited him.

Henderson had hired him because of his ability to motivate people.

"He's supposed to return on Monday or Tuesday. Says he's come up with some new evidence that may support our theory," responded Hal.

"All right then," O'Brien said as he switched off the computer. "We'll all get together when he gets back and hash this thing out. I figure with the four of us we'll make good progress."

Back in Hinton, Thom Beard was talking with one of the constables on duty at the RCMP station.

"Has anything like this happened before?" Thom asked.

"Not since I've been here and I've been here for almost ten years."

"What about the marks? Has the coroner been able to identify them yet?"

"He hasn't got a clue, but the marks strategically coincide with major arteries. Looks like whoever is doing this isn't wasting their time in getting to the source."

"That's my thought, too. From what I've seen of the body it looks like someone used a pair of vice-grips or something to tear the flesh away?"

"That's a good thought, Thom. Come to think of it… I could see a pair of bolt cutters doing that kind of damage. Did you mention that to Hank, the coroner?"

"No, never thought of it until now. Bolt cutters, huh?"

"Yeah. See that's how I lost my two fingers," the Constable said as he held out his left hand showing that two of his fingers were indeed missing.

"Ouch. That must have hurt."

"Oh, it did. It was a long time ago and a long story. Should we phone Hank, and have him take a closer look, at those marks?"

"Probably would be a good idea. Go ahead and phone him. I'm going back to the crime scene again. Let him know I'll be stopping by later."

"You got it, Thom."

Thom Beard arrived back at the Hinton scene thirty minutes later. He took out a tape measure, his 35 mm camera and note pad. He was like O'Brien in that sense, always returning to the scene as many times as it would take to answer one question. Slipping on gloves, he began measuring from the impact point to the place where the body was found. Looking closely at the perimeter surrounding the scene, he searched for tire tracks or footprints that the assailants may have left behind, but found nothing. As with all three scenes, no other tracks of any kind were found.

Beard snapped a couple of pictures and headed back to his car. Noting the time, he drove to the Hinton mortuary.

"Have you come up with anything new for me?" Thom asked the coroner.

"Not so far. I'm still trying to match the characteristics of those laceration marks on the body. I've tried bolt cutters like Constable Blake suggested, but nothing comes close. I don't know what to tell you about them. But I can tell you the corpse dropped a distance of fifty or sixty feet for his ribs to break as they have."

"He's got broken bones?"

"Yep, he sure does."

"No one told me that he had any broken bones."

"That's because no one knew until now. You're the first I've told."

"Why is that?"

"No reason. I only finished up with that test a few minutes before you showed up. I'll be letting Constable Blake know in the morning. It'll also be in my formal report."

"Good enough," said Beard as he jotted down a few quick notes. "So, what you're telling me is that this guy took a fall after death? Is that what caused his ribs to break?"

"That about sums it up, yes."

"And you aren't sure yet what was used to cut up the body that way?"

"Other than it's a quick way to extract blood, not a clue yet. Maybe after a few more tests I'll be able to give you an idea, but so far not an indication, detective."

"You have been a great deal of help. I appreciate what you've been able to come up with so far."

Beard thanked the coroner for his help and returned to his motel room. He called ahead to Hal to inform him of the new findings. Hal mentioned that O'Brien was back from Copeland and he convinced Beard to phone him up as well.

O'Brien and Tracy's kids weren't home yet. They were still out at their Grandmother's. O'Brien was just getting over his jet leg when the phone rang. By the time he got off the phone with Beard, he was almost convinced that they were indeed dealing with a serial killer. The fact that the victim in Hinton had broken bones, from what the coroner assumed to be a fall from fifty to sixty feet, got O'Brien thinking. The case was really starting to get complicated.

They weren't only looking for someone who may have a police or medical background, but someone who also enjoyed torturing their victims. O'Brien knew that once they all sat down and hashed it over, it might make more sense. He thanked Beard for calling. The possibility that someone was stringing up corpses and watching them fall after they had bled to death was really quite unnerving.

O'Brien commenced lounging on the couch for the rest of the evening, Tracy at his side. All the information on the case and the information from Hal and Rory, along with what Beard came up with, O'Brien began to process in his brain until his head hurt. Finally, at 3:00 a.m., he was able to sleep.

Waking up Friday morning, with the same headache from the night before, O'Brien threw some water on his face, brushed his teeth, and popped a Tylenol. Tracy met him outside on their back deck the way she always did during the warmer days of spring and summer. They would drink their first coffee of the day together and listen to the birds. O'Brien told her that he was sorry for seeming so withdrawn the previous night.

"It's all right. I know how you get with cases like this, you know, ones with so many possibilities and theories. Besides, things were nice until Bluebeard phoned," she added with a smile.

They were ten minutes into conversation when they heard the ringing of the phone. Neither one of them really wanted to answer it so they decided to leave it for the answering service to pick up. Besides, if it was important, they'd phone back.

They talked for another half an hour before O'Brien finally left for the office. Kissing Tracy goodbye, he headed to work. He arrived in the parking lot at the same time as Henderson did. Together they walked into the office. During their meek conversation, Henderson turned to O'Brien and unexpectedly said, "How would you like to become the Co., in Henderson & Co.?"

O'Brien was taken aback and before he could reply, he watched as Henderson entered his office. *What did he mean by that?* He thought as he turned and walked to his desk. Henderson hadn't even asked when he got back or how his flight was or anything that was relevant. Just simply, 'how would you like to become the Co., in Henderson & Co.'. Not that O'Brien was complaining; it actually made him feel somewhat good. It seemed odd, however, for Henderson to say something like that.

Sitting down at his desk, he turned on his computer. As the system booted up, he opened his briefcase, grabbed his notes, and began going over them for the hundredth time.

Finally, he phoned up Womarz and asked him if the lacerations to the body found in Fruitmont were at or near the main arteries. Womarz said that they were. O'Brien scribbled his answer down, thanked him, and hung up. He dialled the coroner's office in Copeland and asked him the same question. Indeed, the lacerations were very near and around the main arteries to the thigh and biceps. The case in Grandbluff, however, was too old and the coroner there wasn't the same one who had examined the body. He said he had given a copy of the coroners' report to Hal and Rory. It was all he was able to do. He said the coroner at that time was one Mitch Hagen, now retired and living on the West Coast. O'Brien thanked him for his co-operation and hung up the phone.

Hal and Rory were pulling the night shift so O'Brien wouldn't be able to talk to them until later unless he phoned one of them. However, he knew how annoying it was to be woken up after an eight or twelve-hour shift. He decided he'd wait to talk to them. Instead, he punched the name of Dr. Mitch Hagen into the National Database of Medical Examiners. Within minutes, his address and phone number popped up. O'Brien wrote all the information down in case it was needed on a later date.

Amongst all the commonalties he realised about the killings were that the bodies had obviously been mutilated in a way to extract blood. O'Brien wondered how the perpetrators managed to gather all the plasma or, for that matter, if they had even bothered. *What if these are just homicides with a twist? What if the perpetrators just enjoyed watching the victims succumb to loss of blood,* O'Brien cringed at the thought.

They had evidence that the bodies had been moved from one locale to the other. What they were lacking was why, who and where. Why would someone do it? Who had done it? Where did the murders take place? O'Brien closed his notebook and worked on a few different reports for the rest of the day until Hal and Rory came on shift. He got them to show him the coroner's report from Grandbluff. It was an ordinary report and the drawing showed where the lacerations had been on the body. They didn't differ from the ones of the most recent killings. Again, an unknown instrument or implement had caused the lacerations.

"We have to find out what is being used to do this," O'Brien stated as he gazed at the picture.

"I know. Rory and I are going to work on that tonight."

"It's too bad that the bolt cutter theory wasn't any good, but there are a few other items that we're going to look at," Rory commented.

"If you come up with anything that matches, don't hesitate to call me at home. If you don't, I'll see you guys on Monday," O'Brien responded as he handed the folder back to Hal.

"What! You're not working tomorrow, O'Brien?" Hal asked.

"Not if I can help it."

O'Brien thought it strange that he hadn't seen hide nor hair of Henderson all day. Usually by coffee time, Henderson was barking at him for this, that or the other thing. Today, for some reason, he had left him completely alone. O'Brien exited into the cool evening and walked the distance to his car. His biggest concern was what was being used to tear away the flesh from the victims. Once they figured that out, he knew things would fall into place. Since seeing the first body, he knew that the only solid clues were the victims' wounds. It wasn't animals and now he knew it wasn't bolt cutters either. As for who the murderers were, O'Brien was no closer to that than he was at the beginning of the week. He could only hope that Hal and Rory would come up with something. He was fresh out of ideas.

# Five

O'Brien drove around Fruitmont for almost an hour just to think. It was something he did when he was baffled as he was now. He tried hard to put things into perspective, but kept coming up short. He replayed the two crime scenes he had attended repeatedly in his head. The idea that someone was selling blood on the black market sounded plausible, but not as plausible as the cult idea.

Not being able to come up with anything new, he seriously considered stopping off at the local watering hole to chug back a rye and ginger. The problem with that was that one usually led to another and then another and so on until he was obliterated. Instead, he decided to pick up a bottle of good wine and take it home. Pulling in behind Ed's Liquor Store, O'Brien parked the car and stepped out. Inside he purchased a fifty-dollar bottle of medium dry white wine.

"Going on a bender, O'Brien?" Ed asked.

"Not tonight, Ed. I'm just taking home a bottle so Tracy and I can have a glass of wine with dinner."

"By the way, O'Brien, how are you guys making out with that case?"

"What case is that, Ed?"

"The one where that guy was found over at the train yard. I heard he was mutilated."

"He was."

"I also heard a rumour that there wasn't a drop of blood left in his body. Is that true?"

"Why are you concerned with that, Ed?"

"I'm not. Just curious is all."

"Remember that old saying, Ed? Curiosity is what killed the cat."

"Yeah, I know, but I thought I could shed some light on the case."

Ed was a wannabe cop. He always had been for as long as O'Brien had known him. He'd also helped O'Brien shed light on a case or two. They often played a game; O'Brien would ask him a couple of questions not really related to any one crime. Then, Ed would come up with some good theories. O'Brien always wondered why Ed hadn't become a cop. It wasn't because of his lack of potential that was for sure. Ed was good at coming up with analogies, theories and was extremely good at thought deduction. His weakness was he could go on for quite some time.

"All right, say the victim was drip-dried? In addition, to make it a little bit more interesting, let's say there were lacerations or tears, if you like, all over the body. However, here is the kicker. Whatever it is that has caused the tears has not been identified. What would you suggest, Ed?" O'Brien dared, knowing that he had given out more information than perhaps he should have. Not even the local paper had revealed that much of the case. However, O'Brien knew Ed and he knew Ed wasn't one to say anything in regard to cases they discussed, not because he didn't want to, but because he couldn't be sure if the cases were relevant or if they happened as O'Brien said. O'Brien would never clarify.

"First thing that I'd do is look over the lacerations, tears or whatever you called them to be sure that's what they are. To me a laceration means a deep thin wound; a tear on the other hand means to remove in chunks, whereas a gouge means also to remove in chunks that are deeper than a tear. Once I figured out which of the three it was and it turned out to be tearing, I'd think that maybe the victims were hung say like a side of beef or pork, you know, with meat hooks. Eventually the weight of the body caused the meat hooks to pull out which in turn caused the tears."

O'Brien stood there listening wondering now if he should have even asked. Boy, could Ed ramble on.

"Just from those few what if's you're able to come up with all that?" O'Brien asked dumbfounded.

"Sure, O'Brien, think about it. Try not to confuse yourself with lacerations, gouges, tears and what have you, because each one is caused differently," Ed replied.

"You are incredibly brilliant, Ed, did you know that?"

"Working with the public the way I do, you hear and see a lot of stuff. For instance, farmer Brown comes in and says he gouged his hand on a farming implement. Next day the town drunk comes in and say's he tore the crap out of his elbow when he fell down a bank…" O'Brien cut him off there and raised his hand for him to halt.

"I get your point, Ed."

"Just remember that lacerations, abrasions, bruises, contusions, cuts, gouges, and tears are all different. Each one represents a different cause. Let me give you another example, O'Brien."

*Good God,* O'Brien thought to himself as he chuckled.

"All right, give it to me, Ed."

"The other day I went to the doctor to have a bugger of a cyst on my derriere looked at. The doctor never gouged it out. No sir, he lacerated it so it would drain."

It was a little bit more than what O'Brien wanted to hear, but it was certainly a good analogy, and it left a picture in his head that he wouldn't soon forget. Ed put the wine into a bag and handed it to O'Brien smiling the entire time.

"So you see, O'Brien, one has to look hard at what they're looking at before they can sometime see it."

O'Brien smiled and nodded at Ed as he took the brown paper bag. Thanking Ed one last time, he left. Setting the bottle down on the seat next to him, he started the car and headed for home. It was close to 7:30 p.m. when he pulled into the driveway. There were no lights on inside the house and Tracy's car wasn't in her spot. O'Brien wondered where she might have gone. The note on the table explained all that.

Apparently, she had been called away to Alberta. The phone call that came in that morning was from her friend Gin. Gin's father had died and Gin wanted her to come to the funeral which was scheduled for the following Tuesday.

Gin and Tracy had grown up together and were like sisters. It was only proper that she attend the funeral. O'Brien put the wine into the fridge to keep it chilled and made himself a sandwich, then turned on the TV. It was certainly going to be quiet for the next while. The kids weren't coming back until the following weekend and he wouldn't be seeing Tracy until Thursday, probably.

*Six days without the wife and eight days without the children. What am I going do with all this peace and quiet?* O'Brien thought as he sighed.

The TV lulled him to sleep around 11:00 p.m. When he awoke on Saturday, his back was so tight he could hardly move. He hated it when he fell asleep on the couch. The thing was too short for one and too narrow for another. Slowly making his way to the kitchen, he brewed a pot of coffee. Until it was ready, he decided to have a glass of orange juice. Opening the fridge to get some, the bottle of wine caught his eye and he began to think about the conversation with Ed. He wondered if what Ed said had any merit. Closing the fridge door, he sat down at the breakfast nook and contemplated the entire case again. He figured on two good scenarios to work with. One, some sadistic killer was running around hanging people up with meat hooks or two, some cult was engaging in extreme bloodletting. The third possibility, and one that he was really beginning to doubt, was the possibility that someone was selling the blood as a commodity on the black market.

He preferred scenario number one. It made sense to him now as he sat in the kitchen sipping Java. It also coincided with what Beard had said. Beard stated that the corpse in Hinton suffered a fall after death. *Therefore,* O'Brien thought, *the victim is possibly above the ground strung up like a piece of meat by hooks. The victim gradually dies. The hooks slowly tear away and the corpse falls to the ground.*

He recalled that Beard said that the coroner figured the one victim fell fifty or sixty feet. *That would mean that the victims were hung up at least that high. That would be horrible.* O'Brien thought as he sipped his morning coffee. What made him cringe even more is that he was visualising an elaborate pulley system that the killer or killers would have in order to be able to lift the weight of a full-grown man up that high. O'Brien poured another coffee. He knew that he would have to go over meat hook theory with Hal and Rory. Picking up the phone, he called Hal first.

"What did you and Rory come up with last night?"

"Every two-handled tool that we considered turned out to be a dud. Why are you calling me this early, O'Brien? Don't tell me you wanted to know what we came up with last night. You know that if we had come up with anything substantial we would have called. You want me to come to the office, don't you, you bastard?" Hal questioned with humour.

"I did come up with something interesting. I think we better move on it."

"What did you come up with this time, O'Brien?"

"I'd rather not go over it with you on the phone, Hal. I'd appreciate it if you'd meet me down at the office?"

"Man, O'Brien, I've only had a few hours of sleep."

"I know, Hal. Be grateful. It's more than I get on any given day. Can I count on you?"

"You know you can. What time do you want me there?"

"Within the next couple of hours."

"Good enough. I'll see you then. And O'Brien, this better be good."

Hal chuckled as he hung up the phone.

It took a bit more convincing to get Rory to come down to the office, but he soon submitted to O'Brien's plea and said he'd be along shortly. O'Brien thanked him and hung up the phone. With time to spare before he'd have to leave, he hopped in the shower. He made it as hot as possible to loosen up his back muscles. He let the water beat down on his back until the hot water tank ran empty. After drying himself, he dressed and left for the office.

Stopping off at the bakery, he picked up a dozen doughnuts. Hal and Rory, he knew, would appreciate it; and besides, he hadn't eaten any breakfast yet and doughnuts and coffee sounded good. The smell of the bakery as he opened the door was that of fresh bread and cinnamon buns. As he approached the counter, he began to smell melting chocolate and freshly brewed coffee. It smelled like no other bakery that he had ever been in.

"Good morning, detective. The usual?" asked Mrs. Vandermeir.

"You bet," O'Brien replied as he inhaled deeply, "sure smells good."

"Ah, Horace says he's come up with another recipe. Says it's his Grandmother's. What he seems to forget is that I knew his Grandma, I can tell you that she'd never make a concoction like that. We've been married now going on forty some odd years. Every time he comes up with another recipe to try, he says it's his Grandma's."

"What's he trying to make?" O'Brien questioned out of curiosity.

One thing was for certain, whatever it was smelled good.

"Some kind of blueberry thingamabob or thingamajig; I don't know," said Mrs. Vandermeir. "You want me to call him? Horace!" she began.

"No, no that's all right, Golga."

O'Brien had known Horace and Golga going on twenty years. They had bought the old bakery in the eighties. It was quite run down back then, but hard work and perseverance by Horace and Golga made it what it was today.

"Just tell Horace for me that whatever it is he's throwing together, sure smells good," O'Brien said with a smile.

"Why not you tell Horace yourself?" a heavy Dutch accent voiced.

O'Brien turned around and there stood Horace in his baker attire.

"Horace! How are you doing?"

O'Brien reached out his hand to shake Horace's. The two hadn't seen each other in a while.

"I'm doing; I'm doing. Haven't seen you in days. You better not be buying doughnuts elsewhere," Horace commented as he jokingly shook his fist at O'Brien.

"You'll never have to worry about that, Horace," O'Brien smiled.

"Why are you out and about so early on a Saturday? Tracy making you cook, breakfast? Or as you young folk like to say, brunch?" Horace asked as he chuckled.

"Just on my way to the office. I got some work to go over."

"O'Brien, you work like a baker, you know that? Always go, go, and go. Ah, there is no rest for today's businessman, is there?" he asked, referring to when O'Brien had operated Absolute Investigations back east.

"There sure isn't, Horace; there sure isn't."

"It was nice to see you again, O'Brien."

"It was good to see you too, Horace," O'Brien said as he turned to pay for the doughnuts.

"These ones are my treat."

Golga tapped him on the wrist. O'Brien thanked her. Turned and walked outside to his car. He arrived at the office in plenty of time to organise his presentation for Hal and Rory. Using the extra time, he phoned Womarz. He wanted to know what the possibilities were that meat hooks might have been used.

At first, the coroner thought it was going to be a waste of time. He went on to tell O'Brien that he really didn't have the time and so on. After O'Brien explained the urgency, and why it was important, he was finally able to convince Womarz.

"I'll get the results back to you by midday," he promised.

O'Brien thanked him for his help and willingness and hung up. If Womarz promised to get back to him by midday that would be exactly what Womarz would do. One thing about Cliff Womarz was that he was a man of his word. Not much escaped his trained eye when he was younger, but with age, as with most things, his eyesight was deteriorating. However, his skill, knowledge, and word were still as good as gold. O'Brien knew that if indeed meat hooks or hooks of any kind played a part in the killings, old Womarz would be the guy to discover it.

O'Brien was able to get a message to Beard via the RCMP in Hinton. He asked if they could round him up and to have him call the office ASAP. The Constable said that it wouldn't be a problem. All that was left now was to wait for Hal and Rory to show up. O'Brien was expecting them in the next fifteen or twenty minutes. Erickson, the one guy working in the office, had made a fresh pot of Joe and O'Brien stood to go grab a cup. He noticed a memo he hadn't seen yet. From the memo, he learned that one of Henderson & Co.'s senior detectives in Ridgeville was retiring. It went on to say that detective Wainwright was also one of the founders. Henderson's firm in Ridgeville was small, but so was the town. O'Brien wondered if that was what Henderson was implying that past Friday. Shrugging his shoulders, he pinned the memo up again. Around that time Hal and Rory walked in, each holding a cappuccino smothered in whip cream.

"What do you got for us, O'Brien?" Rory asked as he slurped.

O'Brien explained to them what he had and why he thought, it was so. They compared their notes. O'Brien showed them the diagrams he had as well as the photos he had taken. They went over the old coroner's report from Grandbluff and compared it with the other two. Although the diagram that was supplied with it was old and worn, it was easy enough to see that the marks on the three bodies matched and that they were all in the same basic area. They hashed over it for forty-five minutes before the phone rang.

"Hello, Henderson & Co.," O'Brien responded.

"Hey O'Brien, this is Thom."

"Howdy Bluebeard, what took you so long?" O'Brien asked with a chuckle.

"Snoozing somewhere were ya?" Hal blurted out.

Thom silently laughed.

"Both of them there with ya?"

"Oh yeah. We've come up with something that we really ought to look at."

"I guess you want me to fax you what I've come up with?"

"Yeah that would be great. When are you heading back?"

"Depending on what you come up with between now and tomorrow, I might be back at the office by Monday. Other than that, I am heading back on Tuesday. Unless you need me to stay, there really isn't much more that I have to go through down here."

"Well then, the good news up this way is we might be getting close to what caused all those tears."

"That is good news, O'Brien; the coroner down here is miffed at what might have caused the wounds."

"Well, once we all get together I'm sure we'll figure it out." O'Brien was confident that they would.


Thom Beard faxed what he had come up with, as well as a copy of the coroner's report. The first items that O'Brien's crew at the office received by way of fax were four numbered photos of the crime scene followed by the coroner's and RCMP reports. Then they received the notes that Beard had taken as well as the diagrams that he had drawn. It was a delicious assortment, half of which was gibberish, but nonetheless they pieced it all together and were able to ascertain, that yes, they were getting very close. All they needed now was a phone call from Womarz to seal the deal. If he was able to prove that hooks had been used, O'Brien and his crew were ready to move.

The electricity that he was feeling at that particular moment, knowing that they were that much closer to putting the case to bed, was exhilarating. He could tell that Hal and Rory felt the same. The tasks that lay ahead they knew would be finding out where the murder scene was, how the bodies had been transported if not by train, identifying the victims by dental records, finger prints etc., and last, but not least, determining the motive and finding the killer or killers.

Noticing that it was almost half past two, O'Brien was getting a little antsy as the three of them waited for the call from Womarz. It was like playing poker; they had either a full house or three of a kind. A royal flush would be when they were honing in on the trash that was doing all the gruesome killings. At 3:00 p.m., O'Brien told Rory and Hal that they were quite welcome to take off. It didn't matter if Womarz phoned, as it was too late to do anything after receiving the call anyway. Besides, they had already accomplished a lot in the past few hours. O'Brien wanted them to be fresh before they made their next move.

"Are you sure, O'Brien?" Hal asked.

"Without a doubt, Hal. Go home and get some sleep. You too, Rory. Go on; get out of here both of you. When the call comes in I'll let you know one way or the other."

O'Brien had barely completed the sentence and Hal and Rory were heading out the door.

"I'll see ya on Monday," he hollered after them.

An hour later Womarz phoned.

"O'Brien?"

"Yeah it's me, Cliff. What did you come up with?" O'Brien was excited.

"I did a weight test based on the weight of the guy I have on ice. I don't think I have meat hooks of the same size, but you were right. The tears resemble the ones on this guy almost to a tee. The ones that I've been able to create are a little smaller, which is why I don't think I have the right-sized hook. Other than that, I'd bet my pension that you were right on the money."

"Yahoo! Even though you were only able to make small versions, would you say then that the victims at one time or another dangled on hooks?"

"Most definitely. I'd also be willing to say that the victims were alive during that time. They'd have to be in order for them to bleed out as they have."

"Excellent, Cliff; perfectly excellent."

"I'll have my final report drawn up and sent to you by Monday."

"Thanks a lot, Cliff. I appreciate it."

"And O'Brien…"

"Yeah."

"Get the psycho that's doing this. We need him off our streets," Womarz replied.

"I hear you, Cliff. We're all going to do our best," O'Brien replied with sincerity and conviction.

"I wouldn't expect anything less from you, O'Brien. Goodnight."

"Night, Cliff."

O'Brien was so charged up with the good news that his heart was palpitating. It may have taken almost a week to figure out for sure what had caused the gruesome tearing, but now he knew. Now they had a lead. Hal and Rory were both thrilled at the news. Even though they had spent the better part of Friday's shift going through catalogues and itemised tool categories trying to match something that may have caused the tears, neither one had even considered looking into meat hooks. Then again, neither had O'Brien; that is, not until he had spoken with Ed the 'Wonder Man'.

O'Brien made one last phone call to the Hinton RCMP detachment and left another message for Beard to call him soon. Then, he closed up shop and headed home. The house was cool and silent. Making his way into the living room, he slumped into his favorite chair. He was overcome with exhaustion. He didn't even have the poop to get up and have a bite to eat. Since Monday he'd felt that the entire world was resting on his shoulders and all the people were yelling. Finally, tonight he could rest. As for tomorrow… who knew?

## Six

That Sunday, O'Brien received two phone calls. One was from Tracy. They talked for close to an hour. At 2:00 p.m., Thom Beard called.

"What's up?" he asked.

O'Brien filled him in on the progress they had made and suggested that he drive back. Thom agreed and said he would head back that evening.

In the backwoods of a little train town northwest of Fruitmont called Slocolm, the killer was stringing up victim number four. The blood-curdling screams were like a symphony to the killer, a symphony that he hadn't heard in ten years. Each time he pulled on the ropes that raised the victim, he did so in one fluid motion. Each time he stopped, he gave the ropes a quick jerk causing his victim to scream in excruciating pain.

The killer's name was Anvil Brentwood. Anvil had been only recently released from Matsqui Maximum Penitentiary. He had served ten years out of the fifteen he was sentenced to for beating a man to death with an eight-pound sledgehammer. The man had been beaten so badly that his spine was exposed to the cold earth and bone fragments were embedded in the ground beneath his body.

Anvil's lawyer had managed to get him a plea of insanity because his father had abused him daily as a child and that the victim somehow triggered a regression mechanism that caused him to react. For the first three years, Anvil resided in a mental hospital. When the Psychologist believed that they could no longer help Anvil and he became uncooperative, he was sent to Matsqui where he spent twenty-three hours a day in an eight by ten cell for the next seven years.

As Anvil's fourth victim dangled above his head, he did nothing but stare as his victim bled dry. When the hooks in the body tore away and the victim's corpse landed with a thud to the ground, Anvil smiled.

"That'll teach you, papa," he hissed.

Anvil was not well-educated. As a child, he had endured countless beatings from his father. Because they moved from town to town, as he grew up he was unable to have many friends. He spent most of his childhood cowering in the woods hiding from his maniacal father. The trees and animals were what he called his friends. What he knew about the human body he had learned from the beatings his father laid upon him. He knew where every pressure point was. He knew where the main arteries were because his father had threatened him time and again that he was going to tear them out and watch him bleed. Every time his dad threatened him with that, he would grab Anvil near where the arteries were and squeeze so hard that young Anvil would receive a big black bruise.

As for Anvil's mother, he didn't even know if he had one. When Anvil turned sixteen, his father accidentally fell beneath the wheels of a moving train. From that day on, Anvil wandered through life aimlessly, taking up jobs from here or there. Usually he didn't work for more than a couple of months at any one job and sometimes only for days. Experts had said that Anvil's thirst to kill came at a young age, probably when he pushed his father in front of the train, although that was never proven. It was easy to guess why he might do such a thing.

He was in his early fifties and still he dreamt about the beatings and humiliation his dad put him through. He sat next to the corpse of his fourth victim poking at it with a stick. Standing, he walked over to the blood puddle that was slowly coagulating and seeping into the ground. Looking at his reflection in the dark pool, he smiled.

"Papa is dead now," he whispered.

Sitting on the ridge that overlooked Slocolm, Anvil waited for the next train to pull in. From there he had a view of the train yard as well as the little town. It is why he chose that particular spot and called it home. Hours passed and he only looked blankly ahead at the tracks. At 5:00 p.m., he heard the whistle blow. Throwing the limp body over his shoulder, Anvil headed toward the train yard. He had timed his descent to the yard on many different occasions and he knew that with a corpse that weighed 160 to 180 pounds, he could easily do it in less than fifteen minutes. This left him plenty of time to load up the corpse and jump onboard.

The way the yard was overgrown with weeds and crabgrass offered him all the protection he needed when leaving with his victims. Today the train was heading south towards the town of Applecove, the direction of one of Anvil's favourite pick up spots. There was a small community of homeless people, vagrants, and hobos. Near the outskirts where Anvil knew, he could befriend another victim. Within a day or two, he would convince the victim to come along with him back to his lair.

As the train came to a screeching halt, Anvil crept up to it picking out the boxcar that he and the corpse would share. Slamming the heavy door closed until the train began to move again, he threw the body onto the hard wooden floor and sat down with his back to the wall. In minutes, the train's whistle blew and the train began to chug along down the line. Anvil sat and waited until it began moving faster. Then he cracked opened the door to let the last rays of sunlight in. The next stop he knew was Cassle. It was a pulp and paper town two hours away. That was where he would dispose of the body. At a trestle that crossed over the Nipsu Creek. It would be there that he would toss out the corpse. He would be long gone before its discovery. What Anvil hadn't anticipated was that downstream a group of boy scouts and leaders had gathered to camp for the night. They were on a four-day canoe trip and were working their way upstream to where the Tomaw Creek joined the Nipsu. As if by instinct, Anvil opened the door to the boxcar minutes before the train slowly crossed the trestle. He threw the body into the rushing Nipsu. With the deed done, he closed the door and sat in the darkness of the boxcar, his mind racing with images of his father, his victims, and his life. What a miserable life it had been!

O'Brien spent the majority of the day indoors watching TV. In the evening, he took his coffee mug out to the deck and watched as the moon began to rise. It was a beautiful night. The whippoorwills were beginning to make their presence known, as were the crickets that orchestrated in unison. O'Brien listened intently to the sounds for what seemed like hours. At 11:00 p.m., he retreated to bed.

Arriving at work Monday morning, he found Thom sitting at his desk.

"Hey, Thom how's it going? What time did you get in?"

"Around 6:00 this morning."

"You must be tired. That drive is boring, isn't it?"

"Boring isn't the word; try monotonous."

O'Brien made his way over to the coffee and asked if Thom wanted one.

"Do you want a refill, Thom?"

"Sure, I think I can put down another, two sugars and a cream, please."

"You got it, buddy."

O'Brien brought the cup over to him. He asked if Thom had the time to go over a few things about the case or if he just wanted to go home to bed. He was glad when Thom said he'd stick around. The two of them hashed out the case, chopped it up, ate it, and went over it again. When they couldn't go any further on the case without doing some footwork, they agreed to take up the conversation on Tuesday after Thom had a day to recoup. Before leaving, Thom asked if any dental records on the victims might have shown up. Unfortunately, they hadn't and O'Brien informed him of such.

"No dental, medical, or even prints have come in as far as I know, but the day is still young," O'Brien commented.

"That it is, O'Brien. If something comes in, call me, would you?"

"You know I will, Thom," O'Brien assured him.

"Thanks a lot, O'Brien. See you tomorrow bright and early."

"See ya tomorrow, Bluebeard," O'Brien replied as he stood from Thom's desk and walked over to his own.

One of the things he liked about Beard was that he was always quite thorough. Hal and Rory were still scheduled for graveyard shift for the rest of the week and relaying information back and forth was going to be somewhat pressing. Thom, on the other hand, was on permanent days like O'Brien. For that, O'Brien was grateful. Working a case like this alone would be a pain in the ass.

O'Brien sat down at his desk and decided that for the rest of the day he would go onto something else. There was an array of paperwork to complete regarding the Fogerty case. As well as a few loose ends that needed tying from other cases, he was working on.

He spent two hours finishing up his formal report on the Fogerty case and was reading it over to make sure he hadn't neglected or missed anything when his phone rang. It was Agent Riley from the FBI. He was phoning to see how the case was progressing. O'Brien filled him in on the progress and fed him a couple of lines of bunk. As far as O'Brien was concerned, it really wasn't any of his business on how well or otherwise they were doing, but O'Brien bit his tongue and told Agent Riley what he wanted to hear.

Riley was a nice enough guy and all. O'Brien just didn't like what he stood for. After a twenty-minute conversation and going over the most important points of the case, Riley bid O'Brien good luck and said that he'd keep in touch. *Yippee...* O'Brien thought. They said goodbye to each other on a good note. O'Brien, grit his teeth as he hung up the phone and silently muttered an obscenity. At 4:00 p.m., when the afternoon shift came on and O'Brien was leaving for the day, he ran into Henderson at the front door.

"What? Are you pulling nightshifts now, Henderson?"

"If you'd read the schedule once in a while, O'Brien, you'd know that I've been pulling nightshift since last week."

"That's funny, Henderson. I wasn't even here last week."

"Oh yeah, that's right. When did you get back?" Henderson scratched the top of his balding head.

"What's a matter with you, Henderson? Are you losing your mind? I got back on Friday. I even talked to you. Like I said last week, you better consider taking a holiday."

"I'm sorry, O'Brien. I've been so preoccupied lately."

"Obviously. What's going on?" O'Brien asked with concern.

"Oh, it's nothing; mostly business stuff," Henderson responded.

O'Brien knew what he was referring to. Losing a business partner either through life or death was always difficult. Even though Wainwright was only retiring and was alive and well, the financial burden and finding a replacement for him was probably causing Henderson great concern.

"Yeah, I read the memo. Sorry to hear Wainwright's leaving."

"He's one good detective; did you know that, O'Brien? It's going to be hard finding a replacement for him. As for a business partner, he's to be desired. I got to get going, O'Brien. We'll talk soon," Henderson said as he headed towards his office.

# Seven

It was Tuesday, July 17th; the time was 9:00 a.m. O'Brien was late getting to the office and missed Hal and Rory as they ended their shift. He wanted to speak with them briefly to find out if any ID's had yet been made on the John Doe's who were on ice. He knew that if anything important had come up they'd have emailed him. It was how they corresponded when they worked opposite shifts.

O'Brien anticipated that by now one of the victims would have been identified. He booted up the computer and opened his inbox. He noticed and opened the email marked 'Urgent'. Sure enough, identification had been made on the victim in Hinton. *If only Beard were still there,* O'Brien thought. It was by his request that Thom had returned early.

The victim's name was Ronald Chauncey, age 45. He had no fixed address or next of kin. He was a homeless fellow and had been seen over the years in and around Hinton. Nobody really knew much about him. The RCMP in Hinton had already spoken with someone who claimed they saw him with another man a week or so before the body was found. It was a cashier at a Shop 'n' Go. She was able to give a good description of the man he was with. He had a dark complexion and he was about 6' 2", probably weighed between 200 and 250 pounds. She guessed his age to be in the late forties or early fifties. He was wearing an old green and black checker jacket and torn blue jeans. He had brown eyes and hair. 'He was dressed up like an old bushman' the cops quoted her as saying.

She wasn't, however, able to pick out the guy's picture from any of the mug shots they showed her. One guy, however, resembled the man she had seen. It was a man named Brock Brentwood who had long since been dead. O'Brien was grateful that at least they had a brief description and that one of the victims was duly identified. It was turning out to be a pretty good morning. O'Brien looked at the clock; it was almost 10:30 a.m. and he wondered where Thom was. He went over and poured a fresh cup of coffee. If Thom didn't show up soon, he'd have to give him a call. The poor guy was probably still tired. It was a long drive from Hinton to Fruitmont, easily ten or twelve hours.

Why Thom hadn't taken, a flight was beyond O'Brien. He presumed it was because Thom was too paranoid. Thom always jokingly said to Henderson, 'Put the cost of the flight on my next pay'. Of course Henderson never did. Thom probably saved Henderson & Co., three or four grand a year by choosing to drive. If he could make it there by car in twenty-four hours or less, he'd just drive. O'Brien finished his cup of Joe and was rinsing his cup out when the front doors opened and Thom walked in.

"Bluebeard, you made it. Glad you could join us," O'Brien teased.

"Sorry, O'Brien, the little lady had plans last night. I didn't get to bed until late."

O'Brien knew what Thom meant and he asked Thom if he was still seeing the young lady from Stroh's Fitness.

"Nah, my new love is Debbie," responded Thom.

"No way. The waitress at the Chinese joint?" O'Brien asked with brevity.

"That's right, Debbie Chung Lei, and last night we 'boom boom long time' if you know what I mean?"

O'Brien did. He looked at Thom and shook his head as he smiled.

"Come on, Beard, let's get to work."

They sat down in one of the conference rooms and went over the stuff that Rory and Hal had emailed. Thom was a little perturbed that O'Brien called him back early because if he hadn't, he would have been able to talk to the clerk at the Shop 'n' Go himself.

"I know, but if you were still down there you'd have got no 'boom boom' last night. Be glad I called you back," O'Brien laughed.

"Good point," Thom replied smacking his lips.

The rest of the day went quickly and the last thing O'Brien and Thom did was punch in the possible suspect's description into a few different databases. O'Brien was surprised on how quickly he received the response back. Thirty-five possible matches came up. O'Brien looked over to Thom.

"Got anything over there, Thom?"

"How many bad guys do you think have brown eyes and hair and weigh between 180-250 lbs., and are between forty and fifty?" Thom asked sarcastically.

"I hear you. I got thirty-five matches so far and the numbers are rising."

"I got at least that many." Thom replied.

Together they had accumulated one hundred and fifty-three possible matches and that was only in British Columbia. They weren't going to try Alberta or, for that matter, Canada as a whole. Before they were able to do that, they would have to go through all the names they had already accumulated. If nothing came of it, they'd go the rest of the distance and search all of Canada.

Any lead was better than no lead. If that was what it was going to take, then that's what they were undoubtedly prepared to do. They stayed at the office until 6:00 p.m., checking some of the matches that the databases fired back to them. Henderson barked a couple of times telling them to go home and to let Rory and Hal work on it. Finally, after O'Brien and Thom went through twenty of the names and excluded them because they were either already dead or still in prison, they finally said goodnight. O'Brien quickly sent Hal an email with the remaining one hundred and thirty-three names. Then, he and Thom left for the day. Tomorrow they'd go back at it and tomorrow they would be that much closer.

Arriving home, O'Brien phoned Tracy to see how the funeral went.

"It went all right, I guess. You wouldn't believe how many people showed up. He was sure a well-liked man."

"How's Gin holding out?"

"She's doing okay."

"I'm glad to hear that. She was pretty close to her dad, wasn't she?"

"I suppose, yeah, she was."

"On a lighter note, how are you doing?"

"Pretty good. I'm not looking forward to the drive back tomorrow. It is supposed to get as hot as 35 degrees. Besides, I was thinking if it's okay by you, I'll stick around here for a couple of extra days. That way I can pick up the kids on my way back. I wouldn't mind going for a swim in the lake."

"Yeah, I suppose, if that's what you want to do. I guess it makes sense. No use coming home tomorrow and then having to drive back that way for three hours to pick the kids up. I'll just have to miss you longer."

"I miss you too, Tyler," she said.

O'Brien hated that name and she knew it. No one called him Tyler, not since high school; except for one detective, he had met back east and, of course, his mother. Tracy, on the other hand, did when she was teasing him.

"Hey, what's up with that?"

O'Brien heard Tracy snickering.

"I'm sorry, O'Brien. I just miss you so. I wish you were here. God, it seems like weeks since we've talked or had an intimate moment."

"It has been at least a week. First, I was gone and when I got back, you had to go. It does seem like weeks though, doesn't it?"

"Sure does."

"I'll tell you what. When you and the kids get back and the guys and I finish up with this case, let's take off somewhere. Henderson owes me a three-week vacation. We might as well use it. What do you say?" O'Brien asked with enthusiasm.

"That would be terrific!" Tracy exclaimed. "Do you really mean it, O'Brien?"

"Indeed. I need a vacation. If all goes well, maybe we can take off, say, the weekend of August 12?"

"That would be wonderful, O'Brien. We both could use some R and R."

After a few more minutes, they said their goodbyes and I love you. O'Brien hung up the phone and sighed. He wouldn't be seeing her or the kids for another few days. He wondered if in that time they could have the case put to rest. Somehow, he doubted it.

Wednesday came and O'Brien's crew worked their fingers to the bone. They managed to knock their list of suspects down to fifteen possibilities. Out of the fifteen, only four of them had addresses and worked. The others were going to be a pain to locate because there were no records of any of them working, collecting pensions, or receiving any benefits of any kind. They were able to interview two of the four that day and soon excluded them as suspects.

At 3:00 p.m., they got a call. Another corpse had been found, this time, floating face down in the Nipsu Creek at the point where the Tomaw flowed into it. Boy scouts who were canoeing in the area had discovered it. They would have to drive to the ghost town of Enterprise, which was five miles upstream from the find, then canoe down to where the corpse was. It would easily be a two-hour drive. O'Brien couldn't be sure how long it would take to canoe downstream. Medical personnel had already been dispatched. They considered repelling in from the helicopter, but because it wasn't a life and death situation, rather a recovery, they decided against it. They, too, were going to canoe down.

O'Brien was able to talk to one of the paramedics and tried to convince him to wait until he and Thom arrived. The best the paramedic could do was wait until the Forest Service got there with the canoes that the E.M.S. summoned. O'Brien knew the nearest Forestry Station was in Cassle and that it would probably take them as long as three or four hours to reach Enterprise creek from their direction.

With luck, O'Brien figured he and Thom could make it there themselves easily enough before then. The E.M.S. offered to heli-taxi them to Enterprise, but O'Brien already knew what Thom's choice of words would be to that, so he declined. O'Brien thanked the paramedic and told him that he and Thom would probably be there in a little over two hours.

It was a good thing that Thom owned an SUV. They arrived at Enterprise around 5:30 p.m. The road in was difficult to drive on and Thom's pride and joy ended up with a few more dents and scratches. O'Brien didn't know for sure, if it was because of the road or Thom's driving. He was a maniac behind the wheel and the dirt road was his nemesis. O'Brien's legs were a little shaky when they finally arrived. It was good to feel the ground beneath his feet again.

The E.M.S. Helicopter had already taken off. It apparently was called back because of a more pressing emergency. However, one of paramedics stayed behind to help retrieve the body. O'Brien walked over to him and introduced himself.

"Hi, I'm Detective O'Brien and this is Detective Beard," he said shaking the hand of the sole paramedic left behind.

"Nice to meet you both. I've been expecting you guys. I'm glad you're here. It was getting boring sitting here by myself. Oh, by the way, I'm Dennis."

O'Brien and Thom nodded as they shook Dennis' hand. They shared their thermos of coffee with him as they waited impatiently for the canoes. Within the hour, the forestry truck approached. They watched as a big grizzly of a man stepped out of the Power Wagon. They introduced themselves and shook hands.

"Nice to meet you guys. I'm Ben. We got business to tend to, so step aside whilst I get these boats in the water," the big man said as he took total control.

The three watched as big Ben manhandled the canoes as though they were sacks of potatoes. In less time that it would have taken all three to unload the canoes, Ben had docked them ready for passengers. Thom and O'Brien were in one canoe, and Ben and Dennis in the other. The trip downstream to where the body was bobbing up and down in a logjam took about forty-five minutes and in places was brutal. Canoeing back would be real pleasant.

Finally, reaching the troop of scouts, O'Brien, Thom, Dennis and Ben untangled the corpse and brought it to a small clearing a few yards off the creek where the ten boy scouts and two scout leaders gathered to watch the spectacle. Just by looking at the corpse, Thom and O'Brien knew that the victim had died the same way the others had. Dennis put on a pair of gloves and looked over the corpse for a couple of minutes and then he covered it up.

O'Brien asked Ben what was upstream.

"This creek doesn't run through any town except Cassle and that's still twenty or thirty miles downstream," Big Ben answered.

O'Brien looked at him.

"I don't want to sound rude, but I could care less what's downstream. What the hell is upstream?"

O'Brien was looking deep into Ben's eyes.

"Nothing but a trestle."

"A trestle?" asked Thom as a matter-of-fact.

"That's right. I can also tell you that the last train that went past it was on Sunday."

"Bingo!" exclaimed Thom.

O'Brien knew exactly what Thom was thinking. Obviously, the corpse had been dumped from that train.

"Do you know what direction it was headed?" O'Brien questioned.

"Sure do," said Ben. "It was heading to Applecove. The Sunday train comes from Slocolm and goes right through to Applecove. It makes a brief stop in Cassle, but only for about fifteen minutes."

"You're a wealth of information, Ben," O'Brien responded with glee.

As he reached for but couldn't find his cell, he remembered that he had left it in Thom's SUV. Turning he asked one of the scout leaders how they phoned it in, hoping they had used a cell phone he might borrow. Apparently, when they found the body on Tuesday, one of the older guys canoed back to Cassle and called it in from there. O'Brien nodded and thanked him. They loaded the body into Dennis and Ben's canoe and headed back upstream. An hour and a half later, they were back at Enterprise. They phoned ahead to the RCMP detachments in Cassle, Applecove, and the one closest to Slocolm to fill them in briefly. They asked them to keep their eyes peeled for anything suspicious.

Then they phoned for the E.M.S. It was turning dark when they heard the sound of a helicopter approaching from the south. When it landed, O'Brien and Thom helped load up corpse number four. The E.M.S. was going to take the corpse to Cassle Medical Centre. O'Brien jotted down the information along with the names of Ben and Dennis, as well as the names of the paramedics who were onboard. The helicopter took off minutes later, as did Ben, but not before O'Brien and Thom had a chance to thank him. He nodded and smiled.

"Anytime," he said as he pulled away.

Thom and O'Brien looked at one another and in unison said, "That was one big bear of a guy."

The time was 8:00 p.m.; by 11:00 or 11:30, they would be back in Fruitmont. Tomorrow would be a hectic day, knowing now that the killer could very well be in Cassle or Applecove. Obviously, he was indeed using the train as his own personal hearse. If the scouts hadn't been canoeing in that area, they probably wouldn't have found the victim so soon. It probably would've stayed stuck in the log jam for weeks, maybe even months. O'Brien knew they would have to move quickly now. It would only be a matter of time before the killer read or heard that the body had been recovered.

## Eight

By Thursday, the police artist had come up with a drawing of the possible suspect. She drew it from the description the young lady in Hinton had given. O'Brien knew that it might not even be close to what the suspect actually looked like. Their police artist, Christine, however, was one of the best.

O'Brien faxed copies of the drawing to several different police agencies, and then began to look over mug shots of recently released convicts from the area. Paying attention to those who had been incarcerated, for 10 years or more. It was O'Brien's theory that the killing had stopped in Grandbluff ten years prior because the killer may have been imprisoned. Thom was doing his part as well, looking at mug shots of convicts who were sentenced in the late 80's early 90's. Together, they came up with a big fat zero. None of the photos that they looked at compared to what Christine had drawn. By day's end, both Thom and O'Brien were blurry-eyed and ready to blow gaskets. O'Brien usually didn't get that way. There was something about this case though that wasn't meshing, and it agitated both men.

It came to O'Brien Thursday night as he sat at his kitchen table, that maybe their suspect hadn't been sentenced to prison ten or so years earlier, but perhaps to a mental hospital. There would be no such photos in their mug shot album. Mental hospitals weren't prisons. If their suspect were sent to a mental hospital for one reason or another, they wouldn't have any photos. Photos of the mentally ill were kept at the mental hospital where the person was confined.

O'Brien phoned Hal at his house to let him know of yet another theory. He was surprised when Hal said he'd already been working on it and that he already arranged for him and Thom to meet with a Dr. D. Price at the psychiatric hospital in North Kootenay. Hal said that the doctor claimed to have had a patient for three years that might fit the description. Hal faxed the drawing to the doctor and the doctor told him he'd get back to him shortly, which he did. In fact, Dr. Price told him that he was almost 90% sure that the drawing was that of an aged Anvil Brentwood.

"Brentwood, Brentwood," O'Brien muttered as he frowned and tapped his finger on the counter.

"What's that?" Hal asked.

"That name sounds familiar. I've heard it or read it somewhere."

O'Brien was somewhat perplexed. He thought about it for a moment and then it came to him. The witness in Hinton had picked out a picture of someone named Brentwood.

"Listen Hal, I need you to go back to the police report and the witness' statement from Hinton. I think one of the officers stated that the witness picked out an old photo of someone that the suspect resembled. I think the guy is dead now or something, but I need you to read it over and see if I'm right."

"Sure thing, O'Brien. When I go to the office, I'll check it out. If I come across something like that, I'll either phone you or slip it into your email."

"Thanks a lot, Hal. I appreciate it."

O'Brien hung up the phone and tried to remember where it was for sure that he read or heard that name before. He knew it was recently and after contemplating it, the only place that it could've been was somewhere in the stacks of files they had on the case. If it was there, O'Brien knew Hal would find it. At 9:00 p.m., O'Brien phoned up Thom and filled him in on his latest theory. He let Thom know that they were going to North Kootenay in the morning to the mental hospital to talk with Dr. Price. Thom was enthralled with the possibility. It was true the suspect could very well have been a psychiatric patient.

"That would explain why we couldn't find any matches," Thom commented.

"That's right, but don't get your hopes up. It's only another possibility, Thom. Besides, we really won't be able to say 'yea or nay' until tomorrow."

"I know, but it is a good possibility. I wish we had thought about it earlier."

"I do, too. Anyway, Thom, I'll see ya in the morning."

"You bet, O'Brien. See you in the morning."

Thom and O'Brien met at the office around 8:00 a.m. They put their credentials together, looked over what Hal and Rory had come up with during their shift, and, sure enough, the name Brentwood was mentioned in one of the reports. Hal highlighted it and emailed it. O'Brien threw the information into a database hoping for a response on Brock Brentwood's next of kin, children etc. He and Thom waited for about an hour but nothing came up. They decided to let it float around in cyber space and to look it over when they got back from North Kootenay. O'Brien phoned ahead to Dr. Price to let him know that they were leaving the office and that they would be there by late afternoon. Dr. Price told him that wouldn't be a problem and that he was looking forward to meeting with them.

They arrived in North Kootenay just before 3:00 p.m. The drive to Bedlam Hospital was a nice one. The road travelled along the Kootenay Lake. It was surrounded by plush green hills of grass, and fruit trees. The hospital itself sat on a hill overlooking the beautiful lake and all the orchards scattered here and there. The big building cast an eerie shadow on the north parking lot where they parked.

"It looks like the house in psycho. How fitting," Thom commented as he chuckled.

The pair walked into the lobby and mentioned to the receptionist who they were and that they were there to speak with Dr. Price. Unfortunately, Dr. Price had been called away earlier and wasn't expected back until the evening, probably 6:00, or 7:00. The receptionist said that Dr. Price had left a folder for them. She led the two detectives down a long corridor and into the doctor's lounge, then handed them the folder.

"You can help yourselves to coffee. The cafeteria will be open in about an hour, detectives, so if you'd like something to eat, the food there is good," she said.

They thanked her as she pranced away.

O'Brien set his briefcase down on the oval table and retrieved the comparison drawing of the suspect while Thom began looking over the folder. The picture inside did closely match the sketch from their police artist. They compared the two and agreed that yes, Anvil Brentwood was definitely the guy seen with the third victim, but was he the killer? The two of them read the folder together. It went on to say how Anvil had been abused as a child by his father. He had no known relatives living or deceased other than his father; his mother was unknown. Anvil had been sent to Bedlam because of an insanity plea ten years earlier for brutally killing a man.

"What do you think of that?" Thom asked.

"I think we might very well have a suspect."

Thom stood up and walked over to the coffee machine.

"Can I get you one, O'Brien?"

"Certainly, thanks."

O'Brien continued reading the folder, which consisted of some thirty pages of information that pointed the finger at Anvil. One, he was a convicted killer; two, he had an odd obsession with trains according Dr. Prices notes; and three, he had been sent to Matsqui Penitentiary to finish his sentencing which would have ended two months prior to the discovery of the first victim in Fruitmont. They were awfully close now, O'Brien knew it. They hashed it over for an hour or so and started making phone calls. Thom called to Matsqui to see if indeed Brentwood had been released. The warden wasn't in, however, and the officer on duty said he couldn't reveal that kind of information. He said that it would have to be something asked of his superior. He told Thom to call back in the morning and ask for a Burke Hayward who was the Matsqui Prison Warden.

O'Brien called the office and spoke with Henderson who had just come on shift. He wanted to put an APB out on Anvil Brentwood.

"I'm not going to put no APB out on anybody that we aren't sure has been released from prison or, for that matter, is even a suspect, O'Brien. I can't do that. If you find out that indeed, he's been released and you can convince me that he is a suspect, consider it done. Call me at home in the morning after you find out for sure. Then and only then would I even be authorised to put an APB out."

"I guess you're right. There really isn't any use in doing that yet. Thanks anyway, Henderson."

"Hold on, O'Brien. Do you really think this Brentwood fellow is our guy?"

"If he isn't still in prison, I think he might be. We'll know more after talking to the good Doctor."

"You haven't spoken to him yet?"

"No. He stepped out for a bit before we got here. He's due back later this evening."

"Are you guys going to be spending the night there?"

"I hope not. It depends on how soon the Doc gets back I guess."

"All right, then I'll talk to you tomorrow. Don't forget to call me at home to let me know if an APB should be issued."

"Don't worry; you'll be the first person I call. Goodnight."

"Goodnight, O'Brien," Henderson said as he hung up the phone.

Thom and O'Brien walked downstairs to the cafeteria. The food was quite good. In fact, it was the best hospital food,

O'Brien or Thom had eaten. Even the coffee was fresh, not left over and burnt. They returned to the doctor's lounge a little before 7:00 p.m. and met by Dr. Price.

"You must be the two detectives from Fruitmont, I assume."

"Yes, we are." Thom replied.

"I'm sorry I wasn't here when you arrived. I'm Dr. Price," he said reaching out his hand.

"Nice to meet you, Doctor. I'm Thom and this is O'Brien."

They shook hands and Dr. Price directed them to sit down.

"Come sit down. We have lots to talk about. That picture that was faxed to me is certainly that of an aged Anvil. He was a special case. We thought we were making progress with him until he decided to become uncooperative. He even threatened some of the staff here, saying that he was going to hang them up like pigs in a butcher shop. Most of the staff didn't feel threatened mind you, because Anvil was prone to outbursts like that. As you know, when he was sixteen, his father fell in front of a train," Dr. Price said with doubt. "He said to me on numerous meetings that the train that killed his father brought peace to his world."

Dr. Price thumbed through another folder.

"Was his father's name, by chance, Brock Brentwood?" O'Brien asked out of curiosity.

"Yes it was, but Anvil never mentioned his father's name. His father had already been dead for twenty-six years when Anvil came to be in this place."

"Was he ever questioned about the death of his father?" Thom asked.

"He was, but nothing ever came of it. I myself am one of many psychiatrists that believe he was the cause of his father's death, but it could never be proven without his admitting it. Every time we brought it up Anvil would only stare blankly and was unresponsive to the questions. We stopped asking. Besides, he had been sent here for different reasons. Whatever had happened twenty-six years earlier wasn't one of our concerns."

"I see. You said he threatened some staff members with hanging them like pigs in a butcher shop. Do you think he would do anything or was capable of doing something like that?" O'Brien questioned.

"Oh, he is capable all right. Whether he would follow through with something like that is another story. I would suspect that given the opportunity he would certainly consider it. Why do you ask?"

"Let's just say that the stiffs we have on ice appear to have been strung up like pigs in a butcher shop," replied Thom.

They talked with Dr. Price until 10:00 p.m. and were soon convinced that yes, Anvil Brentwood, if he were out of prison could likely be their suspect. Unable to do much until they spoke with the Warden at Matsqui, they thanked Dr. Price for his time and left the Bedlam Hospital.

"Do we drive back tonight, Thom, or do wait until the morning?" O'Brien asked as they exited the hospital into a cool dark evening.

"I say we drive back."

"Good. I was hoping you'd say that."

As they drove back home, they stopped off at an all-night diner called the White Line to have a late night snack and to pick up coffee and such for the drive back. By 3:30 a.m., they pulled into Fruitmont. O'Brien dropped Thom off at his apartment and headed home.

Six hours later, they were on the phone with one another. Thom had called the Warden at Matsqui and, sure enough, Anvil had been released. He was given a bus ticket back to the last town that he had lived in, which was Birchland. However, there were no records at the Department of Corrections that the ticket had been used, which meant he probably hadn't gone back home.

The Warden told Thom that after a convict left the prison premises, they were no longer responsible for where the convict goes. Their only responsibility was to issue them a ticket. The Warden wasn't much help. What they knew now was that Anvil was released and that he hadn't used the bus ticket. O'Brien phoned Henderson directly to let him know the news. He did what he said he would and issued an APB.

O'Brien called Thom back and had him meet him at the office. They photocopied Anvil's mug-shot from the hospital as well as the artist's sketch and plastered them throughout Fruitmont. Thom faxed a bunch of the real photos to the Police stations in Cassle, Applecove, and the one in North Kootenay as well as the small RCMP detachment in Newton, which, was only a few miles from Slocolm. They knew that if Anvil were the killer, he would probably be somewhere between Applecove and Slocolm. They knew this because of where and when the fourth victim had been found.

O'Brien returned to the office around 2:00 p.m. after stapling Anvil's picture on every telephone pole and bulletin board he could find. The more people that saw his picture the better. Maybe someone would recognise and remember seeing him somewhere.

An hour later, Thom and O'Brien managed to stir up both Hal and Rory and got them to come down to the office. They had a suspect to round up and wasting time could jeopardise lives. There were four possible towns where Anvil could be, Fruitmont, Cassle, Applecove, or Slocolm. He might possibly even be in North Kootenay.

Thom mentioned that he knew of a small guild of vagrants that lived on the outskirts of Applecove and that since the victims were all obviously homeless, it would be a good place to look into.

"Since you know the place, Thom, that's where you should go," O'Brien encouraged.

"Sure thing, O'Brien, I don't mind."

"Great. Rory, I think we'll send you over to Cassle. Hal, you keep things together here. Stay on your toes and be ready to move. I'll head over to Slocolm and Newton. Remember guys, if you get a lead, report to the rest of us immediately. Better yet, let's get back to Hal. He can dispatch from here. Also, if it comes to a confrontation with this maniac, don't shy away from using your piece. It would be better, though, to bring him in alive. Whatever happens keep your wits about you. Remember, he is only wanted for questioning. If he doesn't co-operate arrest him for vagrancy. That's all we can do."

"That works for me," responded Thom.

"Me, too," said Rory.

"Good. I'm glad we are all in agreement."

With the plan laid out, O'Brien called Henderson at home to let him know that he would be missing three detectives for the next couple of days.

"What do you mean I'll be missing three detectives?"

"We've come down with the flu or something," O'Brien jibed.

"Who are we?" Henderson barked.

"Thom, Rory and myself."

"How did you all end up with the flu at the same time?" he questioned with both anger and concern. O'Brien couldn't believe that he'd suckered Henderson and he began to chuckle.

"O'Brien what kind of stunt are you pulling now?"

"Sorry, I was only joking. We're not sick, but we are going to be gone for a couple of days."

"Why is that?" Henderson questioned with authority.

O'Brien explained the situation and what the four of them, would be doing. Henderson finally agreed and gave O'Brien his blessing, not that it would have mattered if he hadn't. The four of them would have followed the plan regardless. That's how sure they were that Anvil needed to be brought in for questioning. They would have dealt with Henderson's wrath afterwards.

"When are you guy's planning on leaving?"

"I think we'll head out today or at least I will," O'Brien replied.

It wasn't until he said that did O'Brien realise that Tracy and the kids were due back later that night.

"Oops, I forgot the wife and kids are due back tonight."

"Can't you leave on Monday then?" asked Henderson. O'Brien thought about it for a moment. He knew that he probably could, but at this point of the game, timing was everything.

"I probably could, but I don't think it would be wise. I'm sure they'll understand. We're close now. I can feel it. We really need to catch up with this guy and get him off the streets," O'Brien responded as he contemplated for a moment. "I'm going to leave today, Henderson."

"Suit yourself. Anything you want me to pass on to Tracy?"

"No. I'll call her at home after I get to Slocolm. She should be back by then."

"Did anyone ever tell you, O'Brien, that sometimes you are too dedicated?"

"I don't know if it's dedication or a gut feeling I have."

"Well then, good luck to each of you and keep me posted."

"We will."

O'Brien hung up the phone and looked over to where the guys were huddling around Hal's desk waiting for the go ahead to move out.

"Henderson gives us his blessing and wishes all of us God speed," O'Brien said with a smile as he stood up from his desk.

"Like it would have mattered?" Thom chuckled, "let's get a move on."

"Here, here," retorted Rory.

"All right, let's move out. Hal you know what to do back here?"

"Sure do, O'Brien," he said giving O'Brien the thumbs up.

O'Brien knew Hal was a seasoned detective and no task was too difficult for him. It was the reason O'Brien suggested, that, he stay back. He was always ready to go and always managed to stay one step ahead of the rest. Another good thing was that the following Monday, he and Rory were once again scheduled for day shift. That meant he would be easy to keep in touch with and that he would be able to multitask around the office. Whenever Hal was on day shift, things got done.

As the three exited, O'Brien looked back at Hal and pointed at him.

"You the man; you the man," he said with jubilant glee.

Hal looked and waved him out. O'Brien stood in the parking lot and watched as Thom and Rory headed west. He, on the other hand, headed north. Slocolm was a good distance away and would take him about five hours. Thom had easily an eight-hour drive and Rory about six. They all agreed to phone into Hal once they arrived at their destinations, just to let him know the location where they would be staying.

O'Brien arrived in Slocolm around suppertime. The motel he was staying at was the Dovetail, which was nestled in amongst some big cedar trees and within a skipping stone throw away from the Slocolm River. It was quite a picturesque place. The town itself hadn't changed in over fifty years. It was an old logging and mining town. The remnants of old lumber mills and silver mines dotted the mountainside revealing this history. Most of the buildings had been standing for generation after generation and only their upkeep was done. The only new building was the Dovetail and it was twenty-some odd years old. O'Brien looked up onto the mountainside and thought it would be the perfect place to hide away from life. There were old buildings that could shelter someone who spent the majority of their childhood hiding in the forests. Someone just like Anvil Brentwood. O'Brien paid for his room. He casually asked if there was anybody in town, who could get him up into the mountains.

"A guide, you mean?" asked the kid behind the desk.

"I suppose, yeah, a guide."

"Sure is. There is a guy goes by the name of Darnell who can take you up. He's lived here all his life. His grandfather used to own the Treachery Silver Mine."

"Treachery? That's a pretty odd name for a mine, isn't it?" O'Brien questioned with sincerity and a smile.

"I guess so, unless you know why he named it that. At first, he named it the Glitter Bowl. He and his crews pulled out a lot of silver. Then one day, the whole thing collapsed killing all but six of his crew of fifteen. He named it the Treachery because it betrayed him."

"That's a good story, kid. Darnell knows the mountains pretty good, eh?"

"Sure does. If you want I can have him meet you here in the morning?"

"Thanks a lot. By the way what's your name kid?"

"I'm Justin."

"Nice to meet you, Justin. My name is Detective O'Brien."

O'Brien reached out to shake his hand.

"Detective?" he asked as a matter-of-fact.

"That's right."

"What brings a detective up to these parts?"

"I'm doing some field work."

O'Brien set his briefcase down on the counter to pull out a picture of Anvil.

"Have you ever seen this guy around here?" he asked as he showed the kid the picture.

"No, no. I don't think so," the kid said shaking his head.

"You don't mind if I tape this to the door do you?"

"Not at all; feel free."

He handed O'Brien his room key.

"You're in room eight, detective."

"Thanks, Justin," O'Brien said as he took the key.

He taped the picture of Anvil up and retreated to his room. It was a cosy room with plenty of light and a magnificent view of the Slocolm River. Setting his bags down, he called up Hal, but got his answering machine.

"Hey, Hal, this is O'Brien. I'm in Slocolm and I'm staying at the Dovetail Motel, room eight. Talk to you soon."

It was still light so O'Brien grabbed a handful of Anvil's posters and began putting them out. He walked from one end of Slocolm to the other, stapling and taping them wherever he could. A few of the stores that were open allowed him to tape the pictures to their windows. He walked along the beach and posted them on telephone booths, docked boats and the like until the ones he had were gone.

Finally, sitting down on a beached log, he looked towards the sunset. It was a beautiful mauve with streaks of white light and an orange tinge. It was different from all the others he had seen. Yet they all had the same effect on him. He loved looking at them. They made him feel alive.

He watched as a couple of seagulls fluttered past and landed on one of the docks to feast on the scrap from a cleaned fish. He watched them for a few minutes, then stood and walked towards the Dovetail. Stopping at a little hotdog cart that was beginning to close, O'Brien bought two hotdogs, a large coke, and a goodnight coffee.

He made it back to the Dovetail before 9:00 p.m. A note from Justin was tacked to his door. Justin had contacted Darnell and Darnell agreed to take him for a hike to some of the older silver mines in the area. O'Brien was to meet him in the front office between 8:00 and 8:30 a.m., pulling the note off the door, O'Brien, entered the room. He set what was left of his coffee on the end table and phoned home, but there was no answer. He punched in the remote code to check for messages. Tracy had called from his mother's house and said that she and the boys would be on their way back Monday. Apparently, O'Brien's Mom convinced her to stay an extra day. He was relieved in a sense and lonely at the same time. At least he knew where she was. She hadn't a clue as to where he was.

He left a message himself, telling Tracy that he was doing fieldwork and that he'd call back Monday and fill her in. Flicking on the little TV that sat at the end of his bed, he stretched out to the 9:00 movie, 'The Good the Bad and the Ugly'. It was one of his all-time favourite Clint Eastwood westerns. Unfortunately, for him, consumed with exhaustion and the excitement of what tomorrow might bring, he fell asleep.

# Nine

On Sunday, July 22, O'Brien woke up at the crack of dawn. The sun was only now beginning to rise and its yellow rays reflected off of the Slocolm River like shimmering streaks of golden thread. He had slept like a baby the night before and was fully energised and ready to face the day. He wondered where Darnell was going to take him. He really wanted to see the old mines that sat precariously on the hillside overlooking the town.

It wasn't his intention when he came to Slocolm to go traipsing through the bush looking for evidence, but when he saw all the old buildings that peeked through the evergreens and dotted the mountainside, he figured it would be as good a place as any to check for evidence that someone may have been using them for their benefit.

It was apparent that Anvil was well versed in wilderness survival by what they had been told about him and from what they read. His instincts told him that somewhere up in those hills was evidence that they were lacking, and maybe even Anvil himself. O'Brien walked out to his car and strapped on his Koflach hiking boots. He grabbed his daypack, which held a compass, waterproof matches, as well as a Buck hunting knife and a first aid kit. At a nearby 7-11, he picked up a large cup of coffee and some power bars and went to the motel's front office to wait for his guide.

He was reading a Times Magazine when he heard a big gruff voice.

"Are you O'Brien?"

O'Brien turned to look who was addressing him. He couldn't believe his eyes. Standing before him was a dead ringer for Kenny Rogers.

"Yes, I'm O'Brien. You must be Darnell?"

"That's right. So you want to take a look around the old silver mines, eh?"

"I sure would, Darnell. I was hoping you could get me up to those old buildings on the west slope."

"I can take you wherever you'd like to go. Justin told me that you said you were up here to do some field work?"

"That's right. I am actually looking for someone that we need to question. He may be in this area. He might even be camping out up there in the hills."

"You think that guy that's posted all over town is staying up in those mines?" Darnell asked with little enthusiasm. "I can tell you that I have been up in some of those hills as recently as last week and I didn't see anything peculiar. That doesn't mean, however, that no one is up there. A good bushman could live up there all year around and not be spotted by locals like me. There is everything a man might need to survive up there, including a freshwater spring."

Darnell opened the door for O'Brien.

"After you," he said as he pointed O'Brien to a beat up two-tone black and grey ¾ ton Ford.

"That's our carriage. We can drive most of the way up to the first mine anyway."

O'Brien walked over to the 4x4 and threw his daypack into the box. The door creaked with age as he opened it. The interior had seen better days. There were remnants of old STP and radio station stickers stuck to the old weathered dashboard, which was cracked and chapped in most places. From the rear view mirror hung an array of car fresheners that were aged and faded, their scent long lost in the past.

Darnell stepped in and smiled.

"She doesn't look like heaven, but she's a good old work horse. We should be at the first mine before ten," Darnell commented as he turned the key and the old Ford coughed to life.

Fifteen minutes later, they entered an overgrown road that cut through a thick pine-clad forest then coursed its way alongside the west slope of the Paradise Mountain to the mines.

As the northbound train from Applecove screeched to a halt in the Slocolm train yard, Anvil and a friend stepped out. They ducked quickly into the undergrowth and darted deeper into the forest to an obscure trail that led to Anvil's killing grounds. The newcomer was oblivious to Anvil's true intentions. All he knew is that Anvil invited him back to his adobe. Anvil promised food, drink, and shelter. The man's name was Bud. He was another faceless vagrant who had landed hard somewhere in life. He had turned to the green glass bottle for solace, but instead found misery. He befriended Anvil back in Applecove and for the past few days, they chummed around like old friends. Bud had no reason to fear Anvil and when Anvil offered him food and drink, he had no reason to decline. When he accepted, Anvil had snagged another would-be victim.

Killer and victim ascended a few small rock bluffs and entered an old mining shack near the entrance of the Big Bang Silver Mine. The shack was equipped with old woollen blankets, a potbelly wood stove, a table and two rickety chairs. In the middle of the table was a wax candle. To the right of the table there was a small counter space with a wash basin, a couple of plates, and tin cups. Bud looked around the room. It was nicer than any cardboard box he had lived in.

"Pretty nice place you got here."

"This isn't my home; it's just where I stay," replied Anvil. His home was the ridge that overlooked the train yard and the little town of Slocolm.

"Where's your home, then?"

"I'll take you there later; for now, let's drink."

Anvil reached into the cupboard and pulled out a magnum of cheap wine. He poured two big cups and passed one to Bud.

"To life, to death, to the forest and the trees," Anvil cheered.

"Let the drinking commence!" exclaimed Bud.

They slugged back half of the magnum in less than thirty minutes. They exchanged stories back and forth, as friends do. Finally, Anvil said he didn't want to drink anymore, but he encouraged Bud to finish off what was left of the wine. Finishing off the last half solo, Bud had no clue about what Anvil was preparing to do. Walking over to Bud, Anvil helped him out of his chair.

"Come on, it's time for me to show you where I live," Anvil said sinisterly.

Stepping out of the rundown shack into the late morning sun, the two friends began to walk up a small incline. It was too much for Bud in his drunken state and he kept stumbling back. Anvil went over to him.

"Put your arm over my shoulder. I'll help you."

Bud swung his right arm over Anvil's shoulder and they continued what would be Bud's last walk.

As they crested over the last part of the incline, Anvil stopped abruptly. He could hear a vehicle in the distance. Looking in the direction of the old dirt road, he could see dust rising. He turned and darted towards the shack, letting Bud fall upon the rocky ground splitting his head and face open as his intoxicated body bounced down the hill. Anvil threw open the door to the shack and retrieved his bag. He grabbed the empty wine bottle and tossed it into a clump of overgrown mountain ash, along with the two cups and plates that he had used in the past. Then, he descended the mountain leaving behind a blood-soaked Bud.

A frothing beast, he crashed down the mountainside, stumbling and adding injury to himself. It didn't slow Anvil down. Pain had always been a part of his life. A few bruises, cuts and contusions, were a minor concern. What concerned him most were the intruders approaching his killing ground.

The next train would be around 5:00 p.m.; in fact, it would be the same one that Anvil had used that past Sunday. The position of the sun as he glanced up told him he had hours to wait. Where could he go until then? He stopped running and like a child began to weep. He began slapping himself in the face until blood trickled out of the corner of his mouth, lips, and nose. Then, he fell upon the ground and lay motionless like a corpse himself, looking up at the trees as dizzy spells and dreams of his past electrified his thoughts.

"This is as far as we can go. We're going have to hike the rest of the way," Darnell said as he put the truck in park and shut it off. O'Brien stepped out of the pickup and strapped the daypack around his waist.

"It's sure beautiful up here," O'Brien commented as he looked up the road and scouted the treeline. An array of honeysuckle blossoms and Indian paintbrushes skirted the road on its higher side. Behind all the orange, purple, and red, a vast forest of evergreens loomed.

"Wait until we get up a bit higher. We can look right across the valley. On a day like this with it being so clear, you might not want to leave," Darnell replied.

"What? And leave behind the conveniences of modern society?" O'Brien joked.

"If I had my choice, O'Brien, you're damn straight. Society today is on its way to becoming one big fiasco. When it happens, I'd give my left nut to be up in the mountains."

"Ouch," O'Brien replied as they started the hike.

Darnell pointed them in the direction they were going to travel.

"Up there, about a half a mile or so, is the Big Bang. It was one of the last mines worked on this side. Not many people go up there. In fact, the last time I was up in that area was probably a year ago. The locals aren't interested in these old mines anymore. Most people that live in Slocolm have already investigated them, either as they grew up as kids or simply by taking a Sunday walk.

Now they have no interest. Some of the hunters from near and far may still hunt around here, but most of the hunters go east, which suits me just fine. Also up at the Big Bang is an old mine shack that still stands. Three or four years ago, some kids went up there and fixed it up a bit. They used to party up there until the road washed out. That's why I figured it to be a good place to check out. If anyone was going to stay up here that would be the place."

"How do you suppose they'd get up there?" O'Brien questioned as they carried on.

"Well, there are a few ways. There is an old trail near town. Plus from the train yard one could make it. It's quite steep, but someone in good shape could make it up in less than an hour."

"How come we never went that way then?" O'Brien commented as he slowed down to take a breath.

"Two reasons. One is we'd be trespassing. The CPR doesn't allow anyone in that yard. It's overgrown and there are pieces of equipment scattered all over the place. One could get hurt quite easily. Second reason is I am not nearly as young as I used to be. A walk like that up those hills would probably kill me."

Darnell smiled.

"Besides, this way is a lot more scenic and we'll be able to check out all four of the mines on this side from here."

"I guess that's a good enough reason for me. How long do you suppose it'll take us to get there from here?"

"Probably the same amount of time as it would take from the train yard. It's just not as steep. It's easy walking from here," said Darnell as he took the lead.

The hike up seemed a lot longer than what it was. To O'Brien, they seemed to hike for hours. They finally came over the last crest and O'Brien could see the roof of a shack.

"That's her," said Darnell pointing at the weathered building. "Up and over another hill, there is a ridge that looks down onto Slocolm and the train yard. When I was a kid, we used to call that place Necking Ridge. The view is so spectacular it didn't take much to get the girls wet," Darnell chuckled as they walked over to the small shack and entered. It appeared as though no one had been there in quite some time.

"It looks as it did last year when I was up here," said Darnell, "except for maybe that candle."

O'Brien looked over to the small table and the candle that was sitting on it.

"The candle wasn't there the last time you were here?"

"Not that I recall," Darnell said as he shrugged and sniffed the air. "I don't recall that stench either."

O'Brien followed Darnell's example and he sniffed the air.

"Yuck. What's that I wonder?"

"I don't know, maybe a dead animal. It smells like something rotten," Darnell replied.

"It's not so bad inside."

"No it's lingering in from outdoors somewhere. Maybe we should look around. It could be coming from the mine itself. Animals sometimes fall into mine shafts and eventually die."

"Yeah. Let's hope that's what it is. God, it's awful," O'Brien commented as they looked around.

They walked closer to the mine entrance but the smell dissipated. O'Brien was beginning to wonder if something other than an animal had died. Every now and then, they could smell the odour as it wafted in the wind and then it would be gone.

"It's coming from over there," Darnell said as he pointed west in the direction of the wind.

"I agree. It's got to be."

They walked a few yards in the direction. Pushing their way through some undergrowth, they were forced to stop dead in their tracks when they heard an unfamiliar sound.

"Did you hear that?" O'Brien asked.

"Yeah, sounded like someone groaning. I think it's coming from up near Necking Ridge," Darnell said as he pointed in the direction.

"Let's get a move on up there then. I think you're right. It sounded like it came from that direction."

Before O'Brien could finish speaking, Darnell had already bolted up and over the small incline. O'Brien followed suit and was close behind when he heard Darnell holler.

"O'Brien, hurry up. There's a guy up here."

"Is he dead?" O'Brien yelled back.

"He's dead drunk, but he ain't dead," came the reply.

O'Brien crashed through brush until he was standing next to Darnell who was kneeling beside a broken and bruised man who obviously had taken a tumble down the embankment.

"He's a mess," O'Brien observed as he caught his breath.

"Sure is. He's got some brutal cuts on his face and scalp. Think I should head back to the truck and get some help, O'Brien?"

"First, let's see if we can get him down to the shack. Maybe we can clean him up and drive him back to Slocolm ourselves."

"What do you think he was doing way up here?"

"Could be he was up here tying one on. Can you recognise him from Slocolm?" O'Brien questioned as they helped the man stand.

"Nope, never seen him before, but I can't be sure 'cause his face is bloody."

They carried the man down to the shack and laid him on one of the beds. Darnell retrieved some water while O'Brien tore some strips from an old blanket that lay on the bed. He washed the guy's wounds and face and bandaged him up as best he could.

"I don't suppose he is what caused that smell?" asked Darnell as he entered.

"Not likely, but I think he was going to be a sacrificial lamb. I have a feeling, Darnell, that he wasn't alone. Let's leave him here. For the time being, he'll be okay. We have to track down that smell."

"I'm with you."

They walked back to where they found the man and once again, the offensive odour came in gusts with the wind. Approaching closer to Necking Ridge, an eerie wind picked up and they heard the distinctive sound of clanking chains. Looking up, they saw a pulley system. O'Brien knew exactly what they were going to find next. In only moments, they were standing beneath two large pine trees. A black crust covered the ground directly beneath the two sets of pulleys. The stench was human blood.

"Holy! Look at all that dried-up blood. It's everywhere. This is the place, Darnel, where those four murders took place. Finally, I've got a crime scene!" O'Brien exclaimed, as he looked over to Darnell who was some distance away, shaking his head in disgust as though he were going to vomit.

"You never said we were looking for a crime scene."

"Sorry, Darnell, but I really wasn't. I presumed that this would be a good place to hide if one needed to hide."

"Apparently your presumption was correct. It looks like it was also a good place to kill. What kind of sick man could do this? I've seen a lot in my life, O'Brien, but this takes the cake. It is plain creepy. The only time I've ever seen that much blood was in a slaughterhouse. It's creeping me out more knowing its human. Can we get the H out of here?"

"Yeah. We're going to have to. This is a job for the crime lab. I'm going to send you back to Slocolm with our friend back at the shack. I'll need you to drop him off at a hospital and tell the doctors that he can't leave until someone from Henderson & Co. gets in touch with them. I'm also going to ask you to phone this number," O'Brien said as he handed Darnell a card. "Ask for Hal and tell him to round up the rest of the crew. He'll know who it is that I'm talking about. Tell him that I need all of them here ASAP. I'll need you to put some flagging tape at the road entrance. I have some police tape that you can use. You're going to have to give them directions on how to get here. If Hal isn't around, then talk to Henderson. He'll know what to do. I'm staying up here until the rest of the guys show up. I think I'll search the area. It could be that Anvil is still up here. He probably heard the truck and it spooked him."

"Do you want me to call the RCMP in Newton?"

"Not yet. Not until after my guys show up. Can I count on you to keep it hush, hush?"

"Sure can," Darnell assured. "How about if after I drop this guy off and get a hold of your office I come back? You could use an extra hand in searching and I know these woods like the back of my hand."

"That would be great, Darnell, and if you got a piece bring it along. I'll deputise you when you get back," O'Brien said jokingly as they continued walking back to the shack. The man passed out on the bed was beginning to come to as they entered the shack to retrieve him.

"Are you all right?" O'Brien asked.

The man looked at O'Brien briefly with a confused look on his face, then his eyes rolled back in his head and he passed out again.

"You know what, Darnell. I think we'll keep him here for now. He'll be okay, but I am going to cuff him to the bed so he doesn't take off."

"Think that's a wise idea, O'Brien? You know, cuffing him to the bed. What if the killer returns, this poor bastard wouldn't stand a chance."

"There are two reasons. One, he'll slow you down. Two, what if it turns out that this is the killer and Anvil has nothing to do with it?" O'Brien responded with a chuckle.

"That's a good enough reason for me," Darnell replied. "I'll take off now. I should be back within a couple of hours."

"Sounds good, Darnell. I'll see you then. Oh, hang on a second. I need to give you the tape."

O'Brien reached into his pack and tossed Darnell the bright yellow tape. Darnell nodded and headed back to the truck. O'Brien watched as Darnell ducked into the forest and out of sight. He reached into his shoulder holster and made sure his pistol was loaded and ready. It held eight shots with one in the chamber. He had one extra clip on his belt and another set of cuffs. O'Brien was ready for bear.

Looking at his watch, he noted the time to be near 1:00 p.m. With luck, Hal would be there by 6:00 or 7:00 p.m. In the morning, Rory and Thom would be close behind. He knew they were going to have to spend the night, if for nothing else, to keep an eye on the murder scene. Deciding to walk the perimeter and pick up wood for the evening, he kept his eyes and ears peeled for sounds or movements. Returning to the shack, he dropped the armful of wood on the ground and looked in on the man cuffed to the bed. He was still breathing, but dead to the world.

Every now and again, the wretched smell of human blood wafted his way making O'Brien's stomach churn. From then on, he didn't travel far from the little shack, not because he didn't want to, rather because he couldn't. All he would need is for the killer to come back and off their witness, that is, if the man inside were a witness and not the killer? O'Brien couldn't be so sure anymore, at least not until he had been able to talk to him.

He knew the Anvil theory was probably the only theory. However, finding this guy so close to the murder scene also made him a suspect. O'Brien would have to wait to be sure. Minutes turned to hours and he thought the day would never end. Finally, Darnell returned. The phone call was a success. Hal told Darnell to pass a message on to O'Brien that the cavalry was on its way.

Just before 5:00 p.m., O'Brien heard a train whistle blow. Curious he walked back to Necking Ridge keeping his distance from the murder scene. From where he stood, he had a perfect view of the train yard and the little town of Slocolm. Squatting to get a better view of the train as it approached, he waited. Then, from the corner of his eye, he spotted another man ducking in and out of the tall grass. Standing quickly he drew his gun.

"Hold it!" he hollered, but the man kept running looking back only once.

O'Brien knew he was way out of range of his pistol. He ran down the slope as fast as he could to get closer with pistol in hand. Before he could even fire a shot, he watched as the man boarded a boxcar and the train began to sputter on its way.

Adrenaline surged through his body as he caught his breath. He counted the boxcars back to the rear engine so that he knew exactly what car the man had boarded.

"Son of a bitch!" he said aloud as he gained his composure.

Obviously, whoever the person was, he was running from something. O'Brien made a mental note of where he had seen the man dart out of the woods. He headed back to the mining shack to wait for Hal; that was all he could do. With luck, Hal would have a cell phone. O'Brien, of course, had left his accidentally back at his room. His only hope was that Hal had his. Then he could contact Henderson and have him get word to Thom and Rory to head off the train.

"What was all that hollering about?" asked Darnell as O'Brien entered the shack.

"Somebody darted out of the bush down below and boarded the train. I didn't even have a chance to fire a warning shot."

"No way," exclaimed Darnell.

"Yeah, that's what I say. There's nothing we can do now, at least not until Hal gets here."

"I could go back down the mountain and make a phone call."

"Nah. By the time, you got back down Hal might already be here. If he doesn't have a cell phone with him, then I'll ask you to do that."

Darnell agreed and they sat waiting patiently for Hal. John Doe was beginning to stir, so O'Brien undid the cuffs. An hour later, they heard the honking of a car horn.

O'Brien walked out of the shack and hollered. "Hello."

"Hello," came the reply. "O'Brien, is that you?"

"Up here, Hal."

He met Hal halfway and filled him in on what had taken place. Luckily, Hal did have his cell phone and before they made it, back to the shack O'Brien called Henderson and filled him in as well. He asked him to get Thom and Rory to meet the train either in Cassle or Applecove.

"O'Brien, they're already on their way back to the office or, at least, Rory is. How about if I get a hold of Thom and have him stop off in Cassle. I'll head down to Applecove myself.

"Excuse me?" O'Brien responded dumbfounded, as he looked over to Hal and raised an eyebrow.

"You heard me, O'Brien. I'll head down to Applecove. Thom is probably closer to Cassle by now."

"Sure thing, Henderson. Are you feeling okay?"

"What? Do you think all these years behind a desk have softened me?"

O'Brien chuckled.

"Not at all. If you're into it, I'd appreciate it."

"Good; then it's settled. Talk to you soon."

The phone went dead before O'Brien could reply.

"Can you believe that? Henderson said he'd go down to Applecove."

Hal looked at O'Brien with a shocked look on his face and shrugged his shoulders. They walked the distance to the shack and O'Brien introduced Hal to Darnell. Then, he escorted Hal up to the ridge and showed him the crime scene. All Hal could do was shake his head in horror. He snapped a few pictures and jotted down a few notes. Just before dark, they headed inside and put together a couple of beds. Hal was tired and O'Brien was fatigued, Darnell was already snoring with his legs up on the table and their friend John Doe was still breathing. All was well.

Within the hour, Hal and O'Brien joined Darnell in a snoring symphony. In the morning, they planned to call ahead to the lab guys and have them dispatch a couple of their technicians. The RCMP would also have to be informed. Hopefully, John Doe would be able to give them some insight.

# Ten

On Monday, July 23, the ringing of Hal's cell phone woke O'Brien up at 5:00 a.m.

"Hello," O'Brien answered.

"Good morning, O'Brien. This is Rory. I'm entering Slocolm as I speak."

"Hey, Rory."

"Where am I supposed to go? I'm just driving past the Dovetail Motel."

"Keep driving on the main highway until you come to some police tape. It marks the entrance to the road. Drive up the road until you come to Hal's car and an old 4x4. Honk your horn and Hal or I will meet you."

"Okay. Talk to you then."

"Talk to you then, Rory."

O'Brien looked over to John Doe who was sitting up in the bunk with a look of 'where the hell am I'.

"Hey, guy, how are you feeling today?" O'Brien asked.

"Like a bucket of shit. Who the hell are you?"

"I'm Detective O'Brien and this is Hal; he's also a detective. That guy over there who is snoring is Darnell," O'Brien said pointing at him.

"What's going on?" John Doe asked as a matter-of-fact.

"We were hoping you could tell us that. We found you yesterday afternoon lying in some bramble, bleeding like a sieve. Do you remember anything about that?" O'Brien asked.

"I was so drunk by 11:00, I don't remember a thing. Where's Anvil?"

"Anvil?" O'Brien questioned with intent.

"Yeah, he's the one that brought me here."

"Where were you coming from?" Hal jumped in.

"Applecove. There was an unscheduled train coming here. Anvil and I hopped it. Otherwise, we wouldn't have got here until today."

O'Brien was taken aback knowing that if the unscheduled train hadn't come by when it had that they might be looking in the eyes of victim number five.

"We were only going to stick around for a couple of days and then head back."

"Head back where?" O'Brien asked.

"I don't know for sure. Wherever the tracks took us. Anvil said we would catch the Wednesday train."

O'Brien looked over at Darnell who was still snoring believe it or not and kicked his chair. He grumbled awake and looked over rubbing his eyes.

"Hey, Darnell, do you know where the train on Wednesday goes?"

"Give me a minute, O'Brien. I got to wipe the cobwebs from my head."

"Take your time."

O'Brien looked back to John Doe.

"By the way, what's your name?"

"People call me Bud."

"Is that your real name?" questioned Hal.

"Yeah, I'm Bud Newberry or at least I was the last time someone asked me that question."

"Where are you from, Bud?"

"Here, there, nowhere really."

O'Brien was beginning to feel sorry for the man. If only he had known how close, he had come to death at the hands of Anvil.

"Do you have a family, wife, and kids? Anything like that?"

"I used to. The only family I have now is the wine bottle and friends."

"You mean friends like Anvil?" Hal asked.

"That's right. Anvil is one helluva nice guy."

"Did you know that he may have killed four men? And chances are that you were going to be victim five," O'Brien stated.

"Get out of here. Anvil wanted for murder. He was one of the nicest folk I've met in a long time. I can't see it. No way."

Darnell spoke up.

"He isn't kidding, Bud. By the way, O'Brien, the train on Wednesday heads north-east to New Kootenay and then onward to Alberta."

He stood and exited the little shack. O'Brien followed Darnell outside leaving Hal to finish up questioning Bud. O'Brien wasn't sure what they were going to do with Bud. It was obvious he hadn't a clue on what had been going on. Their only recourse was to let the RCMP take him back to their HQ. It was a tad early to start making all those calls, not that it would have mattered. The RCMP was always ready and able to move at any given moment. O'Brien figured the longer they kept Bud, the longer they could squeeze him for information. Maybe he'd tell them something that they didn't already know.

At 7:00 a.m., they heard Rory blasting on his horn. He owned a Subaru Forester and the horn sounded like a swarm of bees more than a real car horn.

"Up here," O'Brien hollered. There was silence for a few short seconds and then Rory responded.

"Up where?"

"Hold tough, Rory, I'm on my way."

O'Brien walked down the embankment a short distance to where he could see Rory.

"Rory," O'Brien yelled, waving his arms. "Up here, buddy."

Rory waved back and made his way up to O'Brien.

"How was the trip?" O'Brien asked.

"Not bad at all. It's a nice drive and up here, man, it is beautiful."

"Yeah it is. Too bad this took place up here," O'Brien, said referring to the murders.

"The devil's playground, O'Brien, can be anywhere."

Rory was dead on the money with that. Death, murder, or suicide could take place anywhere and anytime.

"You got that right, Rory."

As Rory approached closer, he looked at O'Brien puzzled and wrinkled up his nose.

"O'Brien, you need a shower."

"Shut up," O'Brien responded with a smile.

Rory hadn't smelled anything yet. O'Brien helped him lighten his load by taking a few items from him. Rory had brought coffee for everyone in a big thermos and some Egg McMuffins.

"What a sight! Fresh coffee and a golden arch breakfast," O'Brien said looking at the egg and sausage sandwich. "Good to see you thinking on your toes, Rory," O'Brien chuckled in appreciation.

"I'm always thinking, O'Brien. Man, you stink."

O'Brien kicked him in his backside. Back at the shack, they all shared some hot Joe and ate the McMuffin thingamabobs. With their thirsts quenched and hunger pangs gone, Hal and O'Brien showed Rory the murder scene.

"Have you guys contacted the lab team yet? The reason I ask is, if you haven't, when you talk to them make sure they send Stacy Lee Brown. This is right up her alley and she's good."

Rory was right; Stacy was probably one of the best crime scene analysts around. She had been asked to join the CSIS on a number of occasions because of her dedication, hard work, and instinctive qualities, but she wouldn't join. Instead, she worked with the RCMP and lesser police agencies like Henderson & Co.

Hal said that he had already called the lab as well as the RCMP, and that, indeed, he had requested Stacy. O'Brien looked at Hal and punched him in the shoulder.

"Right on, Hal. What would we do without you?"

"Probably screw up a lot," Hal said as he snickered.

Three hours later the place was swarming. The RCMP had dispatched four men and the crime lab sent another six, including Stacy. Ben, from the Cassle Forestry Service, was also there to participate in the search efforts. It turned out that he was Darnell's older brother. *What a small world,* O'Brien thought.

Not needed, Darnell bid them all good luck and headed home, but not before telling O'Brien that if he was ever around Slocolm again to give him a call.

"There are still a couple of places I'd like to show you that I know you'd fall in love with. Later, O'Brien," he said as he turned and walked away.
"Later, Darnell, and thanks again."

By day's end the crime lab disbursed and the RCMP had done all that they could. The scene was picked clean and the dried blood washed away with a lime solution. All that remained was the police tape. O'Brien caught a ride back to the Dovetail with Rory. Hal headed back to Fruitmont to meet up with Thom and Henderson to regroup and head back to the frontlines. There was still a suspect to find and detain. They knew that Anvil abandoned the boxcar and that he was possibly in the Slocolm area. Rory and O'Brien stayed back to set up a base at the Dovetail.

The sound of the helicopter that day really put a scare into Anvil as he hid in the bush near Enterprise. He knew that the man on his ridge had seen him. His instincts also told him that the police were looking for him. He had abandoned the train the night before near the place where he had dumped his fourth victim at Nipsu Creek. He decided to walk north along the railway tracks, which essentially would lead him back into Slocolm.

The police, he knew, would be waiting for him southward in Cassle and Applecove, but if he backtracked, he could buy himself some time and perhaps slip out of the reach of the police. If he could board a train that took him into the Rocky Mountains, he'd be home free. He lived in and amongst those mountains on and off his entire life both with and without his father. There he knew he would be safe. What he didn't know or didn't suspect was that O'Brien and his crew had already guessed that he might do exactly that.

The RCMP set up roadblocks at all major intersections and railroad junctions. The Forestry department was notified to monitor all the forestry roads in and out of the Kootenay Region. It was in O'Brien's opinion that they were two steps ahead. He had no idea how hard of an adversary Anvil was going to be.

For two weeks, they had every orifice in and out of the Kootenays blocked off by the RCMP and the Forestry Department using their top guides including Ben. For two weeks, they found nothing. Their home base at the Dovetail turned into a full-fledged Anvil Brentwood-Task Force HQ. They had laptops, desktops and cell phones, but no trace of Anvil Brentwood. The man had simply vanished like mist in early dawn. There was not a billow of smoke in the sky, nothing.

If they didn't get a lead on Anvil soon, they would undoubtedly be faced with another slew of brutal killings. Guy's like Anvil didn't just go away. Henderson showed up at the Dovetail HQ a couple of times, but never stayed long. Usually he only bitched about this or that. O'Brien's wife Tracy and his two boys showed up once and spent the weekend swimming since they were never able to time it right when both of them were home at the same time. It was one of the unfortunate conditions of O'Brien's job.

It seemed to O'Brien that the boys had grown, which they probably had. He wouldn't know because he hadn't seen them in such a long time. The more he thought about them, the more he wanted the case to end. It all seemed so simple on the 22 when they discovered the murder scene. Now, two weeks later, nothing had come of that other than the discovery itself.

Finally, two days before they were scheduled to head back to Fruitmont, a tip came in. A couple of kids who were fishing had spotted a man running through the bush. They had received tips like that daily, but all the ones they checked turned out to be nothing. They were a little bit sceptical. The sighting was only ten miles north east of Slocolm along Trout Creek.

"What do you figure? Should we move on this?" O'Brien questioned with little eagerness.

Thom was the first to speak.

"What do we have to lose? In a couple of days, we have to pull out. If this turns out to be a solid lead, then maybe we can finally put this case to rest."

O'Brien knew exactly how Thom was feeling. He felt the same way.

"What do you guys say?" O'Brien asked Hal and Rory.

"I don't know. We've had so many hogwash tips. Do you think this one will be any different?" Rory commented with doubt.

"Yeah, not only that, O'Brien, but there should be a couple of guys here to man the phones and stuff," Hal suggested. "Maybe Rory and I should hold back here. That way if you guys need assistance, we can dispatch the RC's from here."

It sounded to O'Brien that Rory and Hal were beginning to doubt that they would ever catch up with Anvil. At the same time, he knew Hal was right. Somebody did need to stay behind. After all, who knew what might take place while all four of them were gone.

"I guess you're right, Hal. Rory, are you all right with that?"

Rory nodded.

"All right then, it looks like it's just going to be you and me, Thom," O'Brien said as he and Thom stood and exited the room.

"What do you suppose is up with them?" Thom asked.

"Fatigue. They've been giving it all they got."

"So have you and me."

"I know, but they run on different cells. You and I run on determination and instinct. Hal and Rory, well, they run on logic and facts."

O'Brien and Thom both chuckled. It was true, though, and that's what made the four of them such a dynamic team. There was no one else O'Brien would rather work with than Thom, Hal, and the kid, Rory.

Thom and O'Brien reminisced as they made their way to Trout Lake Provincial Park. The kids were supposedly camping at site four. They drove up to the campsite and parked in front.

Walking over to where the kids sat on a picnic table, they showed them their credentials and introduced themselves. The kids did seem genuine and they led O'Brien and Thom to where they saw the man. They thanked the kids and sent them on their way. Then, they cut across the creek to the other side. It had probably been twenty minutes or so since the call had come in on their tip line. If Anvil was in the area, he hadn't got too far yet.

The brush was dense and full of stinging nettle that reached out and stung their arms and legs. It was so thick, trying to avoid it was next to impossible. Swollen with the poison, they sauntered on, their eyes peeled and pistols ready.

They had been in the bush for less than ten minutes when they came across some footprints crossing the creek. By the look of them, the person had been running at a good pace. They darted back to the other side, but soon lost sight of the prints. It meant one thing to Thom and O'Brien. The man they chased was travelling in the creek. Problem was they didn't know if he had gone upstream or downstream.

Taking their chances, they continued upstream for about five minutes keeping as quiet as possible. Coming around a bend in the creek, they heard the sound of splashing water, then the sound of running feet. Anvil was just ahead, if indeed it were Anvil. Thom and O'Brien sped up, O'Brien on one side of the creek and Thom on the other. O'Brien ducked out of the way of some thick brush and could see the man they were chasing as he tried to cut back across the creek.

"Hold it right there; don't move!" O'Brien yelled.

The man looked back and darted into the dense brush. Thom crashed across the creek and followed him with O'Brien close behind. The whole time they were shouting at the guy to halt, but he kept running like a moose in rut. O'Brien fired a couple of warning shots hoping to startle him into submission. Whoever it was they were chasing kept right on running. O'Brien and Thom kept right on following.

He ran through the bush with the bounce of a deer. God, he could move! After running for ten minutes straight, Thom and O'Brien had to take a quick breather. Thom's face was so swollen from the stinging nettles, it was a wonder he could see at all.

"Thom," O'Brien said in between breaths. "Are you allergic to that stinging crap?"

Thom was panting when he replied. "I guess I am. Man, O'Brien, would you say that guy can run? Did you see how he ploughed through everything?"

The entire quick little break took less than two minutes. Still, it gave the man a two-minute advantage.

"Oh yeah," O'Brien replied, "come on, we got to get a move on."

"Right on your coattails, O'Brien."

They stopped at one point because they heard the snapping of a twig and then another. O'Brien brought his finger to his lips signalling quiet to Thom. He pointed at a bush that he saw rustling. Thom walked quietly around to the other side without as much as kicking a stone. Slowly they moved in closer. Again, O'Brien saw movement coming from the bush. Adrenaline surged in full force through O'Brien's veins. Beads of sweat broke out above his brow.

Moving closer, his mind raced with thoughts of the terror and anguish that the creep had caused, if indeed the man they chased was the killer. At one point as they approached closer, O'Brien was hoping that if it were the killer in the bushes he'd come out swinging. Then, he would have an excuse to riddle him with lead. Realistically though, O'Brien knew all the hatred in the world wasn't worth the legal justice he might face. When Thom and he were within ten feet of the bush and in each other's view, they counted off three digits. Storming the bush, they demanded that whoever it was come out, hands raised. A few seconds passed which seemed like forever and Thom moved in, kicking the bush.

"Get out of there. Come on, get the hell out."

O'Brien moved in from the other side.

"Hands up. Come on, Anvil, we know that's you."

Again, seconds passed which seemed like eternity. Finally, they saw one hand, then two hands. As the man rose, Thom jumped him from behind and slammed him into the soft dirt. Keeping his knee firmly in the small of the guy's back, he cuffed him.

"Stand up," Thom ordered.

The guy slowly rose. Looking at him, O'Brien wasn't sure it was Anvil. This guy was much lighter in both complexion and weight. His hair wasn't quite as dark as O'Brien recalled of the picture.

"Is your name Anvil Brentwood?" Thom asked.

The man stood silent looking up into the trees.

"Is your name Anvil Brentwood?" Thom repeated.

When he got no reply, he gently twisted the cuff's pinching the guy's wrists. Thom had many techniques to make suspects talk and O'Brien hoped that they weren't going to have to go through all of them, but he was patient. If this guy wasn't Anvil, what was he running from?

Shortly thereafter, he finally spoke up.

"I want my lawyer."

At that point, they could do nothing but bring him in. O'Brien read him his rights and they led him back downstream. On the way, the prisoner kept muttering to himself, "Papa's going to be so mad."

At the campground, they contacted Hal and Rory to let them know that they were bringing someone in. O'Brien told Hal that he and Thom would head towards Newton and instructed Hal to radio the RCMP to let them know that they were coming in with a suspect and that they request a backup vehicle to meet them half way.

That afternoon, as they sat at the RCMP station in Newton waiting for a positive identification, Thom and O'Brien paced, both of them crossing their fingers and hoping that the day would end on a good note. They wanted nothing more than to hear that the man they had brought in was none other than Anvil Brentwood. Two cups of coffee later, a constable walked in to the staff lounge grinning from ear to ear. As soon as O'Brien saw that smile, he knew that, indeed, it was Anvil Brentwood.

"Congratulations, O'Brien, Thom. It's Anvil and he's been formally charged with four counts of murder, one of evading police, kidnapping and conspiracy to kill."

Those words were like music to their ears and they hollered in victory.

"Yes, yes."

"Another one down, buddy," Thom hollered.

"You betcha; finally, we can go home," O'Brien related as he called Hal and told him to pack it in, that they were finally going home.

After filling out some paperwork at the station and getting court dates straight, Thom and O'Brien headed back to Fruitmont. Hal and Rory said that they would disassemble the HQ at the Dovetail and meet them back at the office in Fruitmont. The time was 2:00 p.m. They would be back at the office by 6:00 or 7:00 p.m. at the latest O'Brien calculated. He couldn't wait to finally get home. The case had taken a lot out of all of them. With Anvil behind bars, however, it justified the effort. On the drive back to Fruitmont, Thom, and O'Brien sat in silence, each of them in their own glory.

Henderson got the good news and was waiting back at the office to congratulate them and shake their hands.

"You guys have done one hell of a job. I want each of you to know that. Through all the bullshit, you stuck together and followed out with your game plan. That speaks volumes. You are all excellent detectives. Keep up the good work."

O'Brien thought it would be a good time to ask for the three week vacation coming to him. He had already cleared it with Thom, Hal, and Rory and they agreed to pull his weight in paper.

"By the way, Henderson."

"Yes, O'Brien?"

O'Brien looked at him dumbfounded. Henderson never answered a question with a yes.

"Yes, O'Brien?" O'Brien jibed putting emphasis on the yes part as he raised an eyebrow.

Henderson looked at him and O'Brien could tell that Henderson was about to retort, but instead he said. "All right then… what the hell is it, O'Brien?"

O'Brien looked at him and smiled.

"That's better. I was wondering if I could book off my three weeks of vacation I have coming to me?"

"What are you talking about? We still have a ton of work to do on this Anvil thing."

"Not really. Court's not until September. Only paperwork needs to be done."

"Who'll do all the paperwork while you're gone?" Henderson questioned.

In unison, Thom, Hal, and Rory spoke up.

"We will."

O'Brien looked at them and smiled.

"See, Henderson. No problem."

Henderson hummed and hawed for a couple of minutes then finally said, "I'll give you two weeks O'Brien. You'll have to take the other week at another time."

"Fair enough, Henderson. Thanks, I'll take it."

"I expect you back in this office two weeks from tomorrow."

"You bet. Two weeks vacation here I come!" O'Brien exclaimed as he turned and burst out of the office.

## Eleven

One week later, Henderson tracked O'Brien down. He contacted the ranger station at Champion Lakes where Tracy, the kids and O'Brien had decided to spend the first week of his holiday.

Apparently, Anvil Brentwood's preliminary hearing had been set for August 22, Henderson wanted him back a week early to help prepare for it. O'Brien wasn't sure how Tracy and the kids were going to take it. He promised them that they would head to New Kootenay that Thursday and spend some time on Kootenay Lake where they would rent a boat and cast in a line to do some fishing. Now, he would have to explain to them otherwise. He contemplated walking down to the beach to let them know, but decided to wait for them to return. He would be ruining their fun soon enough.

Sitting at the picnic table with a glass of iced tea in his hand, O'Brien wondered why Anvil's second hearing was scheduled so soon after his apprehension. They had put that piece of trash in the clink on August 6, today was Tuesday the 14, O'Brien decided they'd head back that Friday. That way he could start fresh on Monday. It would give the kids a couple of extra days to swim, and Tracy and himself some extra time together before their world was turned upside down again.

O'Brien reminisced about Anvil Brentwood's case. Anvil had killed his victims as viciously as a wolf tears into its prey. Each victim had been lured into the backwoods and viciously murdered. As their blood spewed from their wounds and their screams echoed in the forest, Anvil Brentwood had watched with sickening fascination. They apprehended him a month after they found the first victim and charged Anvil with four counts of first degree murder and kidnapping, one charge of evading the police and five charges of conspiracy to kill, charges that would land him in prison for the rest of his life. Why the second preliminary hearing was taking place so soon after they arrested him was beyond O'Brien.

When Tracy and the boys returned from the beach, he explained to them that he was requested back earlier than expected and that they had to return home. O'Brien was surprised when they said that would be all right and that they understood. Taras said he didn't mind because now he wouldn't miss any more football practices. Zach on the other hand said he missed his cat. Tracy and O'Brien assured him that his cat was fine.

"I know, but what if Neo misses me? I should be there for him," Zach responded with loneliness for his cat.

On Wednesday, the weather turned from bad to worse. They spent the entire day inside the tent trailer playing cards and listening to the radio. Thursday was not any better and by noon, they packed up and headed home to Fruitmont. Although it was a short holiday, it was still some R and R that both Tracy and O'Brien needed, and deserved. They spent Friday, Saturday, and Sunday hanging out in their own backyard. It turned out to be more enjoyable than their time at Champion.

It probably had to do with the fact that a little over a month earlier, O'Brien had shot and killed Norm Bradley, a murderer of two young girls from nearby Hudu Park. O'Brien wondered now why he had suggested going there. The only thing he could think of was so that he'd be close to work. Sometimes he was more dedicated to his job than to his family. How Tracy managed to put up with it was beyond him. Nevertheless, she did and for that, O'Brien was most grateful.

O'Brien arrived early to work on Monday although it was a statutory holiday. In his business, holidays didn't matter. He and his three associates Thom, Hal, and Rory converged to prepare the evidence and files they had on Anvil Brentwood for use against him in court. They wanted nothing less than to have him put away until he died. They were informed that the prosecution was seeking four life sentences, but the defence lawyers were looking at an insanity plea which, if not overturned, meant that Anvil would probably be free in five or six years. He'd only be 58 years old and able enough to kill again.

By late Tuesday afternoon, they had managed to put together quite an onslaught of information they hoped would turn the tables on the defence. They had photos, reports from all the forensic pathologists and an array of information obtained from Stacy Brown, their crime scene analyst at the murder scene. She determined that it was unlikely Anvil was insane at the time of the murders. It was in her opinion that he was way too deliberate to be insane and that an insanity plea in his defence was utterly precarious. Did they have enough, though, to convince the judge? That was another question and one that could not be answered until the following day.

O'Brien and crew went over everything one last time before having it sent to the prosecution and defence lawyers. At quitting time, they agreed to meet the following morning at the *"Big Cup of Joe"* which was the coffee shop they frequented. That night was the first night since they arrested Anvil that O'Brien dreamed about the case and the horror they found.

The murder scene in his dream was as graphical as it was in reality. Even the stench of human blood wafted up his nostrils. His mind raced with images of what the victims must have gone through. He visualised Anvil as he set the meat hooks into his victims the way an angler sets a hook. He watched in horror as Anvil hoisted them up with his elaborate pulley system. Blood formed in red pools and O'Brien watched as each drop landed like rain in puddles brought on by its own downpour. He watched as Anvil knelt beside the bodies and grinned.

So real was the dream, that he awoke with a dry mouth and shivering in a cold sweat. He sat up shaking his head then headed to the bathroom tap for a drink. It was 4:00 a.m. O'Brien knew that getting back to sleep would be next to impossible. He retreated to the kitchen and watched the sunrise. An hour later, he was looking through the Fruitmont Source, the local newspaper that delivered on Mondays and Wednesdays. Flipping through the classifieds, he briefly looked at a couple of the news stories. Setting the paper down, he brewed a pot of coffee.

The rising sun reflected through the many prisms Tracy had hung strategically when they bought the house two years prior. They reflected an array of rainbows that danced on the walls. O'Brien smiled at how precisely she positioned them to catch the early sun, the midday sun, and the evening sun. No matter what time of day it was, the kitchen danced with rainbow colours. Outside the kitchen window, wind chimes gently blew breaking the silence. He poured himself a coffee and exited to the back deck. The day was starting well.

At 7:30, Tracy met him out on the deck and drank a coffee with him before he had to leave.

"How long have you been awake, O'Brien?" she asked.

"I had a stupid dream and wasn't able to go back to sleep."

"What did you dream?"

"Ah, it was nothing."

"Yeah, right. That's why you couldn't get back to sleep, huh?"

They talked for a few more minutes before O'Brien got ready to head to the office. Kissing Tracy goodbye, O'Brien told her that he would see her around 6:00 p.m., hopefully with news that Anvil would stand trial for the hideous crimes he committed. O'Brien, Thom, Hal, and Rory met as planned and headed to the courthouse after downing a couple cups of coffee.

"Think Anvil will stand trial?" Rory asked.

"I sure hope so. If he doesn't, it'll make me wonder why we didn't fill him with lead," Thom replied.

"Come on, Thom, you know we can't just shoot bad guys."

"I know, O'Brien, but if he gets an insanity plea it'll sure piss me off."

"I think it'll piss all of us off," Hal commented.

"Let's hope the defence sees it our way. I mean, the evidence proves or at least I hope it does, that he is a completely sane man," O'Brien pointed out.

"Yeah, but that lawyer… what's his name?"

"Edwin Lacomb."

"Edwin… yeah, him. He is good at talking through his hat," retorted Thom.

It was true. Edwin Lacomb was good at what he did. He was one of the best defence lawyers around. How Anvil was able to afford him was beyond O'Brien and the rest of the crew. Chances were he agreed to do it pro bono. It was something he did on occasion to keep his good name.

"Let's hope this is one of the times he listens to reason," Hal mentioned.

They drove in silence the rest of the way to the courthouse. O'Brien was relieved when he noticed who was reigning as the judge that day. It was Judge J. W. Reinhardt. They knew him as the hanging judge. He was fair, precise, and swift to sanctify justice. Making their way to the aisle that was closest to the front of the courtroom, they sat waiting for the hearing to take place. Rarely did they speak to one another.

Finally, the sheriff entered with three RCMP Officers and one Anvil Brentwood. The sheriff took his position at the judge's chamber door.

"Will everybody please rise? The Honourable Judge J.W. Reinhardt is presiding."

Silence fell in the courtroom as everyone present stood. The judge made his way to his podium bowed for everyone to sit.

"Anvil Brentwood, you have been charged with four counts of murder, evading police, and five counts of kidnapping and conspiracy to kill. Do you understand these charges?"

Edwin Lacomb stood.

"Your Honour, as the defence attorney for Anvil, we understand the charges. I would like to request that Mr. Brentwood undergo an evaluation at Bedlam Hospital in New Kootenay. Mr. Brentwood has a history of psychological tendencies. At age 42, he was remanded at Bedlam for an assault he committed in a rage of mental instability. A Dr. Price, who is the administrator of Bedlam Inpatient Care, has stated that during Mr. Brentwood's detainment, he found Anvil to be suffering from possible paranoid schizophrenia."

Edwin grew silent for a moment before continuing.

"Your Honour, it is stated in the pre-sentencing report, paragraph 2 line 6 and right through to page three as a matter-of-fact, that Anvil was physically and mentally abused as a child.

It states that he was beaten so badly at one point during a lonely school year that he could no longer attend school. Because of his abusive father, he was forced to leave school by the time he was in grade six. Your Honour, it is my opinion that Anvil is a man living with resentment and aggression towards his father and his peers. I believe that a twenty-one day psychological evaluation is in order. It is the least we can offer this man who has suffered so greatly, your Honour."

Edwin bowed and took his seat.

Judge Reinhardt looked over at the prosecution with a look of dismay.

"Does the prosecution have anything to add?"

"Yes, your Honour, we do. May I reiterate the fact that where and how these murders took place entailed a great deal of lateral thinking and planning. Your Honour, may I put forward to you a document numbered 1539 in both my possession as well as in the defence attorney's possession from one Stacy Lee Brown, a highly knowledgeable, and much sought after crime scene analyst?"

"Yes, you may. Please step forward Mr. Ottis and bring forth the submission."

"Thank you, your Honour."

Pete walked over to the podium and set the file in front of the good judge. Stepping away, he bowed and returned to his seat. Silently the judge read over the folder then looking at both Anvil and Edwin, he rose and called for a recess.

"Court will commence in one hour. Mr. Lacomb, I suggest that you refresh yourself with document 1539."

"Yes, your Honour, I will."

When the judge left the courtroom, the defence and prosecution talked amongst themselves. O'Brien and his crew exited the courtroom and had a meeting of their own. So far, it was looking as though the judge might quash the defence's request. If that happened, then Anvil would stand trial. Perhaps justice would be served.

O'Brien made his way into the sheriff's office to retrieve four coffees. Sheriff McAdams was sitting in his swivel chair.

"What do you think, O'Brien? Think Anvil is going to get sent for an evaluation?"

"I sure hope not, Gary. Only Reinhardt knows the answer to that."

"I don't think the judge wants to play around with this guy. When I spoke with his Honour earlier, he already guessed that Edwin was going to pull that line of hooey and request an evaluation. He wasn't buying it then. I doubt he's buying it now."

"Personally, Gary, I don't think he's keen on that idea either. I think after he goes through that folder that Pete gave him more thoroughly, he'll deny Lacomb's request."

"Oh, you do?"

O'Brien heard the voice come from behind. He turned to see Judge Reinhardt standing there. His face grew flush.

"Sorry, your Honour. Gary and I were just having friendly conversation."

"Not to worry, O'Brien, as long as you're not bribing the good sheriff," the judge chuckled. "By the way, you were one of the detectives working this case, weren't you?"

"Yes sir. Thom Beard, Hal Beady, Rory Clemmens, and I worked on it."

"Tell me, O'Brien, while you worked the case, did you ever think that the suspect could be insane? Did he seem to know exactly what he was doing?" the good judge asked.

"No and yes, your Honour. No, I didn't think he was insane, rather I thought him to be quite analytical. Yes, I believe he knew what he was doing."

Reinhardt looked at O'Brien and nodded then returned to his chambers.

"Well, he didn't reveal much, did he?" Gary retorted.

"Certainly not. I wonder what that was all about."

Gary just shrugged his shoulders. O'Brien patted him on his back then picked up the coffees and slipped out. Thom, Hal, and Rory had congregated in the library and were sitting with Pete when O'Brien arrived. He gave them their coffee and they had friendly conversation until the time to head back into the courtroom was upon them. Sitting patiently once again, they waited until the judge was ready to preside. It seemed like forever until they heard the sheriff tell everyone to rise.

"Will everyone please rise? The judge is ready to proceed. Court is in session."

Reinhardt approached his bench and looked sternly at the defence.

"Mr. Lacomb, have you familiarised yourself with document 1539?"

"Yes, your Honour, I have."

"Very well then, could you please read to the court what it says?"

"Yes, your Honour, I shall." He read it aloud; "'Whereas, I find it inconceivable, that for a man who is insane to be able to follow through with these methodical and concise violent acts that have been committed to the four victims. A man who suffers from somatic delusions or other mental or physical impairments, could not, and would not, act as precisely and with the cunning needed to perform these gruesome acts. The precise locations where the suspect had impaled each individual with the meat grappling irons proves to this writer, that, the defendant Anvil Brentwood, at the time of the killings was in a state of mental and physical awareness and that he was also in complete charge of his own actions.'

I understand, your Honour, what Miss Brown is stating here. Nevertheless, let's also remember that it is only the opinion of a crime scene analyst. It has little relevance to the true prognosis of the illness Mr. Brentwood suffers from."

Judge Reinhardt lowered his head and slipped his eyeglasses onto the bridge of his nose.

"Mr. Lacomb, I am aware that document 1539 is only the opinion of a crime scene analyst. However, I favour her opinion more than I favour yours. It is in this Court's opinion that Mr. Brentwood shall undergo an evaluation, however not at the Bedlam Hospital in New Kootenay. Nor shall it be for twenty-one days. He will be detained at the Fruitmont Psychological Observatory where he will undergo a fifteen-day evaluation, not a day longer and not a day less. He will be in the care of Dr. S. Randol who will endorse or refute the findings that have been introduced to the Court today. If Dr. Randol finds that Mr. Brentwood can stand trial, then, judge, or judge and jury shall try him, on a later date convenient to this court. If Dr. Randol finds Mr. Brentwood incapable or otherwise unable to stand trial, he will be committed to an infirmary of the courts choosing. Any questions?"

"No, your Honour."

"Mr. Ottis, does the prosecution have anything to add?"

"Your Honour, the prosecution would like to let the court know that at this time we are also considering another charge of murder for the death of a John Doe in Grandbluff ten years ago. We are also considering an investigation into the death of Mr. Brentwood's father, one Brock Brentwood. There is an implication, your Honour, that Anvil Brentwood may have also played a part in that death. It is an implication that the Prosecution is ready and willing to investigate. With that, your Honour, the prosecution rests."

Edwin Lacomb stood up in a huff.

"Your Honour, as Mr. Brentwood's lawyer I'm going to have to ask for the courts agreement in seeking an injunction on those presumptuous charges. It is the first I have heard of them. It is bias to Mr. Brentwood and to the people," Edwin pleaded.

"Mr. Lacomb, you have fifteen days to familiarise yourself with the situation. As for the injunction, this court denies your request. That is all. Court will be adjourned for fifteen days. Sheriff McAdams, please escort Mr. Brentwood to holding cell eight until we can transport him."

"Yes, your Honour."

O'Brien looked over to Thom who was sitting next to him. He could tell by the smile on his face that Thom was impressed with the hearing's outcome. O'Brien, himself, was more impressed with Pete's closing argument. If Anvil did get convicted of the two extra murders, there would be no way he would live long enough to be released, not even if he were sent to an asylum. He would have to live out rest of his life there or in prison.

# Twelve

By Friday, Anvil was settling into his environment. The room was a pale blue and the bed had not been slept in. He preferred the cool vinyl covered floor. At 10:00 a.m., Dr. Randol made his first appearance. He unlocked the corridor leading to the locked door of room twelve. It would be the first time he and Anvil laid eyes upon one another since Anvil's arrival that Wednesday. The corridor door closed automatically. After he punched in the security number, it locked with a click and buzzing sound.

Dr. Randol was a tall man with a dark mop of thick hair and blue eyes. He had assumed the day to day operations of the Fruitmont Psychological Observatory six months prior. Dr. Randol was not a newcomer to the field of psychology and neurology. Although Anvil was his first patient sent to the Observatory under the order of a Judge, Dr. Randol was well aware of Anvil's shaded past. He knew that Anvil was classified as a dangerous man, a man who would often undergo drastic physical and mental changes.

To Dr. Randol this meant that Anvil was not insane. Rather he thought Anvil might suffer from a possible brain disorder. As he approached the door, Dr. Randol removed the key ring attached to his belt loop and opened it.

"Mr. Brentwood, I am Dr. Randol. I have been assigned to evaluate you by Judge Reinhardt and to put you through some routine tests. I would like to start up a rapport with you. Do you feel like talking today, Anvil?" Dr. Randol asked with empathy.

"Today I say nothing. Maybe tomorrow," Anvil responded never taking his eyes off the floor.

"That's fine. I'm here to help you, Anvil. Maybe together we can figure out what has caused you this great vexation?"

Anvil looked up from the floor. His cold eyes locked with Dr. Randol.

"You people will never figure me out. I have been through this before with doctors that have said they were there to help. How can you help if no help is needed?"

Anvil walked up to the partition of blue rubber coated bars that separated himself and Dr. Randol.

"I say to you, good luck."

Turning, he walked over to the opposite corner of the room where he slid down the wall, his knees upright.

Dr. Randol tried another approach and asked Anvil what his fascinations with locomotives were. It was at that point that Anvil stood abruptly and rushed towards the Doctor.

"Why do you ask? Do I have a fascination for trains?" Anvil hissed as his face contorted and his eyes got big. "The steel horse is what took my father away to a place he deserved to be. It trampled over his evil genius and freed me from his evil grasp."

As abruptly as Anvil neared, he turned and went back to the spot on the floor and sat again in silence. The words he used were words Dr. Randol knew that a man with megalomania would not use in that context. This observation proved to him that Anvil wasn't insane. Dr. Randol decided instead that Anvil might suffer from neural structure degeneration. More tests would have to be done to rule out if Anvil was suffering from glioma or a brain tumour. It was possible that as a child, he'd received concussions, which triggered a minute swelling of his brain, and as he progressed through life, it proceeded to enlarge.

The problem with that was obvious. Not anybody, who went undiagnosed from a cerebrum imbalance, or swelling of the brain, would have lived for more than a few months. Still, was it possible? Dr. Randol jotted down a few notes and excused himself from Anvil's room. He had a theory now, albeit a farfetched one.

When Dr. Randol closed the door and locked it, Anvil brought his knees up and tucked his head. Slowly he began to rock back and forth, his mind racing with his vicious past and the brutal beatings he had received from his father.

It was shortly before noon when O'Brien received the phone call.

"Detective O'Brien?"

"Yes," O'Brien replied.

"This is Dr. Randol from the Fruitmont Psychological Observatory. I have briefly spoken with Mr. Brentwood. His outbursts have led me to wonder if we shouldn't do a CAT scan on him. It's possible, detective, that Anvil may have gliomata. Although this is only a possibility, it's one that has never been looked at."

"Don't tell me that. If there's anything in the world that I don't want to hear it would be that," O'Brien said with disappointment and disbelief.

"I'm sorry, detective. I thought you should be informed. I should say that Judge Reinhardt asked me to inform you. I've just got off the phone with him. He feels the same way as you do. However, it's my job to diagnose these things. You do understand that until we have done the testing I cannot make a firm diagnosis. I wanted you to be aware of the possible prognosis. I have already arranged with the technicians to prepare for this testing later today and will know more shortly thereafter. Would you like me to confirm the results with you or would you rather wait to hear it from the judge?"

"When do you suppose you'll have the results?"

"No later than, I would guess, 6:00 or 7:00 p.m. this evening."

"I'll wait for your call, Doc," O'Brien said as he thanked him and hung up the phone.

O'Brien was discouraged. If Anvil had gliomata, he would never see a prison cell for the crimes he had committed. Instead, he would live the remainder of his life in a hospital.

When O'Brien mentioned it to Thom, Hal and Rory, they too were dismayed. They had all put so much into the case that to hear such a possibility made each of their stomachs churn.

O'Brien could only hope that the good Doctor's prognosis proved otherwise. He wanted Anvil to be put away in prison, not some asylum. He deserved prison, behind walls of concrete and doors of steel, nothing less.

For the remainder of the day, O'Brien went through his roster and made inquiries on a few minor cases he was assigned. One case involved a break & entering. The only thing that went missing was a first edition of 'Gone with the Wind'. It was a stupid case, but there was something about it, that intrigued O'Brien.

A book of its calibre could easily be worth a few dollars. However, O'Brien had received an email from one of the museums he contacted earlier. They reported that the book, depending on its condition, could easily reach $20,000 or more. At that point, he became a bit more interested in the case. He had been working on it for a couple of months.

Another case he looked over before Dr. Randol had called, involved the disappearance of a witness to a drug deal that went terribly wrong. An eighteen-year-old kid was shot and now lay in the Fruitmont General three months after the fact, still in a coma. A witness was summoned to testify in an upcoming trial. However, he had vanished before the summons was delivered, and was now missing for over two months. Everyone who knew him all claimed that they had not seen him.

Finally, at 6:30 p.m., Dr. Randol called with his analysis.

"Detective O'Brien," he started.

"This is he."

"Good news for you, detective. Anvil doesn't have a brain tumour, however he does have a neurological disease."

"And that's supposed to be good news? How?"

"Well, detective, the condition he suffers from will probably kill him in less than six months. It's surprising he has lived this long."

"That is good news, Doc. What is his condition?"

"He has what I believe to be Kuru."

"And what exactly is that?"

"It's a progressive disease of the central nervous system marked by the increasing lack of co-ordination, speech, and thought. Eventually it advances to paralysis and death. It has been thought in the past that this particular kind of disorder has been caused by cannibalistic consumption of diseased human brain tissue."

"What?" O'Brien bellowed. "Cannibalistic consumption of diseased brain tissue?"

"That's right, detective. The disease was first discovered amongst cannibalistic tribes. When cannibalism was abandoned, the disorder became dormant. There have been only rare cases since. That is the only reason it's believed to have been caused by cannibalistic consumption of diseased brain tissue."

"Whew. I'm glad you're telling me that, because none of Anvil's victims appeared to have been cannibalised."

"As I've said, detective, the only reason scholars and such recognised the disease to have been caused by such consumption is because it was no longer diagnosed after cannibalism was abandoned. This, however, does not mean that perhaps sometime in Mr. Brentwood's life he was not subjected to cannibalism. Perhaps that is how the disease spread? There is little known about Kuru to prove otherwise. I, on the other hand, am not one to believe such a conclusion."

"What do you believe, Doc?"

"I believe that Kuru is a hereditary disease. Anvil may have inherited the disorder from his father, but more likely from his mother. Nevertheless, take comfort, detective, knowing that Anvil Brentwood will not see his next birthday. I'll actually be surprised if he lives six more months."

"Thanks, Doc. Keep me posted."

O'Brien hung up the phone as a surge of both satisfaction and sadness engulfed him. The news, although comforting, also caused him to have some sympathy. He wondered how long Anvil might have been suffering. O'Brien sat in thought for few minutes and although it was 7:15 p.m., he finally phoned up the Crime Scene Investigation Lab and left a message for Stacy to call him on Monday.

He wanted her to do some investigating on this thing called Kuru. He was worried at thinking it was possible that Anvil's mother may have had more than one child. If Kuru was a hereditary disease that was transferred from mother to child, he had a legal obligation, especially if they were unaware, to inform them of the possibility of the illness that they may develop. O'Brien already knew that Anvil had never met his mother. Could it be that she continued with her life and bore more children? On the other hand, it could be she died long ago and Anvil was her only child. O'Brien finished what was remaining of his cold coffee, then left the office for home.


The weekend came and went without incident and O'Brien was able to spend it with Tracy and the kids. He even managed to get the lawn mowed and the turtle pond cleaned. It had been a great weekend and time well spent. He loved his home life, but he also loved his job and was anxious to get back to work that Monday. He was hoping Stacy would call with information on Dr. Randol's prognosis of Anvil's condition. In addition, he still had work to do on the disappearance of a witness as well as the disappearance of a first edition book.

O'Brien arrived that Monday to work at his usual time. He proceeded to make a few inquiries with some local used book stores and pawn shops, asking them if they were recently questioned about interest in buying a first edition of 'Gone with the Wind'. None had been.

He talked to a Historical Library asking the same questions with the same results. However, he did manage to get the names of some people who were known collectors of old manuscripts and he wrote them down for reference. He thanked the man and hung up the telephone. It was a start.

Next, he opened the folder marked Missing Witness. Going through the folder, he came up with the same thing as always. There was nothing proving that the witness had been murdered. There was no evidence that anyone with his name had boarded any planes, trains, or automobiles leastwise not in British Columbia. He had simply vanished. O'Brien believed friends and relatives were hiding the guy. Putting the folder on his desk, he dialled Stacy's number. She still wasn't around and they played telephone tag for most of the morning. Finally, at 1:00 p.m. they made contact.

"Hey, O'Brien, sorry I've been missing you. We're pretty busy," Stacy claimed as O'Brien answered his phone.

"That's okay. I only wanted to know if you have ever heard of Kuru, and if you have, what you know about it."

"I've heard about it, but that's not what I specialise in. I am not a neurologist. I'm a crime scene analyst or if you like, a police science research worker. I can tell you that such a disorder is uncommon. I think you should contact Dr. Nebinoff. He has done a lot of research in that field. As recently as five years ago, he had a female patient who died from the type of symptoms that one gets when affected by the disease. He was also granted medical jurisdiction on the woman's brain and has been studying it since."

"Gross," O'Brien retorted. "Dr. Nebinoff, then, you would say is an authority on this disorder?"

"Most definitely. He has also come up with some interesting theories. He can be reached at the Department of Neurological Science at Kingston University. His number is area code 416-555-0033 extension 27. Did you get that, O'Brien?"

"Yeah, thanks a lot."

"No problem, O'Brien. Is there anything else you needed or wanted to ask?"

"Not presently, but if I think of something I'll call."

"I bet you will," she chuckled. "Bye for now."

"Thanks again," O'Brien said as he hung up the phone.

His next step was to call Dr. Nebinoff, but he decided to hold off for a bit and wait for Dr. Randol's next correspondence. O'Brien scribbled in his notebook in big black letters, 'Kuru' what is it and how does one acquire it? In addition beside that he jotted down Dr. Nebinoff' telephone number and extension. He found it curious that as recently as five years prior someone had died from symptoms that were a lot like Kuru. He wondered if maybe that person had any links to Anvil. Currently it was irrelevant, but for future reference who could be sure?

He received a tip later that day via email from an auctioneer that at a book auction, which took place two weeks earlier in Ottawa, sold a first edition of 'Gone with the Wind' to a notable collector in England of all places. The collector's name was Sir Alexander Neilson. He had purchased it for a mere $17,000 Canadian. The book was in fair condition except for a few pages, which had their corners folded. The missing edition that O'Brien was looking for also had some pages folded over. The only thing was, the email hadn't stated which pages. In O'Brien's report, they were pages 76, 92 and 128.

All O'Brien had to do now was contact the collector. What a treat that would be, considering he lived half way around the world. He scribbled the information down and put it with the file. He replied to the sender and thanked him for the information, adding he was curious to know if there were records somewhere that could verify which pages of that said book were folded. Deep down O'Brien was hoping that they weren't the same. The paperwork involved in putting the book back into the rightful owner's hands would then be unconscionable because of who and where the book had been taken, if indeed it were the same book. By day's end, O'Brien was no further ahead in the two investigations or for that matter even close to knowing what Kuru personified. Only time would tell.

# Thirteen

As the last days of Anvil's evaluation quickly approached, Dr. Randol and O'Brien stayed in close contact with one another relaying information back and forth. Although the doctor was unable to ascertain that what Anvil suffered from was Kuru, he was able to conclude that the neurological imbalance would also be the cause of Anvil's death. He guessed that Anvil would succumb to the disorder in less than one year. However, there was more. Anvil also exhibited the antidote to the disorder in his blood. Somehow, the disease that was killing him was also producing a prophylactic interrupter. It was truly uncanny, but that is what Dr. Randol concluded and it was what he wrote in his final report and evaluation.

O'Brien contemplated the good doctor's conclusions. He thought about how unjust it really was. Here was a man who committed violent and inexcusable crimes. Now he was going to become some medical marvel. He would undoubtedly spend the remainder of his life in some medical institution with white cotton sheets, colour television, and all the modern day conveniences of today's society. *How pathetic,* O'Brien thought. Even Dr. Nebinoff was unable to diagnose, what it was that Anvil suffered from. Except, that it was undoubtedly a neurological condition. In the report O'Brien received from Nebinoff, Dr. Nebinoff also concluded that the condition Anvil suffered would likely be the cause of Anvil's demise.

What did this mean to the prosecution? It meant that the case was not going to put Anvil behind bars. Again, he had managed to escape justice. It made O'Brien think about what Thom had said earlier. Why hadn't they put lead into him when they had the chance? It sounded barbaric, but O'Brien was beginning to wonder the same thing. Anvil may be suffering from some neurological imbalance; still, in his books Anvil was a killer. O'Brien had been in this business going on fifteen years; he'd put his share of killers behind bars. None of them compared to Anvil Brentwood's capabilities. To think that his actions would almost be forgivable in the eyes of the justice system because of the imperfections of his brain made no sense whatsoever to O'Brien.

It was O'Brien's opinion that anyone who was as sound as Anvil and who committed murderous crimes ought to be sent to jail for life — no excuses. That wouldn't be the case here though, and O'Brien knew it. The only righteous thing was that Anvil would die in a year or, at least, that is what Dr. Randol and Dr. Nebinoff predicted. O'Brien prayed to God that their prediction was sound no matter how callous that might have seemed.

Finally, Thursday September 6 arrived, the day of Anvil's court date and hearing. O'Brien showed up at the courthouse with Thom, Rory, and Hal at 9:00 a.m. They were all pleased to see that Reinhardt was again presiding as the judge. The four sat in silence, hoping for an outcome that would be satisfactory. At 9:30 a.m., the RCMP and Sheriff McAdams brought the guilty party, Anvil Brentwood, into the courtroom, cuffed and shackled. They sat him down at the defence table while the constables sat directly behind him. Minutes later the judge entered. Everyone rose. He bowed and court was in session.

Judge Reinhardt looked over to the defence table and began.

"Anvil Brentwood, please rise."

Both Anvil and his disenchanted lawyer, Edwin Lacomb, rose.

"I have before me two evaluations from two very well-respected, well-educated psychologists and neurologists.

These evaluations have been sent to and received by both the defence and prosecution. Does the defence have anything to say about the documents numbered 701 and 702?" he asked.

A few minutes passed as Edwin Lacomb briefly looked over the documents.

"Yes, your Honour. I have received them and I have read them thoroughly. Both documents will prove to the court that at the time of these vicious crimes, my client, Anvil Brentwood, was in a confused state of mind."

"Is that what you believe, Mr. Lacomb?"

"It is, your Honour."

"Very well. Please be seated. What would the prosecution like to say about these documents before we get started in today's proceedings?"

"Nothing, your Honour."

"Please be seated, Mr. Ottis."

"Thank you, your Honour," Pete said as he bowed his respect and took his seat.

The judge shuffled through some of the files and folders piled on his podium. He called upon both the defence and prosecution to approach his bench. Some whispering and nodding went on. Finally, the defence and prosecution retreated to their seats.

"Anvil Brentwood, you have committed depraved and violent crimes. Your acts of impurity have caused suffering and torment to the public and men of your peers. These acts will not, go unnoticed by this court. Do you have anything to say, Mr. Brentwood, before I continue?"

Anvil sat in silence for a few seconds then whispered to his lawyer. Mr. Lacomb rose.

"Your Honour, Mr. Brentwood has nothing to say presently. He has asked that we continue and that after he has been sentenced, he will speak."

"Very well. I will grant Mr. Brentwood what he has requested. To begin this hearing, I would like Dr. Randol to please step forward and tell the court what his evaluation of Mr. Brentwood has perceived."

Dr. Randol stood and walked over to the witness stand followed by sheriff McAdams.

"Please raise your right hand and put your left on the bible. Do you swear to tell the truth, the whole truth, and nothing but the truth, so help you God?"

"I do."

"Please state your name to the court and your occupation."

"My name is Dr. Scott Randol. I am the chief psychologist at the Fruitmont Observatory Hospital."

The sheriff set the bible on the stand and returned to his seat.

"Dr. Randol, would you please tell the court what the results of Mr. Brentwood's evaluation consists of," ordered Reinhardt.

"My time with Anvil was less than adequate to make a firm diagnosis of his neurological imbalance. It appears that Anvil suffers from a degenerating disease called Kuru," he stated.

There was a brief silence in the courtroom.

Edwin Lacomb stood.

"Is it your opinion, Dr. Randol that Anvil Brentwood was not in control of his state of mind when he committed these horrible crimes? Could you please elaborate on this degenerative neurological disease called Kuru?"

"I shall. First, I do not believe Anvil was incoherent when he committed the crimes. This type of impairment does not affect that part of the brain that makes us act out. It causes thought degeneration yes, but only in its final stage. Anvil's disorder is only at the elementary stage."

"When you say elementary stage what do you mean? Does this disease come in stages?" asked Edwin.

"Like most diseases, yes, it does as a matter of fact."

"You say it appears that that this disease is only in the beginning stages. Do I detect some uncertainty from you, Doctor? Are you even sure that Anvil Brentwood suffers from this Kuru thing and not some other neurological problem?"

"I assure you that what Anvil Brentwood suffers from is an unknown form of a neurological degenerating disease. It shows symptoms of Kuru to a greater extent than any past or present known neurological disorder."

"Ah, so then, you are unsure of what he may or may not suffer? No further questions, your Honour," Edwin said indignantly as he sat down.

The judge looked over to the defence table.

"Mr. Lacomb, from your questioning I assume that you have not read the documents as thoroughly as I would have expected you to. If you had, you would have read that the disorder your client suffers from was stated in the documents as an unknown form of disorder that acutely resembles 'Kuru'. I would suggest that you do not waste time like that again in my courtroom. Is the prosecution ready to question Dr. Randol?"

"Yes, your Honour, we are."

"Please start, Mr. Ottis."

The prosecution shuffled through some folders and briefly talked with his friend of the court.

"Dr. Randol, you spent fifteen days with the accused. You subjected him to numerous tests and tasks, didn't you?"

"Yes, I did."

"One of those tests, or should I say, during a conversation with the accused, you asked him why he had such a fascination with trains. What was his response?"

"He became hostile and replied that the 'steel horse took his father away to a place that he deserved'. He said it released him from his father's grasp and in addition, trampled over his father's evil genius. From that statement I knew that he was not insane or otherwise."

"Did you do tests to investigate the possibility of a brain tumour?"

"That very day."

"What were the results?"

"We discovered that Anvil had a neurological imbalance. No tumours of any kind were found. We also discovered that not only was he suffering from this disorder but also that it resembled a degenerating disease called Kuru and that he would eventually succumb to it. We also did blood work on Anvil and discovered that he also carries in his plasma the antidote for the very disease that is killing him. It is the only way he manages to stay alive."

"You say he also carries in his blood the antidote? If that is the case, why do you suppose he will succumb to it?"

"It is scientifically impossible for him to continue regenerating this antidote while his body is weakening from the symptoms. It is a very complex degenerating disease. There are virtually no texts written on it. The disorder Anvil suffers from is progressing at a slower rate than what would be expected from such a neurological disorder. It is an educated guess that he will die in less than a year. To be absolutely sure of his condition, more testing would have to be initiated."

"Okay. With that aside, Dr. Randol, is it your opinion that this disorder caused Anvil Brentwood, the accused, to act as he did?"

"Not at all."

"Thank you, Dr. Randol. The prosecution has no further questions at this time."

"Does the defence wish to cross-examine the witness?" asked Judge Reinhardt.

Again, there was a long silence in the courtroom while Mr. Lacomb prepared his next tactful retort.

"Actually, your Honour, it does."

"Please begin, Mr. Lacomb."

"Umm, Dr. Randol, you just stated to this court that this disorder is practically an unknown subject, that not much is known about it. If that is the case, how do you not know that it may or may not have contributed to my client's recent behaviour?"

"If Mr. Brentwood was in the later stages of this disease and his thought process had deteriorated, he would not have been able to commit these crimes. One who cannot think is incapable of reaction, correct. If he was in the later stages and his physical abilities were hindered, again he would not have been able to commit these crimes. The disorder he suffers from, you see, deteriorates these mechanical aptitudes in our brains. So far, they have not deteriorated to the point where he would not know what he was doing. The symptoms are not yet that far advanced. In fact, what he suffers from in my professional view does not constitute any reason for him to have committed these crimes other than his own thirst to kill. I am not denying that the man suffers from a neurological disorder, but I do not feel it is what caused him to act as he did. Does that answer your question?"

"Not really. For now the defence rests, your Honour," replied Edwin Lacomb.

"The court will now call a recess so that I may review and unify what has come about in this morning's proceedings. Court will take a two-hour break and will begin again at 1:00 p.m., this day September 6, 2001," said Judge Reinhardt, as he rose and entered his chamber.

It was a neck in neck race. The hearing brought to the attention of all those present the fact that the disorder Anvil suffered from could not be related to the initiative he took to kill his victims. What the defence was able to argue was that no one could be sure of the extent of Anvil's disorder. It was a neck in neck race; there was no doubt about that.

O'Brien, Thom, Hal, and Rory headed down to the local café for a bite to eat and some coffee and conversation.

"You know what? I think our friend Anvil is going to get his walking papers and spend the rest of his life in some elaborate medical facility. That pisses me off to no avail."

"I hear you, Thom. That is a good possibility. It is comforting to know though that he'll eventually die, isn't it?"

"The only problem with that, Hal, is that no one can be sure that he will die."

"I don't know about that, Thom. Dr. Randol seems to think he will and so does Dr. Nebinoff. He said in the text that I read that it would probably kill him just as it did his patient. That means at least two scholars agree that he isn't going to live to see his next birthday," O'Brien responded.

"Yeah, but are you forgetting that he also seems to be making his own antidote to the disorder. That alone will land him in a medical facility."

O'Brien knew Thom was right. He was encouraged though, knowing that Dr. Randol said he wouldn't be able to continue making the antidote as his body slowly deteriorated. He said it was scientifically impossible, what if it wasn't. That question would haunt O'Brien until the day Anvil Brentwood died.

"You know what gets me? We spent all that time investigating only to be rewarded with the possibility that our friend Anvil may very well die, but he'll die in a resort compared to a penitentiary. Why should he?"

"It doesn't seem fair at all, Rory, but that's justice for you," retorted Thom.

At 12:45 p.m., they made their way back to the courthouse. They sat in silence waiting for the judge to preside. Finally, after what seemed like a leap year, the judge approached his bench and again the courtroom rose.

"Please be seated. The court is ready to conclude. Mr. Lacomb, is your client prepared to carry on?"

"Yes he is, your Honour."

"Mr. Ottis, is the prosecution ready to continue?"

"We are, your Honour."

"Very well, let us begin. The court would like to call upon Dr. Nebinoff from the University of Kingston's Neurological Science Department. Dr. Nebinoff, please step forward."

O'Brien and the others were shocked that the judge called upon him. They had no idea that he had even been summoned. Dr. Nebinoff made his way to the stand. After the swearing in and oath, the judge began the questioning.

"Dr. Nebinoff, you have as recently as five years ago had medical dealings with a woman who suffered from this disorder that Mr. Brentwood suffers from or one like it, correct?"

"As a matter of fact, your Honour, I did."

"And what was your prognosis at the time?"

"Well to begin with, your Honour, the woman I cared for was not capable of anything more than a laboured speech. I ran numerous tests, as did my colleagues, on both her neurological brain pattern and her blood plasma. We were able to ascertain that the symptoms came on fast and without mercy. The patient died from the disorder only two weeks after we diagnosed her. At first, we were certain that she too suffered from Kuru. The symptoms were so alike that it was impossible to diagnose her with anything but that. The only difference was that she did not acquire a blood disorder or deficiency as one gets with Kuru. That was the only difference. All the other symptoms were identical.

I have recently run tests on the defendant Anvil Brentwood's blood as well. He too has the exact symptoms, with the exception that it is occurring in him a great deal slower. Not to mention, your Honour, or to harp on the fact that the accused harbours the antidote in his DNA. I would say the symptoms he has should be scientifically sorted out. It could ultimately prevent others from dying. Whether he is a killer or not, your Honour, he needs to be studied."

"Would you say, Dr. Nebinoff that this disorder could be what induced him to kill earlier in his life as well as latterly?"

"Not at all your Honour, I think that suggestion is utter nonsense. The illness does not make one violent, not when the symptoms commence nor at the termination. It is a fallacy to believe such drivel."

"I see. Thank you, Doctor. Does the defence wish to question Dr. Nebinoff?"

"No, your Honour, nevertheless, I would like to quote what he said in regards to my client's mental state. 'He should be studied scientifically and thoroughly. That, his DNA may very well contain the antidote.' That, your Honour, in itself, should proclaim, the fact that my client needs special medical attention that he will not receive in prison, but at a medical facility. Both Dr. Randol and Dr. Nebinoff have stated that they cannot be sure of his condition until the scientific community has had the time to study the condition that has befallen my client.

Your Honour, if what they predict is true, chances are he will be with God soon. Therefore, I believe that the court should consider a lengthy stay at Bedlam in New Kootenay where Anvil has stayed before. They are the closest entity he has to any sort-of family. Your Honour, if you were a dying man, would you not want to be in the presence of family?"

"Mr. Lacomb, the evidence that has been brought forth and introduced to me, as well as the scientific data this court has received, will not allow the court to sentence your client to anything less than an asylum. You, Mr. Lacomb, of all people must have been aware of this. You know and so do the people know that any criminal who suffers from life threatening abrupt changes in his or her mental or physical state cannot be sentenced to a prison. It would be unjust and

immoral. You do know that, don't you, Mr. Lacomb?"
Reinhardt asked in disbelieve at Lacomb's recommendation.

"Yes, your Honour, I do. I was only trying to benefit my client."

"Trust me Mr. Lacomb, that did not benefit your client; nor do I believe that is what your intent was. I believe your intent was to belittle this court. Any further sympathy pleas from you in that manner will not be tolerated. Understood?"

"Yes your Honour, it is understood."

There was a long silence in the courtroom while Judge Reinhardt continued staring at and intimidating the defence and his client. His stern look made mincemeat out of most people just as it did to Edwin Lacomb. The intensity that the judge provoked in the courtroom was extreme. That was why he had been called the hanging judge. Edwin tried his hardest not to fold and held his stare with the judge until finally he broke eye contact.

"Now, Mr. Lacomb would you like to try again? Is there anything you wish to ask Dr. Nebinoff?"

"No, your Honour, presently the defence rests."

"Mr. Ottis, is there anything you would like to question Dr. Nebinoff?"

"Your Honour I believe that both Dr. Randol and Dr. Nebinoff have answered and revealed all that they can without further testing the defendant's neurological anatomical structure. I also believe that if the defendant's DNA can be studied for an antidote that may help or prevent this disorder. Then I would say that I have no further questions, but rather a request that Anvil Brentwood spend the remainder of his natural life in a medical institution where he will be studied by an array of scientists and medical personnel. Bedlam Hospital in New Kootenay is an option, but not the only option, your Honour. The prosecution would request that the court consider such a place as the Neurological Science Department at Kingston University.

They are well equipped to handle this type of disorder and are the only medical facility that has extensive interaction with it."

At this point, everyone in the courtroom began getting antsy. The Neurological Science Department at Kingston University was the closest thing to a real prison for the mentally ill in all of Canada, compared to all the other medical institutes. Usually patients were kept at the Kingston Penitentiary in the psychiatric hospital. Inmates were brought to the facility for two to three week stays, then they were sent back to the infirmary at the Penitentiary. The psychiatric hospital at the Penitentiary was no different than a twenty-four hour lockup. If Anvil were sent there, it would certainly sit all right with those in attendance.

"Your Honour, to send my client to the Neurological Science Department in Kingston would be nothing less than if he were to be sent to a twenty-four hour lock up in a prison. Your Honour, that is completely unjust; you said it yourself. Are you recanting your statement? What kind of justice is that?"

"Mr. Lacomb that will be your last chance. Any more outbursts such as that will not be allowed in my courtroom another time. You have been warned. Understood?"

"Sorry, your Honour. May I reiterate?"

"No. You may be seated. Dr. Nebinoff, you may step down. This court will again recess for fifteen minutes until closing arguments and the verdict of the court. Mr. Lacomb and Mr. Ottis meet me in my chamber directly."

As Reinhardt exited and the audience rose, O'Brien and his crew smiled and nodded at one another. The case was looking good in their regard. They huddled in the aisle and quietly discussed what was taking place.

"It looks like our friend may be sent to a place he deserves after all. If the judge rules in Pete's favour, Anvil will get exactly what we hoped for. The Kingston Penitentiary is no picnic. He will be in twenty-four hour segregation and will have minimum interaction with others. It's perfect."

"You got that right, O'Brien. If he gets sent down that way, I'm getting drunk," Thom commented.

"And I'll follow your example. But if he doesn't get sent that way, I'm still getting drunk."

"That a boy, Rory. I'll be sitting right beside you."

"Yeah, you can count me in too," said Hal.

"What about you, O'Brien. Will you join us for a stiff one when this whole charade is over?"

"I don't know, Thom. I haven't been drunk in such a long time. I don't think I would be much fun. The last time I got drunk, I was sick for a week. I might join you for one, but don't count on it."

"We'll accept that, buddy. Oh, looks like court's about to start again. This is it, boys. Keep your fingers crossed."

The four returned to their seats and waited impatiently for the outcome.

The defence and prosecution made their way to the front of the courtroom and took up their assigned positions, the prosecution on the right and the defence on the left. O'Brien noticed a glint of shine coming from Pete's eye when he looked at him. Pete nodded with a smiled. He always gave that signal when the judge saw things his way. O'Brien's heart was pounding fast and loud with excitement and anticipation. A few minutes later Judge Reinhardt approached his bench. He looked sullen and committed. A silence engulfed the courtroom as all that were present sat waiting for him to start. He shuffled through his papers with intent and diligence. Finally, he looked at both the defence and prosecution then began.

"This court will now proceed with its findings and implications. We will start with closing arguments from the defence. Mr. Lacomb, do you have anything to propose?"

"Your Honour, I would like to propose that my client be treated for his condition and when such condition can be resolved, we once again put forth the evidence to the court that my client at the time of these crimes was not in a sound state. The defence would like to ask the court for an adjournment so that Anvil Brentwood, the said accused, may face a fair and just sentencing. That is all the defence wishes to state."

"Mr. Lacomb I will take into consideration your request and will rule on it after the prosecution makes its recommendations. Mr. Ottis, will you please rise and state your closing argument and summary."

"Your Honour, the prosecution would like to recommend that the defendant, Anvil Brentwood, be sentenced to The Kingston Penitentiary's infirmary for the remainder of his natural life, where he will undergo exclusive testing at the Kingston Neurological Science Department at the Kingston University. The prosecution believes there is little sense in adjourning this case for a later date. The prosecution feels that would be an endangerment to the defendant's physical and mental being.

The evidence has already proven that Anvil Brentwood killed these men with no remorse and that his mental disorder is not what caused him to react as he did. Dr. Nebinoff has stated that it is not possible the degenerating disorder Anvil suffers from could be what caused his actions on those horrific days that he mutilated his victims. Dr. Randol has stated that it is scientifically impossible for such a disorder to cause one to act violently. The evidence and data has proven to the prosecution beyond a reasonable doubt. That the defendant isn't insane, nor is the disorder Anvil suffers from, a cause for his behaviour. The evidence proves that not only was he of sound mind and body when he committed the crimes, but also that he murdered his victims in cold blood for his own gratification and amusement."

Pete paused as he looked directly at Anvil.

"The prosecution would also like to state that if the defence wishes to proceed with this case, we are prepared to charge his client with two extra counts of first-degree murder for the death of his father as well as that of a John Doe ten years ago in Grandbluff. If the defence is willing to agree to the people's request then we will have no need to further that investigation and will hold it in lieu of his sentencing today.

The people are aware that because of the defendant's disorder, he cannot be sentenced to a federal prison atmosphere. Otherwise, the prosecution would have petitioned for four life sentences, a life sentence for every murder he committed. Therefore, we the prosecution, leave the final verdict and sentencing in the hands of his Honour. With that the prosecution rests."

Pete bowed and gently took up his seat.

"Thank you, Mr. Ottis. The court has listened to and has read countless submissions from doctors, detectives, analysts, the defence, and the prosecution. With the authority vested in this court, I will now state the verdict and sentencing of this court and her Majesty the Queen."

Judge Reinhardt cleared his throat and with authority put forth the verdict.

"Mr. Anvil Brentwood, please rise to hear the court's orders. You have been charged with four counts of first-degree murder, five counts of kidnapping with intent to kill, as well as evading police. Because of your unfortunate disorder, the court cannot, nor will it, impose sentencing to a standard federal prison. It is this court's decision that you shall undergo further testing at a medical facility.

Perhaps your ability to produce an antidote to this neurological phenomenon can be your way to give back to your peers what you have taken away, which was hope and life. For that, the court sentences you to life in a psychiatric hospital where you will undergo experimentation and testing until you succumb to this illness, whether it takes a year or a hundred years. I hereby sentence you to the Kingston Neurological Science Department in the care of Dr. Nebinoff until your death. You will be sent to the psychiatric hospital of the Kingston Penitentiary where you will undergo minor testing at that facility one week out of every month. You will spend three weeks out of each month at the facility of Neurological Science Department at the Kingston University. Upon your death, your body will be donated to the University. For further scientific testing by all those scholars who analyse neurological disorders. Do you understand this sentencing?"

Anvil only nodded.

"Very well. Now Mr. Brentwood, as I stated earlier, I will grant you your say in this matter. Would you like to say something to the court before the sheriff escorts you to a holding cell?"

The courtroom grew cold and silent as all waited to hear what Anvil had to say.

"What you see before you is a demonic abomination of a man that once was. I will not succumb to death as easily as the court and its people wish. I will seek my revenge on all of those that have forsaken me. Anvil Brentwood has not even begun the terror he is capable of. Your sentencing is only a reminder to me on how weak you and the justice system are. You have not heard or seen the last of me."

With that said Anvil sat and waited for the sheriff to escort him away.

"Sheriff McAdams, please escort Mr. Anvil to a holding cell."

As the sheriff rose and escorted Anvil to his holding cell, Judge Reinhardt raised his gavel and slammed it down.

"The court has ruled and therefore it shall be. Court dismissed."

Therefore, it was that Anvil was sentenced to exactly what he deserved. To top it off, the judge did the unthinkable and ruled that his brain after death would remain the property of the Kingston University. All those involved rejoiced with cheer.

"Isn't that something?"

"It is the best."

"It sure is. I feel like a million bucks now."

"That's a good analogy, Rory. I feel like a million bucks, too. I am glad not all that work was lost. He's getting exactly what he deserves," O'Brien replied unsympathetically.

"Here, here," said the others in unison smiling from ear to ear.

Justice did prevail.

# Fourteen

By Friday September 7, 2001, it had been only a day since Anvil's confirmation hearing and sentencing, but the tension that enveloped O'Brien since they first arrested Anvil was finally dissipating, this time, he hoped, for good.

That day, O'Brien went over numerous documents and folders of cases that he had avoided working on during the whole course of the Brentwood investigation. He arranged these cases in priority sequence, making them ready and accessible for his indulgence.

The first one he set on his plate was, of course, the one with the most information involving the missing first edition of 'Gone with the Wind'. He read over the file and pieced together bits of information that he believed were relevant. The book, it was stated, was not museum quality. There were three pages in the book with their corners folded over. The book cover, over the years, received a few inconveniences. Such as a burn from a hot coal that jumped out of an open fire, a stain near the bottom left corner close to the spine, as well as the name of Vada Kleef written in small lettering in blue ink which had faded away to the letters …a Kl… were the only identifying marks.

The book was not going to be easy to locate. O'Brien had one lead and that was the email, he had received from an auctioneer in Ottawa. Who stated that a prominent book collector from England had purchased a first edition of 'Gone with the Wind' for $17,000 Canadian. The reason the collector was able to purchase the book so cheaply was that it too had a few pages with their corners folded over. The email hadn't stated the page numbers. O'Brien had replied to the sender, but so far, he had not yet received a reply. He hoped that would change come Monday. If it didn't, he knew that he would have to locate the book collector himself, which he knew would be a pain in his backside.

Hal and Rory would be on afternoon shift and Thom's hands were full with a case of mail fraud, so neither of them would be able to assist. There would be only a couple of clerical workers and O'Brien running the ship for the entire week. O'Brien was beginning to step away from his desk to grab his last cup of coffee for the day when Henderson approached him.

"O'Brien, I need to have a couple of words with you. Grab yourself a coffee and meet me in my office," Henderson instructed.

"What's up?" O'Brien asked anxiously.

"I'll fill you in when you get to my office," Henderson responded as he scurried away.

O'Brien poured a cup and followed him into his office.

"Sit down, O'Brien. I have a favour to ask and would like to congratulate you on a couple of things."

O'Brien pulled a chair up to the desk and waited for Henderson to continue.

"You've done a great job for me since you started with me back in '98. This Anvil Brentwood case was one I knew you would get to the bottom of…"

O'Brien cut him off there.

"Whoa, Henderson. I didn't pull this off without Thom, Hal, and Rory. They deserve as much recognition."

"Oh, they'll get their recognition, O'Brien; don't you worry about that. This is not the only case that you have done an exceptional job on. There are many others. I wanted you to know that I appreciate your work."

"Thanks, Henny Penny. I try to do my best," O'Brien responded with wit.

"And you do, O'Brien; and you do…that's why I have a favour of you to ask. Before I do that, however, I want you to know that whatever you decide, I'll accept."

O'Brien knew then that he was up to something.

"All right, Henderson. What is it you want to ask me?"

O'Brien held his breath hoping Henderson was not going to ask what he suspected Henderson was going to ask. Nevertheless, he did.

"To start with, O'Brien. How do you feel about a short move for a couple of months? A year tops."

"Let me guess, to Ridgeville?"

"That's right, O'Brien. Since Wainwright retired, our agency there is suffering. The Police aren't even using the agency anymore. We still have a few good clients down that way, but we also need the bones that the Police Agencies toss us occasionally. I need a good detective down there, someone who can get the place back in order. Henderson & Co. will keep up with the mortgage payments on your house. I will even consider paying for a house sitter. That is how badly I need someone there with your abilities. What do you say?"

"You know how badly I hate being put on the spot. I am grateful you feel that way about me. I just don't know if I want to take on an assignment like that. After all, the kids start school this coming week. I'm not sure what Tracy might say."

"Come on, O'Brien. A position as head detective increases your pay by thirty percent. In addition, a nice five-bedroom house was once the Henderson & Co. main office that comes with the deal. It has a large backyard in-ground swimming pool; Taras and Zach will love it. There are a couple of nice lakes nearby as well. The schools are very nice and well-equipped. I'll only need a guy down there with your stature until I can find a permanent replacement."

"It sounds interesting, but I'll need to think on it for a while," O'Brien responded as he contemplated the offer.

"That's fine. I can give you the weekend to think about it."

"The weekend? I need more time than that. Come on Henderson, it's a big decision."

"Gotcha," said Henderson. "You can take as much time as you need, O'Brien, as long as you get back to me in the next three or four days."

"That doesn't sound like I can take as much time as I need, now then does it?"

"I'm sorry, O'Brien. I need someone ASAP, in the next couple of week's max. You've got to understand that the longer it takes you to decide, the more money the company is losing."

"I'll think it through. As for the thirty percent pay hike, if I accept I want that amount to be divided among Thom, Hal, and Rory. That'll be one of my conditions."

"You're a maniac, you know that, O'Brien?"

"Gotcha," O'Brien jibed. "Seriously though, Henderson, that is what I want if I decide to take it up."

"That's fine with me, O'Brien. I don't have a problem doing that."

"Good," O'Brien responded as he stood to exit. "I'll talk to you soon."

"Thanks, O'Brien. Thanks a million. I hope you make the right decision."

"Whatever decision I make, Henderson, will be the right one."

"I know, O'Brien, thanks again," Henderson said as O'Brien exited his office.

O'Brien walked over to his desk and slumped into his chair. He had a lot to contemplate. What would Tracy and the kids say? A new school, a new town, and another move seemed almost intolerable. O'Brien knew Henderson was really counting on his decision to be yes. Chances were it would be. The distance to Ridgeville was about six hours. O'Brien knew that if Tracy and the kids weren't into it, he could still head down and do what he could to get the agency back on its feet.

They could commute back and forth. That wouldn't be a problem. However, the thought of being away from each other for long periods, of time. Was something he didn't desire. That evening before heading home, he drove around Fruitmont for about an hour. His mind raced with possibilities and unmade decisions, decisions he knew that he could not make alone. He'd have to go over them with Tracy and the kids.

O'Brien pulled into the driveway a little before 7:00 p.m. The kids were outside playing and when they saw him pull in, they darted over to where he parked.

"Hey Dad, are you going to do it?" they asked in unison.

"Do what?"

"Come on, Dad, you know," said Taras.

"No, I don't," O'Brien replied dumbfounded.

"Mr. Henderson said he was going to ship us all down to Ridgeville to a great big house with a pool. He said he was going to put you in charge of his agency down there," exclaimed Zach.

"He did, did he?"

"Yeah, he did. Said you would make a great Lieutenant, probably the best ever. That's what he said, Dad, he really did."

O'Brien smiled to himself. He should have known that Henderson would have pulled something like that.

"What else did he say?"

"I don't know," said Taras as he shrugged his shoulders. "You'll have to ask Mom."

"I know what else he said. He said that he has a big surprise for you, except that he couldn't tell you yet or something like that," Zach said as he darted past in a heated rush to catch his cat.

"Well then, I guess I'll have to go and see what your mother has to say."

"She's waiting for you in the kitchen."

"Thanks, Taras," O'Brien said as he turned towards the house.

He was amused by Henderson's tactics and at the same time grateful. Henderson had done this type of thing to him before. That is, phoning ahead and clearing it with Tracy before even asking him. O'Brien swore the two of them were allies. He concluded a long time ago that it probably had to do with the fact that the two of them were forced to put up with him on a daily basis. O'Brien had that kind of impact on people. He was already planning ways to get back at Henderson as he approached the front door. First, he wanted to toy with Tracy for a while. As he opened the front door, she came strutting down the hallway with a big smile on her face.

"Oh O'Brien, I'm so happy for you. Congratulations!"

O'Brien looked at her dumbfounded as though he had no idea on what she was talking about.

"Congratulations on what?" O'Brien questioned.

"Didn't Henderson talk to you today?" she asked in a quiet sympathetic voice. Her face turning shades of red as though she ruined a great surprise.

"I didn't see him all day. What's going on?" O'Brien asked as he set his briefcase down on the foyer hutch.

"Umm, nothing. I just wanted to congratulate you on that Brentwood case."

"That was yesterday, Tracy, you already congratulated me."

"That's right, I did, didn't I? Well congratulations again."

"Thank you again. Are you all right?"

"Yeah, I'm fine. I just wanted you to know how proud you make me."

"Really?"

"Yes, really. You're the best thing that has ever happened to me."

"You're the best thing that ever happened to me as well," O'Brien said as he soaked it up.

He kept her talking like that for a couple of minutes and then said. "By the way what do you think about a move for a while?"

She looked at him not sure, where he was going with that question.

"A move. Where?"

"Ridgeville."

"Ridgeville. You did talk to Henderson today didn't you? You made me feel like such a jerk."

"I'm sorry."

"Oh yeah, you will be, O'Brien!" she exclaimed as she pounced on him and threw him onto the couch laughing the entire time.

"You're so bad, O'Brien. I'll get even with you one day. You wait and see."

O'Brien was laughing so hard he ended up with hiccups.

"Okay, okay," he begged between hiccups, "you win."

After their little wrestling match, they sat down together and talked about Henderson's offer. They decided that it was an opportunity that they did not want to let slip away. All they had to do now was convince the kids. Somehow, O'Brien knew that would be the easy part. They had already expressed their feelings when he pulled into the driveway. After all what kid would turn down an in-ground swimming pool, a five-bedroom house, and a huge backyard? None that O'Brien knew of, especially not his.

By 10:00 p.m., their minds were made up, their firm decision being that they would take Henderson up on his offer. The amount of money they would save was a good reason, especially since Henderson & Co., were going to take up the slack on their mortgage, a staggering amount of $989.00 a month and they would be living in Ridgeville mortgage and rent-free. They would save nearly $12,000.00

if they stayed for a year. However, it really wasn't about the money. That was the little picture. It was about the opportunity and the possible advancement in the firm. O'Brien visualised the metal nametag on a big oak door that lead to his private office. 'Detective Lt. Tyler O'Brien,' it read. O'Brien smiled.

The following morning Tracy and the kids began packing. O'Brien strode around the yard making sure that everything that needed to be packed or locked up was. O'Brien wondered if they were not jumping the gun a bit by packing so soon. He finally decided that it was probably a good idea. After all, it wasn't going to take just one day, not with all the junk they owned.

That entire weekend they packed and by Sunday, there was still a lot to do. As for hiring a house sitter, they decided against that. Instead, O'Brien would have the guys swing by occasionally. If there were anybody he wanted to watch his house, it would include Thom, Hal, and Rory. O'Brien wouldn't even have minded if Thom crashed there. He was single and lived in a quaint two bedroom apartment on Rosewood Drive. O'Brien contemplating telling Thom that if he wanted to he could move in while they were gone, but decided he would simply let him know that if he wanted to use it he could. O'Brien arrived at work on Monday to an array of congratulation letters and a banner draped above his desk.

"What is this all about?" he asked with surprise.

"It's a congratulation party for you, you lucky bastard," stated Thom. "What are you going to do with all that extra pay?" he jibed with a chuckle.

"I'll never see that."

"What do you mean? A promo to Lieutenant automatically boosts your salary thirty percent," said Hal.

"Yeah, I know, but I turned the pay raise down."

"Why would you do that?" asked Rory.

"You'll figure it out," O'Brien chuckled.

"Figure what out?" questioned Thom. "If you seriously turned down that pay raise you're a maniac. That's good coin."

"Funny, Henderson said the same thing," O'Brien replied.

"You did turn it down, didn't you?"

"Sure did, Rory. I figured since it is only temporary I didn't want to get too comfortable in receiving that extra amount. Besides, who cares? We're not in this business for the money, are we?"

"Yeah, I suppose I see your point."

"By the way, how did you guys hear about it? Henderson only asked me on Friday. I haven't even given him my answer yet."

"We were informed last week, O'Brien that you had been promoted and were taking a transfer down to Ridgeville to organise the crew there and to redeem the good name of Henderson & Co.," Thom chuckled.

"You mean to tell me that you all heard about this last week and didn't let me know?"

"That's right, O'Brien," retorted Hal with a smile.

They all cheered, "O'Brien he's our man. If he can't do it, no one can."

They were kidding him that was for sure. He was surprised at how well the guys were actually taking it. He thought that there would have been some animosity floating around. O'Brien realised then that was selfish; he felt feebleminded for even considering it. They were the best crew he ever worked with. The more he thought about all the cases that the four of them had resolved together, he realised that saying goodbye to them was going to be the hardest part in accepting the offer.

He knew they would eventually work together as a team somewhere down the line and that they would all stay in close contact regardless. It was just something about the words — see you all later that made O'Brien appreciate exactly what each of them represented and that was a kinship.

"Look, I appreciate all this, but who is going to take over all my cases?" O'Brien asked with gusto and jubilance as he threw one of the folders he held in his hand into the air and all the papers inside fluttered to the floor. Laughter broke out again and they all began chanting and yippee ii yaaaing.

Henderson came over with a big cake.

"Thom," he asked. "Would you do the honours?"

"Certainly."

O'Brien was half-expecting what happened next. Thom took the cake from Henderson and began reading it aloud.

"Congratulations on your Promotion as Lt. Detective…" he broke out laughing, "they misspelled your name, O'Brien. They got it down here as Lt. Detective Tyrone O'Brien."

"Ah, that's not as bad as some names I've been called," O'Brien responded.

"Really that's what it says, O'Brien. See, check it out," Thom said as he approached closer.

O'Brien reluctantly looked a bit closer and Thom slammed the cake into his face. The entire entourage burst into laughter. Even O'Brien thought it to be somewhat comical as he turned to wash up.

Henderson approached him.

"O'Brien, what have you decided?" Henderson grinned. O'Brien looked at him and shook his head his eyes sparkling with pride.

"What do you think? Of course, I'll accept."

"All right, O'Brien. Listen up, everyone. I want all of you over here while I swear O'Brien in as Lieutenant."

At that point, they all cheered and told O'Brien how deserving he was.

"Wait a minute, Henderson. What do you mean swear me in? Is this official? I thought it was only a temporary position."

"That's what happens when you do your own thinking," Hal jokingly retorted from the back of the room.

"Why did you think that, O'Brien? Do you think I would promote you and then demote you?" asked Henderson.

"To tell you the truth, that is what I thought. I thought I was doing this for you as a favour."

"Oh, you mean by going to Ridgeville. That is a favour, but you were still going to be promoted regardless."

At that point, O'Brien could have sworn that his jaw dropped to the floor and his eyes popped out. He was completely thunderstruck.

"What's the matter, O'Brien? Being a Lieutenant just means you can boss us around when Henderson's not here," Thom said as he chuckled.

"That's right, O'Brien, and you do that anyway."

"Like hell I do, Rory," O'Brien said as he laughed.

He couldn't believe that this was an actual promotion. It was then that it dawned on him that he had given up a thirty-percent pay raise for real. O'Brien chuckled at his dumb luck. *Oh, well such is life,* he thought to himself.

"All right, everybody settle down. I need to swear O'Brien in as Lieutenant."

During the swearing in, O'Brien didn't hear a word Henderson said. His mind was too busy sorting it out. He was however able to repeat the oath.

"Congratulations, O'Brien," said Henderson as he shook O'Brien's hand.

Then he entrusted O'Brien with the insignia-ranked badge that acknowledged him with the empowerment of Lieutenant.

"Speech! Speech! We want a speech," everyone present began to holler.

"I don't know what to say, but I do know that I couldn't have come this far without each of you. Each of you has enlightened me one way or another. You have all been the hardest working crew I have ever worked with. In addition, I thank all of you for this opportunity to become your Lieutenant. Thank you," O'Brien replied as he held up the badge.

The room filled with clapping and smart-ass remarks. O'Brien bowed, turned around, and mooned the whole lot of them. The place went hysterical. By the end of the day, he had been insulted, abused, and tormented, all in good fun, of course. He cherished every moment. That was September 10.

Four days later O'Brien was standing out on his front lawn in the early morning waiting for the moving company, wondering what lay ahead in Ridgeville and what kind of criminal element he might face there. Fifteen minutes later the Ridgeville Moving Company showed up. It took three hours to load up their belongings and off they set to the town of Ridgeville. They arrived at 1309 Mountain Rd a little after 7:00 p.m. The house Henderson boasted about was exactly as he described it. There was a large swimming pool. The fact that it needed cleaning and looked as though it hadn't been used in years was beside the point or at least it was to the kids.

"It won't be all that bad. We just have to clean it up. There's still some summer left," Taras commented.

"Yeah, I know. We will clean it and get some use out of it before it gets cold. First, let's get moved in. We'll deal with the pool tomorrow."

The house itself was immaculate, as were the front and back yards. In the garage there were pool cleaning tools and gardening tools. The house sat on top of a grassy knoll that overlooked Ridgeville. It was surrounded by a wrought iron fence and a gate, which over the years had become inoperable. The driveway had seen better days. The asphalt was cracked and pieces were missing here and there. Other than these few inconveniences, the house was quite comfortable.

Henderson had given O'Brien two days from the time, he arrived to get down to the Ridgeville agency. He wanted O'Brien to call him as soon as he arrived at the office. O'Brien, Tracy and the kids unpacked into the wee hours of the morning, finally stopping for the day at around 4:00 a.m. All that was left was organisation. That was something O'Brien would leave to Tracy. He elected himself to clean up the pool.

They awoke later that day around 10:00 a.m. and by 11:00 a.m., O'Brien was trying to figure out how the pool pump worked so he could dispose of the rancid water and they could begin the task of scrubbing it down. He gave up a couple of hours later realising it was a lost cause. Off the boys and he went to the local spa and pool. O'Brien spent four hundred dollars on a pump and some chlorine. By 4:00 p.m., the pool was drained and they began the task of scrubbing it down.

They scrubbed, re-scrubbed, and scrubbed again until the concrete was no longer covered in the slime that had formed over the years. The pool sparkled when they were done. It took another three hours to fill and at 9:00 p.m., the task was finished. That night they sat in the comfort of their New World and what a world it would prove to be.

# Fifteen

Sunday, September 16, 2001 was a hot and blustering day and O'Brien and family spent it in the pool. It was hard to believe that within two weeks they would no longer be able to use it as fall approached.

O'Brien arrived at the Ridgeville office that Monday at 8:00 a.m. He had been to the office on numerous occasions running errands for Henderson and he knew most of the detectives there. They were well informed about his arrival.

"Good morning, Lieutenant," said a young rookie whom O'Brien hadn't met before.

"Good morning, and you are?" O'Brien responded.

"I'm Mick, Mick Ross. Glad to make your acquaintance Lt. O'Brien. I've heard a lot about you."

"What have you heard?"

"Not to worry, O'Brien," O'Brien heard the big booming voice of Mathew Henninger say. "He's only heard the truth," Matt chuckled.

"Hey Matt, how ya been?"

"Pretty good, O'Brien. Congratulations on your promotion."

"Thanks, Matt."

"How long has the kid been working here?" O'Brien asked referring to Mick Ross.

"I've been here for almost three months," Mick himself replied.

"Well then, welcome aboard."

There was something about the kid, O'Brien already liked.

"What's the first part of business you want to take care of, O'Brien?" asked Matt.

"I'd like to get everybody together so I can reiterate why I'm here. Can I get everybody into the coffee room?" O'Brien asked Matt.

"Sure can. I'll round them all up. Meet you there in, say, ten minutes."

"Thanks a lot, Matt."

Minutes later the crew of six met O'Brien in the coffee room. As they settled, he introduced himself.

"I know we have met a time or two before, but for those who can't remember me, I'm Lt. Tyler O'Brien. I would like all of you to just call me O'Brien. I was asked by Henderson to come down here and fill in for Lt. Wainwright until we can find a permanent replacement. I would like each of you to see me one on one so that I can familiarise myself with your faces and your current cases. I would also like for all of you to continue as though I have been here forever. In other words, don't hesitate to approach me on any matter. If I can help you, I will. Are there any questions?"

There was a brief silence.

"All right, then. The first person I'd like to talk with is Detective Henninger. Matt will you meet me in my office?"

"Sure thing, Lieutenant."

"Can you also please show me where it is?"

The crew chuckled a bit as it disbursed. O'Brien shrugged his shoulders. He really had no idea where his office was.

"Follow me, O'Brien," said Matt. He led O'Brien to a glass door with dull white blinds covering it. It was a nice office painted a weird colour of green called apple blossom or something like that. There were two chairs in front of the big wooden desk. The chair that sat behind it, 'O'Brien's chair,' had a tall back and was tilted. There was a three-person couch against one wall with a small end table and magazine rack. In the corner sat a computer.

"Not bad; not bad at all," O'Brien said as he sat down.

Matt pulled a chair up to O'Brien's new throne and opened a folder.

"I've been working on this case. It involves some purse-snatching that has been going on. Fortunately, no one has been hurt. I'm getting close to nabbing the suspect and, if you can believe it, it's a young lady."

"A young lady?" O'Brien asked as he picked up the folder and began thumbing through it.

"Yep, actually a delinquent. Her name is Sharla Buchworth. You could say she is homeless. We have had dealings with her before. Her parents don't seem to care about her much, which is really too bad 'cause she is a good kid. They're too busy though snorting nose candy to pay any heed to the young lady's needs and wants."

"Do her parents live around here?" O'Brien asked straight out.

"Oh yeah, they live on the north side near the Wal-Mart. They kicked her out. Every time the kid goes back, they throw her out again. It really pisses me off."

"How come no one has tried getting her into a foster home?"

"She's been to them, but because she's sixteen she doesn't stay long. The judge is actually fed up with her antics and this time when I pick her up, she will be sent to Willington Youth Detention Centre. I know for a fact that WYDC is not the place for this kid."

"Do what you can, Matt. When you pick her up, I want to talk with her in person," O'Brien stated with concern.

"Sure thing, O'Brien. Is there anything else?"

"Yeah, can you please send in the rookie; what's his name… Mick?"

"You bet. Talk to you later," Matt said as he exited O'Brien's new domain.

O'Brien scribbled down Sharla's name and circled it. He was going to check out her parents himself. If he could find something to charge them with he certainly would, no ifs, ands, or buts about it. Only before he jumped to any conclusion, O'Brien wanted to talk with the young girl to see what she could tell him about her situation. There was a knock on his door and Mick Ross entered.

"Lt. O'Brien, you wanted to see me?"

"Come on in, Detective. Did you bring your current case load with you?"

"Yes I did, Lieutenant."

"Good. Have a seat. Fill me in, Detective Ross, on what you're up to."

"I'm investigating some mail fraud."

"Mail fraud?" O'Brien questioned. How coincidental, Thom was investigating mail fraud as well back in Fruitmont.

"Tell me about it."

"Not much to tell, sir…"

O'Brien cut him off before he could finish.

"Hold on, Detective. Please don't call me 'sir'. It makes me sound old. How old are you, Mick?"

"Twenty-seven."

"I'm only nine years older, Mick. Therefore, you can call me Lieutenant or O'Brien, but I'd really prefer not to be called 'sir'."

"Sorry, sir," he replied.

O'Brien couldn't stop himself from smiling.

"That's okay. Please continue with what you were going to say before I so rudely interrupted."

"I've been investigating this mail fraud thing going on two weeks and I haven't got any evidence whatsoever on who or why yet."

"What kind of mail is being taken?"

"Mostly tax return cheques and credit card applications, that sort of thing."

"I think you should contact Thom Beard at the agency in Fruitmont. He is also working on a mail fraud case. Perhaps he can give you some insight. I'm actually surprised you two haven't already collaborated," O'Brien commented.

Obviously, one of the things he'd have to address was lack of collaboration between both agencies.

"I'll get right on it, Lieutenant. Do you want me to send in someone else?"

"Yeah, please send in detective Ilene Williams."

Mick nodded and exited.

Ilene didn't even knock on the door; she simply entered with a big smile.

"Hey, O'Brien, how have you been? How's Tracy and the kids?" she asked.

Ilene was the only female detective that Henderson had the opportunity to hire. O'Brien had met her on three or four different occasions and she and Tracy were good friends. Whenever Tracy came to Ridgeville to do shopping or on occasion to run errands for Henderson when O'Brien himself was unavailable, she and Ilene always met somewhere and went out for coffee and a chat. She was as tough as nails and was one hell of a sharp shooter. She was a smaller woman, with well-groomed black hair and crazy green-blue eyes, aquatic almost. Her body was firm and lacked nothing.

'Dynamite came in small packages,' she always said and she was right. "Not bad; we're all doing fine. How about you? How have you been?"

"Same as always."

"Good. What does Henderson & Co. have you working on?"

"I'm in the midst of court hearings involving a couple of DUI's. Same guy, same car. This time he was involved in a motor vehicle accident and ended up in someone's living room. It was a good thing no one was home at the time. He went right through the living room window. The car stopped short of the gas fireplace. If he had hit that, who knows what kind of mess he would have been in. Luckily, he only sustained some cuts and bruises, but he caused over one hundred thousand dollars in damages."

"I hope this time we're going to nail him hard," O'Brien said with disgust. He always classified drunk driving right up there with attempted murder. Second and third offences were even more vulgar in his eyes.

"Oh yeah. He will be losing his license for good this time. He'll probably do some time as well. I talked to the prosecution on Friday and they're pushing for a minimum of nine months' imprisonment with conditions."

"Awesome, Ilene. I'll let you get back to it then. Pop up sometime to the house. I'm sure Tracy would love to see you."

"You can count on that."

"Great. Can't wait to see you when were both off duty sometime. Can you send in whoever wants to be next?"

"How about Slappy?" she asked.

That wasn't his real name. His name was Art Slapinski, a seasoned detective and probably the most ruthless of all of them in Ridgeville including O'Brien.

"Yeah, sure, send him in."

"Okay Lieutenant, I'll yak at you later," Ilene said as she exited.

O'Brien leaned back in his chair and waited for old Slappy to enter. He wondered what the old fellow had been up to. He too worked back east years ago. It was from there that he and O'Brien were acquainted. It was only by coincidence that they both ended up working for Henderson & Co. in two different offices.

"Hey, Slappy. How have you been?" O'Brien asked as he entered.

"Not bad, Ty; not bad at all," Slappy said as he reached out his hand to shake O'Brien's. He was the only person O'Brien let call him Ty, probably because he wouldn't have stopped if O'Brien had asked him to.

"I hope this job isn't going to make you soft, Ty?" he chuckled.

"The day that I become soft will be the day you quit frowning."

"Good to see you, Ty. Want me to run by you what I've been working on?"

"Please, Slappy," O'Brien said as he gestured for Slappy to sit.

"A couple months back two local hikers went missing up in the Kelly Creek Mountains. We've been able to locate a backpack that belonged to one of the hikers. There is a small amount of trace blood on the shoulder strap which has been sent for DNA analysis," Slappy sighed. "Other than that we don't have a clue on their whereabouts or what might have become of them. Not much, eh?"

"Have the K9's been up there?" O'Brien asked.

"Both the K9 units, as well as search and rescue and a slew of volunteers have spent time up in the area. The thing is, there is nothing up there, nothing that we can find, leastwise. I've been contemplating calling up the Elliot Bloodhound Team. Maybe they can come up with something."

"How come that hasn't been done yet?" O'Brien questioned with disbelief.

"Need authority to do that, O'Brien, and every time I called Henderson myself, he always told me he'd get a guy down here that could authorise it."

"Guess what, Slappy? I'm that guy," O'Brien smiled. "I authorise it. Get going on it as quickly as you can, today, as a matter of fact."

There was something else O'Brien realised he'd have to address while he was empowered to do so. The lack of communication and authorisation. O'Brien was somewhat disappointed on how Henderson had been handling things.

"Thanks, O'Brien. It's about time," Slappy said as he stood and exited.

O'Brien still had to talk with Detective Abe Myles and Detective William Jerome, but decided to take a coffee break first and phone Henderson. He exited his office and walked into the coffee room where he poured himself a cup of hot brew. Returning to his new office after looking around at all the busy bodies working, O'Brien phoned up Henderson.

"Afternoon, O'Brien. How is the first day going?" Henderson asked.

"Pretty good. They are not as disorganised as you had first thought, I can tell you that, other than a few problems with authorisations which could've been done from there."

"I know, O'Brien, but I still need a guy down at that office to make sure everything runs smoothly until I can get someone more permanent."

"Did you ever consider Art Slapinski?" O'Brien asked with sincerity.

"Indeed. He doesn't want the position. If you can convince him, O'Brien that would be super."

"Yeah, right. You know if he doesn't want it, he isn't going to take it; he's too stubborn."

"Is there anyone else you can think of, because to tell you the truth, O'Brien, I really don't like having to hire an outsider."

"What are you saying, Henderson? Are you trying to tell me that you want me to pick someone for you? Is that why you sent me?" O'Brien said as he snickered. It would be just like Henderson to do pull something like that.

"I was hoping you would. I mean, I know we've got a lot of good talent down there. It would be a shame to hire someone we don't know."

"You're an ass, Henderson," O'Brien chuckled.

Henderson had got him again.

"However, you know what? I think after I've been here a while I'll be able to pick someone."

O'Brien was already thinking of Ilene Williams. That would throw off Henderson. She was a good detective and had been working for Henderson & Co. going on five years. Why Henderson hadn't asked her after old Slappy turned down the position made O'Brien wonder.

"What about Detective Williams? Did you think of her?"

"I did think of her. She told me to hit the road as well."

"Really. Damn. Well, maybe I can convince one of them in time?"

"I sure hope you can, O'Brien. Keep your eye on that kid, Mick. Check out his arrest record. He has an awesome one. He'd be a good candidate; he only needs a little more guidance."

O'Brien was beginning to get the picture. Henderson wanted him to take the kid under his wing.

"He's only twenty-seven, Henderson. Do you think that would go over well with the others?"

"Who cares? If in six or seven months you think he is capable, what difference would it make?"

"I suppose you are right. I am not guaranteeing anything, though. I'll work with him and help him out. He isn't going to be treated any differently from anyone else here."

"I wouldn't expect that, O'Brien."

"Good. As long as we are clear on that?"

"Of course."

"All right, then. I'll talk to you soon, Henderson."

"You bet, O'Brien. Talk to you soon. Oh, by the way O'Brien, how do you, Tracy and the kids like the house and pool?"

"The house is fine. As for the pool, I'll be sending you a bill," O'Brien chortled.

"What kind of bill?" Henderson asked.

"I'm only kidding, old boy. Talk to you soon," O'Brien said as he hung up the phone.

Finishing his coffee, O'Brien exited the office and began looking around for Detective Myles who had already slipped out of the office to do some legwork. O'Brien then searched out and found William Jerome. Everyone called him BJ because of his uncanny resemblance to the actor in the old television series 'BJ and the Bear'.

"How are you doing, Detective Jerome?" O'Brien questioned as he put his hand on Will's shoulder.

"Hey, Lt. O'Brien. How's it hanging?"

"Do you always answer a question with a question?" O'Brien laughed.

"Would you rather I didn't?" the witty bastard questioned.

"Some things never change," O'Brien said as he reached out his hand to shake Will's.

"By the way, congratulations, O'Brien, on your promotion."

"Thanks, Will. Think you can swing by my office. I'd like to familiarise myself with your caseload."

"I'll meet you there in five minutes, Lieutenant."

"Perfect."

O'Brien returned to his office and in a few short minutes, Will arrived. He was working on a homicide that had taken place a while back. It was first thought to be a five hundred thousand dollar insurance scam involving the wife of the victim and her late night boy toy. When the local RCMP was unable to prove the charges, they no longer had a suspect. The case was then handed over to Henderson & Co. Will had been working on it for the past three months.

O'Brien looked over the folder and was dismayed at the little evidence Will had. All he really had was a victim with multiple bullet wounds. That about summed it up. There had been no murder weapon found. Although the calibre of the gun was identified as a .32, there appeared to be no motive and Will was working on the possibility that the victim was accidentally shot because of mistaken identity or something along that line. He was certainly going through all the steps and was indeed doing a bang-up job.

"It looks good, Will. Nevertheless, I think we should get you some help. Cases with lack of evidence and motive are a pain, I know. I've had quite a few."

"I'd like the extra help Lieutenant, but there isn't anyone who hasn't already got a full plate."

"I'll tell you what. I'm going to see if I can't rearrange a few cases. Ilene is finishing up a case; all she has left is court and that's tomorrow. She's free and clear after that. Therefore, if there is nothing pressing, I am also going to assign her to the case. She'll be a great help, I assure you."

"No problem, O'Brien. She and I have worked together before. In fact, she saved my ass once."

"I know. I've familiarised myself with some of the arrest records. You two did a marvellous job on that case," O'Brien commented with sincerity.

After a few minutes of friendly conversation, Will stood and exited. By 6:00 p.m., O'Brien was able to talk with all the detectives, even old Abe who was working on a minor bootlegging investigation. Overall, it had been a good day.

# Sixteen

That Thursday, Matt finally caught up to Sharla Buchworth. He arrested her for four counts of purse theft, which actually fell under and pertained to the charge of aggravated assault. O'Brien met with Sharla and questioned her on numerous points. She seemed to be a bright enough kid and O'Brien felt sorry for her. He really didn't want her being sent to WYDC. Matt was right; it would certainly ruin any chances of her redeeming herself. O'Brien could tell by her quivering voice when he questioned her that she was fed up with the way things were going, that now she was ready to make a change.

He instructed Matt to hold her for a day or two until he had a chance to talk with Tracy and a judge. He was seriously contemplating asking the judge to release her into his and Tracy's care, at least until they could do a more thorough investigation into the poor kid's home life.

She told O'Brien that her parents were forcing her to steal for them as well as deal for them and that her dad even threatened her with pimping her out. O'Brien was appalled at these allegations and knew that they would have to be checked out.

He always hated child abuse cases. If what Sharla was saying turned out to be true, then that is exactly what it was, child abuse. He had seen over the years what kind of monsters it could create. It would destroy a girl like Sharla. Matt agreed with O'Brien and he halted processing the charges and delayed informing the authorities that sat higher up. They detained her in one of their own cells used for overnight prisoners. Ilene found a female guard who the agency used on occasion. O'Brien contacted a judge, a lawyer, and a bigwig from child welfare. They were willing to accept the terms he put forth to them especially under the circumstances. All O'Brien had to do now was convince Tracy.

At first, Tracy seemed leery about the whole thing. After she met Sharla that Friday, she had a change of heart and agreed. She and Sharla spent the majority of the day together and apparently, Tracy really wanted to help the poor kid. She said it reminded her of how a friend's life was when she was growing up in Alberta. One day her friend was found dangling from the garage rafters. She said that on that day she promised her friend that she would do whatever it took to prevent that from happening again to anyone. O'Brien's best guess was that Tracy was fulfilling her promise.

O'Brien was not prepared, though, for how far she was willing to go. He imagined Sharla spending a month or two with them. However, Tracy had different plans. When Sharla finally came to stay with them that following Monday, Tracy began a one-woman crusade to seek legal guardianship. Although O'Brien thought that they might have bit off more than they could chew, he let Tracy run with it from there on in. O'Brien knew he couldn't encourage her to stop. Why would he? Sharla was a good kid. She had only been pointed in the wrong direction, no thanks to her ailing parents. Moreover, every kid deserved a break in O'Brien's opinion. If they could turn Sharla around, he would be proud of the accomplishment.

O'Brien led the investigation into Sharla's implications about her parents. After a short investigation, he was able to nail her father with possession of a controlled substance, namely cocaine. O'Brien found four ounces tucked behind a pillow on the old dilapidated couch that sat in the middle of the filthy living room. They were able to charge Sharla's mother with possession, as well as child endangerment and neglect. It took three weeks, but they did it. During those three weeks not only did they unfold that case, but also solved the mail fraud case.

They also made some headway on what may have happened to the two missing hikers. The Elliot Blood Hound team spent a good day in the mountains two days after Art called them. They were able to find a tattered shirt with what appeared to be a large bloodstain. The shirt was sent for analysis and the Elliot team headed for home. They would return later when Dean himself, could dedicate more time.

As for the mail fraud case, with Thom's help through collaboration, Mick was able to arrest the young man who was responsible. He also inadvertently solved the case back in Fruitmont because he turned out to be the same guy. Thom was a bit discouraged and called it beginner's luck. However, O'Brien knew better. The kid had done his homework. Even though he solved the case, Mick didn't let it go to his head as some rookies would. Instead, he picked up the next case and plunged in. Perhaps Henderson was right. The kid certainly had a passion for his work.

O'Brien decided he was going to put Mick on the case with Art. He still didn't have much to go on other than a few new pieces of evidence on which they were currently waiting for results, mainly the bloodstained tattered shirt. What lay ahead of him was a lot of unravelling and foraging in the woods. The bloodhounds were scheduled to return in less than two days and who better to send up with them then a fresh young detective? It would do the kid good, and who could say that, he would not find something everyone else missed.

That would leave Art free to investigate other possibilities. Perhaps one of the hikers killed the other and headed to the States? On the other hand, perhaps both of them were attacked and killed by someone else? It could be that they made it look that way and both of them had split to the States. That kind of thing was becoming commonplace. It was a form of insurance fraud that was really beginning to take off, one might say. O'Brien couldn't say that was the case here, not with the evidence they had. Nevertheless, he couldn't say it wasn't either. Art was beginning to lean that too. Others were leaning towards an animal attack. Both possibilities were quite conceivable; both needed further investigating. O'Brien called Mick into his office.

"Detective Ross?" he began.

"Yeah, Lt. O'Brien."

"I'm putting you on this missing person's case involving the two hikers. I think we need a new insight overall. Are you up to it?"

"Certainly. I do have a few opinions on the case…"

O'Brien interrupted him there.

"I'm glad to hear that. However, I don't want you to muddle your mind until you have a chance to help up on the mountain. The bloodhounds are going to be here in a day or two so how about reading over some of the investigation reports that Detective Slapinski has. Be prepared to head up to the mountains when the dogs get here."

"Does Slappy know about this?" Mick asked a bit hesitantly.

"No, but once you tell him that I requested it, he'll be more than helpful. Listen closely to what he tells you. You'll have to learn to take some things with a grain of salt."

"Not to worry, O'Brien. I already got the old guy figured out. I also know that he is seasoned and that to anger him is not a good thing. I think Detective Slapinski and I will get along fine."

"I like your attitude, Mick. Keep it up. I wish you lots of luck with old Slappy. Remember to be mobile when the dogs get here. I'll let you know exactly when that will be after I talk with Dean Elliot sometime later today. I'll keep you posted, Mick."

"Thanks Lieutenant, I'll be ready," he said as he exited O'Brien's office.

O'Brien turned on the old computer that sat in the corner and waited while it booted up. Finally, after what seemed like eternity, the thing was up and running. He punched in the password that was given to personnel of his stature or higher up in order to access different files, folders, and organisations, as well as funding and authorisations. It was only a formality. Every time a new Lieutenant or otherwise took over the position the password was again changed by the Director of Police Commissioners and delivered via registered mail.

O'Brien had received his letter two days prior. This was the first time he was able to access anything on the old dinosaur. For the past month since he had been there, it had sat in the corner collecting dust. It took O'Brien over two hours to access past financial records and other history. The agency was not suffering. O'Brien worked on a few figures and came up with a surplus of over $160,000.00. It really wasn't a substantial amount. However, when you added up what the agency had as a surplus and what the agency in Fruitmont might have, Henderson & Co. was certainly not sweating. Being one of the most influential, investigating agencies in British Columbia. Even Police Departments contracted work to them. Along with private clients, they were not in the red.

O'Brien checked out a couple of the detectives' past and recent arrest records that were confidential. He was impressed with all of them. The Ridgeville Agency in the past two years had only one criminal death and it was Ilene Williams, who fired the shot in self-defence. She underwent counselling in this regard for a few months. Other than that, it was a clear case of self-defence. After about three and a half hours and only being able to access the three or four different folders on the old 486, O'Brien shut it off. It would be a long time, he decided, before he would use it again. Noting the time, he called up the Elliot Blood Hound Team. After the fourth ring, the answering machine came on.

"Hello, you've reached the Elliot Blood Hound Team. This is Dean Elliot. Sorry I can't come to the phone right now. I do page in every hour. Please leave your name and number and I'll get back to you shortly."

"This is Lt. O'Brien in Ridgeville. I am calling to confirm your arrival. Please get back to me at 250-555-0121. Thanks."

O'Brien hung up the phone and headed into the coffee room. He poured a cup and sauntered around the floor talking with the detectives. He needed to stretch his legs. The three or so hours he had spent in front of the computer caused him anxiety. He wasn't that patient when it came to computers. The short walk was something he needed. After a few brief friendly conversations, he retreated to his office and waited for the phone call from Dean Elliot. At last, the telephone rang.

"Hello, this is Lt. O'Brien."

"Yeah, Lt. O'Brien this is Dean Elliot. How are you today?"

"I'm pretty good, Dean. How about yourself?"

"Couldn't be better. I'm returning your call in regards to when I can get back that way. According to my itinerary, I've got you guys down for Tuesday, October 16. Is that okay?"

"Humph. I thought it was this weekend. Nevertheless, yeah, the 16 works. You said that's Tuesday?"

"That's right. This coming Tuesday to be exact."

"No problem, Dean. Detective Ross is going to accompany you along with Art, of course. How many days are you going up for this time?"

"I'm hoping until that Friday. If the weather allows, we might stay a day or two longer. The new detective you're sending along with Art, has he been involved with this type of search effort before?"

"He went through all the same training as the rest of us did. He is a young guy. However, he's full of piss and vinegar and quite quick on his feet. You could say he's in need of some practical experience. I wouldn't be sending him if I didn't think he could handle it."

"What about yourself? Are you going to come along?"

"To tell you the truth, Dean. If I could, I would. Currently, though, my hands are tied with a guardianship case."

"That's right. Art was telling me about that. You are the guy who is helping that young girl. I have to tell you, I think that you're bold. There aren't many people or, for that matter, many families that would step forward like you have. I know that kid. Her parents are trash. I wouldn't trust either one of them as far as I could throw them."

"How do you know the Buchworth's?" O'Brien asked.

"My dogs and I were hired by Lt. Wainwright about three or four years ago to track the kid's old man down after he beat her and her so-called mother. He headed into the bush armed with a pistol. We were or, I should say I was, half-expecting to find him with his head blown off. That would have made my day," Elliot said with sincerity. "It took us a couple of days to track him down and when we found him instead he was strung out on heroin. He never got charged. They simply sent him to rehab for a year. Unfortunately, I caught a glimpse of the girl and her mother after the old man laid the beating on them. It is a picture that has haunted me ever since. I commend you for the initiative you and your wife have taken."

"Thanks, Dean. That was nice to hear."

"Not a problem. I have to get going now. Make sure the detectives are ready for the 16th. I'll pick them up from the office at around 6:00 a.m. Maybe I'll see you then, Lieutenant?"

"You just might, Dean. If not, I'll talk with you when you guys get back."

"You bet. Talk to you soon," he said as he hung up the telephone.

O'Brien was taken aback by the conversation. He was also encouraged. He had only met Mr. Elliot one other time and to hear those things coming from an otherwise perfect stranger seemed unusual. However, O'Brien took it all in with great satisfaction. Dean was right he was doing something that could make a difference.

O'Brien relayed the information to Mick and Art about when Dean was going to pick them up at the office. An hour later, he received a telephone call from the head office in Fruitmont. It was Thom Beard.

"O'Brien, we got a problem."

O'Brien could tell by the tone of Thom's voice that he was not kidding.

"What's up, Thom?" O'Brien hesitantly asked.

"Anvil Brentwood escaped this morning. He killed Dr. Nebinoff and his nurse."

"You got to be kidding?"

"I wish I were, bud. We got word not more than five minutes ago."

"Son of a bitch! Do we know what direction he's heading by chance?"

"Not a clue, O'Brien. Toronto is a big city. They have all the plainclothesmen and city cops that they can spare trying to track him down. So far, they have nothing. Hal, Rory, and I are heading to Toronto tomorrow. Henderson suggested you round up a couple of people from there and follow behind. We have rooms at the Sheridan on the west side. Henderson already booked two double rooms for you as well. So get packing and we will meet you in Toronto. That's all we can do for now."

"I can't believe this has happened, Thom."

"Believe it, O'Brien. This time we have also been authorised by the commissioner to use extreme force if necessary. You know what that means; this is an operation Code One.”

“Good enough. I will put together a team down here. We’ll get out of here as soon as possible. See you at the Sheridan, Thom.”

“We’ll be waiting, O’Brien,” Thom said as he hung up the phone.

O’Brien scribbled into his notebook in big, black letters: The Sheridan, west side, Toronto. He quickly decided on who would accompany him, Ilene Williams and Art ‘Slappy’ Slapinski. O’Brien pressed their corresponding extensions and asked them to come to his office. He went over the details with them, explaining to them both that it was a Code One and that extreme force would be tolerated.

“Every time we face guys like this Anvil fellow it should be a Code One,” replied Art. “Count me in.”

“Yeah, me too, O’Brien. I’m up for the task.”

“Good. I appreciate it, detectives. I’ll make the final arrangements. We’ll have to catch the next flight. Is Canadian Airlines still flying out of here or do we have to head up to Fruitmont?”

“They’re still taking off from here, but not frequently. I believe they fly out tomorrow evening,” said Ilene. “Do you want me to check into it, O’Brien?”

“Would you do that, Ilene?”

“I’m on it, O’Brien.”

She returned shortly thereafter.

“Flight 202 to Toronto leaves tomorrow at 7:00 p.m. There is a stopover in both Edmonton and Winnipeg. It arrives in Toronto late Saturday afternoon. I booked it.”

“All right then. You two might as well head home and pack. Take tomorrow off and rest up. The excursion we are about to embark on is going to be a pain in the ass, I assure you. With fall approaching, Toronto is going to be getting cold. Make sure you pack a sweater. On your way out send in

Will please. I'm going put him in charge here while I'm gone."

"You got it, O'Brien. We will meet you at the airport tomorrow night. Remember the flight is scheduled to leave at 7:00 p.m. and it's flight 202."

O'Brien scribbled it all down as fast as Ilene said it.

"I got it, Ilene. Thanks."

"See you tomorrow, O'Brien."

"You betcha," O'Brien replied as his two colleagues exited and shut the door.

Detective William Jerome entered.

"You wanted to see me, Lt. O'Brien?"

O'Brien directed Will to a seat and told him what had taken place, that he was going to use the powers vested in him to put Will in charge until he returned or Will was relieved.

"You'll be in charge of the day-to-day operations, Will, until Art, Ilene and I return. I'll take up the slack when I boomerang back. I am entrusting you with a five thousand dollar kitty to be used accordingly. You may need to use it in upcoming cases. Who knows?"

"Sounds like you're planning to be gone for quite some time?"

"I hope not, Will. Nevertheless, it may turn out that way. Anvil has a tendency to vanish into thin air. With all the places he has to hide in Toronto, we may never find him. I've written down the Sheridan phone number for you, where we will be staying. I'll remember to call in if we move from that location. In addition, you have my cell number as well as the paging number. The head office in Fruitmont is shooting you a copy of the case file on Anvil Brentwood. I would ask that you familiarise yourself with it. Keep your eyes peeled for any weird stuff that might go on. Anvil is cagey as a rabid coon. For all we know he could be on his way back to the general area where he committed the murders. He seems to like it there.”

O’Brien leaned back in his chair, and briefly reminisced.

“Any questions, Will?”

“It’s fairly straightforward, O’Brien. I think the four of us can hold down the fort. Everything we need to know about Anvil is likely in the case file. We’ll manage.”

“That’s what I like to hear, Will. I am confident in your abilities and I’m certain you will be fine. I have no doubts. Keep, Detective Ross working on the missing person’s case. He’s going up into the Kelly Creek Mountains with Dean Elliot and his Bloodhound team on Tuesday. It is important that he goes. In addition, you are more than likely going to have to appear in court on my behalf in regards to that Buchworth case. I am leaving you that file as well.”

O’Brien smiled.

“The hearing is on the 18th.”

“Not a problem, O’Brien. I’ll see to it.”

“I guess that’s it then. I’ll be taking off in a few minutes for home and I won’t be in tomorrow. We’re catching flight 202 to Toronto tomorrow night. It arrives at Toronto International Airport late Saturday afternoon. I’ll call in and leave a message with the answering service once we arrive.”

“Sure thing. Is that all, O’Brien?”

“That’s it for now, Will. I’ll talk to you when I talk to you, I guess.”

Will nodded and exited. O’Brien drew his attention to what Tracy and the kids were going to say. By now, he could imagine they were as sick of Anvil Brentwood as he was. O’Brien grabbed his briefcase and headed home. Tracy could tell by the look on his face that he had been called away on some job.

“Where are you off to this time, O’Brien?” Tracy asked with concern.

O’Brien explained to her the situation.

"Are you forgetting we have a meeting with Child Services next week in regards to becoming permanent guardians to Sharla?" she reminded him.

"Look, Tracy, I'm sorry about that. You'll have to go ahead without me. Anvil is a killer and we need to get him off the streets. Don't you agree?"

"Oh, I agree, don't doubt that, O'Brien."

"I wish I could be there too, Tracy. However, I am confident it is going to go our way. Judge Leroy is going to recommend it, not to mention the legalities our lawyer has worked out. We even got the backing of the Social Services head honcho. It's in the bag."

"I just hope that all the heads I've busted have been worth it. Sharla needs our help. I feel for the kid. You know what I mean, O'Brien?"

He did.

# Seventeen

On Friday October 12, O'Brien met up with Ilene and Art 'Slappy' at 6:30 p.m. at the Ridgeville Airport. The three sat drinking coffee in the small café until their flight was called.

"All those for Canadian Airlines flight 202, Edmonton, Winnipeg and Toronto, please begin boarding at gate three."

"That's our flight," said Ilene. "Come on, guys, let's get moving. We have a long flight in front of us, not to mention two rather extended stops."

Locating their seats, the three of them sat in silence while the flight attendant ran through her script. The big engines roared and in moments, they were aloft. As the sky darkened that evening, they could make out the countless lights that dotted the earth under their wings. Big towns, little towns and cities scattered the land mass below.

The first layover in Edmonton was a three-hour break. The Edmonton airport was alive with the bustling about of people going here or there. It was like a miniature city that existed beneath glass and concrete. People were lined up at ticket booths and baggage departments. The food court, with its late night cafés and fast food restaurants, was packed. O'Brien walked over to a vending machine and grabbed a coffee and some peanuts. It would have to do.

Three hours later, they were again in the air, next stop Winnipeg, Manitoba. O'Brien closed his eyes and wishfully tried to sleep. As luck would have it, within the hour they hit some atrocious turbulence. That was one of the problems, though, in flying over the desolate plains. O'Brien wondered how Thom faired. He hated to fly and more times than not elected to drive. He chuckled at what he reckoned Thom's retorts to be as he flew blindly over the same plains. He envisioned Thom keeping his eyes closed the entire flight, panic-stricken and unable to move. The little bell began to ring and the senior pilot interrupted the soft music playing.

"This is the captain. Please fasten your seatbelts. Bring your seats to the normal upright positions. Dim all lights and turn off all laptops. We are approaching Winnipeg International Airport. Estimated time of arrival, seven minutes and counting. Thank you."

It seemed to be the longest seven minutes of O'Brien's life. He was beginning to get jet-lagged and he felt queasy as the big plane circled the airport. Finally, they taxied to the tarmac near the building and as the plane slowly came to a stop, the captain came on again.

"The layover in Winnipeg will be for refuelling and an early breakfast break. We will take to the sky in four hours at 9:15 a.m. Thank you."

O'Brien looked at his watch. It was 5:00 a.m. They had four hours to kill and he knew how he was going to kill them. Sleep. Ilene and Art decided to head to one of the café's to have breakfast. O'Brien tilted his seat all the way back. He wanted only sleep.

"Can I bring something back for you, O'Brien?" asked Art.

"Nah. I'll get something later. I am just going to sit back for a few and maybe catch some Z's. I'll meet up with you guys in an hour or so."

The next voice that O'Brien heard was the captain's. He had slept the entire four hours.

"This is your captain. Please prepare for takeoff. Put on your seatbelts. Bring all seats to the upright position, turnoff all cell phones, laptops, and electronics. In addition, please pay attention to the flight attendant as she explains the emergency exits. The next destination is Toronto. Thank you."

Five minutes later, they were taxiing down the runway. As the airliner rose vertically, they could see in the distance the forming of big, black clouds. O'Brien nudged Art who was sitting next to him.

"What do you think of that?" O'Brien asked pointing at the clouds.

"I think we're headed for some nasty turbulence."

"I hope that's all," said Ilene. "Those are pretty dark clouds."

"The worse it could be is probably a thunderstorm, maybe some hail."

No sooner had Art finish that sentence when the plane began to be pelted with hail. The captain came back on.

"Ladies and Gentlemen, please be advised that we are experiencing a brief hailstorm. We are going to ascend above the cloud cover. Please remain seated. The weather office has advised that the storm is travelling south by south-west. We will be away from it shortly."

O'Brien looked out his window and could see the grey mass of cloud cover, which seemed to go on forever. However, at the altitude they were flying, the sun shone brightly and the sky was blue. There was little or no turbulence. Up here, it was a beautiful day.

Back in Toronto, Thom, Hal, and Rory's plane had just landed. Hal and Rory had to wait for the plane to empty before they could help Thom off the plane. He took a Valium during the flight and then another. When the three of them finally made it to the Sheridan and their rooms, Thom collapsed on one of the beds and passed out.

Hal and Rory contacted the Ontario Provincial Police to inform them that they arrived and to find out if there was any news on Anvil. There wasn't. Somehow, he miraculously eluded all roadblocks as well as the All-Points-Bulletin sent out. This wasn't unusual for Anvil. It was 72 hours since his escape, but in that, much time a man like Anvil could have certainly been well on his way out of the province. A fugitive could hide out in the concrete jungle of Toronto for years and never be found. The detectives knew that Toronto was the place where they must begin their search. Thom, Hal, and Rory decided that they would wait for the rest of the crew before pursuing any further. The OPP were still searching so all facets of the search were still being conducted, just not by them.

An hour later, Thom began to rustle.

"Are we there? Or did we crash and I am in Hell?" he asked jokingly. "My head is pounding."

"Well you were in a drug-induced slumber for the past 24 hours. Your head should hurt."

"I hope it doesn't explode," retorted Thom.

"We hope not too. Crap would get on the walls," replied Hal.

"Shut up. What time is it?"

"It's nearly 12:00 noon. Are you guys hungry?" asked Rory. "I saw a Mr. Mikes down the street on our way here."

"Yeah, I could use some sustenance. What about you, Hal?"

"I suppose we should go have a bite to eat. Maybe it will clear your head some, Thom."

"I don't know about that, but a Mr. Mikes burger sounds good to me. Let's go. Lead the way, Rory."

They exited into the cool, clear afternoon. The restaurant wasn't as busy as one might expect. They were in the west end and out of the downtown core. The restaurant was only partially filled with patrons. Finding a quiet table in the back, they ordered coffees and burgers.

"That brisk walk from the Sheridan certainly cleared my head. I feel like a million bucks. By the way, do either of you know when O'Brien's flight is scheduled to land?" questioned Thom.

"Sometime later this afternoon."

"After we eat, are we going to go over to the OPP Station or are we going to hang tight for O'Brien?"

"We might as well wait," replied Rory.

"I have to agree with Rory, Thom. I think we ought to wait."

"Good, so do I. I wanted to make sure we were all on the same brain wave."

The three of them ate and then returned to the Sheridan. Thom made a few phone calls to the Kingston Penitentiary's Psychiatric Ward, seeking information on Anvil's past activities etc. The information relayed back to him was information he really was not anticipating. Over the past few weeks Anvil's disorder seemingly had changed state. According to his weekly EEG's, his brain pattern was now equal to that of an above average man. The disorder was no longer a disorder. Anvil was either faking or he had completely circumvented the odds.

The University of Kingston's Neurological Science Department stated the same. Although they were still mourning the death of Dr. Nebinoff and his nurse, they assisted with as much information as they could at that time. After things settled down a bit and they were again operating at full capacity, they would be of more assistance. 'A week or two,' they said. The information that Thom was able to come up with however, proved one thing, they weren't going to be facing the same man.

"Can you believe that? Anvil has gone into complete remission. There's nothing wrong with him now."

"What? You got to be kidding?"

"I wish I were, Hal. That is what I was told by both the Penitentiary and the University. He isn't going to be as easy to catch up with this time."

"I don't know about that, Thom. If he has been faking this illness, then I guess he's as smart as he was when we first apprehended him. Correct?"

Thom looked over to Hal who was sitting on the bed.

"The kid has a point, doesn't he, Hal?"

"He sure does. It's a good one, too. Whether Anvil has been faking or not, we'll catch him."

"I suppose you're right. We will have a better idea on what to expect from him once we all get together and get going on it. O'Brien will be here soon. He's going to flip when we tell him though. I can just imagine," said Thom.

After an hour's flight above the cloud cover, O'Brien's flight finally descended, breaking through the last of the grey clouds. The hailstorm vanished and they were again flying in clear skies. O'Brien asked the flight attendant that was walking down the aisle with refreshments and such when they would be landing.

"We'll be landing at the Toronto airport in one hour and fifteen minutes, sir. Can I offer you something to drink or eat in the meantime?"

"Sure I'll have a coffee and a turkey sandwich if you have one?"

"White or whole wheat, sir?"

"Whole wheat works for me," O'Brien responded. "What do you have to drink in way of alcohol?"

"Rum, vodka, rye and wine."

"All right, cancel the coffee and I'll take a rye and ginger instead with the sandwich."

"I'll have to return with your beverage and sandwich, sir. This is only a snack cart."

The flight attendant shuffled down the aisle and disappeared into the back lobby. She returned shortly with O'Brien's turkey sandwich. What seemed like only minutes later, the Captain announced that they were approaching the Toronto International Airport. Fifteen minutes later, they were standing in line at Budget Rent A Car. Lastly, with the car loaded, they headed to Toronto's west side and the Sheridan. It was 2:45 p.m.

By 4:00 p.m., the entire entourage was sitting together. O'Brien introduced Ilene and Art. Although they all had crossed paths at one time or another or talked on the telephone, they shook hands and smiled. There was a glow in both Thom and Ilene's eyes, which O'Brien noticed during the introduction, and he smiled to himself.

"So has O'Brien been treating you guys nicely or has he been a son of a bitch?" asked Thom with a chuckle.

"He's been a son of a bitch," replied Art as he punched O'Brien in the shoulder.

"O'Brien and I go way back," he began.

"No way," said Rory, "really?"

"You bet. I knew him when he was a rookie detective. I never thought then that he'd be a Lieutenant."

Art laughed as he proceeded to tell them how long he had known O'Brien.

"That proves it, doesn't it? That it's a small world," said Hal.

"It sure does," O'Brien replied. "With all that said, what do you all figure our course of action ought to be to catch up with our friend Anvil?"

"We got some news for you, O'Brien, that isn't good," replied Thom.

"What's that?" O'Brien asked.

"The EEG tests that he has been subjected to prove that he has gone into remission. Not only that, his brain perception is above average. The disorder he supposedly had isn't a disorder anymore; it is turning him into a friggin' genius."

O'Brien couldn't believe what he was hearing.

"How does a man who suffers from a brain disorder all of sudden become well again?" O'Brien asked with annoyance.

"We can't answer that, O'Brien, not until we start investigating."

"It's too late to pull a miracle out of our hats right now. Is the OPP still doing what they can?"

"They are indeed, but they haven't got any news yet."

"Chances are then things aren't going to change by morning. We might as well wait until then to deal with the problem directly. It'll give us some time to come up with a plan."

"No doubt about that," said Ilene. "I could use a hot bath and a good night's sleep, not to mention something to eat."

"I agree," said Art.

So did the rest of them. It was settled, they would all unwind, and go out for supper at around 7:00 p.m. In the morning, they would embrace the manhunt, fresh and primed.

O'Brien went to the phone and dialled the Ridgeville agency, leaving a message for Will so that he would know they had arrived. They ate supper at a nearby Earl's and by 9:00 p.m. they were sitting in the coffee shop at the Sheridan going over what their plan of action would be as they hunted down Anvil Brentwood. It was decided that Hal and Rory would take care of the clerical and dispatching, Ilene and Thom were paired up to investigate Anvil's stay at both the University and the Penitentiary. Art and O'Brien would hit the pavement and search out the neighbourhoods that they knew Anvil might frequent, such as divey hotels, disarrayed train yards and skid rows, which, of course, Toronto had in abundance.

The following morning, after they all downed some breakfast and coffee, Art and O'Brien headed downtown to catch a subway or train to the lower eastside where they decided their search for Anvil should begin. Thom and Ilene taxied over to the Department of Neurological Science at Kingston University to begin their investigation. Hal and Rory stayed behind to keep in touch with the OPP and CSIS who were only getting light of the escape and the urgency to recapture Anvil.

Art and O'Brien arrived in the lower eastside around 11:00 a.m. They began showing the mug shots of Anvil to passersby, hotdog vendors and the like, but no one had seen their friend. Stopping at a corner café, they grabbed a couple of coffees and continued with their crusade to find Anvil or any evidence that he was still in Toronto. However, they came up short and returned to the Sheridan at around 6:00 p.m.

Ilene and Thom retrieved a couple of journals that Anvil had left behind in his cell. In one of his entries, O'Brien's name came up. It read Detective O'Brien - Fruitmont. Seek O'Brien… They knew what it meant. Right away, they contacted Henderson who sent out a couple of guys to O'Brien's address in Fruitmont. O'Brien was glad that they currently weren't residing there and that Tracy and the kids were safe in Ridgeville. Anvil was a sick man and if what they ascertained from his journal was correct, he swore to kill O'Brien. O'Brien had received a few death threats in his time, but this one from Anvil was one he took to heart. He wasn't sure whether Anvil was still in Toronto or not. Nevertheless, they had to be certain that he wasn't before they could head back.

By 8:00 p.m., Henderson contacted O'Brien. His house back in Fruitmont was still locked up tight, and it all looked as it had a day earlier when Henderson himself did a drive by. O'Brien was relieved. Henderson told him that they would keep a close watch on the premises and if anything seemed out of the ordinary, he would let him know.

It was creepy to think that Anvil was possibly on his way back to that area. That night as O'Brien tried to sleep, he kept thinking of the death threat found in Anvil's journal. Anvil was the type of person who would, if given the opportunity, make good on his word. O'Brien was able to put it out of his mind knowing that Tracy and his kids were safe in Ridgeville. There would be no way Anvil could know that?

At least that is what O'Brien made himself believe. Finally, with heavy eyes he found sleep.

On Monday October 15, after waking the crew, he was able to arrange to rent a couple of cars. They still had places to search and people to interview. Thom and Ilene headed over to the Penitentiary. Art and O'Brien went to the skid row area of Toronto. That whole day O'Brien couldn't stop thinking that Anvil was well on his way back home to Slocolm or the New Kootenay region. If that was the case and Anvil had managed to board a plane, he could very well be sitting on his ridge in Slocolm where he had killed before.

Although Hal and Rory had been doing a bang- up job in contacting airports and Greyhound stations all through Toronto, it was possible Anvil may have boarded either one under an assumed name. O'Brien called Hal on his cell phone.

"Hal, this is O'Brien. I was thinking, maybe you and Rory ought to take a couple of mug shots of our friend over to the airport. Could be he boarded under an alias. Maybe a few pictures will jar someone's memory. What do you say?"

"I'm already on it, O'Brien. We are just waiting for that call from the Ontario Provincial Police. I'm glad that you called because they found a body last night in the lower eastside. We're not sure if it's Anvil's handiwork or not, or if it's Anvil himself. If you and Art are close to the area, you might want to check it out. The address is 1120 East Meyer."

"Thanks, Hal, we'll check it out. So you and Rory will head over to the airports?"

"You can count on it, O'Brien, as soon as we get the call from the OPP and our car rental arrives."

"All right. We'll talk to you later, Hal."

"You bet."

Art and O'Brien arrived at the crime scene on 1120 East Meyer shortly thereafter. As they slid under the police tape, an OPP officer greeted them.

"This… this is a crime scene, gentlemen; you can't enter."

O'Brien reached into his pocket and showed the kid his credentials as he introduced himself.

"I'm Detective O'Brien and this is Detective Slapinski. We are from British Columbia checking out the possibility that this homicide was committed by an escapee from the Kingston Penitentiary and to confirm that the dead body isn't his, that being one Anvil Brentwood."

"Oh, you're the Detectives from Fruitmont and Ridgeville. Glad to make your acquaintance. I'm Roger Mills, OPP special agent," he said reaching out his hand. The kid could not have been older than twenty-five, maybe twenty-six.

"Pleased to meet you, Roger. Are you in charge here?" asked Art.

"No sir. That would be Special Agent Riley from the FBI."

"Special Agent Riley from the FBI!" O'Brien exclaimed.

"That's correct; he flew in last night non-stop from Seattle. The person who is lying dead up there was a dignitary, some political figure, special science guy or something from back in the States."

"Really."

O'Brien knew then that it wouldn't be Anvil's handiwork. Nevertheless, decided to have a few words, regardless, with his old friend, Riley. Art and O'Brien walked up the five flights of stairs. What a dignitary would be doing in a dive like this was beyond O'Brien. As he opened the door to the crime scene, O'Brien spotted Riley kneeling down, looking at where the corpse had laid.

"Special Agent Riley?" O'Brien asked cautiously. Agent Riley just knelt there, looking at the chalk outline of where the body had been.

"That's right," he said not looking back.

"You're double-parked, sir." O'Brien said disguising his voice. Riley stood abruptly and turned to look who was addressing him.

"O'Brien! What in God's name are you doing here?"

"A better question," O'Brien said, "what is a political figure science guy from the States doing in a place like this?"

"Only thing we can assume is that he picked up some hooker, brought her back here, did his thing and then she shot him right square between the eyes, took some personal papers and possibly some classified information."

"You don't think it was an assassination."

"Nah, this bigwig wasn't that important a guy. He's been here in Canada for the past three weeks doing conventions on Neurology."

"Neurology?" O'Brien questioned.

"That's right. He did his last one on Friday and was supposed to be back in Washington on Saturday."

"I guess you haven't heard that Anvil Brentwood escaped on Thursday last week? That's why we're here in this great city of Toronto."

"Anvil Brentwood?" Riley questioned quizzically.

"That's right our old friend from the summer," O'Brien commented as he refreshed Riley's memory.

"You mean that guy who killed all those homeless?"

"The one and only."

"Hmm, I do recall hearing that someone escaped, but I didn't hear the name. You don't suppose this killing has anything to do with him, do you?"

"I doubt it, but I can't be sure. Do you know if the victim here had any dealings with a Dr. Nebinoff from the Neurology Department at the University?"

"I'd have to check it out. I imagine so. After all, he was down here for that reason. You know, neurology."

"Are you able to reveal to me the name of this victim?" O'Brien asked, knowing he could cross-reference the name to the passenger list from the airport and bus stations before the FBI and perhaps the CSIS. It was a shot in the dark, but it was a shot.

"I'll tell you what, O'Brien. Leave me your number and I'll let you know this evening 'cause I'm going to have to run it by my superior. You see, there is more to this guy's death than I can let you know."

*Of course,* O'Brien thought as he gave Agent Riley his cell number. They shook hands and Art and he exited the room.

"That guy seems to be a bit of an ass, doesn't he, O'Brien?" Art commented as they descended the stairwell.

"He's FBI. What can you expect?"

"I hear you," Slappy replied.

As they entered the daylight from the dank hotel, OPP special agent Roger was still standing guard. O'Brien and Art sauntered over to him and asked if he knew who the victim was. O'Brien told him that he already forgot the name, because there was so much on his mind. He was hoping Roger would take the bait.

"Wasn't it Dr... umm, what the hell was it Slappy?" O'Brien brusquely questioned Art.

"I can't recall it either. It was Dr. something or other..." Slappy said shaking his head and following O'Brien's lead.

"No, no. It was Professor Golbart Linquist," replied agent Roger.

"Ah yes. Yes, that was it," O'Brien said as though he really knew. "Thanks a lot, Roger, it saves me the trip of going back into that dark, dank hotel and asking Agent Riley a second time. Wouldn't want to bother the FBI."

"No problem, detective."

They thanked him and returned to their car. Quickly O'Brien jotted down the name and phoned Hal. Rory answered.

"Hey, Rory, this is O'Brien."

"No," he replied jokingly.

"Listen, I have a name I want you to cross reference to the passenger list of the airport and Greyhound. Got a pen handy?"

"Sure do, O'Brien, fire away."

"Okay, the name is Golbart Linquist, a Professor. Let me know instantly if you find that name," O'Brien instructed.

"You got it, O'Brien."

O'Brien clicked the cell phone off while he and Art pulled out from the curb. They drove a few blocks away then parked. They walked around the slums for a couple of hours flashing the mug-shot of Anvil to as many people as they could. No one had seen him. By now, O'Brien was curious to know why Rory or Hal hadn't called him yet. When he looked at his cell phone, it became clear. The cell phone battery was dead.

"We have to find a pay phone," O'Brien commented. They walked to a nearby café and used the telephone. The phone rang once, then twice, then three times and so on.

"They must be at the airport," O'Brien responded when there was no answer. The only thing left to do was to head back to the car. Art and O'Brien walked the seven or so odd blocks back and showed that many more people Anvil's mug-shot, but, of course, it was fruitless.

"You know what, Art?"

"What's that, O'Brien?"

"I've come to the conclusion that Anvil is three steps ahead of us. I can't figure out why no one has seen hide or tail of that maniac. I'm beginning to believe he's on his way out of this province or he's already in another."

"Come on, O'Brien. It's only been two days since we started looking for him. Toronto is a big place. He could be anywhere. He could be looking at us right now."

O'Brien knew old Art was right, but he was confident that they weren't going to find Anvil in Toronto.

"I know. I'm just chided that he has pulled the wool over everyone's eyes for this long. I hope when we catch up with him, he gives us an excuse to end his meagre existence."

O'Brien knew it was his annoyance and temper talking.

"Those are pretty harsh words, but I agree with you."

They walked the remaining distance to the car in silence. O'Brien's mind was swirling with the possibilities that Anvil may very well be back in Fruitmont. It was a probability that O'Brien wished didn't exist. However, in all actuality it did. As soon as they arrived at the car, he plugged his cell phone in to recharge. Not five minutes later, the phone rang. It was Rory.

"What, you decided to answer your phone?" he jibed.

"Ah, the battery went dead."

"I got some news for you. A Professor Golbart Linquist boarded a plane to Edmonton on Friday evening. What's with that name anyway, O'Brien?"

O'Brien told him about the run in with Riley at the crime scene at 1120 East Meyer, moreover that the victim was Professor Golbart Linquist. The pieces were coming together.

"What you're saying then, is that Anvil or the perpetrator who killed this Professor has boarded that plane?" confirmed Rory.

"That's what I believe. I think Anvil may have seen this person at the University. The Professor may have even interviewed him. I think Anvil was already planning an escape. When the opportunity knocked, he took it. I think he tracked Linquist after his escape on Thursday to the hotel on Meyer where he shot the Professor, stole his ID, and headed straight to the airport. The Professor probably had the flight ticket on him. I don't know if any of this will come out in the wash, or where Anvil may have come up with a pistol, but my instincts tell me that is how it went down. How else would a dead guy board a plane?"

"That's a good assumption, O'Brien, but a number of different people could have done just that."

He was right, of course. The assailant may not have been Anvil. Somebody, however, boarded a plane under the dead man's name. It was circumstantial, but it was their only lead.

"The only thing we can do right now Rory is check out the possibility. It is too late to send a fax to the airport in Edmonton. We can do that first thing in the morning. How did you guys make out at the Toronto airport?" O'Brien asked.

"Hal went on alone. He hasn't called me yet. Mind you, I've been predisposed in the bathroom for a few. He may have called then, but there is no message on my cell or pager."

"Okay. So you don't know what the results are or if anybody identified Anvil as boarding a plane?"

"Not until Hal calls back. He only left a little over an hour ago; he might be stuck in traffic. I'll let you know as soon as he calls in."

"Nah. Art and I are on our way back to the hotel anyway. You can fill me in when we get there."

"Sure thing, O'Brien. See you soon," he said as he hung up the phone.

Art and O'Brien arrived back at the Sheridan at 5:15 p.m. Rory had some news for them all right. Anvil was identified boarding the flight to Edmonton and of course under the assumed name of Professor Golbart Linquist. The other news was that Hal was already on his way to Edmonton. He had boarded a plane shortly after 4:30 p.m. with nothing but the clothes on his back.

Immediately O'Brien made arrangements for the rest of his crew to take the flight to Edmonton the following morning. Hal said he would meet up with them at the Hilton on 26th and Gerard on Edmonton's west side near the Edmonton Mall. They made telephone calls to all the police agencies in the Edmonton area and filled Henderson in. Henderson said he would relay the message to Will Jerome back at the Ridgeville Agency.

O'Brien knew it was a long shot that Anvil was still in Edmonton. Anvil could hitchhike from Edmonton to Fruitmont or the Kootenay Region in less than two days. However, they had to follow his every movement. Assumptions that Anvil may very well be heading back to Fruitmont wouldn't cut it. He knew they had to track his every movement from the time Anvil arrived in Edmonton until they finally caught up with him. It was going to be a lengthy process, no doubt. The plus side was that now they had a reason to use extreme prejudice.

Thom and Ilene arrived back at 6:30 p.m. They managed to question a number of different doctors and a psychotherapist. They all had the same thing to say, that they were befuddled at Anvil's progress. It made no sense to any of them how the disease could go into remission. Thom and Ilene also found a number of different packages of flowers, which seemed odd. One of the doctors informed them that it was part of Anvil's rehabilitation. They wanted to study how he would interact with animated living objects. They were surprised at how well he cared for the flowers. This proved beyond a reasonable doubt that Anvil was a feeling, thinking, caring and capable individual. To O'Brien it was a bunch of nonsense. Who was he, though, to judge psychotherapists and the like?

The flowers turned out to be White Hellborne and Black Hellborne. Ilene, being a bit of a botanist, looked up the flower varieties in her botanical bible as she called it. She heard somewhere that the White Hellborne flower had been used in mediaeval days to cure madness and was fed to young children to improve intelligence whereas the Black Hellborne was believed to bring bad luck to whomever consumed it. After a few short minutes, she concluded that what she heard was true.

"Can you believe that? It says right here that the White Hellborne flowers were used as a cure for madness and other neurological imbalances. Do you guys think that our friend Anvil could have been versed in this knowledge?" she questioned.

"I don't know," O'Brien replied. "It certainly wouldn't surprise me. Whether it has any bearing on his mental well-being now or, for that matter, his recovery, only Anvil knows that answer, at least for now."

It was definitely something to consider. Anvil had toyed with all of them for this long. Who could say that Anvil didn't know? Whatever the case might be, first they had to track him down, ask questions later. The five of them boarded flight 302 to Edmonton early Tuesday morning October 16. O'Brien did not receive any telephone call from Riley. It didn't matter anymore. He would be in contact with him as soon as they caught up with Anvil and they were able to prove that he had killed the Professor. The FBI would figure out soon enough that the escape of Anvil and the death of the Professor coincided with one another.

The flight to Edmonton was not nearly as long as the flight to Toronto and the stopover in Winnipeg was only 25 minutes. They arrived in Edmonton shortly before 6:00 p.m. Again, they waited for all the other passengers to exit before they could help Thom exit. He had taken a Valium for the flight and wasn't quite able to walk off the big plane by himself. As O'Brien helped him off, Thom mumbled.

"If we have to go from here to somewhere else," he slurred. "Then I'm driving… "

O'Brien knew he meant it. After the five of them made their way through the checkout and grabbed a car rental, they loaded Thom and the luggage up, then headed to the Hilton on 26th and Gerard.

They found Hal sitting in the café of the Hilton slurping a cappuccino and reading the Edmonton Sun. He didn't yet noticed them and Ilene walked over to him and put her hands over his eyes.

"Guess who?" she said.

"It's about time you guys showed up."

"How did you know it was us?" asked Ilene.

"I'm not expecting anyone else and I'm sure as hell not that good-looking for a pretty lady that smells as sweet as you to come over to my table and put her hands over my eyes," he replied. "Come on over, team, and sit down. The table is big enough for the six of us. Where is Thom?"

"The Valium fairy got him again." O'Brien replied, "he's up in your room snoring."

"I did book you all rooms. Didn't the desk clerk give you the keys?"

"No, Ilene just asked for your room number. Thom was beginning to get grumpy and needed a nap," said Rory.

"Have you come up with any news on Anvil?"

"Not a thing," replied Hal as he shook his head. "The guy is like the invisible man. I showed off his portrait, but he hasn't been seen. The RC's don't even have a lead. All we know for sure is that he was here in Edmonton. The airport records show that indeed a Professor Linquist was on Flight 110 Friday evening. The paper trail leads to the front checkout of the airport. From there it is a mystery as to where he may have gone. The good news is that I convinced Henderson to put a Canada wide APB out on him. All the police agencies are on alert and have been informed to use extreme caution."

"What about the FBI and CSIS?" O'Brien asked as though he cared. "Are they aware of what's going on?"

"Who cares about the FBI? As for the Canadian Secret Intelligence Service, they're giving us complete reign. They say that they can't get involved yet. Something to do with circumstantial evidence. You know all that bureaucracy that they have to go through to make a move on something like this. If we can put him in the hotel room when the Professor breathed his last breath, then they will get involved. Who needs them, anyway?" Hal chuckled.

They finished their coffees then headed to the front desk to get room keys. Two rooms were double occupancy and one was a single. O'Brien would room with Rory leaving Art and Ilene with a room each to themselves. They decided to leave Thom where he was in Hal's room. Once settled, they booked one of the smaller conference rooms in the hotel for the following morning so that they could be left alone while they discussed a strategy.

Deep in the pit of O'Brien's stomach, he knew Anvil wasn't even in Alberta. If he were, chances were that he was likely up in the Rockies somewhere. As O'Brien closed his eyes that night, his mind tortured him with visions of Anvil's destruction. The crime scene in Slocolm that summer before they arrested him played out like a movie in O'Brien's fatigued state. He woke up in a cold sweat; it was 3:00 a.m. He lay awake in bed until 6:00 a.m., his mind racing with all kinds of possibilities. He thought back to the journal Thom and Ilene found and he envisioned Anvil himself sitting outside his house in Fruitmont vengefully watching and waiting for the right opportunity to strike…

At 9:00 a.m., they gathered in the conference room. They discussed over breakfast what their logistics should be, even though they weren't sure that Anvil was even in Edmonton. They decided to stick with the same plan as they used the day before and split up.

"We have to figure out if he is even here," O'Brien said.

Finishing their breakfast, the six of them decided to cover the city streets from east to west showing Anvil's picture to as many people as possible. Of the three teams showing off the portrait, it was Hal and Rory who got a hit. Art and O'Brien were entering a divey hotel when O'Brien's cell phone went off.

"Hey, O'Brien, guess what?" asked Rory.

"What?"

"Hal and I are over in the lower eastside. We've come across a guy who claims he has seen our friend. Says Anvil ripped off his wallet the other night at the Arlington Hotel on Bing Street. We are heading over that way right now. Maybe you should meet us there?"

"Thanks a lot, Rory. You can count on it."

O'Brien shut off his cell.

"Excellent," he blurted. "Hal and Rory might have a lead on Anvil's whereabouts."

"Good. Where are they?" Art asked with excitement.

"Over on the eastside. They're heading over to the Arlington on Bing."

"That's about a thirty minute drive from here," stated Art. "Let's rock and roll."

They walked back to their rental car in anticipation of what they might find at the Arlington. The drive through downtown was hectic and nerve-racking, but they made it to the Arlington in less time than they expected. They found Hal and Rory standing at the bar talking with the bartender.

"What have you guys come up with?" O'Brien asked as he looked around the dirty bar.

"Anvil was here all right. In fact, he checked out this morning," Hal replied with discontent.

"How long was he here?"

"Since the 15th."

"You got to be kidding," O'Brien exclaimed. "Where was he headed?" he asked the bartender who was now at the end of the bar.

"Beats me. I only work here, man. He was blabbing last night that he was sick of Edmonton and was heading back home, wherever that might be."

"Back home, eh?" O'Brien observed.

"Yeah, that's what he said."

O'Brien knocked on the counter and looked at Hal, Rory, and Art.

"Come on. I think I know where he's heading."

They were only about four hours out of Birchland and that was the last known address of the Brentwood clan. It could be that was the home he was talking about.

"Remember the warden told us in the summer that they had given him a ticket to his last known physical address in Birchland. Could be he is headed that way. Rory, you want to get a hold of Thom and Ilene. Have them meet us back at the hotel ASAP."

"Sure thing, O'Brien."

"I'm going to get in touch with the RC's and tell them to keep their eyes peeled."

Rory and O'Brien made telephone calls and then the four of them headed back to the Hilton. The crew of six arrived within minutes of each other.

"You think Anvil might be heading to Birchland?" asked Thom.

"I don't know for sure, but I think it's a good possibility. It is where he's from. We are going to need to check out the Greyhound to see if a person by the name of Lance Billingston might have boarded. That is the guy's name whose wallet was lifted, isn't it, Rory?" O'Brien double-checked.

"It is, O'Brien."

"Good enough; let's get rolling."

They phoned the three Greyhound lines that were in Edmonton, but no one by that name or with the description of Anvil had boarded.

"Do you think he might hitchhike?" asked Ilene.

"That's a good question," O'Brien said as he raised an eyebrow.

"Maybe we ought to head that way. There are three ways to get there and we have three cars," Hal pointed out. "We can meet up in Birchland later this evening."

"That's an excellent idea. Let's do it," Thom replied.

"I'm game. Where should we meet?" O'Brien asked with enthusiasm.

"How about at the Gravy Train? You know the truck stop west of the outskirts."

O'Brien nodded.

"All right then, the Gravy Train it is at, say 8:00 p.m. That should give all of us plenty of time to get there."

Two hours later after making arrangements with the car rental agency to take the cars out of province and letting the Ridgeville Agency and the Fruitmont Agency know that they were on the move; they set out in the three directions. The RCMP agreed to co-operate with their efforts and would closely watch the highway out of Birchland. If Anvil were headed in that direction, he would be stopped, they hoped.

# Eighteen

Thirty miles west of Edmonton, Anvil was standing on the shoulder of highway 2A West, his arm outstretched and his thumb in the air as the big diesel approached. It was the tenth big rig he had seen that afternoon. Anvil hollered obscenities as the truck sped by. Minutes later, he could see in the distance a vehicle approaching. Walking backwards, he reached out his thumb again. It was a camper and truck. The truck slowed and pulled up beside Anvil, then stopped. Anvil smiled as he entered the cab.

"Where you headed?" the driver asked.

"Fruitmont," replied Anvil.

"Whereabouts is that?"

"A ways west of the BC border."

"I'll get you close. I'm headed to White Swan to do some hunting."

"Hunting? What are you hunting?"

"I got myself a couple a deer tags and a moose tag."

"You're hunting moose and deer?"

"That's right. Have you ever done any hunting?" the driver asked.

"Nope. I don't like the taste of wild game. By the way, my name is Lance," Anvil said as he reached out his hand.

"Pleased to meet you, Lance. My name is Wayne," the driver said as the two shook hands.

"It was nice of you to stop for me. I have been standing out there since early this morning. I was beginning to think I'd never get a ride."

Wayne looked over to Anvil and smiled.

"Ah, I figured I could use the company. I've been driving for almost ten hours. Some friendly conversation will keep me awake."

"Yeah," Anvil said as he looked out the window nodding his head. His mind was devising a plan. He didn't want to hitchhike anymore and this ride was perfect for his purpose. All he had to do was get rid of the driver.

"When you hunt for moose and deer," he began, "what kind of rifles do you use?"

"My favourite is a 30.06, but I like using the .270 as well. The 30.06 is good for the bigger stuff, but it might make a hell of a mess out of a deer. The .270 might down a moose, but then again it might not, so I use the 30.06 for the moose and the .270 for Bambi," Wayne chuckled.

"I see," replied Anvil still looking out the window.

"You don't mind if we make a brief stop at the next rest area do you? I ate at a crappy truck stop this morning and I need to use a can," Wayne spoke out.

"Not at all, you're the driver."

"Good. There is a rest area up ahead, oh about twenty miles that has some shit houses. We'll stop there."

"Yes, yes, that is a splendid idea," replied Anvil.

In the back of his mind, he knew it would be the perfect opportunity to strike. Then he could continue alone to Fruitmont. Fifteen minutes later, they pulled into the rest area.

"Here it is. If you have to piss, piss now or forever hold your piss," Wayne chortled as he pulled up close to the restroom and shut off the truck.

Stepping out, he absently left his keys in the ignition.

"I'll be back."

Anvil watched as he entered the outhouse, then he silently opened the passenger door and stepped out with the keys in his hand. He checked the camper door to see if it was locked, but the door opened. Inside he could see the two rifle cases lying on the floor. Picking up the bigger of the two, he quietly searched for the key on the key ring he held in his hand to unlock the case. Finding it, he silently unlocked the case and picked up the rifle. The clip was also inside and he slammed it into the rifle. He pulled back the bolt and the bullet injected into the chamber. Then he walked the short distance to the outhouse.

Wayne didn't feel a thing as the bullet ripped through his chest splattering blood and tissue on the wall behind him. The sound of the big gun echoed in the woods and then silence fell all around. Not even a bird chirped. Anvil smiled.

"That's got to hurt."

He removed the body and put it in the back of the camper. Leaving the wall covered in blood and tissue, slowly he pulled out onto the highway and continued west in the direction of Fruitmont.

Art and O'Brien were the first to arrive in Birchland. They had seen no one hitchhiking. O'Brien's only hope was that one of the others had. He and Art drove around the sleepy town keeping their eyes peeled hoping to see Anvil, but to no avail. Stopping off at a little café, they ordered coffees.

"I sure hope this doesn't prove to be fruitless," O'Brien replied. "I'll kick myself if we don't come up with something."

"Come on, O'Brien. We just got here."

"True as that might be, I have a feeling this is a dead end. My guts keep telling me that Anvil is on his way elsewhere."

"We're not going to know that until the others get here."

"I know, Art."

Finishing their coffees the two of them drove around until it was almost 8:00 p.m. As expected, they didn't see hide or hair of Anvil. They even talked to a few locals. One old-timer knew where the Brentwoods used to live on occasion and he pointed them in the direction. It was a rundown shack by now and no tenants had lived in it for almost six years according to the old fellow they spoke with. The yard was overgrown and the building was dilapidated.

"So there's where Anvil and his papa used to live," O'Brien commented as he looked on.

"It's hard to believe a little Anvil used to run around that yard, isn't it?" questioned Art.

"Yeah. Should we take a closer look?"

"Might as well. What time is it? We have to meet the others at around 8:00 p.m."

"We have a few more minutes before we have to head towards the Gravy Train. Come on, let's go have a closer look."

Exiting the car, they walked over to the old house. The wooden siding was a cloudy grey colour and most of the windows were broken out. The front door was barely hanging on by the hinges and it creaked as O'Brien opened it. Inside was a musty smell and a few mice skirted across the floor as they entered. Garbage was scattered throughout the two-bedroom shack and an old rotting couch sat up against the far wall of the living room. Remnants of a flower pattern 1960's - 70's wallpaper were peeling off the walls and an old picture dangled from a nail. The floorboards were coming up and they were twisted and warped.

"What kind of childhood do you suppose a guy could have in a place like this?" asked Art.

"I'm sure in its prime the place wasn't all that bad. It is chilling being in here though. It's hard to believe this is where he lived for a short while on and off," O'Brien said as goose pimples formed on his arms and a chill ran up his spine. "I don't think we're going to find anything here."

"Probably not. Come on, let's get over to the Gravy Train," Art lamented.

They exited the run-down shack and headed to the car. O'Brien turned and took one last look. He pictured old man Brentwood sitting in the yard, a beer in one hand, and a big stick in the other, waiting to lay a beating on his son for whatever reason he could muster.

As they pulled into the Gravy Train parking lot, O'Brien saw that Thom and Ilene's rental car was there, but not Hal and Rory's.

"I wonder where Hal and Rory are."

"Beats me. Maybe Thom and Ilene know," replied Art.

"Let's hope so."

They walked into the truck stop and over to the table where Ilene and Thom were seated.

"Hey, any luck?" O'Brien asked as he and Art sat down.

"Nothing, O'Brien."

"Humph. Have you heard from Hal and Rory?"

"Nope."

"I guess we'll sit and wait. What's on the menu?"

Ilene handed O'Brien a menu.

"Where did you guys go? We drove around for about twenty minutes before we came here," Thom mentioned.

"One of the old-timers pointed us in the direction of Anvil's old homestead. We checked it out. There is no way he would want to come back to that. It's just a rundown piece of scenery."

The waitress came over and took their orders. O'Brien ordered a steak sandwich and fries, as did Art and Thom. Ilene ordered a veggie burger and onion rings. The four were finishing up when Hal and Rory rolled in.

"Over here, Hal," O'Brien said waving them over. "Did you guys come up with anything?"

"A big fat zero. We didn't see one hitchhiker."

"Neither did we."

"I guess we should get a hold of the RC's and let them know. What do you guys think we should do now?" O'Brien asked as he sipped his coffee.

"The first thing I want to do is have a bite to eat," Rory spoke out.

"Yeah, me too. What did you guys have?"

"Steak switches," replied Thom.

"Yum, sounds good. I think I'll have that too."

"Make that two," Rory added.

As they ate, the others continued discussing their next course of action. They decided to spend the night in Birchland. There was a motel across the way from the Gravy Train with vacancies. It was there that they decided to spend the night. In the morning, they would have no choice but head back to Edmonton. Maybe they could pick up Anvil's trail again. O'Brien phoned the RC's once they got the rooms and told them the bad news that they didn't have any success in tracking Anvil to Birchland.

"That's too bad, detective. At least we'll all be able to sleep tonight," the Constable replied. "We'll keep our lines of communication open though. Could be he's somewhere close. Besides, there is a Canada-wide APB out on this guy so we have to stay alert."

"That's true, but I don't think he's coming this way. Thanks for all your help anyway."

"No problem, detective. If anything comes up don't hesitate to call."

"I won't. If you people hear anything don't hesitate to call us. We'll be staying at the Glendale Motel until tomorrow and then we are heading back to Edmonton. My cell number is 555-0121 if you can't reach me at the motel. Once again, thanks for your help," O'Brien said as he hung up the phone.

He looked at his watch. It was going on to 10:00 p.m. He contemplated phoning home because he wanted to hear Tracy's voice, but he decided not to, as it would only make him miss her more.

They all gathered in his room a few minutes later. They talked and played cards until midnight then returned to their rooms. O'Brien was asleep for only a little over an hour when he woke up in a cold sweat. He dreamed again that Anvil was sitting in the bushes behind his house in Fruitmont waiting

like an animal for its prey. It took until 4:00 a.m. to finally
fall asleep.

## Nineteen

On Thursday, October 18, O'Brien and crew were feeling the chill of fall when they awoke. During the night a cooling system settled in Birchland and the frozen ground was a reminder of what they would be in for if they didn't apprehend Anvil soon. Granted it was only six days since his escape, still he could be anywhere. O'Brien had a hot shower and then met the others over at the Gravy Train for breakfast.

"Think we should head over to Grandbluff? It's only a few minutes east of here. It could be Anvil decided to head that way. After all it is where that first John Doe was discovered ten years ago," O'Brien asked.

"We're not going east at all, buddy," started Thom. "Early this morning an elderly couple stopped off at a rest stop about four hours west of here. They found one a hell of a mess. Apparently there is blood, bone, and flesh splattered all over the wall in one of the restrooms. I'm thinking our friend is heading back to Fruitmont."

"What? You think Anvil is somehow involved?" O'Brien asked.

"Not only me, O'Brien, we all do."

"We think Anvil is headed that way to follow out the threat referenced in his journal," responded Hal.

"You don't seriously think he'd follow through with that gibberish?" O'Brien asked, although he felt the same way. "How do we even know if he had anything at all to do with this latest situation? Was there a body found? Come on, you have to persuade me with a bit more than pure speculation. What we have to do is find out if what was found on the walls is that of human origin, then we have to find a body. Did you guys ever think it could be that some hunter left that mess behind? Maybe it was from a grouse he might have been cleaning."

"O'Brien, you should hear yourself right now. Two days ago you would have been the first to move on this," exclaimed Thom. "You don't think we wouldn't have checked that out. There's a 30.06 slug embedded in the fucking wall and a casing outside the entrance."

O'Brien sat in silence, feeling embarrassed.

"Listen, I apologise to all of you. I should have listened closer. If Anvil is headed to Fruitmont, then we better stop him before he gets there. Tell me how did you guys find this out before I did?" O'Brien asked jokingly trying to break the tension that he created.

"We only got word of it not more than twenty-five minutes ago. The RC's tried calling you but you didn't answer your cell. They called directly to the Motel. The manager roused me and I took the call," said Ilene. "When I knocked on your door and you didn't answer we presumed you were in the shower. Was our assumption correct, O'Brien?"

"Yes, it was."

O'Brien smiled nodding his head feeling like a dork for being such a jerk.

"How do you guys suppose we should handle this?"

"First, we've got to get over to the scene and check it out. The RC's are going to be there all day. The crime scene people are expected there this afternoon. You are right, O'Brien, about the body. They haven't found one. Still they're treating this like a homicide," said Thom.

"Well then, let's finish up our breakfast and get a move on. It's going on to 9:00 a.m. now. If we take off soon, we can beat the Crime Scene Unit. I wouldn't want to get in their way."

In the back of his mind, O'Brien was convinced this was the handy work of Anvil. He also knew, hell he had known from the beginning, that Anvil was probably headed west. He was just unwilling to admit it out loud. They had to find him before he found them. Until then, they were all in jeopardy. One question that they couldn't answer was that where did Anvil come up with a 30.06 rifle. By 9:30 a.m. O'Brien and crew were on their way with all three-rental cars in a convoy, heading west. They got a surprise at around 11:00 a.m. when O'Brien's cell phone rang.

"Hello, O'Brien?"

"Yeah, this is he," O'Brien responded.

There was some static and then O'Brien heard what sounded like Henderson's voice.

"O'Brien, this is Henderson. I'm headed east of Cranbrook. There's been a murder there."

"Yeah we heard. We are all headed there right now. How come you're headed that way?" O'Brien was curious.

"I thought you guys were still in Birchland and were going to head back to Edmonton. Don't you ever answer your phone I called this morning, but couldn't get through?"

"I wonder if it has anything to do with the area. How far do you think these cell phones go anyway?" O'Brien chuckled.

There was some more static and then Henderson responded.

"Listen, these cell phones suck. I didn't hear a word you said. If you're headed that way, I'll meet you guys there."

The telephone fell silent as O'Brien shook his head.

"Henderson is going to meet us there."

"What is he going to do that for?" Thom was curious now.

"He said he thought we were headed back to Edmonton. Apparently he tried phoning me this morning all the way from Fruitmont on his cell phone."

"Like as if you could even get a signal. Boy, he has a lot to learn about today's technology. That word scares him. He figures if it's technical it ought to work like everything else," Thom said as he chuckled. "The poor bastard is getting old."

"I wonder why he didn't send one of the other guys," O'Brien questioned as he looked out the passenger window and contemplated.

"Like I said, he's getting old. He's probably getting tired of sitting on his ass barking orders," replied Thom as they fell silent.

Finally, they arrived on the scene at 1:00 p.m. The RC's were still there of course and they had cordoned off the entrance to the rest stop. O'Brien showed his credentials to the constable who stood at the entrance and the RCMP constable allowed them to enter. They parked a short distance away from the scene so as not to disturb the ground.

"Well, here we are," O'Brien, said as Thom shut the car off.

They waited for the others to pull in behind and then all six of them proceeded over to the scene. It was a bloody mess; there was no doubt about that. The blood on the wall was beginning to turn a black crusty colour. O'Brien's intellect raced with the scene he had discovered that summer when they were first introduced to Anvil's sick mind. What appalled O'Brien the most were the fragments of bone that stuck out of the wall like porcupine quills.

"Doesn't leave a very nice picture in one's head does it?" asked the young RCMP rookie who was sitting on the hood of his car.

"It sure doesn't, kid," replied Art.

"I've never been to a crime scene like this before. Don't get me wrong. I have seen body parts scattered here and there, but that was at an auto accident. This here is plain murder. To think that whoever did this is still running around freaks me out," said the young officer.

"Does the RCMP have any kind of lead on what might have happened here?" O'Brien asked as he turned to face the young rookie.

"Nope, not a clue. We know that a truck was parked about where you are standing. It also had a camper. We can tell that by the depth of the tracks. Could be it was an accident, but I doubt it."

"An accident?" asked Thom. "How do you suppose it was an accident?"

"It could be he or she brought their gun in with them say for protection or to clean it while they did their business and it accidentally went off. Whoever was with them grabbed them and headed for help?" the rookie offered as an option to plain murder.

"Have you guys received notification from any nearby hospitals that someone has been brought in with a 30.06 rifle injury?" O'Brien asked knowing that the kid could very well be correct in his description of what may have transpired.

"No, sir. We haven't heard anything of the sort. It's only a theory I have been speculating. It could be it was a suicide attempt as well. Maybe they were fighting with their spouse and decided to end it all. Their spouse freaked out grabbed the body and headed…well who knows where. It's another theory."

"Those are valid points, kid," O'Brien replied.

It could have happened that way. The rookie rather reminded O'Brien of himself when he was a rookie, never wanting to look at any crime one way. In time, however, he learned to go with instinct and observation. Nine out of ten times he was right.

"You have some good potential, kid. How long have you been on the force?" O'Brien asked wanting to know more about the rookie standing in front of him.

"Sixteen weeks tomorrow."

"What's your name?"

"I am Constable Riley of the Cranbrook RCMP," he stated with pride.

"Constable Riley?" O'Brien questioned. "Are you related to Agent Riley of the FBI?"

"Yes sir. He's my dad."

"You got to be kidding," O'Brien exclaimed with laughter. Thinking how unlikely it was to actually meet a father and son both of whom worked in policing of one kind or another and more times than not on opposite sides.

"Yes. I am, as a matter of fact," the rookie said as he smiled.

"Jesus Christ, kid, don't do that to me. So you're not related to Agent Riley then?"

"I've never heard of him. Riley is my first name, not my last. My last name is Fell."

"What kind of name is Fell?" asked Thom.

"I've been told it is Dutch."

"I should have known you were Dutch by how tall you are. How tall are you kid?"

"Six foot four," Riley responded, standing now and towering over them.

"Wow. Your old man must be one big Dutchman."

"I never met him. He was killed on duty."

"Oops, sorry to hear that."

"Hey, it was a long time ago. Don't worry about it," Riley stated.

O'Brien reached out his hand.

"Nice to meet you, Riley. Welcome to police works 101," O'Brien commented as they shook hands. "I'm Detective O'Brien."

O'Brien took it upon himself to introduce the rest of the crew to the kid.

"How long have you been at this godforsaken scene Riley?" O'Brien asked after the introductions.

"Web and I," he said pointing at the RC standing at the entrance, "we were the first on the scene; we've been here since 8:00 a.m. As soon as the Crime Scene Investigators get here we can take off."

"Where are they coming from?" Hal asked.

"Both detachments from east and west are on their way."

"What's their ETA?" O'Brien asked.

"Anytime now," Riley replied as he looked at his watch.

O'Brien walked over to picnic table and dialled Henderson's cell number.

"Henderson here. How can I help you?"

"Hey, Henderson, how close are you to the scene?" O'Brien asked.

"Who is this?" he retorted.

"It's me, O'Brien."

"O'Brien? What are you talking about? How close am I to the scene? I'm at the office."

"What? Aren't you on your way here?"

"Here? Here, where?" Henderson asked.

O'Brien thought he was funning with him.

"Don't kid around Henderson. Didn't you call me about an hour ago?"

"Nope."

"You got to be kidding," O'Brien stated with annoyance.

"What's that?" Henderson asked.

"Well, someone called me not more than an hour ago. I could have sworn it was you."

"I haven't called anyone today, O'Brien. I think you got a trickster on your hands."

O'Brien thought for a moment and it became clear.

"Not any trickster, Henderson. I think it was Anvil."

"What are you babbling about, O'Brien?"

O'Brien explained to Henderson where they were and what had taken place.

"I haven't heard a thing about that. So it's possible that he has killed again?"

"We don't know for sure, but somebody has either killed someone and has high-tailed it with the body and all or on the other hand, it could be there was a gruesome accident that took place here. I'm betting it was Anvil. I'm also betting it was Anvil who called me. He knows what we're up to. I have a feeling Henderson, that he has definitely headed back to Fruitmont. He killed whoever it was that might have died here, then took the body so he could dispose of it somewhere else. Pretty coy of him. He knows that without a body we are going to have a tough time figuring out who the victim is."

"I think you ought to put a request into the Wild Game Commissioner, being that it's hunting season it's quite feasible that some hunter may have picked him up. Maybe we can find out how many hunters could be heading this way from out of province. I know it is a big leap of faith, but we might come up with some names. It is a start. In fact, I will do that from this end. I have a friend that might be able to get me some names quickly," Henderson said with speculation.

"Sounds like a plan. I'll ask the RC's if they have done that. Even if they have, Henderson, you might as well go ahead. Maybe we'll come up with some different names."

"I will, O'Brien. When I call I'll use a code name so you know it's me. How does 'bird-dog' sound?"

"Good idea. Bird-dog it is."

"I'll be in touch."

"Okay, talk to you, Henderson," O'Brien said as he turned off his cell phone.

"Hey you guys, come here."

O'Brien waved the rest of the crew over.

"That call I got earlier wasn't Henderson."

"What?" asked Thom.

"It wasn't Henderson. He's at the office."

"You don't suppose it was our friend Anvil, do you?" asked Rory.

"It's exactly what I'm thinking. Anyway, Henderson is going to find out how many hunters from out of province could be heading this way. He has a good theory. He figures some hunter may have picked up Anvil. It would explain where he got a 30.06."

"It's probably the best theory we got. That would also explain the truck and camper idea that Riley over there has," Thom said as he pointed at the rookie.

"I think we should also see if we can't get a trace on where that call you received came from," replied Ilene. "I'll get in touch with communications and see what they can come up with."

"That's a good idea. How long do you think it will take?" O'Brien asked.

"An hour or an hour and half tops."

A few minutes later the crime scene investigators arrived in their white vans. They took tire castings and picked through the scene with a fine-tooth comb. Constable Riley and his partner took off shortly thereafter. They waved as they headed back to Cranbrook.

"Good luck," Riley hollered as they sped away. O'Brien and the others waved and watched as rookie Riley and constable Web disappeared into the day.

"I think that kid is going to make a good cop," O'Brien commented as he looked at his watch. It was almost 4:00 p.m.

"Do you figure we ought to head west? On the other hand, should we hang tight here for a bit and see what Henderson comes up with. There is a little coffee shop down the road about five miles. We could head there and wait. What do you say?" O'Brien mentioned to all.

"Yeah, I'm all for a nice cup of Joe. It's getting pretty chilly out," Hal commented.

He was right. The temperature was dropping and a cold wind was beginning to blow.

"All right then, come on guys, let's get going," O'Brien said as he turned and began walking back to where they had parked. The crime scene investigators were heading out as well. They had gathered all the information that they could until a body was found. They taped up the outhouse with police tape and put a 'Do not enter' sign on the door.

"As if that will deter anybody from entering," Thom said. He was right of course, but as long as the investigators got all they could, it really didn't matter. It was police policy to tape a scene up. In the morning chances were the Parks and Recreation people would be out painting anyway. The restroom would be ready for public use in less than a day.

O'Brien and crew pulled into the Big Burger and Coffee Shop at 4:30 p.m. It was warm inside and the placed smelled of fresh brew and greasy burgers. They found a table near the back and ordered a round of coffee. At 5:15, Henderson phoned.

"O'Brien, this is bird-dog. I have a list of names of possible hunters heading into the interior. However, the count is at twenty-five. I've contacted the RCMP and their list is twice that amount. I think you guys should head into Cranbrook. I have booked you all rooms at the Cranbrook Motel. It's off highway 3A, west of the Cranbrook Furniture building. We are going to try to contact the spouse's, family, and friends of all the names we have. Maybe someone was supposed to phone home, but hasn't yet. I will contact you as soon as we have any solid leads. Until then while you are in Cranbrook, you might as well check out any possibilities that someone may have seen him driving or something. If he is driving, he has to stop for gas somewhere right. I am also putting Erickson on watch at your address. If he sees anything, I'll be the first to let you know."

"Thanks, Henderson. I appreciate it."

"I know you do, O'Brien. I have also notified Tracy. There are a couple of our guys from the office in Ridgeville keeping a close watch on the house back there."

"Who did you send over?" O'Brien asked out of curiosity.

"Will and Abe."

"Excellent choice. Thanks again."

"No problem. I'll be in touch, O'Brien," Henderson said as he hung up the phone.

"That was Henderson," O'Brien reported as he put his cell into his pocket. "He and the others have come up with a list of twenty-five hunters who might possibly be heading this way. They're going to make some phone calls and try and find out if perhaps one of them was supposed to phone home, but hasn't. We've got motel rooms booked in Cranbrook. Henderson wants us to head that way and check a few things out. Said he'll contact us there if they come up with anything."

"And if he doesn't?" asked Art.

"If he doesn't, then I guess we'll do what we can. If Anvil is driving, he has to get gas. We'll check out every gas station from here to Fruitmont."

"Most definitely. We'll catch up with him one way or another," Art responded.

"You got that right," Thom spoke out, although they were not sure if indeed they were on Anvil's trail. It was all speculation. Sitting in silence they finished their coffee and headed outside into the cold dark evening. As they were pulling out of the parking lot, Art and Ilene flashed their headlights. O'Brien stopped the car and waited for them to approach.

"O'Brien," Art hollered out his widow, "we got word that call you got this afternoon came from Cranbrook. If it was Anvil, he called from there."

O'Brien nodded and hollered back "Thanks a lot, Art. Let's get a move on."

"We're right behind you," Art hollered as he rolled up his window.

"Our friend was in Cranbrook?" questioned Thom.

"I don't know if he's still there, but at one time he was. We're getting closer, buddy."

O'Brien dialled up Henderson in hopes that he was still at the office.

"This is Henderson; can I help you?"

"Yeah, this is O'Brien. We received word that the call I got this afternoon came from Cranbrook. Do you think that's a good enough reason to have the RC's put up a roadblock?"

"Not unless we know for sure it was him. Not much we can do until we find that out. What time is it now?"

"It's almost 6:30 p.m."

"He could be anywhere by now. I think we should stick with the first plan. If it turns out that it was him, I'll have roadblocks put up quicker than you can say Anvil Brentwood."

"All right. We're heading to Cranbrook as I speak. We should be at the Motel in less than three hours."

"Good enough, O'Brien. If we come up with anything between now and then I'll call."

"Sure thing, Henderson," O'Brien said as he turned his cell off.

O'Brien was anxious with titillation at the possibility that indeed they were on Anvil's coattails. It would be a stroke of good luck, undoubtedly, if they happened to come across someone who might have seen him.

"What's new at Henderson's end?" asked Thom.

"Nothing. He said we ought to follow out with the first plan. If we can put Anvil in Cranbrook at noon then he'll have the RC's put up roadblocks."

"I sure hope this isn't a wild goose chase," blurted Thom.

"You and me both."

They drove in silence for about an hour.

"I'm getting so tired of tracking this maniac. You know that, O'Brien?"

"I hear you, Thom. I'm sick of chasing him around too. I hope it all ends soon."

An hour later, they could see the bright city lights of Cranbrook.

"It sure looks big in the dark, doesn't it?"

"That it does, O'Brien."

They pulled into a 7-11 on the outskirts and on a whim O'Brien brought a picture of Anvil into the cashier.

"Excuse me. Have you by chance seen anyone that looks like this guy?" O'Brien asked, pointing at Anvil's picture.

"No sir. I haven't. I just got on shift. If you like I can call the person who was working here before my shift. He only lives a half a block away."

"Thanks. That would be appreciated," O'Brien remarked.

Fifteen minutes later a tall kid walked in.

"Sir," the cashier started, "this is Rett. He was working this afternoon."

"Thanks," O'Brien said. "Hello, Rett. I am Detective O'Brien. I was curious to know if you have seen this guy today?" he questioned as he pointed at Anvil's portrait.

"Yeah, he does look familiar. He was driving a two-tone beige and brown Chevy 4x4 with a camper."

"You wouldn't have happened to note the licence plate number would you have?"

"No, but, on the roof of the camper there was a set of deer antlers, plus the front window had a nice size crack in it."

"Excellent observation, Rett. Thanks a million."

"No problem."

"He didn't mention where he was off to did he?"

"Nope he just filled up, paid, and left. He was heading west though."

"What time would that have been?"

"11:00-11:30 a.m.; something like that."

O'Brien had no doubt in his mind now that Anvil was heading west.

"Thanks Rett, you've been a great help."

"What's the guy wanted for?" the kid asked.

"We need to question him is all. Nothing to worry about. Thanks again," O'Brien said as the kid exited. O'Brien called over to Thom.

"Hey, Thom, the kid said he has seen Anvil; said he was here between 11:00-11:30 a.m. this morning."

"Talk about getting lucky or what," he exclaimed.

"You got that right. We best phone Henderson and let him know. What do you think?"

"Yeah, I guess we should. Maybe he could order some roadblocks, especially since we don't know for sure where the bastard might be?"

"True enough, Thom. If we have roadblocks put in place at the bottom of the Creston cut-off and out at the ferry dock in Balfour, we might stand a chance in stopping him."

"The problem with that, O'Brien, is there are still two other routes that he could go, one through the Pend d'Oreille and the other up through Kimberly and Fairmont."

"Good point, but if we don't stop him at either of those two places, we can make a good assumption where he is headed next."

O'Brien picked up the cell and dialed Henderson again to only get his answering machine. O'Brien left a message anyway and decided that he would call Henderson at home once they got to the motel. They were getting into the car when Hal and Rory pulled up. They filled them in to what they had discovered and they too said they talked with someone at a nearby A&W that claimed to have served him at lunch.

"It's obvious then that he was here, there are no two ways about it," replied Thom.

"Yeah. Still, we don't know for sure in what direction he headed after his visit here," stated Hal. "What did your guy tell you?"

"Said he was headed west."

"Well then, we already have a conflict. The waitress we talked to said he mentioned White Swan and that's north," said Rory.

"Yeah, north through Fairmont. I think we should head to the motel where we can figure this thing out. It'll be a lot more cosy discussing it there rather than in this freezing cold," O'Brien replied. "Art and Ilene are probably already waiting."

O'Brien waved Hal and Rory on and Thom and he got into their car.

"I'm really beginning to hate Anvil more with every minute that passes by," said Thom as they pulled into the street.

"Don't worry, Thom, we'll catch up with him sooner or later. I think we are going about this the right way. Let's not get too concerned on where he may or may not be. For now, let's think of all the possibilities and eliminate them as we can."

"Yeah, but every day that goes by, he's laughing at us. I'll guarantee it."

"First off, 'yeahbuts' eat lettuce," O'Brien started. "Secondly, we're not days behind him anymore. We're only hours. Lighten up a bit. His days are numbered."

Thom managed a smile.

"Yes they are," he responded.

"Good. Let's not get discouraged. We'll discuss our next course of action with rest of the crew and we'll follow it out accordingly. Agreed?"

"Agreed," said Thom.

Neither spoke a word after that. O'Brien was beginning to get concerned about Thom. For the past few days he had been showing the stress of being overworked. Finally, they pulled into the Cranbrook Motel.

"Excellent, they're all here," O'Brien said as Thom found a parking spot. Hal met them in the parking lot and handed them their room keys.

"We're all in my room, sixteen. We'll meet you there when you get settled."

"You bet, Hal," O'Brien responded as Hal turned and walked away. Thom and O'Brien grabbed their baggage and headed to their designated rooms. O'Brien was in eleven and the rest of the crew had rooms corresponding in succession. It was good to have their own rooms for a change. O'Brien entered his and slumped down on the wicker chair. He looked around. It was cosy enough. Tossing his bag onto the bed, he headed over to room sixteen.

"Well, what does everyone figure?" he asked. "We have four possible ways Anvil may be travelling. He is going west through Creston, or onward to Balfour to the Kootenay Lake Ferry, or, the Pend' d'Oreille and through Fairmont Hot Springs. Any suggestions?"

"I think we should split up and head towards Fruitmont on the four routes. It will mean renting another car and that two of us will be going solo. I know the Fairmont area quite well and wouldn't have a problem heading that way," said Thom.

"That probably is our best bet. I know the Pend' d'Oreille area. I'll cover that route," O'Brien responded. "That leaves the Creston-Salmo route and the route to Balfour open."

"We'll take Creston unless you and Art want that route?" Hal asked of Ilene and Art.

"Nah, we don't have a problem with the Balfour route do we, Ilene."

"Not at all. It works for me," Ilene said in agreement.

"All right, it's settled. I'll cover the Pend'd'Oreille. Thom is going to cover Fairmont. Hal and Rory are doing the

Creston-Salmo route. Ilene and Art are taking on the Balfour route. Correct?"

O'Brien asked to make sure there were no second thoughts. There weren't.

"Well that will put all of us in Fruitmont at around the same time. With the exception of you, Thom, you'll probably arrive a day later. If we leave early tomorrow after we track down a rental for Thom, the five of us should arrive in Fruitmont tomorrow evening. Remember we are looking for two-tone beige and brown Chevy 4x4 with a rack of deer antlers on the roof. That ought to scream out," O'Brien said as he snickered.

"No doubt how boisterous," replied Ilene. "It screams redneck."

"Whatever it screams that's what we're looking for. It is a two-tone Chevy 4x4. If anyone comes across anything like that, make sure you call it in. It might not be wise to try to apprehend him alone. That is a decision I leave up to each of you. Also remember this is a Code 1 and extreme force will be tolerated. In other words, if he tries anything on you and you have a clean shot do not hesitate; blow his brains out," O'Brien authorised.

"Here, here," they all clamoured.

After participating in friendly conversation for about an hour, O'Brien headed back to his room to telephone Henderson again. On the fourth ring Henderson answered.

"Hello."

"Hey, Henderson. I didn't wake you did I?"

"Not at all, O'Brien. I guess you have some news for me?" he asked.

"Nope, just wanted to phone," O'Brien jibed.

"Come on, O'Brien. What do you got for me?"

"I do have some news. Anvil was here in Cranbrook between 11:00 a.m. and noon. We have two witnesses that claim to have seen him. He was driving a camper and truck, a

Chevy 4x4 that is brown and beige to be exact. Get this: it has a set of antlers attached to the roof. We're not sure in which direction he might be headed. The person I talked to said he was heading west out of Cranbrook. However, Hal and Rory spoke with a waitress and she said he mentioned White Swan. We're going to split up tomorrow and head towards home. One of us might come up with something. I would like you to request a roadblock at the bottom of the Creston cut-off and one out in Balfour. If we don't corral him, then he is definitely going via one of the other routes. Thom and I are going to cover those two routes."

"Sounds to me like you guys have a good plan. However, did you consider the two routes through the states? You know Kingsgate and Rykerts. He could pop up in either Waneta or Rossland."

"Dumb luck. I didn't even consider that," O'Brien pointed out.

"Don't worry about it. I will take care of that possibility. You guys just follow out with your plan."

"You got it, Henderson. We will."

"Good enough. I'll expect to see you guys sometime tomorrow evening. I'll get those roadblocks up, O'Brien."

"Thanks, Henderson. By the way have you had any luck tracking down any possible hunters who haven't called home and were supposed to?"

"Nothing yet, so far the names we've cleared have all been in contact with their spouses. The new information about a two-tone beige 4x4 may speed things up."

"Unless of course the owner of the vehicle doesn't have a spouse."

"Yeah, that is possibility," Henderson replied with sigh.

"Well, we'll keep things going until we hear from you or find the vehicle or find Anvil himself. That is all we can do."

"Yep, keep on with the objective."

"You can count on it, Henderson; you can count on it," O'Brien repeated as he hung up the phone.

He thought about the border crossings. If Anvil managed to get into the States he was more brash than he anticipated. O'Brien convinced himself that there was no way Anvil would manage that. He stood and walked into the bathroom and turned on the shower. He stepped in and as the hot water beat down on his skin. He envisioned again the dramatic gruesome crime scene he discovered in Slocolm that summer. Then his mind raced to the last scene at the rest stop, and how the small bone fragments, protruded out of the wall. It was a sickening feeling and he felt a chill rush up his spine. At that instant the hot water ran out and cold water pierced O'Brien's skin like a million tiny pins and needles.

"Holy crap!" O'Brien hollered at the top of his lungs as he turned the shower off.

Moments later Thom came bursting in.

"What's going on? O'Brien, are you okay?" he yelled.

"I'm fine, Thom. The hot water ran out and it startled me, not to mention pissed me off," O'Brien replied through the bathroom door.

"Jesus. It sounded like you were being killed!" Thom exclaimed.

"Hey, thanks for your concern, buddy, but I'm all right."

"Okay then, I'll see you in the morning. Night, O'Brien."

"Goodnight, Thom," O'Brien hollered behind him as Thom slipped out and closed the door.

Dragging his freezing body out of the bathroom, he turned up the room thermostat. Finally, after a few minutes of standing close to the warm, blowing air, he began to warm up. He put on a pair of jogging pants and a T-shirt, climbed into bed, and shut the lights off. Sleep took him as quickly as the hot water had turned to cold.

# Twenty

That night as they all slept, an early snowstorm passed through the East Kootenay region and covered the ground with the first snowfall of the season. They awoke to three or four inches of the white stuff. O'Brien turned on the radio and listened for the day's forecast. It was expected to get above 5 degrees and remain clear. There was no chance of precipitation and the temperature was going to be seasonal.

O'Brien was relieved at the forecast. He knew that the East Kootenay region was famous for early winter. Snow could fall for days and complete road closures were quite frequent. Today, however, that wouldn't be the case. Shutting off the radio, he headed to the bathroom to brush his teeth and slap water onto his face. Packing up his belongings, he exited the little room and headed over to Thom's.

"Rise and shine, daylight in the swamp," he hollered at his door.

Thom's muffled and dreary voice answered back.

"Be right there."

By this time Hal, Art, Rory, and Ilene were outside sweeping off the cars.

"Good morning," O'Brien said with satisfaction and glee.

"Morning, O'Brien. You seem chipper today," responded Ilene.

"That's because today is going to be a great day."

"What makes you so sure of that?" asked Rory. "Did you have a wet dream last night or what?"

"Shut up, Rory," O'Brien chuckled as he threw a snowball at him.

"Look up to the sky. It's a beautiful blue and the sun is beginning to shine. That, in itself, ought to mean it's going to be a great day."

O'Brien gazed to the sky and he smiled; today would indeed be great. A few minutes later, Thom came out of his room, his overnight bag in hand.

"I got a car rental from Budget. I can pick it up any time after 7:00 a.m. What time is it now?" he asked.

"It's 6:30. We have time to get some breakfast and coffee. I'm famished," replied O'Brien.

"Yeah, me too, and coffee sounds good," Thom replied.

"Well, let's drop off the room keys at the office and get on our way," Ilene chorused.

Ten minutes later, they pulled out of the Cranbrook Motel parking lot and headed for the nearest greasy spoon. They settled for an early morning diner that was called the Blue Lagoon. It was a nice establishment and it served wicked blueberry pancakes with whipped cream. The amount on O'Brien's plate was enormous and he wasn't able to finish the whole helping. He looked at his plate and shook his head.

"I'm not going to have to eat for days. I'm stuffed."

"No kidding. That was a big helping of sausage and eggs that I had too," replied Art.

They finished with coffee to go. In the parking lot, they went over their plan one last time. Satisfied that they were all in accord with each other, Thom and O'Brien bid the four of them goodbye. Then he and Thom headed over to the car rental agency and picked up Thom's rental. It was a two door Mercury LTD, teal blue in colour with power everything.

"Nice car," O'Brien replied as he shook his head. He knew all too well how Thom could run a car into the ground.

"It's nothing like my SUV, but I bet I can drive it like one," he said jokingly.

"No, please Thom, whatever you do, don't drive it like your SUV," O'Brien responded with a smile. "I don't think Henderson & Co. needs another car."

The two of them finally went their separate ways. O'Brien went west and Thom went north.

O'Brien was about ten miles out of the city limits when his cell phone began vibrating. Pulling to the shoulder, he reached into his jacket pocket and retrieved the annoying thing.

"Hello, this is O'Brien."

"Detective O'Brien?"

"Yes, this is he," O'Brien replied wondering who it was on the other end.

"Detective, this is Constable Miller from the Cranbrook RCMP detachment. I'm calling to let you know that we have found the Chevy truck you have all been looking for, as well as a corpse which, was in the camper. How far out of town are you?"

"About ten miles," O'Brien said as the telephone went dead. Curious he dialled the Cranbrook RCMP as quickly as it took him to realise that his cell phone was fully charged, therefore, there was no reason for it to have died. The telephone rang once, then twice; finally on the third ring someone picked it up.

"RCMP. This is Constable Burbach. Can I help you?" the voice said on the other end.

"I sure hope so. This is Detective O'Brien from Henderson & Co., out of Fruitmont. One of your people, a Constable Miller, called me. He said that you guys have found a Chevy truck with a corpse in it?" O'Brien questioned.

"Sorry, Detective. There is no Constable Miller at this detachment. Are you sure he said he was from Cranbrook?"

"Yeah," O'Brien said hesitantly. "I thought he said he was from the Cranbrook detachment. I guess I was wrong. Sorry about that."

"No problem, Detective."

O'Brien thanked Burbach and turned off his cell. It was then that he realised that the caller might very well have been Anvil. He was checking up, trying to find out O'Brien's whereabouts. That meant one thing to O'Brien, Anvil was likely in the vicinity. He glanced around at all the possible advantage points hoping to see a Chevy truck. Instead, he saw nothing.

"Where are you? You maniac," O'Brien said out loud.

"Where the hell are you?" he said again as he slammed his fist into the dashboard. *So you want to play games, eh? Well I guess I haven't a choice but to play along,* O'Brien thought to himself as he turned out onto the highway and continued out of town. He contemplated calling up Hal and Rory to let them know about the latest call. Instead, he held off. After an hour of driving and paying close attention to every vehicle and its driver that passed, O'Brien concluded that Anvil was not following. Was it possible that he was ahead? Pulling to the shoulder, he dialed Hal's cell number.

"Hello, Rory here," came the reply from the other end.

"Hey Rory, this is O'Brien. Where are you guys?"

"Near Yahk. What's up, O'Brien?"

"I got another one of those calls. Anvil is toying with us again."

"What did he say this time?"

"He said he was an RC Constable at the Cranbrook detachment. Then he went on to say that they found a pickup and camper with a corpse in the back. What I need you and Hal to do is turn around and head back my way. I think he is ahead of me. I'm east of Moyie. I figure if he is, we might have a chance to catch him off guard."

"That's a good idea, O'Brien. We're turning around right now," Rory said as he gave the turnaround sign to Hal.

"Great, keep your eyes peeled. Wherever we meet each other is where we'll stop," O'Brien instructed. "As I said, I'm east of Moyie; my ETA is probably twenty minutes."

"I hear you, O'Brien. We're on our way," Rory said as he turned off the cell.

O'Brien pulled out onto the highway and proceeded west. He decided to take a quick detour into the Moyie Lake

Provincial Park. It was only three hundred yards off the main highway. Driving into the park, he couldn't believe his luck. Low and behold—there it was as plain as day, a two-tone Chevy 4x4 with a camper and a set of antlers on the roof. O'Brien's car skidded to a halt and he dialled directly back to Hal and Rory.

"Step on it. I found our truck."

"You got to be kidding!" exclaimed Rory. "What's your location?"

"I'm at the Provincial Park in Moyie. On a hunch, I decided to take a quick detour and there it was. I don't know what I'm going to find, but the truck looks abandoned."

"Yeah, well, be careful, O'Brien. Our ETA is about thirty minutes."

"I'll tell you what, leave your phone on and I'll put mine on the hood of the car. That way if you hear any shooting you'll know what's going on."

"Very funny, O'Brien. Just be careful."

"I will be," O'Brien said as he exited the car.

"Hello, is anybody there?" O'Brien asked as he walked towards the vehicle with gun in hand somewhat reluctant to continue without backup.

He knew Hal and Rory were on their way and this somehow gave him courage to walk closer.

"Hello, is anybody there?" O'Brien asked again as he approached the cab. He looked inside to see if the keys were in the ignition, then walked up to the camper door and tried to open it. Of course, the door was locked. He tried looking through one of the windows and saw only blackness. Someone had covered the windows with black garbage bags. He contemplated smashing one of them but then decided against it.

Someone had even removed the plates and VIN. Whether it was Anvil or not remained to be proven. He knew this much for sure. Whoever had parked the truck, did what they could to prevent it from being easily traced. O'Brien sat down on the hood of the car his eyes and ears tuned to any movement or noise. However, silence was all that he heard. Finally, a car approached. Looking, he spotted Hal and Rory speeding in his direction. Precisely at that moment, his cell phone rang. O'Brien quickly reached for it and answered.

"Hello, O'Brien here."

There was an eerie silence, some breathing and then the dial tone. O'Brien threw the telephone as hard as he could onto the ground pieces of it scattered in all directions. Hal and Rory were pulling up by now and Rory jumped out of the car.

"Are you okay, O'Brien? What are you doing throwing a perfectly good cell phone into the ground?" he asked quizzically with humour. "You had another one of those calls, didn't you?"

O'Brien looked at him and nodded.

"Goddamn it! Where the hell is that son of a bitch?" Rory exclaimed.

"I haven't got a clue," O'Brien shrugged.

Hal walked over to the camper and he tried the door.

"It's locked."

"I know," O'Brien replied, "even the plates are gone as is the VIN."

"Someone wants to keep this truck from being traced, I'd say," Hal replied.

Rory walked over to the camper door and pulled out his gun.

"Fuck it," he hollered as he fired a round into the door handle.

The gun echoed and the door swung open.

"Look at that. There is a corpse in here," Rory commented as he stepped away.

The smell of decay and human excrement overcame the pine-scented air.

"I guess we better call this in."

O'Brien sat on the hood of his rental car and nodded. He was totally overwhelmed.

"Yeah, we better," he replied.

Hal called up the RCMP in Cranbrook and told them of their discovery.

"The RC's are on their way. They should be here within the hour," he said as he shut the phone off.

"Good thing we didn't smash a window, otherwise we'd be barbecued."

"What do you mean?" O'Brien asked in horror.

"Check it out, O'Brien. The windows are rigged to explode."

Rory pointed out the set up. Had anyone smashed any of the windows it would have been the last thing they did.

"I was going to do that," O'Brien said with hostility and at that point wanted nothing more than to empty his magazine into Anvil.

"Someone must have been looking out for you," Hal responded.

"Yeah and thank God that they were," O'Brien replied as his mind turned to his family.

The three of them stepped back from the camper and sat on the hood of O'Brien's rental car. They stared blankly into the unlit little camper shaking their heads.

"If Anvil can rig something up like that, then we're all in for a big surprise. Where do you guys suppose he came up with that?" O'Brien asked dumbfounded.

"Magazines, books, who knows? The fact is that he has," retorted Rory.

"The way he has that rigged took a lot more than guess work. There is no way he could've come up with that out of the blue."

"I agree, Hal. It does seem professional, doesn't it?" O'Brien lamented.

Hal nodded his head in agreement.

After what seemed like forever, the RCMP finally arrived. One of them walked over to the camper and looked inside, then stepped back.

"Best call the bomb squad. This camper is rigged to go airborne. You guys are lucky it didn't explode. How did you open the door without it going boom?" he asked as he looked over the door. "I see," he said noting the bullet hole in the door handle. "Well your unorthodox way of opening the door," he smiled, "inadvertently saved you. If you picked this door to open it you would have been blown all over kingdom come. I'm surprised the bullet didn't ignite something," he stated.

"What?" O'Brien questioned. "We knew the windows were rigged. The door was too?"

"It sure was. Come over here and I'll show you."

The RC pointed out how Rory's bullet entered the door and in the process snapped a wire that was attached to it.

"See, if you had opened the door any other way, that wire would have pulled on the end cap of that propane tank," he said pointing at the twenty-five pound canister, "and at the same time it would have been ignited by the pilot light from the stove. The door is rigged similar to the windows except opening the door would have been a lot messier. It is rigged to unplug those three gas cans. That oil lantern would have fallen and smashed on top of the stove, making the whole lot ignite. You guys or anyone who might have tried to break in or pick the lock wouldn't have stood a chance. It could have been kids. That Anvil guy you are tracking is a diabolical SOB."

The three of them stood in awe as the constable explained how near to dying they had come.

"There's not much we can do until the explosive unit gets here. They say it will take them about two hours. We're supposed to stay clear of it until then. Anything could trigger it apparently," commented the RC who contacted the bomb squad.

They all turned and walked over to where the RCMP parked.

They began making friendly conversation when they heard a rifle shot. Instantly, the camper exploded, smashing the windows out of O'Brien's rental car and igniting the interior. The front end began spewing fluid and the paint lit on fire. Pieces of camper and truck littered the ground as a ball of flames shot up into the air catching a few cedar boughs on fire. They jumped for cover and waited until the truck and camper were nothing more than smouldering pieces of metal. Two more small explosions followed which they decided to be ammunition that was left in the camper. Lying on the ground, O'Brien looked in all directions for whoever fired the deadly shot. At the entrance of the park he saw a black car as it sped away heading east. It was a Cadillac and he made a mental note of it.

The few seconds that passed seemed like eternity. When it was safe, they stood and looked at the mess that was strewn all around. O'Brien's rental car was still smouldering and the interior completely gutted by the flames. The only way it would be leaving there was on the back of a tow truck.

"Man, did you see how that camper came apart? It was like an aerosol can in a fire," exclaimed Rory.

O'Brien's ears were still ringing from the sound and he shook his head trying to relieve them. The RC's were on their radio calling ahead to their dispatcher.

"This is Constable Burbach. We need immediate assistance out at Moyie Park. There has been an explosion. Send the Fire Department and a couple of tow trucks."

Burbach hung up his radio and walked over to where O'Brien and the others were standing.

"Did you guys happen to see anybody who might have fired that shot?" he asked.

"I didn't see a thing," O'Brien replied. "it all happened too fast. What about you, Hal, Rory? Did you see anything?"

"Nothing."

"It sounded like a high-powered rifle; there's no doubt about that. The son of a bitch could've fired from up there," Burbach said pointing to a clearing on the other side of the highway, "or for that matter from anywhere in the bush. We're going to have to search these areas thoroughly. I'm going to call the dispatcher again and have him send a few more guys, with luck, maybe a couple of K9's."

"Yeah, we better get in touch with our associates as well and let them know what's going on. We are expected back in Fruitmont this evening. I don't think that's going to be the case now," O'Brien responded.

"If you like, I can have our dispatcher call ahead for you," said Burbach.

"Sure thing. Here's Henderson's number," O'Brien said as he handed Burbach the card. "Have him call Art, Ilene, and Thom. They're ahead of us. Once he gets a hold of them, they're going to have to turn around and come back this way."

"You got it, detective."

"Thanks."

O'Brien walked over to where Hal and Rory were standing.

"It looks like we're going to be here for a while. Once the rest of the RC's arrive, we'll help them search, but I don't think we're going to find anything."

"Why is that?" asked Hal.

"I glanced up to the entrance as soon as that shot echoed; I noticed a black car speeding away and heading east. He's not going west anymore," O'Brien responded eerily.

"Why didn't you say something earlier?" asked Rory.

"Cause I want us to catch this maniac and when we do… I know that what I'm about to say could get me in a lot of hot water. I want him DEAD. Don't even look for an excuse if you run into him. Just aim and fire."

"O'Brien, are you sure you mean that? We could lose our licenses."

"Yes, I do, Hal. We won't lose our licenses, not if Henderson has anything to say. He'll cover our asses."

"Are you sure about that?" asked Rory.

"Yep. Remember we have been given authority to use extreme force. And that's exactly what it will go down in the books as."

"I'm all for that," commented Hal.

"You bet," replied Rory.

"Good. Now let's see what kind of assistance we can be to the RC's."

The three walked back to where the RC's were.

"How long until the K9s and extra guys get here?" O'Brien asked.

"They should be here shortly," replied Burbach.


By 6:00 p.m. that night they had searched the entire area where one might have a clear shot at the camper, except, of course, the park entrance. The bomb squad as well as the Crime Scene Investigators finished up and both O'Brien's car and what was left of the truck and camper were loaded up and sent to the impound for further investigation. All that could be used to identify the corpse now was DNA and dental records. As the RC's and other agencies men began to disburse, O'Brien waved and nodded to them as they faded into the early evening.

"What are we waiting for?" asked Rory. "Come on, let's get moving."

"Hold up a minute," O'Brien said. "Grab a flashlight and follow me."

"Where are we going?" asked Hal.

"We're going to walk up both sides of the road to the highway. If whoever was in that vehicle I spotted earlier fired that shot, then up on that road somewhere is a spent shell casing, maybe two," O'Brien replied. "If there is a shell casing, then we'll have the calibre of the gun and perhaps a partial fingerprint."

"What do we need that for? We know it was a 30.06. We know that it was Anvil who fired the shot," Rory mentioned with intent.

"That's all true, Rory; no doubt about it. If we find what we are looking for, it will only benefit us when we fill him with hot lead. Besides I'm sick of this game and I want to be 100% sure that indeed it is Anvil. Some of the things that we have been seeing make me wonder. I don't recall him being that smart or brash."

"It's definitely out of character. Remember though, that he has been in treatment for the past while. We'll never know what might have transpired while he was in care," commented Hal as they walked along the north ditch of the road to the highway.

They finally came to the area where O'Brien saw the vehicle.

"Stop. This looks like the area where I saw that car. Look around for tracks or anything unusual."

The three of them shone their flashlights on the ground. Minutes later, O'Brien spotted a footprint leading off into the bramble.

"Over here," he said waving Hal and Rory over.

"What do you got, O'Brien?"

"A large-size footprint, probably a size twelve."

O'Brien looked closer and found another partial print that lead up to a stump.

"Looks like he used this stump to bead down on the camper. It's in perfect line of where it was parked. There has to be a casing around here somewhere," O'Brien said as he shone his light onto the ground.

"Yeah, unless he picked it up," Rory commented.

"Quit being so negative, Rory," O'Brien began as he looked at Rory. Rory was standing with his mini-mag flashlight stuck in his mouth like a jack-o-lantern.

"You're a nut bar, Rory," O'Brien said as he smiled at Rory's antics shaking his head.

"Just getting into the Halloween spirit, O'Brien. It's not too far away you know."

"Yeah, I know," O'Brien replied.

"Hey guys, check this out. I've found three casings. Nope, make that four," exclaimed Hal.

"What," Rory and O'Brien clamoured in unison.

"He fired four shots man," Hal replied matter-of-factly.

"I only heard one," O'Brien responded as he traipsed over to where Hal was standing.

"Maybe we only thought we heard one. Remember those other smaller explosions when the camper was floating out of the sky. What if they were pot-shots at us?" Hal questioned.

"What a thought! That's probably exactly what they were. Holy," said Rory in awe.

"No doubt. Let me get this straight. The shooter who is probably Anvil leans up against this stump. He aims at the propane tank, or whatever, to cause the explosion. He fires hitting his target. He watches as we dive for cover. He is pissed now because he knows we're all right. The camper is still popping like corn. He figures he knows where we're lying on the ground and in succession, before all the noise of the explosion has dissipated, he fires three more rounds hoping to tag somebody, anybody for that matter," O'Brien replied analytically.

"O'Brien, I bet you're dead on the money with that," Hal said as he thought in contemplation, bringing his hand up to his chin.

"That was one heck of a theoretical account," Rory responded.

"Thanks, no clapping. Just throw money," O'Brien said as he bowed in humour.

Picking up the four spent casings and putting them into an evidence bag, Rory began counting, "One, two, 30.06, four," as he put them into the bag. Hal and O'Brien could only roll their eyes in the back of their heads.

"Why are you so chipper, Rory?" O'Brien asked.

"I love life, O'Brien. Today we could have been dead on more than one occasion, but by God, we are still standing. For that I am grateful. It means I get to live for another day and hopefully for many more to come," he chuckled.

"That's an excellent view, buddy," Hal said.

The three of them walked back to the one rental car they had left and piled in.

"Where do we go from here?" asked Hal.

"To a hotel, James," replied O'Brien.

They decided to stay at a hotel in Moyie called The Double Oaks. It was quite posh and it cost Henderson & Co. $270.00. They figured they deserved a treat; besides, most of the other establishments didn't have any vacancies. The ninety bucks per night per room at the Oaks was quite a sum for most. It was no wonder the other hotels and motels were full.

O'Brien phoned Henderson shortly thereafter to let him know where they were and what had been going on, as well as to have him tell the others where to meet.

"Whereabouts in Moyie?" he asked.

"The Double Oaks Motel."

"The Double Oaks," he blurted out.

"Yeah," O'Brien said as he chuckled.

"That place is going to cost me a fortune. I don't deny you guys deserve it. Enjoy your goddamn stay. I'll let the others know where they can find you. By the way, what's going to be your next course of action?"

"Well, after we regroup and I get another rental, I guess we will split up again. This time, though, we'll concentrate our efforts in and around here for a day or two, keeping our eyes peeled for a black car."

"Black smack," said Henderson. "Do you know how many black cars are out there these days?"

"A lot more than I could ever count," O'Brien responded. "This one, though, is special. You see, Henderson, not only did I notice its colour. I also noticed that it was a 1998 Cadillac Deville."

"That's a little better, O'Brien. Did you tell Hal and Rory about that yet?"

"No. I'm going to wait until we're all together. That way I am assured that they don't all hear something different."

"That's acceptable. I wish you God speed, O'Brien, and stay in touch. If there are any changes of venue make sure you let me know. We will keep the borders locked up tight."

"I hear you. Thanks a lot, Henderson. I'll talk to you soon."

"You bet, O'Brien. Goodnight."

At 8:00 p.m. Hal, Rory, and O'Brien met in the lounge and put back a couple of drinks, something O'Brien hadn't done in years. Tonight however, he really needed some sauce. After a few shots of Tequila and a couple of shooters each, it dawned on them that it had only been one week since Anvil escaped. In that little amount of time, they had seen more crap happen than what they were used to seeing in a regular month. By midnight, they were sauced and O'Brien crawled up to his room. Once the bed stopped spinning, he fell into a drunken slumber.

# Twenty One

O'Brien awoke Saturday to the annoying sound of a phone ringing. It didn't ring like most phones. This one buzzed. Sitting up in bed, his head began to pound causing his forehead to involuntarily frown. Blurry-eyed, he looked towards the desk where the phone sat. The first step he took towards the obnoxious buzzing almost caused him to fall down; his legs were like rubber. *What have I done to myself,* O'Brien thought as he made his way to the telephone.

"Hello," he answered.

"Hi, O'Brien."

It was Tracy.

"Hey, how's it going?" O'Brien asked.

"A lot better for me than for you it sounds like. Are you sick?"

"Oh yeah, I have a hangover big time."

"You tied one on, eh?"

"I guess you could say that. Hal, Rory, and I did put down some sauce last night. I feel like I have the flu… again. Now I know why I haven't guzzled in so long."

"You had good reason to celebrate. Not only are you still alive, everything went according to plan when I attended court to get guardianship of Sharla. We have custody of her until she turns nineteen. Isn't that awesome?" she questioned.

"Yeah, it is kind of neat. I'm glad."

"Oh, I almost forgot, Will told me to tell you that when he attended court in regards to Mr. Buchworth's sentencing on those drug charges you nailed him with, he was sentenced to five years."

"That's excellent. I'm starting to feel better already. What about Sharla's mom? What happened there?"

"I believe she was remanded or something. Will, never mentioned it."

"All right. How are things going back in Ridgeville? Do you have snow yet?" O'Brien asked.

"Not yet, but it's sure getting cold. It will probably snow in the next couple of days. I miss you."

"I miss you, too. Don't worry; this Anvil thing will end in the next little while. We're all getting sick of him. I guess Henderson mentioned to you what happened yesterday?"

"Yes, he did. That is also one of the, reasons, I wanted to talk to you. I'm scared for you, O'Brien."

O'Brien could hear the concern in her voice.

"Ah, don't worry. I think we've got him figured out."

O'Brien was lying through his teeth. They didn't have a clue on what to expect next from Anvil.

"I hope so. I don't want to become a widow."

"Don't worry about that; that'll never happen," O'Brien hoped.

You couldn't be sure in his line of work.

"I wonder how many dead cops have said those exact words to their wives?" she questioned.

"Listen, if it'll make you feel better, I'll promise to wear the vest."

"What good is that? Remember, Ryan was wearing his vest when he was shot."

"I know, but he was killed with a cop-killing bullet. You can't just pick those up anywhere. I don't anticipate that Anvil is equipped like that."

"How do you know for sure?"

"I don't. I can only speculate. Regardless, I will wear the vest from now on. How does that sound? Does that put you at ease a bit?"

"Not really. I'll feel better when you're home and safe."

They continued talking for almost an hour before hanging up and saying their goodbyes.

O'Brien looked at his watch the time was 10:00 a.m. He wondered why Hal and Rory hadn't come by yet, he dialed Hal's room. A disoriented and sick sounding Hal answered.

"Yeah, what is it?"

"It's O'Brien, Hal. How are you feeling?"

"Like a bucket of horse crap. What time is it?"

"A little past ten. What time did you and Rory finish drinking last night?"

"If it's ten now, seven hours ago. We closed down the lounge and then we ordered some off sales and finished upstairs."

"So you guy's drank until three this morning?" O'Brien questioned as he felt his own gut wretch.

"Something like that. Listen, O'Brien, I have to go. I feel like I'm going to puke. Rory and I will pop over in a bit."

"Okay, I'll see you in a bit."

O'Brien had a hot shower to clear his head. He was feeling gross. He had quit drinking at around midnight and feeling the way that he did, he could only imagine that Hal and Rory were feeling a lot worse for wear. O'Brien looked into the bathroom mirror and decided to shave, the first in almost three days.

After he cleaned up, he wandered over to the window and opened the curtain. He looked out onto the street. Parked on the other side was a black car, a 1998 Cadillac Deville. O'Brien couldn't tell if it was the same one he saw, that is until he was able to take a closer look. Bolting out of his room and out onto the street to where the car was parked, he walked to the rear looking it over. Sure enough, it was the same car. He could tell because the plates were gone and when he looked inside through the window, the VIN was also removed.

O'Brien's first thoughts were to open the door, but he couldn't be sure if it was not rigged. Instead, he walked to the rear of it again and looked up to the gas tank. Unsurprisingly the tank was rigged. He noticed a dirty red liquid dripping out of the trunk. He was unsure if it were blood or transmission oil. Not wanting to leave the scene, he pulled Rory's cell phone out of his jacket pocket and called again to Hal's room.

"Hey Hal, you and Rory better get your backsides out here. I'm across the street from the Motel. We have a big problem," O'Brien said with conviction.

"I'm on my way, O'Brien."

Hal hung up the telephone. Five minutes later the three of them were standing in the street looking over the black Cadillac.

"That's definitely blood dripping out of the trunk," Rory said as he touched some and rubbed his fingertips together. "Think we should pop open the trunk and have a quick look see?" he asked.

"No way. We can't be sure if popping open the trunk won't cause it to explode. We have to get in touch with the bomb squad again," Hal commented as he began dialling the RC's.

"Hello, this is Detective Hal Beady from Henderson & Co."

"Hello, Detective. What can I do for you?"

"We found a 1998 black Cadillac Deville across from the Double Oaks…it's rigged to explode. There also appears to be some blood dripping out of the trunk. Umm… can you send the bomb squad?"

"Most definitely, detective, I'm dispatching them right now."

"Thanks a lot. We'll keep everybody a safe distance away from the vehicle. Is there anything you want us to do until the squad gets here?" Hal asked.

"Can you read off the plate number to me?"

"Sorry, the plates are gone and so is the VIN."

"I guess keep people away from that side of the street. Cordon off the perimeter. The bomb squad will take it from there when they arrive."

"Consider it done," said Hal as he shut off his cell.

"The RC's Bomb Squad will be here shortly. We have to keep everybody clear of the area. I think our best bet is to cordon off this entire side of the street."

"No difference of opinion here," O'Brien commented. By the time they cleared the street of people who began to swarm, the RC's bomb squad showed up followed a few minutes later by two RC Constables.

"What do we have?" O'Brien questioned the leader of the bomb squad, whose name coincidentally was Captain T. Flint.

"Just something that looked like a bomb," he said as he showed O'Brien the contraption. "It's a plastic box with a couple of wires. We have checked out the vehicle. It's safe, but what's in the trunk is awful."

O'Brien walked over to the car and glanced into the trunk. The body inside was mutilated to such a degree it was hard to decipher if it was male or female. Too many bullet holes riddled the corpse.

"Oh, my God. Is it a man or a woman?" O'Brien looked over to Flint.

"Your guess is as good as mine, detective. Undo the pants and take a look," Flint said as he joked with black humour. "Looks like he or she was used for target practice, doesn't it?"

O'Brien looked again at the messed up corpse. It did look as though it had been used for target practice. Each hole represented a different distance. At least that is what the entrance holes were telling him. Some were smaller and some were bigger. Meaning a distance change took place each time the victim was shot. He counted nine holes or one might say entrance wounds. The one to the victim's head tore off the scalp, which caused the victim's face to cave in making it impossible to know if it were male or female by the face alone.

"Yeah, no kidding," O'Brien replied as Rory and Hal came over.

"What do you mean target practice?" Rory looked inside.

At that point, he turned green jumped back and puked.

"Oh my God. That's the sickest thing I've ever seen!" he exclaimed between gasps of air.

Hal was standing next to O'Brien looking in awe.

"We have to take care of this maniac soon. Who knows what he's going pull on us next."

"I know," O'Brien said as he closed the trunk. "Are you okay, Rory?" he asked half-chuckling.

"No. That was nauseating. I hope I never see anything like that again. What are we up against?"

"We're up against the same maniac who we took down in the summer, Rory. He's a bit more sadistic now, though," O'Brien half-smiled.

"A bit?" questioned Hal. "What he did to that victim is the most brutal thing I've seen."

"It is brutal; still we have to keep our wits. Somehow, he has been able to tail us. What we have to do is find out how. Once we have that figured out, we can put an end to all of this. I'm thinking he has a police scanner and has been keeping tabs on us that way. I say we talk it over with the RCMP and come up with a bullshit plan with them to send him into an ambush of sorts. What do you guys think of that?" O'Brien asked.

"It's certainly worth a try. I say we wait for the rest of the crew though. It'll be more convincing if we're all together. He probably knows that they're on their way by now. If we were to do something rash without the others it might make alarm bells go off in his head. I do think that is what our next course of action should be. I mean, it's obvious he's either watching us from afar or he's listening in on conversations we've been having with the RC's," replied Hal.

"What I don't understand," began Rory, "is that we haven't contacted the RC's by radio. We've always called them by cell phone. How do you guys figure he's scanning our conversations when we're not using a radio?"

"That's a fair question, Rory and I'll tell you how. We do call them with our cells, but they dispatch from the radio," O'Brien said as he chuckled and shook his head.

"Oh yeah, right…sorry O'Brien, I'm still feeling drunk from last night. I should have realised that. I feel like an idiot."

"Don't worry about it, Rory. I knew the only reason you'd ask a question like that was because you're still feeling all that booze in your system," O'Brien replied.

The three of them converged on the sidewalk and watched as Captain Flint and his crew headed out of town. The two RC's stayed behind. They pulled up behind the black Cadillac and turned on their hazard lights. Looking closely, O'Brien recognised Constable Riley. As he looked in their direction, O'Brien waved and smiled.

"Hey look, it's that kid Riley from the rest stop incident," O'Brien said nudging Rory.

The kid stepped out of his car and hollered over to O'Brien.

"Hey detectives, how's it going? Nice to see you again."

O'Brien, Hal, and Rory walked over to where Riley was parked.

"Yeah nice to see you, too. How's it hanging?" asked Rory.

"I can't tie it in a bow if that's what you mean, but it's hanging," came the kid's reply.

O'Brien looked at the kid in admiration and punched him in the shoulder.

"How have you been, Riley?"

"Not bad, O'Brien; not bad at all. A hell of a mess here too, huh?"

"It sure is. Have you had a chance to look at the body?" Hal asked.

"I prefer not to. Flint filled us in. I don't think I need to see it. Besides, the Coroner will be here any time now. He's coming in from Creston because our Coroner in Cranbrook is attending a convention out of the area."

"What are you guys going do with the car?" O'Brien questioned with curiosity.

"It'll be towed, of course, to an impound yard and the lab guys will go through it. It will probably be transported with the body in it to the Creston detachment. The Coroner has been called to simply verify it is a corpse. Once he's done that, then off we'll cart it."

"Do you have a problem with us going through it briefly?"

"Not at all, O'Brien. Go for it."

"Thanks. The reason I asked was because a lot of the time the RC's aren't too appreciative if we do that before them."

"You won't have that problem with me, O'Brien. As far as I am concerned, the RCMP and detective agencies such as yours should always co-operate on cases like this. Besides, if you think about it, this is truly your case anyway. I think our role should only be for backup."

O'Brien was beginning to like the kid more every time they met. He was certainly right that they should all co-operate. Sometimes though, that didn't always happen.

"Thanks a lot, Riley. That was well put."

Riley nodded and smiled.

O'Brien walked over to the driver side door and after slipping on a pair of latex gloves, he opened the door. The others followed suit and they began looking for evidence that could put Anvil in the vehicle. O'Brien was still not 100% sure, although if he had to make a decision on whether or not it was Anvil, at that moment he would have said yes. They found a couple of gum wrappers and a book of matches with the front cover ripped off, probably so they couldn't be identified. In the back seat, Hal came across a piece of paper with the address of the Double Oaks printed on it.

"Check this out, O'Brien," he said as he handed O'Brien the piece of paper.

"I wonder if that's Anvil's handwriting or not?" O'Brien asked as he looked at the piece of paper.

"We can certainly find out. Where are those journals that Thom and Ilene found?" questioned Hal.

"They were in the trunk of my rental, I think. They're probably toast. Dumb luck or what, eh?" O'Brien replied.

"No kidding," said Rory. "I'd hang on to it though. I'm sure if it comes down to it, we can get another sample of his handwriting."

"Oh, I plan on holding on to it. It's evidence, Rory."

O'Brien put the piece of paper into his pocket. The car, they knew, would be dusted for prints at the police impound and they would have direct access to any that were found.

"I'd say she's pretty clean guys. Let's leave the rest up to the RCMP," O'Brien said as he exited the car.

"Did you find anything interesting, O'Brien?" asked Riley.

"Not really. A book of matches, some gum wrappers; that's about it."

"Maybe the lab guys will come up with something better," he replied.

"Let's hope so. Thanks for letting us have a peek, Riley. We'll probably be seeing you around. Come on guys, let's get some coffee."

O'Brien looked at Hal and Rory and waved to Riley at the same time. They walked back to the motel and headed into the coffee shop.

"Time sure flies when you're having fun," said Rory as he looked up at the clock on the wall. It was going onto 2:00

p.m. "When do you suppose Art, Ilene, and Thom will get here?"

"I would expect in the next few hours. They'll probably get here between four and five," O'Brien replied.

They ordered some coffees and settled down from all the morning's activities. O'Brien mentioned to them that he was the proud guardian of a sixteen-year-old girl.

"You guys did win, huh?" asked Rory. "That's cool. I'm glad for you, O'Brien."

O'Brien smiled and nodded his head. He was glad too.

"How do you suppose the boys feel about it?" questioned Hal. "I can picture them torturing the poor thing with snakes and such."

O'Brien too visualised it.

"She's a tough kid. Could turn out she's going to torture them."

O'Brien took a swig of coffee.

"I know this much," O'Brien started as he put his coffee down, "things at home will never be the same. I mean in a good way, of course. Sharla is a nice kid. She has a good head on her shoulders, too. I hope Tracy and I can provide her with the parenting and direction the kid deserves. She has lived in back alleys and dumpsters, not to mention the pigsty that she called home for too long. She deserves better," O'Brien said with parental authority.

"Here, here, O'Brien."

Finishing their coffees, they headed back outside. They decided to do a quick tour of the little town and maybe come up with a lead on where their friend might be. The coroner, they noticed, was pulling up to the scene and they openly walked over and introduced themselves.

"Pleased to meet you. I'm Dr. Relkoff."

O'Brien watched as he opened the trunk. He bent over to get a better look of the corpse inside.

"What we got here is a mess. He's male, I can tell you that. Age and that sort of thing are unknown for now. I am going have to do a post-mortem examination on what is left. One thing I do know for sure is the wound to the head is what killed him. Judging by the wounds, the shot to his head is the freshest. The poor guy was still living up to that point."

"How do you know that?" O'Brien asked.

"The other wounds didn't hit any vitals. They are just flesh wounds. Each was from a different yardage, too. I'm betting the furthest was 300 yards away, all the way down to… I'm guessing by the head wound, 10 yards, or thirty feet, if you like. I'll have a better idea once the examination has taken place," he said as he closed the trunk.

He walked back to his van and grabbed a business card.

"Are you guys in charge here or is the RCMP?"

Dr. Relkoff scratched his head.

"Ah, it doesn't matter either way. Here's my card. If you want more information on this guy, call me up, say Wednesday next week. I'll have a better idea on who he is and if what I've told you comes out in the wash."

O'Brien reached over and accepted the card.

"Thanks," he said as the coroner entered his van and pulled away.

"Come on guys, let's take a quick tour of town. Maybe by the time we get back the others will be here and we can plan out our next course of action."

The three of them drove around town for an hour when Hal spotted Thom's car approaching from the east. Thom didn't notice he was being tailed until he pulled up to the Double Oaks. O'Brien, Hal, and Rory watched as he pulled up to the curb shut his engine off and yawned. Then he stepped out and stretched.

"Welcome to the Double Oaks," O'Brien blurted at him through the open car window.

"Hey, O'Brien. You guys have had some pretty interesting stuff happen, eh?" he asked.

"You bet."

O'Brien exited the car. Hal and Rory stepped out at the same time and they walked over to Thom.

"Come on, let's get you a room. Looks like you could use a rest."

"What? You're going get another room here?"

"What's the matter with that?"

"One word, O'Brien. Henderson."

"Don't worry. He knows we are here. Come on."

"No problem. Just let me grab my bag."

After O'Brien fixed Thom up with a room, he booked two more for Ilene and Art.

"This is going to cost Henderson a mint," Thom smiled.

"About a grand when it's all said and done."

They walked Thom to his room. Thom unlocked the door and they stepped in.

"Man, nice place. And you're sure Henderson is cool with it?"

"Oh yeah. I talked to him yesterday. Besides, there are no other vacancies. We checked it out yesterday when we arrived."

"Yesterday was quite a bang, I hear," he said sarcastically.

"It was. This morning was pretty interesting too."

"Oh," he asked, "what happened?"

O'Brien explained to him what had taken place and how the victim was riddled with bullets.

"Unbelievable. We have to stop this guy. Man, I can't believe it."

Thom shook his head.

"Yeah, we didn't believe it either," O'Brien replied.

Thom sat on his bed still shaking his head.

"Pretty sick if you ask me. I can't wait to train my sights on him."

"None of us can," said Rory.

They took their conversation back downstairs to the restaurant after Thom settled and seated themselves to a table for six. O'Brien looked at his watch it was almost six bells.

"I guess Art and Ilene should be here in the next few minutes. Let's order some food. I'm getting my appetite back finally."

"Good idea."

Hal raised his hand to signal to the waitress to come over.

"Good evening. My name is Corrine and I'll be your waitress this evening."

She set their menus on the table.

"Today's special is New England Clam Chowder with Caesar Salad and a dinner bun. I'll be back shortly to take your order."

"Thanks," they said in unison as she pranced off.

"What a little cutie," said Thom.

The remark caused all of them to smirk. O'Brien looked at him and shook his head. It was just like Thom to be thinking with his manhood even under those circumstances.

O'Brien picked up the menu that was in front of him and after briefly reading it, decided to go with his all-time favourite standby, which, of course, was a steak sandwich and fries. O'Brien closed the menu and set it down.

"Already made up your mind, O'Brien?" asked Thom.

"Yeah. I'm going with the steak switch and fries. What have you decided?"

"I think I'd like a Corrine and a side order of thighs," he said softly below his breath as not to be heard too far away. "I'm only kidding. I think I'll go with the steak switch as well."

"Hal, Rory what are guys in for?"

"I think I'll take the special. I haven't had clam chowder in eons," replied Hal.

"Rory, how about you. What are you going to have?"

"I don't know, O'Brien. Every now and then when I think of food I feel queasy. I think I'm coming down with the flu. All this driving around and the change of weather is taking a toll on me. Think about it. We've pretty much stayed in a different hotel or motel and sometimes even in different provinces every night since this whole charade began."

"I think that's what's left of a hangover talking," replied Hal. "Have a big bowl of soup. It'll fix you right up."

"I don't know about soup, but maybe something."

Rory opened his menu again. Reading down the menu, he decided to go with the barbecued chicken, garden green salad and pasta.

"I think once we're done here we better find out where Art and Ilene are. I thought they would have been here by now. I am a little bit concerned. I hope there wasn't a problem," O'Brien stated.

"You worry too much sometimes, O'Brien. They'll be here. Relax."

"You're probably right, Thom. I'm just getting anxious to get on with it. We're not going to be able to do much tonight, but I would like us to have a plan together for first thing tomorrow. I know it's Sunday and all and we're all a little edgy and tired, but the sooner we put this case to bed the sooner we can get on with our lives."

"No kidding. Won't that be nice?" Thom replied.

They all nodded.

Finishing dinner, they ordered some coffee, then, headed to their rooms. It was 9:00 p.m. and still no sign of Art and Ilene. Lying on the bed, O'Brien decided that if he hadn't heard from them by 11:00 p.m., he would call ahead. Switching on the television he did some channel surfing. The media had managed to get hold of the two deaths in Moyie and a picture of Anvil. They threw a couple of different disguises on to his face and warned everybody to stay clear of him. If someone sees him, they are to contact the CSIS at their toll free number or the FBI at theirs.

*Great, now we will have a circus,* O'Brian thought. A few minutes later, there was a knock at his door.

"Coming," he said as he sat up and walked to the door.

He was pleased to see the tired eyes of Art and Ilene.

"I'm glad you're here. I was beginning to worry. Come on in. Have you heard what's been going on?"

"It's all over the radio. You would think in cases like this, the media would give us a chance to come up with some facts before announcing it to the bloody world," said Ilene. "How is everybody?" she asked, "did anyone get hurt?"

"No, we were lucky. If it's all over the radio you must've heard how the truck and camper were rigged?" O'Brien questioned.

"Oh yeah. We heard, but from Henderson first then the radio. We stopped off at the scene on our way. That's what took us so long. We knew nothing of the guy you found this morning, though. That we heard straight from the newscast on the radio," said Art.

"That figures. I saw a quick news flash myself. Listen, I got you both rooms. If you're tired, you're quite welcome to go crash. I did want to talk to everybody before tomorrow. Nevertheless, we can do that in the morning at breakfast. I imagine Thom might still be awake. He's in room thirty-seven if you want to stop off and say hi. As for Hal and Rory, I doubt it. We tied one on last night. In other words, I wouldn't be hurt if you did. I think that tomorrow we are going to put a plan together and have it in place for Monday. What do you say?"

"Sounds good. What time should we meet in the ante meridiem?" asked Art.

"I don't know. How's ten?"

"Good enough. At the restaurant, then?" questioned Ilene.

"You bet."

O'Brien handed them their room keys.

"Excellent. We'll see you in the morning, O'Brien. Goodnight."

"G'night and try not to get too sauced," O'Brien retorted as Art and Ilene walked toward the door.

"You don't have to worry about that, O'Brien," replied Ilene. "All I want is a bite to eat, a hot bath and a nice warm bed."

"I don't know about that," started Art. "I could use a drink. Maybe I'll try and twist Thom's arm to come and have a drink with me."

"You won't have to twist too hard. I'm sure he'll be glad to accompany you," O'Brien commented as they headed out of his room.

# Twenty Two

On Sunday October 21, the weather in the East Kootenay
area was starting to turn. A fog hung over the valley in Moyie
that Sunday like steam from hot rocks of a sauna. The
vehicles that were parked along the street as well as in the
many driveways were coated with thin sheets of ice. It was a
cold, grey morning. O'Brien looked at his Timex; it was 8:00
a.m. He had two hours to kill before meeting with the rest of
the crew. He wanted to curl back up in the big bed and wait
for the sun to shine. Instead, he wandered downstairs to the
coffee shop and ordered a large cup of black plasma.

Holding the cup in his cold hands, he inhaled the aroma
and his mind raced with the pleasantries of home. Although
he knew things would be different with the addition of Sharla
as a permanent presence, he longed to be there, back home,
watching his own television in the company of Tracy and the
kids. Taking a sip he smiled and nodded his head, *I'll be
home soon,* he thought to himself.

Finishing the coffee, O'Brien made his way back to his
room. On a whim, he decided to phone up the RCMP
detachment in Cranbrook. To ask where, his rental car was
taken. So that he could retrieve Anvil's journals that were in
the trunk. O'Brien dialed their number it rang once then
twice, then there was some static and it rang again before
someone answered.

"Hello. Is this the RCMP?"

"Yes, it is. Can I help you?"

There was something about the voice that sounded
familiar.

"Yeah, is Constable Burbach in?" O'Brien questioned.

"Sorry," came the reply. "Burbach is off duty today. He'll
be returning next week. Is there something I can help you
with?"

"What about Constable Fell? Is he nearby?"

"Sorry, Neither Fell or Burbach is on duty."

There was some more static on the line and then the voice came back on.

"However, Constable Miller is on duty."

The line went dead. Quickly, O'Brien dialed the number again. On the second ring it was picked up.

"Good morning, this is the RCMP. Constable Burbach here, how may I help you?"

"Constable Burbach, is that you?" O'Brien questioned to be sure.

"Yes, it is. Who is this?"

"O'Brien, Detective O'Brien."

"Hey O'Brien, how are you this morning?" Burbach asked.

"For starters, I just phoned your number and some guy said neither you nor Fell was on duty today. I think it might have been Brentwood. He somehow managed to intercept the call. I figure if we can put a trace on where it was intercepted we might be able to figure out where he is," O'Brien replied with anxiousness.

"You bet, O'Brien. You're still at the Double Oaks, room thirty-one?"

"Yes, I am. I'll wait to hear from you. Thanks a lot, Burbach."

"No problem, O'Brien. Expect to hear from me in less than an hour."

"Thanks again," O'Brien said as he hung up the phone.

Finding out where the call had been intercepted was top priority. O'Brien sat near the phone waiting with anticipation. He hated the waiting game. He couldn't stand it. Looking at his watch, he realised it had been less than ten minutes.

"Come on, phone already, would you," he said to himself.

Minutes dragged on and then finally the phone rang. O'Brien quickly picked it up.

"O'Brien, we have a trace on where the interception occurred. It was intercepted at room twelve at the Double Oaks. I've already dispatched a car to your locale."

"Thanks, Burbach. I'm heading down there right now," O'Brien said as he hung up the phone.

He darted out of his room, down the flight of stairs knocking over a hotel cart and hurting his knee. Continuing on to room twelve and without knocking he kicked the door open. With his gun in hand, he knelt on his good knee and scanned the room.

"Police. Come out," he hollered.

There was screaming in the hallway and people running. Standing O'Brien peered around a corner and looked in the bathroom and the closet, but no one remained. At that moment, Thom came bursting in followed by the others.

"What's going on, O'Brien? Christ, you've scared the entire motel awake."

Thom's pistol was drawn.

"Our friend has been staying here. He somehow managed to intercept a call I made this morning. Can you believe that? He was right under our noses. Hal go and find out to whom this room was rented and if anyone has seen that person leave in the last twenty minutes."

"I'm on it, O'Brien."

"The rest of us are going to have to block off all exits and sweep this room clean. The RC's will be here shortly. They have already been dispatched."

The five of them split-up, Rory, Art, and Ilene headed for the exits while Thom and O'Brien began sweeping through the room. It didn't appear as though anybody had slept in the bed. There was an indent on the rug where it looked like someone might have been lying at one point.

"Check it out, Thom." O'Brien pointed at the impression.

"Looks like whoever was in this room decided to sleep on the floor rather than the bed. Weird," Thom replied.

Things were about to get even weirder when O'Brien entered the bathroom and began looking around. On the wall he spotted some writing, but only because of the way the light was coming through the obscured glass window. It wasn't in ink or pencil. In fact, had the light not been shining on the wall, he would never have been seen it.

Someone had written on a piece of paper and they pushed hard enough to cause what was on the paper to make an impression of the words on the wall. It was what was written that made O'Brien's skin crawl and fear for the safety of Tracy and his kids.

'The days in Ridgeville are getting longer. Winter is getting close. You may get closer, but you'll never be close. AB.'

To see if he was correct, O'Brien took a pen and a piece of paper from his pocket notebook. He put it up against the wall and began to write 'Anvil Brentwood is a prick'. Sure enough, it left an impression of an exact copy of what he had written on the paper. O'Brien called over to Thom.

"Thom, you have to see this," O'Brien said as he waved him into the bathroom.

"What've you got?"

"You can't see that?"

"See what?"

"Hang on a second. You have to be standing over this way a bit," O'Brien said as he pushed Thom along. "Can you see it now?"

"The writing? Yeah I can, but only when the light hits it."

He walked over to it and began to read it aloud.

"'The days in Ridgeville are getting longer. Winter is getting close. You may get closer, but you'll never be close. AB.'

Holy, O'Brien, how does he know anything about Ridgeville?"

"I haven't a clue," O'Brien shrugged.

"We better get on the phone and get someone down there to keep an eye on Tracy and the kids," Thom exclaimed as he reached for his cell and handed it to O'Brien.

"They already are and have been since this whole thing started. Besides, I don't think he's going there. Notice the way that little piece of poetry reads —you may get closer, but you'll never be close. That reads to me like he's daring me to head that way or he expects me to head that way and that I might be closer to where he is, but I won't be close."

Thom was looking at O'Brien with a 'what in God's creation are you talking about' look.

"I know it sounds absolutely ridiculous, but think about it for a minute."

"I have. It still makes no sense," replied Thom.

"Maybe if I explain it this way," O'Brien started. "He presumes that if I read this, I'll head back to Ridgeville. He knows sooner or later one of us would have found this little masterpiece and we'd head to Ridgeville in a panic. Meanwhile, he heads somewhere else. We're all freaking out that he is in Ridgeville, and we've started concentrating on that area alone and he's back east or up north somewhere. Do you get the picture now?"

Thom looked at O'Brien, raised a brow, and nodded. "I get it now. You think this is a ploy to get us to head back west. It makes sense. He's been fooling us for this long I guess he could be thinking like that."

"Exactly," O'Brien said. "Do you have your knife handy?"

"What for?" Thom asked.

"To cut this out of the wall. It's evidence and we can have the handwriting experts take a look at it if we need to."

Thom reached into his boot and removed the lock-blade knife he always carried there.

O'Brien slipped on a pair of gloves, walked up to the wall and etched around the writing. Thom's knife cut the drywall better than a drywall knife would. The piece popped out perfectly. O'Brien put it on the bathroom vanity and handed Thom back his knife.

"You wouldn't happen to have any evidence bags handy, would you?"

"In the car I do. Do you want me to grab a couple?"

"Thanks, Thom. That'd be great."

"No problem, O'Brien. I'll be back in a minute."

As Thom exited into the hallway, O'Brien read the poem over for a third time. He questioned his intuition that he first had that Anvil wasn't heading anywhere near Ridgeville. What if he was? There it was, one of those 'what ifs' that O'Brien hated so much. Stepping out of the bathroom, he looked around the room again. He still couldn't believe that, Anvil had been there. He wondered why they hadn't seen him. Maybe they had. They just didn't know it at the time. It brought O'Brien back to a comment Hal made awhile back that Anvil was like the invisible man. It was then that Thom came back with the bags.

"Here you go, O'Brien," he said as he handed O'Brien the bags.

"Thanks, Thom."

O'Brien put one of the bags into his pocket then stuffed the drywall piece into the other.

"Any sign of the RC's yet, Thom?" O'Brien asked as he walked out of the bathroom.

"Not yet."

"Did you see Hal anywhere?"

"Yeah, he's still talking it up with the manager. He said he'd be along shortly."

"How about getting on your cell phone and see if we can get an RC telephone technician over here. They should have been here by now. We're going to have to know what box Anvil might have used to jumper out my call and what kind of equipment he used. If he bought it locally between here and Cranbrook, we might get another lead on him. I'm going to head over to the front desk. You know the procedure. Don't let anyone in here except cops."

"You bet, O'Brien. I'll get a hold of the technicians right now."

O'Brien nodded and exited the room. He hadn't walked ten feet when Hal came around the corridor.

"The guy who rented room twelve was a guy by the name of Jack Wheeler. I did a check on the name. There is no one listed in the BC directory or anyone with that name that has so much as a parking ticket. No one even knows what Mr. Wheeler looks like. Apparently, he rented the room with his Visa and received the key from the electronic night auditor. The room was paid in full right up until today. He rented the room Thursday. The hotel cleaning staff said that every time they came to Mr. Wheeler's room, it looked as if no one had even been there. They said the bed was always made and that there was never any sign that anyone even used the toilet or shower. I don't know what to make of it."

"That's because he didn't sleep in the bed and he probably didn't shower," O'Brien replied.

"What do you mean, O'Brien?"

"We found a spot on the rug that looks like someone was using it as their bed."

"He's that screwed up that he doesn't sleep in a bed?" Hal questioned quizzically.

"I guess so," O'Brien said as he tossed his hands up in the air, "probably because of all those years he spent in Matsqui before we were introduced to him this past summer. Maybe he slept on the floor rather than the flea-infested mattress. Who knows?"

"Things that make you go hmmm, eh O'Brien?"

"Yeah, things that make you go hmmm," O'Brien replied.

He and Hal turned and walked back to room twelve. Thom called the technicians, and because it was Sunday was told it would take a good three or four more hours, before they could expect one.

"Three or four hours, is better than tomorrow," O'Brien said. "We'll wait."

Moments later, two RCMP Officers showed up. They informed O'Brien that a few members of the CSIS were on their way. When O'Brien questioned why, they stated it had something to do with the murder of Professor Linquist back in Toronto. O'Brien thought, *Great, now we'll have to deal with them and their antics.* Although O'Brien preferred Canadian Secret Intelligence Service over the FBI, he knew either one could throw a monkey wrench into the work that they had so far conducted.

"Well then," O'Brien started, "I guess you guys won't mind if we take off? We have a few other leads to follow," O'Brien said.

"Not at all," said the RC's. "We're only here until the CSIS gets here anyway. They said once they get here, they'll be taking over this part of the investigation."

"What part is that?" O'Brien asked.

"I couldn't tell you, detective, that's just what they said." replied the one RC as he shrugged his shoulders.

O'Brien looked over to Hal and Thom and said, "Come on, let's G.T.H out of here."

They rounded up the rest of the crew and headed to the restaurant. They selected a quiet table near the back and started hashing over a plan to get to Anvil before the CSIS or FBI managed. This was their collar and they were going to get it.

"What do you suppose this Linquist fellow has to do with it? He's not even breathing anymore. Didn't our friend Anvil put a bullet in his head?" asked Thom.

"We presumed it was Anvil 'cause that's the name he boarded the plane with to Edmonton. It might not have been Anvil at all who killed the Professor and that's why the CSIS want him, so they can question him on where he might have picked up the Professor's ID" O'Brien replied. "Or maybe it was Anvil and he's holding some vital information that the CSIS wants. Who knows for sure what's going on there?"

"This whole thing is turning into a mess. If the CSIS pulls rank on us and takes over this case, I'll freak," Rory retorted.

"Let's not give them the chance. I suggest we contact Henderson. Run all this by him, put together all the evidence we've come up with and ship it to him via courier. If it's not in our hands, the CSIS can't take it away without a bit of a fight. Dr. Relkoff said he would talk to us on Wednesday with more information on that John Doe who bled through the trunk of that Cadillac. I know that the CSIS will probably want to get that information first. Maybe we'll get lucky and we'll get to it before they do."

They all agreed. O'Brien contacted Henderson who was all for the idea.

Then they did the only thing they could and that was head to Creston. O'Brien didn't know what would come of it all, but Creston was where Dr. Relkoff practised and he was the only one who could give them the information on who the John Doe was. How much it really mattered remained to be seen. O'Brien knew that if Anvil were anywhere in the Moyie area, once the CSIS arrived they too would be watching for him. O'Brien's instincts told him that Anvil had vacated the area shortly after intercepting his call. What direction he might be going was anybody's guess.

Until they got more information on who the last victim had been, and where he was from, they were at a stalemate, unless by some coincidence Anvil emerged from the bush somewhere between Moyie and Creston. Other than that, O'Brien was confident that Anvil was long gone. O'Brien thought back to the writing he had found on the wall, 'you may get closer, but you'll never be close'. O'Brien knew that Anvil's whereabouts were somehow hiding in those words.

He repeated them over and over again in his mind. He sat on the passenger side of Thom's rental car watching the scenery go by as they drove west to Creston. *What was Anvil trying to say in those words? Was he even trying to say anything?* O'Brien thought about the possibility that Anvil would head over to the Slocolm Valley area where they captured him that past summer. He couldn't see it, but it was something they would have to check out in the days to come.

They arrived in Creston before dark that Sunday evening and grabbed rooms at the first motel they found. It was called The Cherry Orchard. It wasn't nearly as nice as the Double Oaks, but the price would keep Henderson at bay.

## Twenty Three

The week of Monday, October 22, would turn out to be more challenging than the previous week. O'Brien made contact with Dr. Relkoff early that morning to check on the progress he might have had so far in identifying the person who was discovered in Moyie.

"To tell you the truth, detective. I haven't come up with anything solid. I cannot even find any medical records on this person. It's as though he doesn't even exist. There are a couple of other tests I'm going to run, but I can't get to those until Tuesday. His fingerprints aren't in any database. Therefore, I can tell you for sure that he hasn't been charged with any criminal offences nor does he belong to any government agencies, none that are admitting it, at least. I will know more once I complete the remaining tests. I suggest you get back to me, say, early tomorrow evening."

"Sure thing, Doc. What would be an appropriate time?"

"I speculate around 5:00 p.m., if that works for you?"

"All right. By the way, Doc, I'm sorry for calling earlier then we discussed. It's just that we are in Creston now and I figured what the heck."

"No need to explain, detective. Do call back tomorrow night and perhaps things will have changed."

"Thanks, Doc. I'll talk to you then."

O'Brien sat in silence looking out the window. For October, Creston was sure a pretty place. The town was covered in a light dusting of snow. This made the many orchards and pasturelands that surrounded the town sparkle in the morning sun. It wasn't nearly as cold as it had been in Moyie, but you could tell all the same that winter was on its way.

He decided to offer the crew a day of R and R. They'd flown from one province to the next and so on over the past days that the thought of driving anywhere made O'Brien feel sick to his stomach. God how he wanted this manhunt to end, at one point he was seriously considered turning the entire investigation over to the CSIS. He already presumed that once the CSIS caught up with them, they would pull rank and request all the evidence that they came up with. O'Brien soon changed his tune when he decided that they had all come this far.

"No use giving it up now," O'Brien said to himself. He stood, stretched, and walked outside.

The cool crisp morning air felt good to O'Brien as he walked from room to room rousing the crew.

"Rise and shine," he said at each of their doors.

O'Brien told them that once they pulled their asses out of bed, there was a nice diner down the street called The Main Street Diner, and that they should congregate there to discuss the day's activities.

It was a beautiful morning. The diner was only two blocks away and O'Brien decided to walk the distance. The thought of driving even that far didn't sit well. It was a good thing he walked. What happened next left him with no choice but run back to the Motel, and take Thom's car.

He was walking down a hill that led to the downtown core. He was close enough to the diner that he could even read the sign. When a brown Chevy 4x4 van pulled up on the other side of the street. It slowed down to a crawl. At first O'Brien thought that the driver was slowing down to ask for directions. He looked over to the van and watched as the driver raised his left hand and gave him the finger and then sped off, but not before O'Brien got a good look. The driver was none other than Anvil Brentwood! O'Brien turned and ran back to the motel busting in on Thom as he brushed his teeth.

"What the hell is going on, O'Brien?" he asked in awe as O'Brien grabbed the keys from the bed stand.

"It's Anvil. He's driving west in a brown Chevy 4x4 van. The SOB just gave me the finger!" O'Brien exclaimed as he bolted out of Thom's room and over to the car. With no time to waste, he ripped out of the parking lot heading west. Three or four minutes had passed and O'Brien knew that meant Anvil had a good head start. Which direction he decided to head was anyone's guess. O'Brien was betting he continued west. The look on Anvil's face at that brief moment on the street when their eyes locked was the look of fooled you again, didn't I?

O'Brien continued due west until he came to the bottom side of the Creston cut-off. He saw nothing. Turning around, he pulled into a Husky station that was off the main highway. He asked if anyone had seen a brown Chevy 4x4 van scooting by. No one had. Using the phone on the counter, O'Brien dialled Thom. The phone rang only once before he answered.

"Hello, Thom here."

"Thom, this is O'Brien. Listen, I am at the bottom of the Creston cut-off. I'm not sure if Anvil went this way or not. I'm at a Husky station and no one here saw a brown van go by. I am still going to head over the top. I'll phone you from Salmo. I want you guys to separate. Send someone to Balfour, someone down to Rykerts Border crossing. You know, much like the same plan we had before. If I don't contact you in, say, two and a half hours, whoever is left in Creston has to follow this way 'cause it will mean I didn't make it to Salmo. If it turns out that I head towards the Pend'd'Oreille, I'll leave something along the road to let you all know that I went that way. The spare tire or something. We're getting close, buddy; we're getting close," O'Brien exclaimed.

"I'll probably be the only one left here. Seems someone stole my car. If I don't hear from you in two and a half hours I guess it'll be me who heads that way. And you, you silly bastard with no cell phone. What are you going to do if he causes you grief and you need backup?"

"That's what the time frame is for. If you don't hear from me in that allotted time then something has either gone wrong or I headed south. Have to go, Thom, we're wasting time. Oh yeah, do me a favour and grab my stuff out of my room. Thanks, Thom. I'll talk to you soon," O'Brien said as he hung up the phone.

He filled the car up with gas and grabbed a couple of coffees. Before he headed west to Salmo, he set the odometer to zero. Back at the motel, Thom dispatched the crew and then began to find a rental. His only request was it had to be a 4x4. The first agency that he called up was in the suburb of Erickson.

"Sorry sir, we haven't any 4x4 rental's left. The last one went out yesterday afternoon. It's not due back for a week."

"Is there another agency nearby that might have 4x4 rentals?"

"You might try Wesley's 4x4 Rentals. As the name suggests, he specialises in four wheel drive vehicles exclusively," she replied snobbishly.

Being the smart-ass that he was and not liking the tone the woman took with him, Thom said, "And you might try some Midol. Thanks for your time."

He hung up the phone and looked in the yellow pages for Wesley's. Finding the number, he dialled.

"Wesley's, what can I do you for you today?" the pleasant voice of an old man responded.

"Hello, I'm looking for an SUV or any kind of 4x4. I was hoping you'd be able to set me up," replied Thom.

"It depends. What are you looking for? I have one Chevy 4x4 van left, a couple of Subaru's, an older Jeep Cherokee, a couple of half tons, three quarter tons, whatever your preference. I'm sure I have something that suits your fancy."

"Where are you located?"

"Down near the Little John campground. Do you know where that's at?" the old guy questioned.

"Sure do. I'll be there in say half an hour," replied Thom as he hung up the phone. Not having any wheels and not wanting to call a cab, he headed outside and began to walk the short distance to the campground and Wesley's 4x4 Rentals. The cool fresh air and bright sun felt good as he strolled along. His mind racing with something the old guy said that he had 'one Chevy 4x4 van left.' Thom wondered if the other one was possibly the van that O'Brien saw. He made a mental note to question the possibility once he arrived at Wesley's.

O'Brien, by now, had driven to almost the summit of the Creston cut-off when he saw a set of tracks heading up a lightly snow-covered road that coursed into the mountainside. He pulled to the shoulder to have a better look at the tracks. Maybe he would be able to determine the size of the vehicle. Walking to the road entrance, he knelt down at the tracks. He determined that the vehicle that jetted up the forestry road was definitely not a car. Could it have been the 4x4 van? There would be no way O'Brien could follow with the car he was driving. He decided to walk up the road a short distance and listen for any sounds of a vehicle. Finding a nice clearing where the sun was shining and he could look down onto the highway, he heard only silence and the wind. After a few minutes, he turned and began to walk back to the car.

He turned a corner when a door slammed and a vehicle started up. O'Brien barely had time to react before the van was on him. Jumping clear, he reached for his pistol and managed to fire off two shots. The van sped around the corner sliding this way and that on the lightly snow-covered surface, then it was out of sight. Moments later, the sound of metal on metal riveted the silence. Running now, he came around the corner. To his horror, the rental car was t-boned and pushed into the middle of the highway, fuel spewing from its ruptured gas tank. O'Brien noticed that the skid marks from the van ended on the other side. Running across the highway and over to the embankment he looked over the 100 to 200 foot drop. Amongst the brush and bramble, he could faintly make out the van as it sat on its roof, the wheels still spinning.

Flagging down a logging truck, he got the driver to radio ahead to the RCMP to report the accident. He couldn't phone Thom; however he knew that once Thom heard the sirens heading westerly he'd know what to do next. Twenty-five minutes later, the RC's showed up. The tow truck followed as did the paramedics and fire trucks. O'Brien explained to the RC's who he was. They watched as one of the Paramedics repelled over the embankment. Everyone present agreed that no one could have survived.

A few minutes later, the Paramedic came over the radio.

"There is no one here. The van is empty. There isn't even any blood anywhere. I'm going to walk down a bit further towards the creek. Could be the driver got thrown. Over."

"That's a ten four. Keep your eyes peeled. If by chance the driver is alive, it could be he is dangerous. Over," said the EMS guy standing on the bank.

"That's a copy over and out," was the response, then silence.

O'Brien couldn't believe what he had just heard and he walked over to where the EMS fellow was standing.

"Did I hear your buddy correctly? That no one is in the van?"

"Apparently not. Could be he was thrown out. Put it this way. Chances that he may have survived a crash like that are next to nil, if that is what you are worried about."

O'Brien looked at him and nodded.

"It gives me some comfort knowing that, but what if he did? Do you think he could've gotten away without an injury?"

"Nope."

There came another squawk over his radio. "You're not going to believe this," responded the Paramedic at the bottom of the bank. "I've found footprints heading across the creek. It looks like he's running. Over."

"I guess head back up. We'll have to leave the rest to the RC's. Over."

"Ten four. I'm heading back."

The radio went dead.

O'Brien squatted and looked across the draw. The rugged terrain on the other side looked so barren and desolate that he cringed at the thought of having to track Anvil. Regardless, though, that is where they were heading; O'Brien knew it. The RCMP radioed ahead and requested that their helicopters get in the air ASAP and to begin flying a grid up and down the mountain. They dispatched Thom, Ilene, Art, Hal, and Rory for O'Brien from their office and informed Henderson who eventually got through on the RC's radio channel.

"Detective O'Brien, I have a call here for you from Henderson," the RC said as he waved O'Brien over to his car. Handing him the mike, the RC stepped out and signalled to him to go ahead and sit down.

"This is O'Brien, over."

"Are you okay, O'Brien? Over."

"Yeah, I'm fine. A little bit shook up. Over."

"Listen, O'Brien. Sounds like you guys have to head into the Kootenay Pass Mountain range and that's rugged territory. I've spoken with an outfitter in Creston and have set you up with an account. You are going to need some gear. The name of the place is East Kootenay Outfitters. Over."

"I know the place. Over."

"Good, then you'll have no problem finding it. Listen, don't spare any expense. You are all going to need some good gear. Over."

"The thing is, Henderson, I'm forty-five minutes away from the place. Detour Hal and Rory that way. I would prefer to sit here and wait for them. Who knows? Anvil might decide to pop out somewhere and I'd hate to miss that. Over."

"All right, I'll do it that way. O'Brien, no hesitating. Remember, this is a Code One. Over and out."

The radio went dead. O'Brien looked at his watch and he noted the time to be 1:00 p.m. *We still have a few hours of daylight,* O'Brien thought as he stood up and walked over to the bank where he watched the tow truck slowly inch the demolished van up. Minutes later an old blue and white Jeep Cherokee came to an abrupt stop. Low and behold if it wasn't Thom. He darted over to O'Brien's side of the road.

"Are you all right, man? I saw what was left of rental being towed. Good thing you weren't in it."

"Yeah, I'm fine. Take a good look across the way, Thom, 'cause that's where we're headed," O'Brien replied. "By the way, good choice in a rental," he said nodding towards the Cherokee.

"I figured before this thing was over we'd need something like that. Besides, I hate cars. She's not a rental either. I bought it."

"What?" O'Brien questioned.

"It was at Wesley's 4x4 Rentals. With a price tag of thirty eight hundred, I couldn't turn it down. I probably could have got it cheaper, but once I heard the sirens in Creston heading west I ran out of time to dicker. It's still under old Wes's insurance 'cause I never had time to get any, but she's bought and paid for."

Looking at him O'Brien shook his head.

"You're crazy."

Thom smiled. They walked over to where the van was being loaded onto a five-ton truck to have a closer look. It had been destroyed. Thom stood there shaking his head.

"Old Wes is not going to like this."

"What do you mean?"

"Yesterday he rented this van to a guy who fit Anvil's description to a tee. The guy rented it for two weeks. Paid cash and went by the name of Jack Wheeler."

"Unbelievable," O'Brien started as he again shook his head. "So that SOB has been here as long as we have. Man, he's coy."

"That he is, O'Brien. That is why we have to stop him. Should we head back into Creston and pick up some stuff for this next little excursion?"

"Nope, Henderson already took care of that. He rigged us up an account at the outfitters in Creston. He's going to have Hal and Rory swing by there before they head up this way."

The big five-ton tow truck with the van loaded up took off, followed by the fire trucks and paramedics. The RCMP set up roadblocks on both sides of the cut-off. The border crossings were notified and put on alert. Two helicopters buzzed overhead for about two hours and then reported to have seen nothing. When the rest of the crew showed up, it was starting to get dark and they decided to head to the top of the cut-off.

The Forestry Department granted O'Brien and the rest of his crew permission to use the cabin at the top that was a tourist attraction for their HQ. They would stay there for the night. It was too dark to start a foot search in such rugged terrain. The cabin was maybe ten years old and was in immaculate shape. The RC's were going to continue with the roadblocks until O'Brien and crew or the RC's either apprehended Anvil or laid him to rest. In the morning, they were going to send a dog team in and a couple of RCMP scouts at the point where Anvil had crossed the creek.

O'Brien and his men were to cross the creek from the top and proceed downstream to where there would be some flagging tape so they would know where the RCMP team took up the search. From there, they were to follow behind and meet at a snow-clearing shack that was about five hundred meters up from the creek. The plan seemed simple enough. However, as morning came and they geared up and began their search, it was clear to all that they were no competition for Anvil and his adept abilities in the bush. For starters, the dogs lost his scent at the point where he crossed the creek, which meant he was travelling in the creek. Was he going upstream or downstream? The RCMP scouts didn't find any tracks on either side of the creek downstream or upstream a half a mile in both directions. Anvil again had simply vanished like a misty fog on a hot day.

By noon, the helicopters were in the air again. This time they were concentrating on the creek and they patrolled up and down for a few hours until a fog began to settle on the mountain making it unsafe to continue. As their luck would have it, at 3:00 p.m. a snowstorm rolled in and they were all forced to call off the search. O'Brien had the RCMP drive them back to the cabin where they settled in for yet another cold night.

O'Brien tried calling Dr. Relkoff with Thom's cell phone, but because of the weather, he couldn't get through. By 6:00 p.m. they were experiencing a full-fledged blizzard. The wind whistled outside relentlessly for almost three hours and by 9:00 p.m. that Tuesday, the ground was completely covered in fresh snow. The temperature dropped and ice formed on the cabin's windows with an abstract array of different designs. It reminded O'Brien of his childhood when his mother would point at the kitchen window of their farmhouse during those cold winter mornings and say, "Jack Frost has been here." As a kid, O'Brien always wondered who Jack Frost was. *To be young again*, he pondered.

O'Brien turned to the crew and pointed at the window.

"Jack Frost is out in full force tonight. We better prepare for a cold one. Let's gather up some wood and get that fire roasting."

With flashlights in hand, they headed outside to the woodpile. The snow covered their ankles and the brisk wind caused them to shiver. The darkness of the evening seemed eerie and silent. Moreover, behind the dark grey clouds they could see the brightness of the moon. Once the cloud cover dissipated, it was going to be cold.

O'Brien looked across the way to where the Kootenay Creston Highway Dept. had a year-round shop and dispatching office. The silence was broken by the sounds of the big loaders and sand trucks as they started up, preparing for a long night of snow removal. It was somewhat comforting to know that they weren't the only ones that night on top of that mountain pass. It also posed a threat. If Anvil managed somehow to commandeer one of the trucks, he would be a great danger. The roadblocks at either end of the valley wouldn't stand a chance. Neither would pedestrians, vehicles, or buildings. He could become quite a menace with that kind of power and weight.

Once they got back inside and unloaded the wood they had gathered, O'Brien questioned the crew. "Who wants to brave the cold with me one last time tonight and head across the road to inform those who are working over there about Anvil? I would hate for one of them to pick him up hitchhiking or something. Could you imagine the carnage he'd create?"

"No doubt, O'Brien. I'll head across with you," said Thom. They exited again into the cold evening air. A few minutes later they were talking with one of the sand truck operators. They had been informed by the RCMP that a fugitive might be in the area and that they were to report any hitchhikers.

"There's no way anyone here tonight will pick up any male hitchhikers. We see one though, we'll be reporting it to the RC's. We are all keeping our doors locked, and have agreed to radio in every ten miles of black top that we plough. Basically every fifteen or so minutes we will be radioing in. Not to worry, detectives; we'll be careful."

"Good enough," O'Brien said as he knocked on the fender. "We're just across the way. If you guys see anything, let us know, would you?"

The driver nodded that he would. Thom and O'Brien darted back to the warmth of the cabin.

"She's a brisk one tonight," O'Brien said as they entered the cabin.

"You got that right," replied Thom as he shook himself off.

"How did it go?" asked Art.

"They've been informed. I guess the RCMP mentioned it to them earlier," O'Brien replied. For the next hour, they huddled near the wood stove eating power bars and slurping percolated coffee. At 11:00 p.m., they set out their sleeping bags. Blowing out the candles, the entourage closed their eyes and listened to the whistling wind, each in their own world of deep contemplation. Would they ever stop the maniac Anvil Brentwood?

# Twenty Four

On Wednesday, October 24, the snowstorm from the night before reduced traffic on the pass to a crawl. Although the sun was shining, the ice-covered ground was slick and remained frozen. Of the three cars, Thom's was the only one that started. After boosting the other two, they headed back into the cabin leaving the vehicles running and at the same time keeping an ever-watchful eye on them as their windows began to thaw.

A few minutes later, a RCMP Sergeant pulled up next to their vehicles and flashed his red and blue lights. He obviously wasn't too keen on walking the distance to the cabin. O'Brien walked over to him and the RC informed him that during the night someone managed to steal a vehicle in Salmo. He said that they couldn't be sure if it was Anvil. After all, how could he have passed through the roadblock unchecked?

To O'Brien it was simple.

"If it was Anvil, he probably hiked through the bush. Has anyone checked that out?" O'Brien asked. He felt a little embarrassed when the RC Sergeant replied that someone had and that any tracks that might have been left behind were covered by the snowfall.

"It snowed down below as well?" O'Brien asked.

"That it did, detective."

"I guess we're stuck between a rock and a hard place. What is the make of the vehicle?" O'Brien requested. "I'm thinking my crew and I ought to see if we can't track it down."

"That's why I'm here, detective, to let you know that we have this place pretty much covered. We will continue keeping it that way until this guy is caught. We have been told to keep the roadblocks in place until such time that he is.

If you and your crew have a couple other ideas to follow through with, you might as well get them covered. The vehicle was a 1999 Dodge Ram. The plate number is 2657-BH. It's blue in colour and has a matching canopy. All the RCMP stations right down to the coast and as far as the BC-Alberta Boundary are on alert. BC is going to be tightened up like a screw and even more so now."

"What do you mean even more so now?"

"Oh yeah, I guess you haven't heard. Sorry about that detective. The memo just came in this morning. The guy you found in the trunk of that car in Moyie has been identified as a Jack Wheeler, a very prominent Neurologist. He and a Professor Linquist managed to get a court order giving them the authority to transfer your friend Anvil to a scientific research lab in Vancouver. You probably know the rest of the story that he managed to beat the odds on some brain disease he was suffering from all because of some serum Linquist and this Wheeler fellow concocted."

"That's a lot more than what we had. We were aware of the brain issue thing, but we had no idea how Linquist or Wheeler fit in the circle of things nor did we know about any serum."

"Like I said, detective, this stuff just came in. It is also why the CSIS has got involved. You do know they are concerned about finding this Anvil fellow as well, don't you?"

"Oh yeah, we know that much, but we don't know why."

"It's because apparently Linquist was the only guy who had the formula for the serum. When he was found, the blueprint wasn't, nor were any notes that he kept on his person. The CSIS believe Anvil has them. I guess it is some kind of miracle cure for Alzheimer's and other brain infections. In addition, this Jack Wheeler fellow suffered quite a bit before he died. His body was riddled with several high-powered rifle slugs all of them being a 30.06. The

Medical Examiner said that the shot that killed him was the one to his head fired at a range of 10-12 feet; can you imagine the blood spatter at that range? You'd have to be pretty sick to do that. The other bullet wounds, from what the examiner is stating, must've been done while Mr. Wheeler was still breathing. It is my guess that he was sighting in a scope. Either way, the victim didn't die until the shot to his head. Well, detective, I'm expected at the bottom. I hope this new information comes in useful. Good luck and we'll stay in touch."

O'Brien thanked him for the information and waved as the Sergeant backed away.

At least now, they had an idea why the CSIS were involved and how the two victims fit into the scheme of things. Whether or not Anvil was in possession of the notes and formula was anyone's guess. What O'Brien's crew knew for sure was that if the CSIS apprehended Anvil before they did, Anvil would be shipped off to a resort-like hospital in Vancouver. There he would be compassionately studied. There was no way O'Brien's crew was going to let that happen. They all agreed on that point.

Loading up their gear, O'Brien proposed a plan. They were back to three vehicles and there were three ways out of Salmo. Anvil either headed west to Fruitmont, east to New Kootenay or north-west to Slocolm. It was decided that Thom and O'Brien would head that way. The roads up in that area could be ugly at this time of year. Since Thom had a 4x4 who better than he and O'Brien? Hal and Rory were going to head to New Kootenay while Ilene and Art would head west to Fruitmont. They all agreed that once they arrived at their predetermined zones they would call each other via cell phone. If that failed, they would call the office in Fruitmont and inform Henderson who would then have to work his magic and relay the messages among them.

With the plan set out, they embarked on tracking down a 1999 blue Dodge Ram license plate # 2657-BH. The driver may or may not be one Anvil Brentwood, a wanted felon and murderer. It was the only lead they had and could follow at the time. The RCMP did have the Kootenay Pass region well blocked off and they would continue searching in and amongst that area. They had dogs, snowmobiles, and helicopters. O'Brien knew that if the RCMP found Anvil they would hear about it, and whatever happened after that happened.

It was now a cat and mouse chase. To the cat would go the mouse.


By 11:00 a.m., the crew finally made their way to the bottom of the cut-off where the roadblock was set up. The RC's nodded them through as they held up their badges. If it were Anvil who had stolen the pickup, then he had quite a start. In those hours, he could have easily grabbed another vehicle or may already be at his destination, wherever that may be. O'Brien's crew's first priority was to seek out the stolen truck. Once the whereabouts of the vehicle was determined, they could set out to investigate if it were Anvil. If it proved to be, then they could proceed with phase two, which, was seek and destroy.

Hal and Rory arrived in New Kootenay shortly after 12:00 p.m. They phoned O'Brien and Thom's number first.

"We're in New Kootenay, O'Brien. We didn't spot the truck. We're going keep our eyes peeled and maybe go a bit further up the lake, maybe as far as Balfour. What do you think?"

"Actually Thom and I still have a distance to go. I guess if you guys only go as far as Balfour that'll put you there closer to the time that we'd be getting to Slocolm. Yeah, go for it. Contact us when you get to Balfour."

"You got it, O'Brien," Rory said as he turned off the cell.

O'Brien dialled Art's number. After a couple of rings, he answered.

"Art here."

"Hey Art, this is O'Brien. We got word from Hal and Rory they are now in New Kootenay. They didn't see a thing. They're going to head up Balfour way. Have you seen anything?"

"Nothing, O'Brien. Anvil could be as far away as Vancouver by now."

O'Brien knew he was right. It was possible. The only thing they could rely on was the number of RCMP detachments. More RCMP meant more eyes.

"I know, Art. I am betting he is not going to want to go that way, not yet at least. He is going to want to wait for the heat to die down. Unless, of course, the perpetrator turns out to be someone else. If it is Anvil like we all hope it is, he doesn't plan to leave the Kootenays. He'd rather hole up in the mountains than risk a move like that."

"I sure hope your assumptions are correct, O'Brien. Otherwise, the SOB has bedazzled us again."

"Let's hope that isn't the case. By the way, what's your ETA to Fruitmont?"

"I'm guessing between fifteen and twenty minutes."

"Very well. Once you arrive, head over to the office, and contact me from there. I'm sure Henderson would like to hear what's going on."

"Yeah, I wouldn't mind seeing Henderson; haven't seen the old fart for a while. I'll contact you once we get there."

"Thanks a lot, Art."

O'Brien looked over to Thom as he drove, noticing that Thom had a stern and puzzled look on his face.

"What's up?"

"Don't look now, but if you can believe it, there is a blue pickup coming up on us. It's been following us for almost ten minutes," he replied.

O'Brien continued looking ahead as not to startle the driver.

"Can you tell if it's a Dodge Ram?"

"No, it keeps lagging. I'll let you know once it gets closer and I get a better look."

They began to pull off highway 3A and onto highway 6. The blue truck followed them in unison. Turning into a Shell station they kept their backs to the road so the driver of the blue truck, if it were Anvil, wouldn't recognise them. A couple of minutes later it passed. Their hopes were dashed when they noted the truck to be a Ford.

"That isn't our perp," commented Thom. "While we're here, let's grab something to eat and drink. I need a hot coffee and maybe a couple of pepperonis. What do you say?"

"For sure I could use a coffee, but I think I'll have jerky."

Minutes later, back in the Cherokee, as Thom and O'Brien were sipping their coffees Thom's cell began ringing. O'Brien reached for it on the dash and answered.

"This is O'Brien."

"Hey O'Brien, this is Art; we're at the office. Henderson says hi. Listen, we didn't see any blue pickups. How's it going from your end?"

"We had a blue truck following us, but it turned out to be a Ford. We're probably about 30 minutes from Slocolm right now. I still haven't heard back from Hal and Rory. Maybe call them up, Art. They should've been in Balfour by now."

"Yeah, I'll see if I can't get them on the phone. If anything has changed with them, expect to hear back from me. Otherwise, I'll talk to you when you call in from Slocolm."

"You got it, Art. Talk to you soon."

A few miles later, just before Thom and O'Brien passed the Valhalla Bridge, they spotted another blue pickup.

"Could it be the same one we saw back yonder?"

"I don't know about that, O'Brien. It looks like it has more road clearance. Let's try and see if we can't get a tad bit closer without alerting whoever is driving it," Thom replied.

"Let's do it!" O'Brien exclaimed.

It did appear to be a different vehicle. Slowly Thom increased the speed of his Cherokee and in moments they were close enough to read the plate number and the vehicle make. It was a Dodge Ram. Plate Number 2567-BH.

"It's the vehicle!" exclaimed Thom.

"Pull back; pull back. We don't want him to think we're tailing him," O'Brien responded.

Thom slowly decelerated the powerful Cherokee.

"We know which way he's going. Let's get in contact with the others and seal this deal once and for all."

"Man, O'Brien, my heart's pounding. I'm having an adrenaline meltdown."

"I hear you, buddy. Me too."

A few deep breaths later, O'Brien was able to follow through with contacting the others. He tried Hal and Rory first because they could head straight up to Kaslo then turn back into Silverton and meet them up the Slocolm Valley somewhere. O'Brien tried three times; however, the mountains weakened the cell phone signal. He dialled the office instead, which was a shorter distance and not so obscured by the mountain range in that area. He spoke directly to Henderson.

"Henderson, listen, this is O'Brien. We have a visual on the stolen vehicle. There is one driver. It's heading up into the Valley towards Newton. Send Art and Ilene up to Cassle and have them go up through Pass Creek and over into Slocolm. Could be he will try an escape that way once he knows we are on to him. I couldn't contact Hal and Rory. I need them to go up past Balfour and into the Kaslo area. They can detour back through Silverton and meet up with us somewhere between here and Slocolm Park, which is where I'm betting he's heading," O'Brien said, all in one breath.

"O'Brien if you were talking any faster I wouldn't have understood a word. Nevertheless, consider it done and be extremely vigilant. According to what I have heard, our friend has become quite the sharpshooter. Be careful," he said as he hung up his phone.

"Have you calmed down a bit, Thom?"

"Oh yeah. What is the plan? Can we simply pull him over and shoot him?" Thom asked half-joking.

"I think we'll be a bit more tactful, but I'm sure that will be the end result. We'll follow him for now and wait until we meet up with the others. If I have it figured right, we can box him in before he gets to the ferry dock that heads across the Arrow and into Revelstoke. We might have this thing tied up by early evening."

"That would be a dream come true."


They continued onward and stayed within a half a mile of the truck. They knew Anvil couldn't possibly know that they were following him especially since they were driving in a Jeep Cherokee. Then it dawned on them that Thom picked the Cherokee up at the same rental agency as Anvil picked up the van. They decided to play it safe and kept their distance.

Twenty minutes later, Anvil pulled into a Thrifty Gas Station.

"Perfect. Now is our chance to see if the driver is who we hope it is," said Thom. They drove past the Thrifty Station looking closely at the man walking into the doors. By physical appearance both Thom and O'Brien were able to make an educated guess that it was indeed Anvil Brentwood.

"Damn. We never got a good look at his face," said Thom.

"No we didn't, but I'd say it was Anvil by his gaunt appearance and how he walked."

"I'm pretty sure it was him, too. Think we should pull off somewhere and wait for him to drive by so we can get a better look?"

"I'd say so. Pull up here," O'Brien said as he pointed to a road that turned off the main highway and was obscured from passing traffic.

"Perfect," said Thom as he pulled into the road. Manoeuvring the Cherokee, they parked behind some bramble. For ten minutes they sat there waiting and watching, but no blue pickup passed. They decided that perhaps Anvil goosed around and headed to Valhalla or some other nearby forest-clad road. Backing out from where they parked, Thom stopped at the entrance of the road and was about to signal back south when Anvil finally drove by. He looked at them and with a stunned look, recognised O'Brien. Anvil gunned the big Dodge as Thom gunned his Cherokee. The road being somewhat slick caused the Cherokee to fishtail and end up in the ditch. Thom gunned it a couple of times almost making it out.

They were wasting precious time. The two of them jumped out on either side and locked in the hubs. Jumping back in, Thom gunned it one last time and the Cherokee, now in four-wheel drive, shot out of the ditch like a bat out of hell. They didn't even bother unlocking the hubs. It had taken at least three minutes and that meant Anvil had a three minute start. There were numerous different back wood roads in the area and they knew Anvil could have taken any one.

O'Brien called Henderson to let him know that it was definitely Anvil Brentwood and that he made them out. Henderson suggested that they should head straight for the Arrow Lakes Ferry. If they didn't come across Anvil between where they were now and the ferry dock, then Anvil was definitely holding up in the Slocolm Valley Mountains. Henderson told O'Brien that the ferry wasn't due on that side for another forty-five minutes and that they could easily make it there before it landed or took off.

"Excellent, Henderson. Thanks a lot."

"Remember, stay vigilant. Do you think I should inform the RCMP?"

"I think it would be better if you didn't. If they're informed of Anvil's whereabouts, then so will the CSIS and so on. You know what will happen if the CSIS hear about it before we apprehended him. They'll shut us down."

"All right, O'Brien, we'll play it your way for as long as I can keep the RC's at bay. However, once they hear of it, there isn't much I can do."

"Thanks, Henderson. We'll be in touch."

O'Brien turned off the cell.

"Henderson figures we ought to head to the ferry dock. The next one isn't due to land on this side for about forty-five minutes or so. If we can make it there before it leaves and we don't come across Anvil, we'll know for sure that he took one of the forestry roads into the hills."

"Beautiful. Is your seat belt on?" asked Thom as he gunned the big 360 high-performance engine of the Cherokee.

"No," O'Brien fumbled with the belt, "but it is now," he exclaimed feeling the G-Forces of the Cherokee as the four-barrel kicked in. "What about the hubs. They're still locked in."

"Not to worry, O'Brien. These old Cherokees can handle it. If the hubs don't make it, I'll replace them. Right now my only concern is making it to that ferry dock. If he gets on that and we can't flag it down, we'll have no choice but to call the RC's to intercept him on the other side and if Anvil ever clued into that, he'd have an entire ferry that he could hold hostage. Personally, I don't want that. Besides, if we happen to see some tracks heading up some road, we'll be ready."

"The only problem with that, Thom, is what if they turnout not to be his tracks and he boards the ferry without us having a clue. He'll have a good chance of slipping away. I say we don't even bother and head straight for the ferry. Once we know he isn't there we'll come back this way and really check out these roads."

"Good point, O'Brien."

They arrived at the dock, as the ferry was halfway across to their side. They pulled to the shoulder and exited the Cherokee. There was a line-up of traffic of twenty or so vehicles. They walked along the line-up making sure no blue Dodge Rams were waiting to board the ferry. None were.

"I guess he did detour up one of those roads."

"It looks that way. Nevertheless, we can't leave here. It would be our luck that he boards the next one," Thom said shaking his head.

"I know. We have to get someone here to watch while you and I head back. I'll contact Henderson and have him send Hal and Rory directly here. With luck, they will be here before too long. We're also going to need someone at the junction of 3A and highway 6. Art and Ilene I know, are headed up through Pass Creek, so that takes care of that route. Hal and Rory are coming in from the northwest so that route is covered. Unless Anvil slips by either one, I'd say he's going to be in a panic and will probably ditch the truck and head off on foot. We have to find that truck, buddy."

O'Brien opened the passenger side door of the Cherokee and reached in for the cell.

He walked over to a clearing that overlooked the mighty Arrow Lake where he knew reception would be better to call up Henderson. The problem with that was he was a sitting duck for Anvil. O'Brien heard and felt the sting of gunshot all at the same time. The bullet entered his left shoulder spinning him around and knocking the cell phone into the water. The pain was excruciating. O'Brien did though, manage to pull his pistol, and looking at the wound briefly, he was relieved that the bullet had exited clean. Seconds passed and Thom was standing beside him and as quickly had a tourniquet wrapped up under O'Brien's armpit and across his collarbone. Instantly, the bleeding slowed.

"Jesus Christ, O'Brien we got to get you to a hospital."

"Look. It hurts like hell, but I'm not going to any hospital until he's down. He fired from right over there," O'Brien said pointing at a clump of mountain ash.

"Can you stand?"

O'Brien grimaced in pain then stood.

"Come on, let's go."

The two of them crept over a little knoll as the blue Dodge began backing up onto the highway. O'Brien, forgetting about the pain he was in, with adrenaline pumping, he and Thom fired an array of bullets into the truck and into the driver. There was no reason to ask him to surrender. Not now. Anvil had fired upon them first and that gave them the right to fire back. The whole thing ended in less than two minutes from the time O'Brien was shot until Anvil lay over the steering wheel, his lifeless body twitching for the last time.

"Are you ready to go to the Hospital now?" asked Thom grinning from ear to ear.

O'Brien looked at him and quoted Shakespeare.

"All things are ready if our minds be so," he managed to say before he slumped to the frozen ground.

Checking to make sure Anvil was no longer alive, Thom walked over to the pickup and checked his pulse. Looking back to O'Brien, he gave the thumbs up sign.

"He's as dead as dead can be."

O'Brien remained sitting on the ground as Thom headed back to get the Cherokee. He was way too weak to move. He was beginning to feel the pain again that he so abruptly stopped feeling in those few brief moments. Squinting, he watched Thom skirt across the highway. People were standing all over the place trying to get a glimpse of the action that they had heard and seen.

All of a sudden, the horn in the Dodge went off. O'Brien looked over to it fear stricken and pointed his gun. He was relieved when he realised Anvil's dead body had simply fallen forward again after Thom had checked his vitals and was now resting on the horn. The sound was an eerie reminder of what Anvil had been. Raising his pistol, he fired relentlessly into the grill of the truck until he managed to put the truck's horn out of commission.

He felt an array of sensations at that point, all of which were that of relief. As silence fell, he could faintly hear the crashing waves of the Arrow Lake as they smashed against the rock bluffs. Then, darkness swept over him as he passed out from loss of blood, pain, and exhaustion.

The next thing he remembered was waking up at the Trail Regional Hospital that Friday, his left shoulder aching from the wound he'd received. There were cards and flowers throughout the room. He opened the one from Thom. There was a little ditty and then two words. *Case Closed.*